C000040203

'If you like your crime fiction to ̰____ ,
Green has your measure.' — *THE GUARDIAN*

'J.M. Green knows just how to use black humour, irony and
underplayed sarcasm to perfection.' — *THE SATURDAY PAPER*

'Green is a welcomed addition to the growing coterie
of Australian female crime writers.' — *THE AGE*

'A rattling good story.' — *THE WEST AUSTRALIAN*

'A social worker by vocation, Hardy is the sort of laksa-loving,
inner-city woman who fits into the role of accidental detective with
considerable aplomb.' — *THE NEWTOWN REVIEW OF BOOKS*

'A compelling story of drugs, shady criminals and murder
in the Western suburbs of Melbourne ... Green captures
experiences wholly and honestly. Her characters are complex,
engaging and, most of all, real.' — *LIP*

'What a fantastic new voice in Australian crime fiction! I loved every
word written on these pages ... This is crime fiction at its most human
level.' — *READING, WRITING AND RIESLING*

'*Good Money* is simply a great yarn, offering a mixture of humour,
heart and action.' — *FAIR DINKUM CRIME*

'This is a powerhouse debut, full of excitement, jokes, brutality and
scenic flights over Australia's dangerous red centre, and the very bad
use of very good money.' — READINGS BOOKSHOP

TOO EASY

J.M. Green is a crime writer based in Melbourne's western suburbs. Her debut novel, *Good Money*, the first hardboiled-crime novel featuring Stella Hardy, was shortlisted for a 2016 Ned Kelly Award, the Sisters in Crime's Davitt Award for best debut, as well as the 2014 Victorian Premier's Literary Award for an Unpublished Manuscript. She divides her time between writing in her backyard studio and working as a librarian. *Too Easy* is her second book.

TOO EASY

J.M. GREEN

SCRIBE
Melbourne • London

Scribe Publications
18–20 Edward St, Brunswick, Victoria 3056, Australia
2 John St, Clerkenwell, London, WC1N 2ES, United Kingdom

First published by Scribe 2017

Printed and bound in Australia by Griffin Press

 The paper this book is printed on is certified against
the Forest Stewardship Council® Standards. Griffin
Press holds FSC chain of custody certification
SGS-COC-005088. FSC promotes environmentally
responsible, socially beneficial and economically
viable management of the world's forests.

Scribe Publications is committed to the sustainable use of natural
resources and the use of paper products made responsibly from
those resources.

9781925322026 (Australian edition)
9781925548181 (e-book)

A CiP entry for this title is available from the National Library of
Australia.

scribepublications.com.au
scribepublications.co.uk

For Doreen
for the love and the stories
(1931–2016)

1

FOOTSCRAY, MIDWEEK, the sun sneaking away as the street lights flickered to life and the coloured bulbs outside the kebab shop burst into a frenzied circuit. To the untrained eye — a visitor, say — the sweep of assorted humanity strolling in the warm evening was a scene of cosmopolitan excitement. To folk who tucked into tabloids, the sight was of the end of days. To an officer of the law, it was a landscape of latent court appearances. To a community worker, such as myself, I surveyed the elaborate greetings and handshakes of this place, as likely to comprise colleagues as clients, with great affection. These were my people.

I was waiting on the street downstairs from the Narcissistic Slacker, an above-shop studio, domicile, and barely-functional commercial art gallery belonging to the artist known as Peter Brophy. Next minute, Brophy was beside me, hair damp and combed down. There was just time for a quick smooch, then I looked him over. He'd missed a spot shaving, and I couldn't have loved him more. The shirt was his favourite — brown cotton with white piping, still good after many washes. He tapped his top pocket. 'All set.'

'What's in there? Ear plugs?' I asked hopefully.

'Cyanide.'

We laughed, linked arms, and walked through the alley to the car park where he left his van.

'I like Phuong,' Brophy was saying. And I knew where he was going with that.

Phuong was a detective with Victoria Police. She was also my oldest friend. How that came about was a mystery. We met at uni, and not long after that, she dropped out and became a cop — yet, we stayed friends. Since then, whatever new directions our lives took, no matter how divergent, we remained tight. She was everything I wasn't. The epitome of composure, fun without being crazy, straight without being boring. It was her blowhard boyfriend that Brophy and I were bracing ourselves to endure. I had a limit of ten minutes with Detective Bruce Copeland before I felt that one of us had to die.

The radio on low, we drove to Kensington in silence. We skirted the racecourse, dotted with spring racing marquees, and behind them the twinkling lights, and joyful screams, of the Royal Melbourne Show. My hand out the window, fingers spread to catch the rush of warm air.

Phuong's apartment was an entire floor of a warehouse conversion, a bohemian pad with a fake log fire, large driftwood sculptures, and a meditation room.

'Detective Phuong,' Brophy said as they embraced — his term of endearment for her. My theory was that it served as a reminder. After all, she was a cop, and he an ex-junkie.

'Peter, nice to see you.' Phuong took off the apron she'd been wearing over a black dress: sheer in places, bling at the neck. She pointed to the fridge, and Brophy went to stack his beer inside. Yma Sumac sang from concealed speakers. Steaming away atop Phuong's fancy European appliances was evidence of a Vietnamese banquet.

If I'd made a banquet, it would consist only of Pringles. I'd be running around, possibly screaming, and things would be on fire. Phuong's kitchen, on the other hand, was ship-shape, and the food, no doubt, would be wholesome. And the good news was that Copeland had not yet arrived. Champagne!

Phuong served a plate of tasty-looking things, fried in batter. Brophy hesitated. 'Tofu and mushroom,' she said. His eyes widened. 'Everything is veg,' she assured him.

I spied a bottle of French champagne in the fridge, and began to tear the foil.

'What's the occasion?' Brophy asked, removing the cap on a beer.

'I was going to wait for Bruce so we could tell you together.' She glanced at her watch, blinked. 'We're taking the plunge.'

'What?!' I shrieked as if I'd been smacked. 'What plunge? Not the *marriage* plunge?'

She took that as excitement, and smiled. 'Is there another kind?'

'But ... but ... I mean, this is so sudden.'

'Not at all. Truth is, we've been waiting for his divorce order to be finalised. He had some financial issues to straighten out in the settlement, but that's all taken care of now.'

'But ... what about your parents? What will they say? Have they even met Copeland? And where will you live? You can't move out. This is your sanctuary, your refuge of serenity. Where's Copeland live? Bloody Woop Woop. Come on, Phuong, have you thought this through? You're not rushing, are you? When is this plunge?'

The smile slipped. 'You mean, *congratulations*.'

'Of *course* I mean that. This really is just so ... great. Such great news.'

Brophy had consumed most of the hors d'oeuvres. He wiped his hands and gave her a peck on the cheek. 'Congratulations to you both.'

'Thank you. It's been hard to make plans. Since the restructure, Bruce and I hardly see each other.' Phuong directed her words towards him.

'You moved out of homicide?' I was stunned.

'Cybercrime,' she said to Brophy, like I wasn't there. 'Bruce is with Guns and Gangs.'

'Good name, "Guns and Gangs",' he said. 'Nice alliteration. The gangs are, what? Teenagers?'

She drew her hair back, looped it into a neat bun. 'Outlaw motorcycle gangs.'

Brophy brought me a tofu ball thingy. I dipped it in the sauce. 'How's he like that?' I said.

She checked her watch again, and didn't answer. I hoped she wasn't going to ignore me all night. She sniffed and went to the kitchen. 'He likes it,' she said to the stove. 'But some cops in the unit are leftovers from the drug squad. They're not exactly … effective.'

'Leftovers' was a euphemism. She didn't need to explain that these individuals had relaxed attitudes to the law. And had dodged every previous attempt at a crackdown.

The door opened and Copeland stumbled in. The middle-aged, gone-to-seed look suited him, made him seem hard-working yet genteel. The black-rimmed glasses made him appear intelligent, almost bland — and that was why, looking back, I'd misjudged him at first. I had failed to see the dangers, failed to grasp that Bruce Copeland had the principles of a cage fighter. 'Couldn't find my keys.' He jangled them, then went to Brophy, hand out. 'Mate.'

Brophy stood up straight, shook his hand, and offered him a beer.

'Mate,' Copeland said again.

'Where were you?' Phuong asked.

'West Sunshine. Anonymous tip-off about a hydroponic set up. Uniforms found a body in the bathroom. I hung around with the FSD people. Lost track of the time.'

Forensics, my arse — he stank of the pub. I shot Phuong a look, but she was busy setting table, with twinkling glasses and rolled napkins. I began filling the champagne glasses.

Copeland registered the movement and boomed at me. 'Stella Hardy, the woman of the hour. How're things on the migrant front? Still saving lost souls?'

The 'migrant front' was referring to my job, and 'saving lost souls' was an insult. Compassion was for losers, apparently. What an age we lived in. For Phuong's sake, I was responsive. 'Hello, Bruce,' I said from a distance.

He turned to Phuong. 'Never guess who the deceased is. Give up? *Ricky Peck.*'

Phuong's sharp inhale startled me. 'He's a Flower.'

'A *flower*?' I snorted.

Phuong looked at me at last. I caught the full impact of her ferocious displeasure and turned away.

'A member of the Corpse Flowers,' Copeland said. 'Motorcycle gang.'

'Odd name for a bikie gang,' Brophy was saying. '*A flower by any other name would smell of a decomposing animal.*'

'Laugh all you want,' Copeland said.

'But *Corpse Flower*,' I said. 'How bad can they be?'

'They're dangerous people,' Phuong said. 'Ricky Peck was untouchable.'

'Someone fucked up,' Copeland said, drank some beer, and noticed me using a napkin to mop up some wine. 'What have you done now?'

'Nothing. Congratulations, by the way.'

He squinted at me.

'To you and Phuong.'

'Oh. Right.' He raised the stubby to Phuong. 'Thanks.'

She gestured to the table. A fragrant broth with floating wontons awaited us. I was at an age when food was everything. It surpassed all joys and entertainments, and this dish was nirvana in soup form. Its magical soothing effect filled me with good will to all. I turned to Copeland. 'I hear there's a few bad apples in the ranks?'

He released a beery puff and patted his chest. 'That is so,' he said. 'But we've got it covered. New accountability rules, cross checks for money and evidence.'

Rules. Yeah, that'll work. I topped up the champagne glasses.

'How do you even get evidence?' Brophy asked. 'Bikie club houses are like a fortress — armour and cameras — how do you infiltrate that?'

Copeland laughed. 'Informant. An insider's turned.'

'A bikie?' I asked, incredulous.

'No. A go-between, dogsbody type. A low-level dumb-arse.'

'But a guy who knows where the bodies were buried,' Phuong said.

'Literally, right?'

'His intel's been top notch. Details on deals and names,' Phuong said. 'And some —'

'The investigation's ongoing,' Copeland cut her off. 'Can't say too much.'

'Is it Jeff Vanderhoek?' Brophy asked, as he cleared the empty bowls.

I stopped collecting the spoons and watched Copeland. He sighed. It *was* Vanderhoek.

Phuong realised it too; she stared at Brophy in disbelief. 'How did you figure that?'

'Just guessed. I used to know him years ago. Hadn't seen him for ages, then I bump into him at the market. Surprised he was still alive, to be honest. Said he's busy as stink working as a go-fer. Cashed up.'

Copeland shook his head. 'Dumb junkie.'

It wasn't clear if he meant Jeff Vanderhoek or Brophy.

'Nice friends you have,' Phuong muttered.

I dumped the spoons in the sink. Phuong knew Brophy no longer used, not even methadone. I didn't appreciate the inference.

Copeland sniffed. 'Any chance of another beer?'

'In the fridge,' I said.

He cocked his head at me as he stood. We locked eyes.

I don't remember when this antagonism started. A couple of years ago, maybe? We'd had a bit to do with each other over a murder investigation involving one of my clients. Probably because I'd done a better job of sorting out the situation than the homicide department had. To be fair, I did bait him sometimes. It had something to do with him dating my best friend, and his being entirely unworthy of her.

Copeland brightened, went over to Brophy, gave his shoulder a slap. 'What have you nerds been up to?' he asked. 'TV binging? Playing Dungeons and Dragons?'

Brophy took his question as genuine. 'No time for that, I'm afraid — flat-out painting. I've got a show in early November.'

'It's a huge deal,' I said, because Brophy wouldn't. 'A solo show at a major gallery.'

'Don't you have your own studio gallery space?' Phuong asked. 'What's it called?'

'The Narcissistic Slacker,' Brophy said.

Copeland smirked and detached a beer from the plastic wrapper.

'This exhibition is too important for that space. It's at a Fitzroy gallery, very prestigious.' I could be his manager at this rate. 'This Is Not A Drill has international connections.'

'Is Stella your muse?' Copeland asked. 'She's ideal, if you want a bolshy feminazi.'

I allowed him an obligatory hoot. 'He doesn't need a model.'

'Actually, I've been working with one for a while. I'm working with her again tomorrow,' Brophy said.

'Wait, who is this person?' I asked.

'Her name's Felicity. I did a guest lecture for an art class, and she said she liked my work.'

'Did she?'

'She modelled for the class, and I had an immediate response to her poses. I've started a completely new series of paintings.'

An immediate response to her poses. What kind of bunkum was that?

No further conviviality could be squeezed out of the evening, and it wound up soon after that. Brophy said he was working early, first thing. And Copeland was falling asleep in his chair.

Brophy flipped the blinker at Union Road. 'How about Jeff Vanderhoek?'

'How do you know him again?'

'Dunno, years ago. We hung out together.'

'Hung out?'

'Scored, used. He saved my life once.' He looked over to gauge my reaction.

I stayed calm. 'How?'

'Called the ambos and gave me mouth-to-mouth till they got there. They hit me with Naloxone and I walked away.'

Brophy nearly dead — I hated to think of it.

He parked the van, and we headed up to his studio.

'We survived,' he said, grinning.

'Copeland though,' I said. *Not the plunge, Phuong. Not with him.*

2

FOR AN artist's bedroom, Brophy's was surprisingly tidy. I gave him a gentle nudge and gathered my clothes from the floor. He hauled himself upright in a tangle of sheets. 'Time is it?'

'Early. I'm going home before I go to work.'

His bedroom looked onto an alley. Somewhere below, a baby was crying, or a cat perhaps. I leaned out the window, but could see nothing other than industrial-sized bins, and piles of rubbish bags. I closed the window and put my undies on.

'Better get up, too. Get started before Felicity arrives.' Brophy stood naked, staring into his wardrobe. 'What to wear ...'

I checked my hair in the mirror: semi-tamed, clean at any rate. I blew Brophy a kiss. 'Have a good day with your muse.' I went through the studio, and down the ancient staircase to the street.

The sky was rosy-pink and the air already balmy. There were a few locals about. I waited for the tram, watching a cop grill a couple of street kids. A girl in a windcheater five sizes too big, pants dirty and frayed. She had a septum piercing and smokes, so there was some money, but worn-out shoes, so cash was mostly tight. The boy next to her looked stunted. He was taking deep drags on a cigarette, which probably didn't help, but I couldn't help wondering if childhood malnutrition could be possible in a city like Melbourne.

'What brings you here, sunshine?' the young constable asked, acting friendly but ready to press charges if need be.

'This isn't *Sunshine*,' the boy said, looking about him, arms spread to display the Paisley Street sights. That's when I remembered him. He and his mother were regulars at a foodbank I used to take my clients to. He'd been about ten then and shy. He looked older than thirteen now; his black hair was cut short, shaved on the sides.

The girl shook her head, as though the cop had disappointed her. 'This is Foot-*scray*,' she said, and sighed. *How could the cop not know that?*

'Smart arse,' the constable said, but not with real anger.

'Dickhead,' one of them shrieked, and they turned to leg it.

They were running straight at me. On impulse, I put out a hand to stop the boy. 'Cory? Remember me?'

They both stopped short, and I moved closer. 'I'm Stella,' I said, in my certified non-threatening voice. 'Remember me? I knew your mum.'

He darted a sharp up-and-down look my way, acted perplexed, then spoke to the girl. 'Pull out your smokes on a Footscray street, and you might as well rip a flare and say, "Come up to me, weirdos."'

I didn't like the way the girl laughed, pointing her finger at me.

He flipped open the pack, some cigarettes slid forward. 'You don't know me, love, but, yes, you can have a ciggie.'

The girl bent over, shrieking out laughter. Sheesh.

I held up my hands. 'I don't smoke.'

He shrugged. The girl pulled on his arm to turn him around. 'Let's go, Cory.'

'I *knew* it!' I said.

'He's here,' the girl added, pointing to a late-model Commodore that was pulling in across the road. The driver rested a thick arm out the window. A lot of muscle, a lot of tattoos — all the way up to the neck hair. A bikie type that was too big and too old to be messing with kids.

'Wait,' I said — no plan, other than to stop them.

Cory turned back, grinning. 'Nothing you can do, miss.'

What did *that* mean? And what were they doing with a goon like that? I watched them run to the car and get in. It cruised away, windows down, speakers up, rap beats waking everyone in the street.

A tram rolled into the terminus. I hopped on, and as it trundled away, my thoughts turned to Phuong. Me and my big, stupid not-faking-happiness for her. I had to fix that blunder. Today. At my stop, I jumped out and jogged up Roxburgh Street to Pine View, a white stucco block of flats where my one-bedroom flat on the third floor awaited.

Someone stood in the long early morning shadows of the front yard of my building.

'Nice night?' asked Brown Cardigan, my third-floor neighbour. A lead went from his wrist to a Shih tzu that I'd never seen before, urinating on the pine tree.

'Nope,' I said.

3

IN THE staff kitchen, someone had made a sign of taped-together A4 paper that said *TEN YEARS OF WORMS!!!* The 'Western and Outer Region Migrant Services' was having a lunch party. We weren't going to just do cake and sing the song. My boss, Brendan Ogg-Simons, known as Boss, wanted the occasion to be a media event. He'd invited all our clients, other agency people, local paper journos, and photographers. No politicians, we told him, or the staff would rebel.

We were all supposed to bring food. I had dip and chips I'd bought at the super on the way to work. The place was in a frenzy of preparation. For my part, I tried Phuong for the tenth time, but she still didn't answer. I left a grovelling message of regret for displaying an unsatisfactory amount of excitement about her wedding. Then I'd tidied the staff room and put out the plates, cups, streamers.

I'd just sat down with the paper, and in came Raewyn Ross of the Flemington Police.

'Hey Rae, how's things in law and order? You being tough on crime or what?'

Since her promotion, she'd asked me to call her by her rank: *senior constable*. A request that repeatedly slipped my mind. Instead of reminding me again though, she slumped into a chair. There was something different about her, something to do with her eyebrows.

'Doesn't your cop shop have a staff room?' I asked.

'I prefer yours.'

I didn't blame her. The numbers there were against her. Too many men, of the sly overgrown school-boy variety, shirking the harassment policies, artfully placing her at the butt of all jokes, including her in none.

She sighed. 'Caffeine — any danger?'

I spooned coffee into a plunger and caught a whiff of perfume, noted the fake tan. 'Have you got a boyfriend?'

'*Had*.'

'Oh, Rae. I'm so sorry.' I put in an extra spoon of coffee and held the plunger under the urn.

She curled her lip. 'He was cheating.'

'What? The bastard.'

'Said he was going surfing, but he was shagging some skank from Gippsland.'

'Well, that's just uncool.'

She lifted her chin. 'Oh, who cares? I'll just get back on the app where I found him.'

'So, a dating site?'

'Yeah. There's lots — Sexrisx, UzeHer, Hi-Wham.'

'Sounds romantic.'

Rae let out a sudden snort and smacked the paper I'd been planning to read. 'Oh my god! He's dead! That paedophile is dead.'

'Who?'

'This guy, Ricky Peck.' She spun the paper around, and pointed to a photo under the headline: *Bikie Kingpin Drowns*. Peck was impressive. A beefy, tattooed man in shorts and a muscle t-shirt. But it was the incongruous pair of Dunlop Volleys that had me curious. Tennis shoes on a vicious bikie? Roofing tilers wore them for the grip, but I doubted this man had worked an honest day in his life. Maybe he played tennis.

'Peck was a child abuser? I thought bikies *beat up* paedophiles. Wouldn't that be kind of rare criminal activity for a bikie?'

'I know, right? I nabbed some local kids a while back — caught them thieving — and, lo and behold, they reckon Peck's been trying to groom them.'

'Did you report that?'

'I told my sergeant, and he just laughed. But he was a dead-set paedo. As well as a crazy gun-nut. Dangerous as they come.'

'Paper says it was an accident.'

Rae shrugged. 'Could be. Even a nut-job can be careless.'

I depressed the plunger, thinking about Cory and the girl I'd seen him hanging out with earlier this morning. It seemed that they were making life choices that were ... suboptimal. I poured the coffee and glanced at Rae, who was picking at a nail. She was not a reliable source. Bikies were two things: thugs and entrepreneurs. Where was the money in paedophilia? I hoped the youth workers were onto it. Or maybe they weren't. *Nothing you can do, miss.* I doubted Cory was on anyone's radar.

Shanninder, my colleague and fellow WORMS galley-slave, swept into the staffroom with a bowl covered with a tea towel, and a couple of Tupperware containers. 'Gather round, children, we're having *pani puri.*'

Everyone in the world could cook except me. I could smell the bowl's delicious contents from across the room. A sudden whim sent me running to my desk. I dialled Brophy's number. Tonight, I'd cook him dinner — that would surprise him. I'd have to learn how in the meantime, but that shouldn't be too difficult.

'Hello?' A woman's voice.

I cleared my throat. 'Is Brophy there?'

'Yes, but he can't come to the phone.' Formal register, posh accent. *Young.* The 'transcendental' model.

'Excuse me?' My reptilian instincts licked the air.

'Who is *this*?' Her voice had a whip-sting of condescension.

'It's Stella.'

'Oh.' Airily, like it meant nothing. 'I'm Felicity.'

'Put him on.'

'I can't break the flow. We're in a creative peak, he's totally absorbed. This is going to be a radically courageous new work.'

'Just get Brophy, will you?'

'No can do. Call back next week.'

The phone went dead. I stared at the receiver in disbelief. Who did she think she was? *We're* in a creative peak. The nerve of her. I had a good mind to go over there right now.

Was I out of my mind? That would be psycho behaviour. But the room swam in red mist and my heart burned black. I put a hand to my forehead: stone cold. I felt unwell, off my food. I should be in bed. With Brophy.

In the staff room, everyone was laughing and toasting and eating. I dragged myself to the kitchen to join the party. On the way, I passed Boss's office — the blinds were drawn and the door shut. I tapped and opened it. 'You coming to this thing? It's your party.'

'In a minute,' he said. Used tissues littered the desk.

'Ten years, Boss. The culmination of your life's work.'

He lolled back in his chair and groaned.

'Are you okay?'

He stared at the ceiling. 'My life's work. *This.*'

'Don't say it like that. This is awesome, you're making a difference in people's lives.'

'Leave me be, Hardy.'

I shrugged and shut the door.

More guests had arrived. The invitations had been taken up on the whole by refugees recently granted a temporary protection visa — like Afshan and Shahid, Hazaras from Afghanistan. They were new clients and top-notch people. They greeted me with wide grins. 'Happy birthday to your WORMS, Stella!'

'Um, thanks.'

'You must have some of our honey cakes.'

I had to accept, though I was feeling nauseous. A bulb flashed, caught me with my mouth full.

Shanninder had arranged her *pani puri* on the table and explained the procedure: you make an opening in a *puri*, a hollow bread puff, and fill it with chickpea curry, then you pour in the *pani*, a delicious peppery sauce. Raewyn Ross made a brave attempt and shoved the puff into her gob whole. Her expression went from pondering, to happy, to one of ecstasy. I was pleased to see a rare Raewyn-smile.

She'd forgotten all about that cheater and the Gippsland skank.

Meanwhile, Phuong hated me, and Brophy was in the thrall of a harpy. I couldn't stand by and let her take over his life. Game on, Felicity, I said to myself as I picked up a *puri* and cracked its head open.

4

I WALKED without light, in the rain and wind. Seven days with no word from Brophy. The storms blacking out the city were nothing compared to the one raging in my heart.

I'd left my car near his van and hurried in the dark night around to Paisley Street. A vehicle flashed by, red tail-lights shining on the wet street. A silent flicker of lightning followed by a rumble that was deep, ominous, judgemental. I found shelter in the doorway of a gangsta-wear shop with a direct line of sight to his above-shop studio. I took up my position and settled in for a stakeout. Headlights approached from Nicholson Street. The car took the corner too fast, and sprayed me in a fine, muddy mist.

Every time I'd tried to call Brophy, *she* had answered. And on each occasion, she had refused to fetch him, preferring instead to harangue me with a lecture on Brophy's need for time, and 'pure artistic practice'. What was I, contamination? Last week, in a fit of frustration, I'd flown up the stairs and banged on the wall. She pulled back the sliding door, which was the heavy industrial sort; it barely shifted two centimetres on its rusted track, but I got a visual: white, blonde, tall and tanned, in a skimpy robe. She told me he was not to be disturbed, then she heaved the door closed.

And tonight, down on the street, in gale-force conditions, I locked eyes on to his studio window, waiting for my chance. The minute she left, I'd run up there.

A gust of wind lifted the awning above me. There was an alarming sound of scraping metal. Just as I shone my phone light up, a rusted downpipe above me burst apart. I jumped too late, and a torrent of cold water gushed down, baptising me into some dark cult: *Join us, crazy stalker.*

Stalker? Alright, yes, I was. But in my defence, it had been a rough week. Boss was a cranky-pants, and Phuong was still refusing to take my calls.

Now my jeans were sodden, my jumper was a sack of wet wool. I moved to another doorway, my eyes glued to the darkened windows of his studio. After a moment, a soft yellow glow flickered — it must have been a candle. How fucking romantic.

Music erupted in my pocket, the tinny first line of 'Prove My Love' by the Violent Femmes. I'd downloaded the ringtone at a happier time, when its brisk percussion seemed optimistic. Now, it felt like mockery. 'What?' I demanded into the phone.

'You believe in ghosts?'

'Phuong. Hey. At last.'

'Ghosts — what's your take?'

'Um, this is actually a bad time.'

'You're busy? Doing what?'

'I'm just busy.'

'You remember my cousin Cuong?'

'I know Cuong.'

'He's freaking out about the power failure. Too much darkness. He's seeing spirits in the dark. A spirit in the sky.'

'Jesus.'

'No. Some dead relative, probably. I'm with him now.'

I thought I heard footsteps splashing across the street. 'Wait.' I put my hand over the phone and stared into the blackness. I was mistaken. 'Sorry, Phuong, what is this about?'

'Cuong has a cool new apartment and I thought you might like to come over. We're in Sunshine; it's practically around the corner from your place. And, well, the thing is, I need your help with something.'

Any other day, I'd be already on my way. And this was my chance to make it up to her. Besides, Phuong rarely required my help. But what if she needed help choosing something for the wedding? I didn't know how long I could keep up a charade of good will.

'Um, so now, you mean?'

'Yes.' I could hear the impatience.

Looking up, I saw shadows move against Brophy's window, and I inhaled. Then I sensed movement closer, and from the corner of my eye, I saw her. Shit. *Her.* Right beside me. I lowered the phone from my ear.

'Stella Hardy. What are you doing?'

She was wrapped in a coat, but odds-on she was naked underneath. Not a gram of fat on her.

'Nothing,' I said, mortified.

She looked to the sky. 'It's pissing down, you bloody idiot, go home.'

I would not be told by her. 'No. I'm coming up.'

'I can't let you do that.'

'What do you mean you *can't let me*?' I said, incensed.

'He sent me down to tell you,' she said, with a malevolent shrug. 'He doesn't want to lose focus.' Then with the long-legged stride of a stilt-walker, a circus freak, she crossed the road, back to the Narcissistic Slacker.

He sent her down? I was shaking, caught by the urge to hit something. I raised my hand, looked at my phone. *Forget you, mate.* 'Phuong? Give me the address, I'll be there in fifteen.'

5

PHUONG SHONE a light on my face. 'You're all wet.'

'Astounding work, Captain Obvious.'

'Detective Obvious.'

People with rank, always with the rank. She held the entrance doors open for me. The automatic doors were useless without power. Places like this were hyper-secure until something went wrong with the technology, and then they became death traps. She pointed her torch to the ground and guided me through the building. 'We have to take the stairs.'

Cuong's apartment on Hampshire Road was about six months old. Built on the site of an old foundry, developers had whacked together ninety-three cheapo studios — twenty floors, with miniature balconies — and named it *La Fonderie*. The suburb of Sunshine looked upon this menhir in its midst and laughed. How long before systemic entropy, starting with graffiti — not art, not your Banksy or Lushsux, but a mush of curse words, all ghetto and no cred — merged the place with its surroundings, with povo-scary town?

Cuong's apartment was on the fifth floor, which was fortunate. Any more stairs and I'd have carked it. He was waiting with his door open, and handed me a towel. He was better at these things than his cousin.

'*Chào anh,*' I said.

He bobbed his head — a bow, or perhaps a nervous tic. 'Haven't seen you for a long time, Stella.'

'It's been a while.' I looked into the apartment. 'You're moving up in the world.'

He shrugged, but then cast a worried glance down the empty hallway. 'Hurry, Stella. Come inside and get dry.'

20

A studio — meaning bedsit, meaning single room divided into 'zones'. For the compact living area, he'd chosen simple elegant furniture, a two-seater sofa, an armchair, a sideboard on which the accoutrements of an altar were spread: an offering of fruit, burning incense, family portraits in wooden frames, tea candles.

'Where were you when I phoned?' Phuong was in the kitchenette, pouring hot water from a saucepan into a mug.

'Out.' I took off my jumper. 'Can I hang this out on your balcony?' I asked Cuong.

He looked horrified. 'Not out there. The friends will get inside it.' He took the jumper from me without further explanation and draped it over a towel rail in the bathroom.

Phuong handed me a mug. The tea had black twigs and bits of burnt rice floating in it.

She looked me up and down. 'So you were out in the rain?' She made being in the rain sound like bourgeois decadence, like it was some depraved lifestyle choice.

'I like rain.'

Cuong now offered me a towelling robe, the heavy, luxury-hotel kind.

'Cám ơn rất nhiều.' I bobbed my head.

He laughed; my pronunciation always made Vietnamese people laugh.

No doubt about it, he was a classy guy. The candlelight accentuated his hollow cheeks and melancholy eyes. He sure *looked* haunted. I wondered how much help someone like Phuong, the ultimate rational being, was to a man with a fear of the supernatural.

I put the robe on, slipped off my sandals, and curled up on the sofa.

Cuong retreated to the sleep area, where his bed and a small wardrobe were sectioned off by sheer curtains. He drew them closed, but I could see him sitting on his bed. He put his earbuds in and opened a laptop.

'You have friends who get on the balcony and put on your wet clothes?' I asked Phuong, rubbing my hair with the towel.

She sighed. 'It's code for *you-know-what*. Saying the G-word attracts them.'

I glanced at him. 'He seems okay now.'

'He's a bit better. We had a couple of cognacs.'

I looked at the sticks in my tea, wondering what I had to do to get an upgrade. 'What was his problem?'

'The power went off. Gets him every time. My parents usually deal with him, but they're away at the moment. I don't understand it. I mean, I understand the ghosts, the ancestors. This is different — he believes there's one ghost that wishes him harm.'

It was comforting to know I was not the only suspicious person on the planet. I sipped the twig infusion. A robust flavour, concentrated like the Queensland sun. A brew tailor-made for me, I had no doubt, and I assumed it contained herbs of restraint. This witch would have me spayed. 'Now,' I said, putting the mug down. 'How can I be of service?' If I could do Phuong a solid favour, it might defuse some of the ill feeling between us since my botched handling of the news of her engagement.

She didn't meet my eye. 'It's Bruce.'

Bugger. We were on dangerous territory again. I'd say the wrong thing again for sure. I decided to try to keep things light. 'I see. Well, I'm no relationship counsellor —' based on that day's activities, I'd say I was downright unqualified '— but you guys seem … okay together.'

She shook her head.

'No? Alright. Let's see. He's into werewolves, you're more of a zombie fan? I've been through that, and don't worry, it can still work.'

'He's under investigation.'

Her words took a moment to settle. 'What investigation? You mean the one he initiated?'

'It expanded beyond his control. The task force had been tapping phones.' She sighed. 'They recorded some pretty damning conversations, evidently. And now the investigation is in the hands of the new integrity commission. They're calling it Operation Raw-Prawn.'

The seriousness of this development was out of my comfort zone. It seemed more feasible to me to suggest that Bruce Copeland was a wizard, or a Greens voter, or a model-plane enthusiast. 'What's he done?'

She sniffed, and I realised she was teary, or had been. Now she was glaring at me. 'Jesus, how can you even ask that? He's not involved.'

'Of course not.' I sipped the tea. I had to admit, it was calming. I could use some respite on the emotional front. 'What do they have?'

'The OTIOSE commission people are very reticent, but the rumours are there's a recording of an unidentified cop, most probably a Guns and Gangs detective, making deals, demanding cash and heroin.'

'Wait, an officer of the law was behaving like a thug?' I clapped a hand to my cheek.

Phuong squinted, a sign she was displeased. 'Your relentless sarcasm, it's food colouring for the soul.'

'Sorry,' I said, and meant it. 'I want to help — any way I can. Please go on. Who is the detective?'

'No one knows for sure. Everyone is paranoid. There's a few likely candidates, but Bruce doesn't have anything to do with the idiots in the unit.' She coughed. 'His problems started with Jeff Vanderhoek, the Corpse Flower informer. Vanderhoek gave Bruce the name of a dealer.'

'*The Corpse Flowers.*' I smirked. 'I mean, seriously.'

'Stella, can you please focus. This is important. This dealer lives in Norlane — that's in Geelong.'

'I know where Norlane is.' Just because I was easily distracted didn't mean I was dumb.

She sniffed again. 'Bruce arrested the guy — drugs and weapons charges. He put the evidence in the unit's safe, and the dealer spent the night in the lock-up. All by the book.'

'Okay, so he followed the new procedures.'

'Yes. Except that, today, someone checked, and it's gone. All of it.'

'What kind of evidence are we talking about?'

'A couple of hand guns, a shotgun, a grenade, and about a hundred grams of heroin.'

'A grenade?' I put down the mug. A *grenade*. It was so bizarre it was almost funny.

'That was sent off to the bomb squad for disposal, but the other weapons and the heroin had been in the safe, or he thought they were, for the last week. Now they're gone. Without the evidence, they had to release the dealer.'

I tried to be reassuring — with any luck, it actually came across that way. 'I'm sure Bruce is thoroughly law-abiding.'

In the flickering candlelight, her face seemed to float in stark chiaroscuro. 'He needs the dealer to testify. Tell the truth. That Bruce bagged it all, and took him to the lock-up. And have the stupid lie blown out of the water.'

'He expects a criminal to testify for him, a cop, while incriminating themselves?'

Phuong shifted, folding her legs under her. 'I understand why you would say that, but the situation is complicated. There are rumours this guy wants to get out of the Corpse Flowers. And he knows a *lot*. If Bruce could just talk to him, a deal might be on the table. The truth about Bruce, as well as other information he has, in exchange for immunity.'

'Then call the investigators and tell them to talk to this guy.'

She bowed her head. 'He's skipped town.'

'Of course he has.' My head dropped back in exasperation.

She stood up, walked to the sideboard, and spoke to the shrine. 'Why do you hate Bruce?'

'I don't hate Bruce,' I said.

'*Intensely dislike.*'

'Not even close. How can I dislike him? I don't even know him, not that well.' As a general rule, I preferred to be honest in my dealings with people. Most of the time I was. This was not one of those times.

'We're going to get married.'

'I know. And I'm happy for you.'

She turned away from the shrine and gathered the magazines on the coffee table into a neat pile. Then she picked up a cushion and started plumping it. 'The dealer's name is Mortimer — Isaac Mortimer — and he *knows* Bruce is innocent.'

'Jeez, woman. Don't be so bloody dramatic. Last I checked, the system works the other way around. They need hard evidence to convict Bruce, and there isn't any.'

She didn't respond.

'There isn't any evidence, right? Is there?'

'What if a cop under suspicion decides to save themselves by making false accusations against Bruce? And the testimony of a colleague would be considered evidence, Stella. If no one knew that cop was corrupt. That's why we need Isaac Mortimer.'

We? *We* need Isaac Mortimer? I took off the robe. My jumper was still damp and steaming on the towel rail in the bathroom. I put it on anyway.

'When have I ever asked you for a favour?' Phuong said.

I stopped. Answer: never. I owed her — how many favours? I wanted to make it right with her.

'This is your forte,' she went on. 'You've worked with street kids. You know the squats, the addicts. You know your way around.'

Child services for a while, then public housing: my career spanned many fronts of the community sector. Phuong had heard me talk about the slog, the cases of hopeless addiction, child neglect, of family dysfunction. I was happier now in migrant services.

25

'Isaac Mortimer,' Phuong said, slow and clear. 'All we need is an address.'

I faced her. Her pleading eyes skewered me. 'You are my dearest friend. I would do just about anything to help you. But you can't flatter me into combing junkie squats for an ice dealer.' Certainly not for Copeland.

I took my mug to the sink, turned on the taps, as mist rose from my wet sleeves.

'He has *fuck yeah* tattooed on his forehead.'

I rinsed the mug.

'If you won't do it for Bruce, do it for me.'

Cuong lounged on his bed. I caught his eye and waved. He seemed startled — possibly because I was surrounded by white puffs of jumper fog. I gestured for him to take out the earbuds.

'Cuong, do you know what tomorrow is?'

He shook his head, shrugged.

I turned to Phuong. 'You better word him up. He sees little vampires and zombies on the street tomorrow, he'll have a meltdown.'

She waved a dismissive hand. 'He knows. Kids in dress-ups don't concern him.'

I wanted to know what *did* concern him. I was curious about the ghosts, with their fondness for wet clothes on a balcony.

'I'm really sorry, Phuong. I hope it works out,' I said, and left, shutting the door behind me.

In the darkened hall, I paused. In some respects, Cuong was on the money. Ghosts were everywhere. I felt them hanging around in the residue of lost romances, and hovering in the memory cringes of insomnia. Or, haunting me on those mornings when I felt like boiled shite, I could hear them in my remorse.

Here, under the green exit lights, a ghost whispered to me of failure. Of relationships gone awry. Of Brophy gradually fading into my past.

6

THE NEXT day, work was hell. I was in the gutter again. Afshan, my bowling buddy, was worried about me. 'Let's use the baby rail,' he said.

Calling it the 'baby rail' had been my stupid idea, back when I thought bowling might be fun and should be played properly. Before I discovered I sucked.

'I'm not five years old,' I said, with my hand over the air vent, waiting for the mechanism to regurgitate my ball. WORMS had booked Sunshine's Funky Town, an amusement centre for go-karting, laser tag, and ten-pin bowling, as part of our new 'Have a Go' program. My colleagues were keen on these events, as we all got to get out of the office on the pretext of assimilating our newest residents into the Australian way of life. So far, we'd been to a football match at the MCG, chartered a fishing trip on Port Phillip Bay, and had a picnic at Hanging Rock. Some suggestions for Have a Go that were deemed unsuitable by management included a trip to a TAB, driving around in a hired truck on hard-rubbish day, and ferreting.

'But I will be glad of it.'

That was a lie; Afshan was taking pity on me. His ball had entered the gutter only once. With his thick, square hands and low centre of gravity, he'd mastered the game after only a brief rundown of the rules. He racked up a commendable beginner's run of sevens and eights that had him in high double digits, and he'd completed an excellent spare.

'I think not.' When my ball bobbed up, I plugged the icky holes with my fingers and hoicked the thing, more in disgust than hope. It bounced and rolled inexorably to the gutter. I turned to Afshan and laughed as though carefree and amused.

He laughed along, rather guardedly. Now he took aim, the seven kilos of polyurethane pressed to his lips. He gave a self-deprecating little shrug, stepped forward, genuflecting on his right knee and swinging his arm. The ball kissed the wood and raced in a curving roll that roamed from one side of the alley to the other until it hit the front pin side on. Strike. In his first ever game of ten-pin bowling.

'Nice,' I said.

'Yes. It was very nice. Now, Stella, for your turn we will set up the ramp?'

'No, thanks. I'm done with this fool's diversion. Let's see if the food in the cafe is safe for human consumption.'

We left the game unfinished and went to a dining area with the ambience of a needle exchange. A twenty-four-hour news channel blathered away from a television on the wall. It crossed to the weather forecast, delivered by a woman wearing a black cape and a pointy witch's hat. Last night's storm had caused major disruption in Melbourne, she said. The power was still out in some places in the western quarter of the city. A tree had fallen on a house. Scenes of residents cleaning up, one collecting a stray trampoline from their neighbour's yard. A montage followed of children dressed as ghosts, pirates, mermaids, and a voice said, 'Children taking food from strangers: five reasons parents should be worried.'

Afshan and I bought coffee and a couple of slices of apple cake. We were taking the plastic wrap from the cake, and our chances, when the drum intro to 'Prove My Love' started up in my bag. Caller ID: *Beloved*. I excused myself and dashed to a private corner.

'Brophy? At last.'

'Hey, you. I've missed you.'

Oh, the relief. 'I've missed you, too.'

'I heard you were hanging around the studio last night.'

Hanging around? That sounded like Felicity's twisted version, making me seem creepy. Well, it was sort of accurate. But still, I was confused. I mean, normally I *would* have just come up and said hi. And why didn't I? Because Felicity told me not to. Brophy's request. I

28

closed my eyes, resisting the urge to argue. Besides, my pride wouldn't let me admit I'd been impeded by that poseur. So, I obfuscated. 'Not me. You heard wrong.'

'Really? Felicity said she saw you.'

'Yeah, but she's got the IQ of an eggplant so ...'

He let that go.

I moved things along. 'You free tonight?' The odds were against it, but I asked.

At his end, a long pause. Considering the possibilities, perhaps. 'Damn, can't tonight. I'm flat out. Worked all last night and I'm worried I still won't be ready for next week.'

'You'll get it done. They'll be amazing.'

'Tell you what,' he said, sounding brighter. 'As soon as the exhibition's over, we'll go out. Or better yet, we'll go away somewhere, a dirty weekend. Daylesford or something.'

I sensed a flicker of hope. Were we going to make it? 'Love to,' I said.

'Great. Gotta go, Felicity's here,' he said, and hung up.

Ugh. Her timing was horrible. Or uncanny. I resolved to change my ring tone — 'Prove My Love' was now categorically tainted.

'How is your boyfriend?' Afshan asked, when I returned to the table. 'He is an artist, yes?'

'I'll tell you how he is: he's holed up in his garret with a woman who poses naked for him seven days a week.'

Afshan looked away and sipped his coffee. 'I'm sorry to hear that.'

'I don't buy it. No one can work *all* the time.'

'Stella, perhaps you should give him the time to do his work.'

'How would you feel if your girlfriend was alone with a naked man?'

'My wife and daughter live in a camp in Pakistan. I haven't held them for four years.'

'I see. Sorry. Bad example.' I really needed to stop complaining to refugees.

Afshan pointed to the TV. 'There is a breaking news.'

Pink-cheeked, I looked at the screen. *Police detective questioned.* The picture cut to a serious-looking woman in the studio. 'Welcome. I'm Yolanda Gilling, and joining me now to discuss this development ...' Cut to an old, familiar face. 'The Minister for Police, Marcus Pugh.' Well, well, well, the right honourable *Mucous Pukus,* as I and my colleagues at WORMS thought of him. What a tosser. WORMS had had the misfortune of having much to do with the minister — and was all too aware of his love of ribbon cutting and credit taking.

'Mr Pugh, isn't it time your government called for a Royal Commission into the Victoria Police?'

'Yolanda, we don't need a royal commission. Incidences of police corruption are rare in this state.'

'Why have you disbanded the Police Honesty Investigation Branch, or PHIB, *and* IBAC, the Independent Broad-based Anti-corruption Commission, and replaced it with one body, responsible for investigating all public-agency corruption, the ...' She checked her notes. 'The "Official Tribunal Investigating Offenders Suspected of Egregiousness", or OTIOSE, which has fewer powers, and is essentially a toothless tiger?'

'The government took the view that IBAC was too expensive and was under-performing.'

'But that's because it was under-resourced — and now you've replaced it with an even less effective organisation.'

'I disagree with that notion, Yolanda.'

Yolanda moved on. 'Operation Raw-Prawn has only just been instituted, and already crucial evidence has reportedly gone missing. And we know there are current serving officers under investigation. It's not a good look.'

'That's my point. A royal commission won't achieve that sort of result. The only sector of our society to benefit from such an expensive exercise is barristers.'

Yolanda Gilling looked unconvinced. 'A lawyers' picnic?'

'Exactly. A royal commission can lead to people being granted immunity from prosecution, suspected criminals. We've done a lot to address the problems that go back to the bad old days of the drug squad, the chemical-distribution days.'

'But you can understand some people think that you have something to hide. Does your government have something to hide?'

'We have nothing to hide. We have a properly constituted corruption investigation body that is accountable to the parliament with sufficient powers the police need to deal with organised crime. I don't know what more they might need that they don't currently have.'

Afshan gnawed on his cake. 'He is saying the police are not corrupt? I think so, they are corrupt.'

My thoughts returned to last night, to the image of Phuong's strained face. 'I can't believe I'm saying this, Afshan, but I agree with Pukus.'

'Who?'

'The minister. There are some greedy idiots in police uniform, for sure. But there's no widespread corruption. Your typical cop is honest and hardworking. Like my friend Phuong, faithfully doing her duty.' What I didn't tell Afshan was that for her outstanding arrest record and her scrupulous honesty she'd found herself sidelined to a cybercrime unit.

He stopped chewing. 'Not all the police are corrupt,' he said, 'but some are … What is the word? Dodgy.'

I considered this. 'Have you had firsthand experience?'

He looked down at his coffee.

'If you need to speak to a cop you can trust, call Detective Senior Constable Nguyen.'

'Perhaps.'

'I have to say, Afshan, I'm rather shocked by your cynicism.'

He shrugged, then tipped his head to the screen, as if that settled the argument. I turned to see footage of Bruce Copeland being shoved into a police car and driven away.

7

ASCOT VALE'S heartland was subdued. My neighbours were a sedate bunch. After work, there was a civilised queue to buy beer at the supermarket, which I joined. And later, with a six-pack and a family-sized pizza, I plodded up Roxburgh Street and went up to my flat to contemplate my existence.

The 7pm ABC news covered an assortment of the day's happenings. Train to the airport? Not so fast. Bandicoots extinct? No, they're making a comeback. Tie up your trampolines, more storms imminent.

Then came a bikie funeral for a chap discovered facedown in a bath in a derelict house bursting with hydroponic flora. The late Ricky Peck had been a popular fellow. Outside the church, his mates pelted the journalists with golf balls. It was the least they could do. Cops were still making inquiries. Cut to a woman I recognised — a mature journalist, with a permanently serious face, and wicked cheekbones. 'Bunny Slipper reporting in Braybrook.'

Back to the studio, where the newsreader added, 'Tune in on Sunday night for part one of Bunny Slipper's three-part documentary on the escalating activities of outlaw motorcycle gangs in Australia.' Segue to Bruce Copeland — the detective inspector had been interviewed by police for a second time and released.

Sprawled on my lounge room floor, full of pizza and beer, I could bear no more. I flicked through the channels and found a movie full of suffering and violence and Leonardo DiCaprio delivering his lines in a nifty South African accent. A linguistic feat like that deserved an Oscar, surely. He was negotiating with a warlord: a plane full of grenade launchers for diamonds. The warlord gives Leo a bag of crap. Leo tells him *no deal*, he will have to use old AK-47s against the government troops. Good luck with that, warlord, I thought. Then a knock on my door ruined the moment.

I hit the remote and discovered that my left leg had fallen asleep. I dragged myself upright and made it to the door without falling down. I put my eye to the aperture. Framed in my peephole was a short person in a rubber mask.

Some blame the Americans, some the Irish, but after a slow start, Halloween had arrived in Melbourne and was now a thing. It was half-arsed compared to the US version. Here it was more a last-minute ransacking of two-dollar shops. Plastic masks, cut-up pillowcases, and cardboard hats. It lacked the authenticity of tradition, having been introduced in my lifetime, so I felt comfortable ignoring it. During my childhood, no filament of fake cobweb had been spread across a single fake tombstone in any Australian front yard.

The masked child bounced excitedly from foot to foot, no doubt anticipating her glycaemic hit. As far as I could tell, she had come as what I could only describe as an ugly old woman. I felt I should not reward that kind of thing.

'I know you're in there, Stella!' the child shouted. 'I heard your TV. You're watching *Blood Diamond*.'

Who was this kid, Margaret Pomeranz? 'Just a minute.' In my pantry, I found a small, unopened packet of sweet airline biscuits that I had must have stashed after a flight. I twisted my deadbolt and pushed the door back.

'Trick or t—'

'Oh, shut up. Here.' I thrust the biscuits in her little hand.

The eyes within the mask took in the impoverished offering, then moved to my face and narrowed. 'I should egg your flat.'

I tried to snatch the biscuits back, but she yanked her hand away.

'If one egg hits my door, just one, I'll hunt you down, you shrunken hag.' But she had fled, no doubt using her witch powers to fly down the three flights to ground level.

'Thanks, Stella,' a maternal voice called from the stairwell.

I mumbled something neighbourly and shut the door. *Blood Diamond* was over. I hit the remote and my lounge room began to emit ultraviolet rays of boredom. Ennui filled every corner, and my weary soul soaked it up like a sponge. As ever lately, my thoughts turned to Brophy. He needed time to himself to work. It was a completely reasonable request, and one I had agreed to. I was a mature, independent woman after all. I had the self-sufficient emotional poise of a religious hermit. Usually in times such as these I'd have gone to bed with a good book.

But these times were not usual. He was gambolling about his studio with a naked woman twenty years my junior.

And so, as I found my car keys and put on my spray jacket, I reminded myself that I'd never said anything about not driving slowly past his place. Late at night. Several times.

I made it to the car park just as the elements exploded in a biblical deluge. Again with the lightning. Spring storms were frequent in Melbourne, but this was beyond a joke. I started the Mazda and cranked up the heater. A sappy love song came on the radio. I changed the station: Pugh droning on. I snapped it off, roared down my street, and cracked a left turn in third gear. It was not me but some mad woman driving across the Maribyrnong with a smouldering ache in her chest. Suspicion gnawed away in there like a starved rodent.

This so-called Felicity, she was no muse. A cerebral lightweight with delusions of profundity, a spray-tanned false prophet, a pretentious boyfriend-stealing goddamn interloper. He said she *inspired* him. Oh God, Brophy, what were you doing with her?

8

THE HEATER gave it everything, but cold came in from a hole in the floor. The rain fell as if being tipped on the world from a million swimming pools. As I got closer to his street, my teeth started chattering. First, I did a slow circuit of the block, eyes on the light in his studio. No movement up there. I parked behind his building and pulled up the hood on my jacket. I passed under his windows, where it would be impossible for him to see me. Not many people about, except for a couple of men dashing down the street, huddled under a raincoat. A woman sat slumped at the bus shelter playing on her phone — then she turned to me and spoke. 'Stella.'

'What the?'

'It's time we had a talk, don't you think?'

'Jesus, Felicity. No.'

'I know this is awkward for you. It's awkward for me, too.'

'Stop saying "awkward". What are you doing down here?'

'I've finished sitting for him for tonight.'

Sitting, posing, seducing. 'Then I might go up.'

'He's working on backgrounds. Probably for the whole night. I wouldn't disturb him.'

I resented this. 'Then we should both go home.'

'I'm meeting some friends for a drink. Why don't you come along? We can have a heart-to-heart, what do you say?'

An evening of claptrap with this ditsy nong. 'Hmm, sounds tempting, but no.'

'One drink.' She was unyielding. It made her seem older somehow, and made me feel infantile, like *I* was the princess here.

'Fine. I'll meet you there.' I would be unable to find the venue.

'I don't have a car. You can give me a lift.'

She was a determined adversary, I'd give her that. And I doubted her invitation was spontaneous. If it was a tactic, then, much as she irked me, it would be to my advantage to find out what this schemer was up to. 'One drink wouldn't hurt, I guess. Car's over here.' I pointed to the alley.

As we buckled up, I said, 'Shouldn't you be dressed as a cowgirl, out knocking on doors and asking for sweets?'

'Halloween is not about sweets. The commercialisation is a recent degradation of an ancient festival that actually has its roots in pre-Christian Ireland.'

'Gosh, Felicity, that is so interesting.'

She tilted her head, blinked, then went on.

'Traditionally on Halloween the gateways between the living and the dead are for a short time open. And while the modern-day zombie costumes send up death, we can't escape it — death awaits us all. According to one study, grief seeks to *stay with* lost loved ones, not distance them. Even as time goes on, people yearn for closer ties to the dead.'

I thought of my father. Time hadn't brought any closure, whatever that was. His crop-dusting plane crashed when I was a teenager, and his presence was still palpable, even now.

'The popularity of Halloween,' Felicity went on, 'has more to do with anxiety about death. Imagine if we were able to really relate to the dead! It happens in Mexico and Japan — in lots of places — and in the lighting of candles to the ancestors in Chinese Confucian and Buddhist traditions. The souls of the dead return home.'

'What are you, some kind of a pagan?'

'No, I did a semester on comparative religion. Turn right, here.'

I turned into Victoria Street, heading south to Seddon. A flock of little witches dashed under a shop awning. I thought of Cuong and how Phuong had said his concerns were not about random ghosts. A single, specific spirit haunted that poor man. A ghost with a grudge.

'Here it is, The Drunken Tweet.'

The place was a single-fronted shop converted into a disinterested and therefore on-trend wine bar. Felicity made an earnest study of the cocktail list. 'One MFW, no ice,' she told the waiter. 'Stella?'

'Two.'

I glanced at the blackboard menu. The 'MFW' stood for 'Mad Fucking Witch', a cocktail of fruit-based liqueurs. It was too late, I supposed, to change my order.

Felicity regarded me with blunt scrutiny; I could almost hear her tiny brain calculating. I didn't like it one bit. 'So,' I said. 'How's your day been?'

She acted dismayed.

'So,' I continued. 'Mine's been tops, thanks for asking. Bowling. Cake. It had everything.'

'I haven't fucked him.'

Ah, candour as a shock tactic, designed to catch me off-guard. What she didn't know was that I was *always* on guard. And normally I'd have given her a pasting. However, I had no doubt that this conversation would get back to Brophy, so I had to hold my fire. 'I don't care either way,' I replied blithely.

She squared her shoulders and took a deep breath. I feared she was about to make a *speech*. I had a fear of public speaking. Not my own, other people's. What if I became bored and started to panic?

'We haven't even kissed, but I think you should know —'

'Stop. Whatever it is, I don't want to know.'

She put up her hands in mild exasperation. 'I thought we could talk, adult to adult.'

Two jars of toilet-blue liquid appeared, each with a striped straw. I seized one and consumed half, sweet as drupe, and alcoholically warming. Oh boy, could I get stuck into these. 'Alright then, let's talk. What are your grand plans?'

She held the jar near her lips. 'Plans? You mean with Peter Brophy?'

'I mean your *studies*.' Dummy! 'Your *future*.'

'This is bullshit,' she said, clearly exasperated. 'I'm trying to tell you that even though I'm not interested in Peter sexually —'

'I heard you, okay? He's a free agent,' I said. Perhaps I'd have more luck using that undergraduate conjectural language she obviously traded in. 'I don't believe in tying people down. Monogamy is a construction of patriarchy. People are free to love whomever they feel like.'

Felicity went stern. 'That's nice, in theory,' she said. 'But I don't think relationships work that way, Stella. We form attachments. It's only human. We need love and family and we feel very protective of those we love.'

Bloody hell. The situation was hopeless. I sipped my Mad Witch juice.

'Are you familiar with Eris? In the Iliad, she's Enyo; she's the goddess of strife, discord, and ...' She paused for effect. 'Jealousy.'

'A lesson in the classics. Thanks for enlightening me.'

'There're certain rituals you can perform that can appease an angry goddess.'

I nearly sprayed the table blue. 'What the heck are you on about?'

She sat back. 'We all have a bit of Eris in us, don't you think? Petty jealousies, competitive instincts turned to bitter rivalry?'

This was what she had to tell me? I'd show her a *goddess*. I'd make up one of my own — a cold, hard bitch who flouted propriety and good manners. The awesome power of righteousness in a bat-shit, bad-arse, crazy mother—

There was an abrupt *dingdong* in my pocket. I acted apologetic as I pulled out my phone. Felicity bowed her head.

Phuong: *Where r u*

'Sorry,' I said to Felicity. 'It's urgent.'

An indulgent hand came out of her sleeve and waved. 'Go ahead.'

Me: *Help! I'm being held hostage at the Drunken Tweet*

Phuong: *Run! I'm at Cuong's*

Me: *15 mins*

'Well, this has been all very edifying,' I said, draining my juice.

Felicity bestowed a slow blink upon me, like a cat in love. 'It has, hasn't it?'

I dropped a lobster on the table, Christ only knew what a witch juice set one back these days. 'I have to see a man about a ghost.'

As exits went, it was *rip, shit, and bust.* I jumped in the Mazda and gunned it.

9

CUONG BUZZED me into his flat. Candles again, despite the power being operational, and that familiar trace of sandalwood incense that had an instant calming effect. It was tempting to ask if I could hang around, have a week-long retreat, right here in his flat. I spied Phuong, hunched over her phone in the kitchenette, and gave her a thumbs-up.

He lit a bunch of incense sticks and went outside. I followed him onto the balcony. A small wooden structure was set up on the floor, about the size of a doll's house, and near it offerings of oranges, a packet of Hero-brand cigarettes, a can of beer. And, on either side, red glowing battery-powered candles.

He bowed with the incense, intoning in muted Vietnamese.

'How's work?' I asked lamely. 'Software development, is it?'

'Nah, economics,' he said without looking up. 'It's okay. No dramas.'

'So ... you're okay?'

He placed the incense in a bowl filled with sand. 'Halloween is not a problem for me.'

I looked askance at him.

'Phuong told me you were worried for me,' Cuong said.

'The dead are supposed to come home, that could be upsetting for anyone.'

'Nah.'

Phuong came to the balcony. Her face was drawn. 'Bruce was on the news tonight.'

'I saw.'

Phuong sighed. 'Come inside. Want some tea?'

'Tea? No. Thanks.' I moved some of Cuong's books off the sofa.

'Has he been charged?'

'Suspended.' Phuong flicked on a lamp and draped herself on the armchair. 'It's a joke. The stolen-evidence claim is baseless and circumstantial.'

'The enquiry sounds like a mess.'

She rolled her eyes. 'I know, right? They're under intense political pressure to sort it out quickly, so they're panicking, letting criminals testify, chasing every claim and counter-claim.'

Cuong, I noticed, was in the kitchenette, his head inclined at an eavesdropping angle.

'How's Bruce coping?' I asked.

'Not well. He's laying low, helping his dad with his boat-hire business in Somers.'

Suspended and hiding. The situation was an order of magnitude more serious than it had been yesterday. How could a bunch of idiot bikies wreak this much havoc in the upper ranks of the police? 'I saw that bikie's funeral on the news tonight.'

She rolled her head towards her shoulder, and a bone cracked. 'Ricky Peck was a violent criminal, with enemies. People like him don't drift away in a bath, they die in a hail of bullets.'

I appreciated her scepticism, but surely even violent people sometimes suffered deaths of quiet misfortune. But now was not the time to debate such things. The moment called for something reassuring. 'Phuong ...'

'You can't help. I understand. It was wrong to ask you. There are certain places that the average person should not voluntarily go.'

Average? *Average?* 'I go to places, all sorts of places.'

'You probably wouldn't have the first clue about those druggy people, how to talk the language.'

'I speak druggy.'

She sighed like she hadn't heard me.

'Have you had dinner, Stella?' Cuong was beside us, resting a hand on my shoulder.

41

Phuong sat up, bright again. 'I'm starving.'

'Me too.' Pizza didn't count; it was a snack food.

'Let's get some *phở*.'

Food was an excellent idea. The witch juice had made me unsteady. And I suspected Phuong and Cuong had once again been nudging the cognac. Cuong was smiling strangely at me, and Phuong seemed slightly manic. I would need to keep an eye on her.

10

THE RAIN had stopped for now, leaving the drains gargling and the road shimmering. Phuong, Cuong, and I skirted the idle souls loitering on the shopping-centre steps and made for a row of *phở* places further along Hampshire Road. Cuong ushered us into one that was busy. Above the tank of writhing fish at the back of the restaurant: greyhound racing on a mute TV.

I didn't order *phở* because of the beef stock, and the beef. Instead, I ordered a plain vegetable soup with tofu. The choice impressed Cuong, and he asked me if I was Buddhist.

'A better one than your slack-arse cousin over here.' A nod at Phuong.

She sighed loudly. 'Eating meat is not against Buddhism.'

I scoffed and winked at Cuong, but he had turned away, and was staring dull-eyed at the races. We had some strange customs in this country. Twice a year, Australians came together to stop and reflect: once to remember the war dead, and once to watch a horse race. I guessed he'd think that was kind of cool.

We ordered some beers, and within minutes, the soup arrived. Phuong blew on a green vegetable suspended in her chopsticks and slipped it into her mouth.

Then she dropped the chopsticks and shoved the bowl away. I, on the other hand, had a healthy appetite, and drank my soup with gusto. A consolation, soup was. I took my consolations where I found them — in a bowl, in television binging, in nursing a private hatred. Phuong started hunting in her bag and muttering to herself.

I noticed she was a little pink in the cheeks, and her gaze was slightly unfocused. I looked over at Cuong. He was staring like a zombie at the races on TV.

'Stella.'

I turned back to Phuong. Her hand was on the table, closed tight. She opened it and revealed two bullets. She lifted one from her palm and turned it around in the light. 'Here,' she said. 'Look. I found them in my letter box this morning.'

I rolled the bullet between my fingers. The casing was engraved: *Nguyễn Phương*. I noted the precise diacritics.

'Are these any old bullets, or the same calibre as police-issue semi-automatics?'

'Police issue. To get at Bruce,' she said, and held out her hand.

I dropped it back in her palm. 'If Copeland's the target, why not send them to him?'

'They know he'd be more worried about me, than for himself,' Phuong said, slurring the last word. She pressed her fist to her lips, white knuckles.

'I paid. Let's go,' Cuong said, putting the wallet in his back pocket. He said something in Vietnamese to Phuong, and we went outside.

The streets were hushed, it was getting late. We passed under the glare of the shopping-centre security lights and out again, into the shadows. Ahead, *La Fonderie* was in darkness.

As we approached, hissing sounds came from somewhere near Phuong's blue hatchback, parked out the front. I squinted and saw a silhouette bending over it. Cuong shouted. The figure cursed and sprinted across Hampshire Road — an effortless spring over the fence, and gone.

Cuong pointed at Phuong's car. Silver spray-painted squiggles on the driver's door: *u r dead*; and on the back window, fat capitals: *DOGS DIE.*

11

'I THINK we should call the —'

'Don't you call anyone,' she said, pointing her keys at me.

I turned to Cuong. 'I'll take her to my place.'

'I'll get it out of sight.' Cuong took her keys and got into her car. 'See you later, Stella,' he said, and drove it into the *La Fonderie* underground car park.

I led Phuong away, towards my car. She stumbled along obediently.

'I was thinking, maybe, I might help you. A bit.'

She blinked. 'Help how?'

I gazed up, seeking a star to wish on, or swear at, but the city haze offered none. 'I'll try to find Isaac Mortimer.'

'Stella.' Phuong seized my hand with the force of a handcuff. 'Thank you.'

'He's probably half way to Kununurra by now, or Fitzroy-bloody-Crossing.'

'No, he isn't.'

I faced her. 'Care to enlighten me?'

'Bruce still has friends who support him within the unit. They've checked. Mortimer's phone's inactive and he hasn't used his credit cards.'

'Maybe Copeland should ask them to find the guy,' I muttered.

She looked stricken. 'But they can't be seen to —'

'Right, right. But why do you think he's still in Melbourne?'

'He came up on security vision at a 7-Eleven. Norlane. Day after he walked out of remand. A week ago.'

'That last known address was Norlane, too, wasn't it?'

'Yes, but he'd spent most of the last few months in Melbourne. He had a strong network in Footscray,' Phuong said. 'You'll have better luck here, with the local kids.'

45

I put her in my car, and then we headed down Ballarat Road; if I kept going, we'd be home in ten minutes. Instead I turned right, towards Footscray.

Phuong bent forward to peer at the side of my head. 'What's the plan?'

'Might as well make a start tonight,' I said.

I parked across the street from the Narcissistic Slacker. The studio lights were still on. I left Phuong in the car and ran up the stairs. Instead of knocking, I tried the door. It shot across, sliding off its tracks, and slammed against the wall. Two square metres of metal door started to fall forwards. I ran around and caught it just before it toppled. I was trapped there, bracing it with both hands on a precarious slant.

I turned my head to see a stunned Brophy sitting on an upturned milk crate, the end of a paintbrush in his mouth. His eyes were wide with, I think, surprise, but it could also have been fear.

'Um. Sorry. Someone must have oiled the wheels.'

He leapt up. 'Stella? What are you doing?'

My heart hurdled the top rib. It had been too long since I'd seen those bare forearms.

Together we manoeuvred the door back onto its tracks. My face brushed his arm, I closed my eyes and inhaled. When I opened them, Brophy was watching me, amusement in his eyes.

'Hey,' he said, and stepped closer. 'This is a nice surprise.'

I spun away. Phuong was waiting in the car; if Brophy and I started something, I might be here all night. Also, as of now, I was committed to assisting her with this matter. Phuong, I was helping. No one else. I started to pace. 'Isaac Mortimer, know him? He's a dealer, sells around here — mainly to kids, I understand.'

He looked tired and, worse, disappointed. He let out a heavy sigh. 'I've told you, that's all in the past. Yes, at one time, I had a problem.'

'What? No, I'm not accusing you. I simply want to know where this bloke deals.'

'Oh. Right.' Bewildered, pretending not to be. 'Did you …

want to score?'

'No! I'm asking you because you hear things. You're still friends with that informer, Jeff Vanderhoek.'

That startled him. 'I saw him on one occasion, first time in years. We said maybe five words to each other.'

'Right. So maybe you know the places where kids are chasing?'

'Is this for work?'

'For Phuong. It's a favour.'

He scratched his chin. 'Try the car park on Droop Street, near the funeral parlour.'

An open space, dark at night, a choice of backstreets and alleyways leading in all directions to run down if the narcs showed. I should have guessed. 'Brilliant, thanks.'

I'd begun, and it felt good. I galloped down the stairs, then paused to regret my haste and the missed chance to kiss him goodbye. I wondered if he cared. Perhaps not, if he was as absorbed in his art as Felicity had claimed.

Phuong was texting when I got back to the car.

'News?' I asked.

'Nothing,' she said, sounding almost sober. 'I'm calling in sick for work tomorrow.'

I drove west on Barkly, to Droop Street. Instead of turning, I continued west and stopped at the next set of lights. Drizzle had built up and I hit the wipers. No one on the streets — Halloween action dispensed with for another year.

A couple of boys rounded the corner on foot, ideal ruckmen at over two metres apiece. They hunched inside their puffy jackets, hoods up, in no hurry. The boys ambled into a bottle shop that was still trading, bars on the windows and the door. The traffic light changed, and I turned right into Donald Street and arced back to Droop.

The car park was lit in places, but there were dark areas in which to hide. I backed into a spot at the rear of the funeral parlour. The headlights captured light rain. I switched them off and cut the engine.

12

PHUONG CHECKED her watch. 'Ten to three,' she said.

'You say that like I should write it down. We are off-*piste* now, Phuong. This is the unauthorised missing-persons patrol.'

She resettled herself in the seat. 'Silver spray-paint — how d'you get that off a car? Soap and water?'

'More chemicals,' I said. 'WD-40?'

'That's a lubricant. I'll probably need a solvent. Acetone, maybe.' She opened her handbag, took out a folded A4 sheet. 'Take this. The VicPol media release on the arrest of Isaac Mortimer. There's some handy details.'

Handy details? I shoved it in my back pocket. 'The real mystery is why Leo didn't win an Oscar for *Blood Diamond*.'

She rubbed the window, creating a smeary circle. 'Why should he?'

'The Afrikaans accent, it's unbelievable. And his Krio is fantastic.' She looked at me.

'Krio — the language of Sierra Leone. I looked it up.'

'Why are we here again?'

'Popular transaction point. We wait for a while, inconspicuous as possible, and see who shows, get a feel for the place. I might know some of them.'

She nodded. 'And offer some inducement, cash for info?'

'Probably. I haven't thought that far ahead. That's usually how these things work. There's an exchange. Like Danny Archer — he's trading weapons and he has to negotiate with the rebel leader, Commander Zero. Diamonds for grenade launchers.'

She observed me for a short time. 'Are we talking movies or are you making a point?'

'Commander Zero gives him bad diamonds.'

'Stella, I'm not giving you bad diamonds.'

'But you are being ... economical with the truth.'

She looked out the window and sighed.

'Shit, it must be bad,' I said.

'Shut up, it's not bad. Okay. It is. Bruce was on a stakeout, a few weeks ago. I joined him for a few hours. Brought him something to eat.'

I raised my eyebrows. 'Whose idea was that?'

'We'd never see each other otherwise. Anyway, we were watching this house.'

'Whose house?'

'Peck's. I'm helping with the recording set up. Bruce wants audio — informant's wired.'

'This Jeff Vanderhoek guy that Brophy knew?'

She nodded.

'That's brave,' I said. I wondered if Jeff had had a choice.

'He goes in, the audio's good. There's some mindless talking. Then they mentioned Bruce. Just once. It didn't seem significant to me, it was such an oblique reference — someone saw him at a sports bar. They were badmouthing him. "*Oh, Copeland, that bloke's a prick,*" like that.' She pulled her hair back and took a hair-tie from her wrist and then looped it around into a ponytail. 'So much for him being in conspiracy with them.'

'Exactly. Nothing illegal about going to the pub. And?'

'And then Bruce goes, "By the way, can you erase that?"'

I blinked, not sure I'd heard her correctly.

'I know,' Phuong said quietly.

'That's —'

'I *know*. I was shocked. Bruce is by the book.'

'What did you do?'

'All we had was innocuous gossip. There was nothing useful in it.' She shrugged. 'I deleted the whole thing. We got back to St Kilda Road and he said the equipment was faulty.'

'You deleted the recording?'

'It's not *that* bad.'

I held the bridge of my nose. 'They'll be able to recover it.'

'No, I wiped it, it's gone.' She paused. 'Well, not gone. First, I made a copy, then I deleted everything.' She looked at me.

'To cover your arse?'

'For my own ... interest.' Phuong's cryptic expression gave nothing away. I wished I could do that, suppress all outward signs of thought and feeling. Instead, I was cursed with a face like an open book — and not a normal book, one of those kid's pop-up books with moving parts. Since I could read nothing from her face, I'd have to come right out and ask her if — in her heart of hearts — she believed Bruce was squeaky. But not now. 'Can I hear it?'

'No way,' she said, and turned her gaze towards the dark car park.

She'd changed since she started seeing Copeland. The old Phuong would never have gatecrashed a stakeout, or deleted a recording. Were personalities really that plastic? If so, I could do with a change. Not a minor adjustment either — I'd have a full reconstruction, my whole personality.

'We've known each other for a long time.'

'No,' she said.

'You can trust me.'

'*No.*'

'Phuong. You know who left the bullet, don't you? And who vandalised your car.'

'Hello,' she said, pointing to the street in front of us. I looked into the gloom. Out of the mist emerged a group of kids: a girl and two boys. The boys — one tall, one short, both thin — were trying to kick each other, sideways, kung fu–style. They appeared to be without a care, none of that jumpy, desperate vibe addicts have. They weren't junkies yet.

They dressed alike in many layers of shabby windcheaters, loose jeans, runners that looked expensive. They entered the car park, and I lowered my window.

The girl was singing 'Turning Tables'. Adele did it better, though I admired the attempt. There were some tough notes in that song. But the boys were apparently against it.

'What's that shit?' the short one demanded. He turned, and his face caught the light. My boy Cory. 'Hey Razz, check it. Yo!'

He made some beatbox beats and rapper-style hand moves, singing some song about wiping the blood off his Nikes. Australian hip-hop style.

The taller boy — Razz, evidently — laughed. He pointed to the alleyway that ran behind the funeral parlour. 'Look out.'

Phuong and I followed the finger. A girl with long hair walked under the street light, about fifteen, give or take. She pulled the zip of her jacket up and down.

Razz waved his hand. 'Yo, Alma.'

The girl beside Cory giggled.

Razz readjusted his pants down to his hips. 'S'up,' he shouted again to Alma.

'Over here.' Alma moved near a tree in the shadows. Razz ambled across the car park.

I lowered the window all the way, but we had no chance of hearing them from here. I turned my attention back to Cory. The other girl was circling him, grinning.

'I like your shoelaces. They have dogs on them.'

'Mighty Bulldogs,' he said.

She came up close.

He held a foot up for her to see. She peered at it. He stepped closer to her.

'Eww.' She screamed and backed away.

Phuong sat up. 'Oh, no.'

I scanned the foggy surrounds and spotted a man, walking along Donald Street. Copeland. He crossed the road and entered the car park. I looked to see if the boy, Razz, had seen him. A deal was in progress with Alma, the girl with the long hair. She was holding her

51

bag open for him to see the contents. Razz was leaning over it.

'Cop!' Cory yelled.

Razz grabbed the bag. Alma snatched it back, and ran down the alley. Razz, Cory, and the girl scattered in all directions.

Phuong jumped out of the car and ran towards Bruce. I got out and zipped up my jacket. I gave them time for a long embrace then dawdled over to join them. He looked unkempt and had let his beard grow. If he'd been holding a cup, I might have thrown in some change.

'You shouldn't be here,' Phuong said.

'What *are* you doing here?' I asked.

He glared at me. 'I'm twiddling my thumbs in that cabin, while Isaac Mortimer is enjoying the free air, and cunts are bullshitting to the commission.'

'I understand you're frustrated, but you can't —'

'But if I get Mortimer to come in —'

'You *can't*. You're under suspicion. You have to live like a choir boy.'

'I know what I'm doing. And I'm careful. Anyway, I can't sit around while —'

'I'll find Mortimer.'

'You told me she didn't want to get involved,' he said to Phuong.

'She changed her mind,' Phuong said, with a grateful nod in my direction. 'Earlier tonight.'

'Why?' He glared at me as if trying to fathom my motives. I glared back at him, and then he caught on. He turned suddenly to Phuong. 'What happened?'

She didn't answer, so I replied, 'She's received threats. And they spray-painted her car.'

'Who? Did you see them?'

'Looked like a big bloke to me. Could be a cop.'

He took Phuong by the shoulders. 'Are you alright?'

'Of course.' She played unconcerned. 'Probably just kids.'

'Would kids write *DOG*?' I asked Copeland. 'Or is that more the kind of thing cops say?'

He folded his arms. I got another look-over for my trouble.

'This is getting out of hand. When you blokes turn, you really go nuts, don't you? Seems like every cop in the department is either crooked or being silenced.'

'I'm *handling* it.' His lip curled. 'I know these people, and I'll handle it.'

'Doing a great job so far. Meanwhile, coming to Footscray tonight shows spectacular judgement on your part. Why would you come to a known drug-dealing area?'

'These kids'll know Mortimer.'

'Maybe.' I looked around. 'But they're gone now.'

'Without Mortimer's testimony, I'm finished.'

'Cops don't do well in jail,' Phuong added quietly.

There she was again, defending him. Phuong sniffed. I wasn't moved. 'Gotta say, I'm starting to regret this already.'

'But Stella —'

'When you locate him,' Bruce was saying. 'Don't do anything. Don't talk to him. Don't call your local police. All you do is tell me where he is. Right? You let me handle it. I'll take it from there.'

Phuong put her arm through his. 'I'm going with Bruce,' she said. 'I'll stay with him, at his dad's.'

'Good idea,' I said. 'Go to Western Port and stay there. I'll get in touch when I find Mortimer.'

Copeland grunted.

'You're welcome,' I said pointedly as I walked away.

'Stella, wait.' Phuong caught up with me. 'The tape. I'll send it to you.'

13

TIME TO go home to bed. I stopped at the lights on Ballarat Road. The passing traffic was partying; music doofed. Then, crossing the road right in front of me, I saw Alma. She must have come straight from the abandoned drug deal in the car park. She walked fast, holding her bag to her chest.

I flicked my left blinker and followed her. She was headed to the Macca's up the road. It had been a long time since my last McNugget. I passed Alma and pulled into the McDonald's car park. She was sitting down in a quiet section near the toilets when I entered the building. Near the entrance to the kids' play equipment, a table of delinquents had chips, eating some and throwing the rest. I stood in the queue behind a man in hi-vis, and studied the board. God help me, I couldn't go through with it. Even the thought of the soft-serve made me want to puke.

I stepped up. 'A cup of tea. Thank you.'

I took my tea to a table near Alma, facing the door. In the eye-aching glare of fluorescent lights, I felt myself sinking. This place was a nightmare. Joy could not survive in here — too much *convenience*. I jiggled the tea bag. My reflection in the window appeared weary and resentful. If I turned my head slightly, I had a view of the girl.

The auto doors parted and a slim woman came in, brown hair in a bun, wearing a professional-looking pants suit, a leather satchel over her shoulder. She scanned the place, looking for someone. Alma raised her hand and the woman hurried over, brushing by me as she went.

'Sorry I'm late,' she said to Alma. 'How's the treatment working?'

Alma touched her cheek. 'Great. All cleared up.'

Intrigued, I moved closer and bent over my phone, pretending to scroll through something on the screen.

'And the new hair colour?'

Alma swished her hair. 'Love it.'

'Great. So tell the others.'

Alma sighed. 'They don't care about skincare.'

The woman pursed her lips. 'What they care about is irrelevant.' She pulled a stack of files from the satchel. 'I need to schedule appointments for the tests.'

An adolescent shrug from Alma. 'I told you, offer them smokes and shit. That's the way to get through.'

'Community workers don't bribe their clients.'

Community workers? What community worker meets clients after midnight?

A pause. The woman straightened her back. 'Right. What can I get you?'

'McFlurry.'

As she walked by, I leaned out of my chair to put my phone in my bag, and we connected hip-to-head.

'Sorry, mate,' the woman said.

I caught sight of a blue tatt on her wrist, uneven scribble. 'Nice bit of ink,' I said.

'This?' She laughed and held it out. 'It really is ink. Biro, actually. A phone number.'

'Oh, right. I thought it was a home-made job, like a prison tatt.'

She ripped her hand away. 'What's *that* supposed to mean?'

'I ... wait, what? I didn't mean —'

'You fucking —' She swiped at my cup, sent it skittering, tea splashing the wall.

'Wow. Okay.' My hands were up, palms out. 'I'm going now —' I was stepping backwards and grabbing my handbag. I had made it to the doors when Crazy in the pantsuit came at me.

'Wait! Listen,' she said. 'I want to apologise.'

'No need. Forget it,' I said, flustered.

'Come on, hear me out. I'm not a bad person. It's just that I can fly off the handle sometimes.'

'We all can. No worries.'

She lowered her voice, almost pleading. 'So there's no need to make a complaint about me or anything, is there?'

'Last thing I would do.'

'Because I've been inside, and I'm a bit touchy about it.'

'That's understandable.'

'Don't need the parole people breathing down my neck.'

'Of course not.'

She pointed to Alma. 'I'm making up for it, working with these kids.'

She stared at me with clear, unblinking eyes. Up close, I saw that some hard years dragged at her cheeks. A tooth was broken at the front. Community workers needed clearance, and jail time was a deal breaker. Whatever this was, it was less than legit.

'Case work of some kind?'

Her laugh was deep, the pack-a-day kind. 'I'm all about the kids.'

Not exactly an answer. 'How's that?'

She paused, appeared pained. 'I don't want anyone to go through what I've been through. I try to reach them early, before they get addicted.'

I acted impressed, thinking that this psycho should not be *anywhere near* kids. On the other hand, right now she might be useful: she might have connections, know people — dealers perhaps. 'So community work? Me too, sort of, a social worker.'

She looked astonished. 'No way! Really? Hey, I'm Josie. Let me buy you another cup of tea.'

I hesitated.

'Come on. We can both have a chat with young Alma.'

I didn't want tea. But Alma, yes, I wanted to chat to her. 'I'm Stella.'

'Grouse.' She lowered her voice as we walked back to Alma. 'This kid, I swear she's got a death wish.' She laughed again. 'We've all been there, right?'

'Ha ha, yeah.'

14

'ALMA, THIS is Stella.'

She cast a slow eye from Josie to me. 'Hi.' Stage-four boredom; she was almost terminal.

'I'm getting her a cup of tea. You want that McFlurry?'

'With Oreo sprinkles. Wait …' Important pronouncement coming … 'No sprinkles.'

Josie left, and I smiled at Alma. She made a blatant evaluation of me, found nothing of interest.

My eye drifted to the files on the table. I couldn't read the labels on any of the tabs. Several papers inside each, paperclips poking out.

'Josie is —'

'I'm bipolar,' Alma said, watching me to gauge my reaction.

'That must be tough,' I said.

She shrugged, 'Yeah. Been in hospital. Taking my meds.'

'Is Josie helping you with that?'

'Pfft. *No*. As if.'

'What does she … do? How does she support you?'

She smirked. 'Don't get all *suspicious*.' Like I was a real square. 'She's trying to set me straight.' The sly look.

I almost laughed.

'Anyway, I don't care, she pays for stuff so, whatever.'

'Stuff?'

She looked away, deaf, the bored act again.

Time to burst this concocted bubble. 'Does she know you sell drugs? How'd that deal with Razz go?'

Her eyes locked onto me like a search light on an escaped prisoner. I held her gaze. She flicked her hair.

'You some kind of creepy kid stalker?'

57

'Should I tell her?'

She leaned over the table towards me, hissing. 'You don't know shit.'

'Whose gear were you selling?

She held out her hand, middle-finger up.

Josie returned. 'All the crazies out tonight, ay? Here you go.' She handed me a cup and slid the dessert towards Alma.

'I'm going to the bathroom,' Alma said.

'Me too.' I followed her into the ladies.

Alma pouted at her reflection, pumping a mascara wand.

I pretended to inspect my eyebrows.

'There's a bloke owes me money,' I said to her. 'Wonder if you know him?'

'Probably not.' She worked the gunk over feathery lashes.

'Isaac Mortimer?'

'Never heard of him.' She zipped up an expensive-looking bag and left.

I looked in the mirror, absorbing the conversation I had witnessed. Josie's shtick seemed somewhat bogus. I had come across volunteer crusaders before, working at late-night soup trucks, handing out blankets to people sleeping rough. They were usually backed up by a church or community organisation. Josie was an unauthorised, freewheeling sort of helper, the kind who often did more to harm than to help. Though perhaps haircuts for the homeless was innocent enough.

Meanwhile, her putative client, Alma, was a trouble on steroids. Unnerving, like the company she kept, and yet she seemed highly intelligent. I had no doubt she was feeding me a crock of nothing-to-see-here.

I had one last look in the mirror, picturing myself with seventeen layers of mascara. As I was leaving, I heard a noise in one of the cubicles.

'Is she gone?' A teenage girl's voice.

'Who?' I asked.

'Alma.'

'Um, yes. It's just me here.'

'Sweet. So you said you're looking for Isaac?'

'Yes,' I said to the cubicle door. This was turning out to be quite a surprising night. 'Do you know him?'

A hacking cough and then the gross sound of inhale and swallow. 'We're mates.'

'You are?' I said, incredulous. I got on my knees and looked under the door. A back blocked my view.

'Don't you believe me?'

'Sure.' I went into the next cubicle and looked under from the side. A pile of blankets, a girl's skinny legs sheathed in black leggings, dirty bare feet, green toenails. She was sitting on the floor with her back to the cubicle door.

'Bikie, face tatt says *fuck yeah*.'

'That's him.' I got up and washed my hands. 'Don't you get disturbed by people coming in?'

'Nah. It goes quiet from now on. They come in to clean about seven, so I've got a few good hours.'

I heard the optimism and the confidence, and I despaired. Tomorrow, I'd have a word with Boss. In the meantime, this was a genuine bite. 'I heard Isaac skipped town.'

'Nah. I saw him yesterday.'

'Really? Where does he hang out?'

She let go another wet cough, a hacking TB-style lung ejector. I waited.

'Corpse Flower clubhouse in Braybrook.'

I would not be walking up to a bikie clubhouse to knock on the door. Not on the word of a green-toed child in a McDonald's toilet at four in the morning. I imagined that Copeland would have ruled the clubhouse out as a hideout in any case. 'Hmm, anywhere else?'

'He sometimes drinks at The Ashbrook, plays poker there.'

I have read about escaped prisoners who were caught at their local pub. Sometimes the lure of the pub outweighs common sense, especially for the extremely stupid.

'Thanks for that.' I paused before leaving. 'You okay in there?'

'Excellent.'

'Alright then. Well, good night.'

'Warm, dry — fucking will be, mate.'

Josie was waiting for me. Alma had gone, leaving her McFlurry untouched.

'Might call it a night,' I said, picking up my tea. 'I'll have this in the car.'

'Yeah, I should go home, too.' She seemed distracted.

'Nice pantsuit,' I said.

'Thanks. I try to be professional.' She smiled, showing a glimpse of broken tooth.

The question was, a professional what?

At the top of the four flights, I discovered my front door was washed in yoke and albumen. The Halloween hag had made good on her threat. The kid must have wasted three-dozen eggs. I swept up the shells, but the ick was stubborn and a quick wipe with paper towel did little.

I had the Spray n' Wipe out when I saw a voicemail message on my machine. '*It's your mum, love.*' My mother, Delia, insisted on the telephone. Never a text or email, no matter how hard I tried to convert her. '*Call me when you get a chance. I need to talk over this Tyler business with you.*'

Tyler was my sister, Kylie's, husband. He was what my father's generation called a no-hoper. He'd trained to be an Anglican minister, but gave it away for lack of interest. Then he tried his hand as a mechanic, but he had no qualifications, and caused permanent damage to a vintage Chevrolet. Then he had a crack at stock agent, but he was unpopular with the farmers who found him apathetic and ill-informed. I didn't know what the 'Tyler business' was, nor did I want to know.

It had been a long day and a rough night. I undressed and stood under a hot shower until I started to relax. I fell into bed, thinking about the girl who intended to bed down for the night in a public toilet. There were stray dogs who lived better than some kids in this city.

15

THURSDAY MORNING at work, I was occupied with typing my name in different fonts to see which I liked best. Stella Hardy in Verdana, Stella Hardy in Traditional Arabic, Stella Hardy in Wingdings. Stella Hardy in Wingdings 2.

Since arriving at WORMS, bleary-eyed and seedy, I'd sent emails to some contacts I had in a couple of youth-housing agencies, and given them the details of the homeless girl sleeping at McDonald's. Then I spent a good hour reading *The Age* online. I read stories of the post-storm clean up — some houses were still without power. Weather predictions for Cup Day were for a cold start with rain, before the sun was expected to out and blast us like an atomic bomb.

I now turned my attention to the task of locating a Mr Isaac Mortimer. If I was honest with myself, *both* sides of the law were as fishy as penguin breath. Frankly, I couldn't care who got investigated; preferably the lot of them. But threats had been made against Phuong, and that changed the whole ball of wool.

I found the police media release Phuong had given me, in a crumpled ball at the bottom of my handbag.

Division Response Unit/Guns and Gangs (DRUGGs) members have arrested a man following the execution of a search warrant in Norlane today.

About $180,000 worth of drugs were seized from the Marsden Ave property and a 32-year-old Norlane man was arrested and charged with the following offences:

- one count of possessing a commercial quantity of a drug
of dependence,
    - one count of possessing cartridge ammunition,
    - three counts of possessing an unregistered firearm,
    - one count of possessing an explosive device.

Detective Sergeant Bruce Copeland said today's operation is a
reminder of the hard work being done by DRUGGs to tackle
drug-related crime.

On the back, Phuong had written Mortimer's last known address:
15 Marsden Ave, Norlane.

The girl sleeping in the toilets at McDonald's had said to try
either the Corpse Flowers clubhouse or The Ashbrook Hotel.

I opened a browser window and discovered that tonight, at The
Ashbrook Hotel in Braybrook, was parma night. A pot and parma
for twelve bucks. Perhaps Brophy could be convinced to leave his
studio and have dinner with me. Not the parma, of course, but
maybe a salad and chips, perchance a buttered roll. Isaac Mortimer
went there for the gambling, not the food, if the kid in the cubicle
was right. And that was a big *if*.

In the meantime, I could start with what I knew for certain about
Mortimer: he was a dealer. It was likely he was also a user. I rang the
needle exchanges and called in a couple of favours from some friends
who worked there, but made little progress. And I figured a person
like Mortimer would likely stick in the memory.

'Oi!' Boss was looking over my shoulder. Open plan offices were
a modern-day tribulation. 'The business cards arrived.' He dropped
a small box on my desk. 'Here's yours.'

Boss had assigned us our job titles. I had lobbied for 'Social
Worker to the Stars' or 'Good-Time Girl', but he'd insisted on 'Client
Liaison Officer'.

'Thanks. Is that all? I'm kind of busy.'

He was unimpressed. 'Doing what?'

'Um. Nothing. I'm all yours.' I stuffed the business cards and the press release in my bag.

'Afshan called. Things are getting heated with the neighbours apparently. The police have been called. Help him sort it out.'

I was concerned for Afshan, naturally, but I was also overjoyed to be getting the hell out of this place. As I was leaving, I popped my head in Boss's office. 'Were you aware that children are sleeping in the toilets of Macca's for want of a bed for the night?'

He stopped typing, looked bored. 'Are they?'

'Yes. Is anyone doing anything about that?'

'I'll check my magic answer-to-everything stick and let you know.'

'You,' I said evenly, 'need a holiday.'

I took the train to North Melbourne, changed to the Sunbury line, and alighted at St Albans.

Ah, St Albans, the best *phở* in the west, halal meat, fresh injera, frozen yoghurt, and the highest murder rate in the state. Personally, I liked the area; it had a crazy high-adrenalin atmosphere. And a high murder rate was relative, right? I pulled out my phone and read up on a few stats: 2.9 homicides per 100,000 people was the Victorian average, while 7.2 per 100,000 people was the average around here. Global average was 6.2; the average in America, 5.2.

I quickened my pace.

The way to Afshan's house cut through the thrumming shopping district, through the supermarket car park, along a council recreation reserve, and down a street of houses that were either neat with well-tended gardens, or rubbish dumps with a couple of cars up on blocks in the front yard. On the way, I tried Afshan's mobile, but it was turned off. His share-house was an austere weatherboard in which seven adult men lived. Two single mattresses in each of the two bedrooms, two in the dining room, and one in a covered back veranda. They took turns to cook in the tiny kitchen, but not, if I remembered correctly, to clean it.

Afshan's house was in its usual condition — unassuming and a little untidy. The place was quiet. I couldn't see any bicycles on the porch or in the driveway. Maybe the bikes were put away in the garage — the roller-door was down. The street was drowsy, no traffic, no parked cars. I'd come this far, I reasoned, so I went up and twisted the doorbell gizmo. Soon, I heard stomping in the hall.

Shahid, a newcomer to the household, opened the door in his slippers and closed his eyes as he nodded me inside. His dark hair was freshly combed, the lines still visible. 'Dude, welcome. What are you doing here, man?'

'I heard the police were here,' I said, a little taken aback.

'The cops have totally gone, dude.'

'Is Afshan home?'

'No, no. He is visiting the neighbour. This lady, her cat was on fire, and she blames us. We would never. Afshan tells her, and the police, it wasn't us. There is a dude in the street who is very, what is the word?'

'Weird?'

'Yes. He is weird.'

'Psychopath?'

'Maybe. For now, say weird.'

False alarm then. I was relieved, not that cat burning was acceptable. The idea shocked me. Although, I was more of a dog person. Cats baffled me. I found them grandiose and capricious. I made allowances for Brophy's cat; Aragorn was pleasant enough.

'Afshan will be back soon,' Shahid said. 'Come, you can watch a movie with me while you wait. Watching movies helps my English.' He shuffled in his slippers to the back of the house where the TV was paused. I picked up the case: *The Big Lebowski*. That explained a lot.

Afshan came home just as The Dude wrapped up the mystery.

'Nice timing. Cat lady okay?' I asked.

'She is still upset. But she believes me, no-one in this house would do such a thing.'

'Are you in trouble?'

His face was serious. 'Nothing you can help me with.'

'You'd be surprised. I can be very helpful. Quite helpful.'

'No.'

'Okay. I'll get going.'

'I'll walk you to the station,' Afshan said.

Shahid jangled some keys at me. 'We can drive you to anywhere you want to go.'

'In what?'

'He's bought an old delivery van. Very cheap. Now he makes a little money driving people and make some deliveries. Black market money.' Afshan winked at me.

'Maybe another time.'

Afshan and I walked through the supermarket car park, where a high school punch-on was underway, in front of a small crowd, all recording it on their phones.

He put out his hand and we shook. A breeze swirled the plastic bags along Main Road West.

'You and Shahid want to have dinner with me tonight? I'm going to The Ashbrook.'

He smiled. 'No, thank you. We are going bowling.'

'What? You liked it then?'

'Yes, it's very relaxing.'

I left him and walked through the shopping strip. I bought a copy of *Blood Diamond* at one of the last video shops in existence. Later, as I waited for my train, I thought about the cat. I didn't even know the poor creature and I was upset about it. Come on, St Albans, you can do better than that. And a murder rate of 7.2. I checked my phone again. Murder rates in specific US cities: Baltimore, 34.9; New Orleans, 53.2; Detroit, 54.6.

I started to calm down. St Albans was a model of community safety and peace.

16

BACK AT WORMS, Boss was in his office with the blinds down and the door shut. I went to my desk, and Shanninder rolled a chair up to my cubicle. 'He's getting worse.'

'Boss? I know.'

'Mid-life crisis.'

I considered that. She was probably right; she was usually right about people.

'What happens next? He leaves his wife and buys a sports car? I can't see him doing that.'

Shanninder shrugged. 'My guess, he'll quit.'

'God help us.'

'Seriously.' She scooted back to her desk. 'By the way, this came for you.'

A parcel with Phuong's hand writing. I dropped it on the desk and rang Brophy.

'Dinner? Tonight? My shout.'

'Great. Where?'

'I'll pick you up at seven. Bye.'

That was better. I ripped open Phuong's parcel. A USB stick dropped on my desk.

I slotted the USB: a sound file, and a word document named *Vanderhoek enters Footscray premises*. The recording Copeland had asked her to delete — along with her transcript of the audio. Phuong was nothing if not thorough. I tapped a finger on my lip. That she was willing to share it with me might mean that she was having second thoughts about Copeland. That was promising.

I clicked on the audio and was informed I would have to download a more up-to-date version of the audio software to my ancient WORMS computer before it would play. I thought about just reading Phuong's transcript, but I wanted to hear the voices for myself. After endless clicking, and agreeing, and restarting, the damn thing finally played.

Phuong's voice: '*Subject enters house at ... four oh eight p.m.*'

The quality of the audio was poor. At times, the voices were faint or muddied by ambient noise. I replayed it and read along with Phuong's notes.

> PECK: Vanderhoek, you fucking junkie, why aren't you dead yet?
>
> VANDERHOEK: Dunno mate, tin-arsed I reckon. [giggling]
>
> PECK: Tin-brained more like it. You're working for us now?
>
> VANDERHOEK: Gorman reckons the jacks don't notice me.
>
> PECK: Yeah? You're a forgettable prick, I'll give him that. Come on then, sit down. I'll get the gear.
>
> [23 seconds of silence]
>
> PECK: ... close to pure so be fucking careful.
>
> VANDERHOEK: I'll cut it down.
>
> PECK: Don't want to kill off our customers. [laughs]
>
> VANDERHOEK: [inaudible] ... old junkies.
>
> PECK: Do they?
>
> VANDERHOEK: [inaudible] ... be okay.
>
> PECK: So Gorman found you, did he? Lifted a rock and there you were, ay?
>
> VANDERHOEK: He's expanding the network.
>
> PECK: [laughs] You dumb fuck, you don't even know what that means.
>
> VANDERHOEK: He's brought in Mortimer. That Asian cunt. I can't keep up.
>
> PECK: Isaac-fucking-Mortimer's a Corpse Flower, you idiot. He's the western sector distributor to the youth demographic.
>
> And you can tell him that the Turk and I would like a word.
>
> VANDERHOEK: I'm not going near the Turk.

PECK: Did I say you had to go near the Turk?

VANDERHOEK: No, Ricky.

PECK: I said *if you see Mortimer*. I'm starting to think Gorman
made a mistake, picked a donkey. Are you a donkey,
Vanderdumbfuck?

VANDERHOEK: No, Ricky. It's just that the Turk scares me,
that's all.

PECK: [laughs] Yeah. He's a fucking lunatic. [inaudible] … me
best mate, the little wog. Seen the world together, Asia, USA.

VANDERHOEK: [inaudible. Counting?] There's four grand.

PECK: [inaudible] … getting serious, online MBA, management
shit. The US-style of fuck-your-competition.

VANDERHOEK: Not that smart. He's always drinking at the
Spida Bar. Jacks drink there, too. Blyton and that bastard,
Copeland.

PECK: That's why he likes it. Checking up on them. Not Blyton,
he's useless.

VANDERHOEK: Blyton's not —

PECK: Ask for your opinion?

VANDERHOEK: No. [yelp of pain] Leave it off, mate. I'll tell
Mortimer, no worries.

PECK: Just keep your mouth shut, Jeffy, you'll live longer.

I read through Phuong's transcript again, taking note of each name.
Jeff Vanderhoek was the addict and dealer who, years before, had
saved Brophy's life. Hearing the fear in his voice, the awful grovelling,
gave him a fresh presence in my mind. I thought about the man I
loved, and his past. He and Jeff must have been friends, at one time
— acquaintances, at least — and yet I couldn't picture it. Brophy must
have changed a lot since then. Or maybe I just didn't know him as
well as I thought. Felicity was making me paranoid. I shook off that
suspicion and focused on the transcript. Jeff had only just joined the

Corpse Flowers, so the conversation had taken place before he had stepped up to the role of police informer. Or, in fact, *mis*-informer. Ricky Peck was horrible, but soon after this recording would die in a bath. And the Turk was an apparent sadist, with a dubious business degree. He sounded like some managers I'd had.

It would be handy to have a hard copy to refer to. I hit 'print' and ran to collect it. Shanninder was standing by the printer, collating a stack of flyers. She looked at me, rolled her eyes. 'How bad is Boss's singing?'

'Atrocious.'

I hung around, whistling a tune. When she left, I pulled the transcript from the tray, folded the paper, and shoved it in my wallet. Back at my desk, I faffed around, rang a few clients, arranged a house inspection after a family of Sri Lankans were unexpectedly deported.

I did a quick online search for 'The Turk'. The internet told me he was indeed a sadistic thug. A string of vicious assaults. He was often associated with, but not a member of, the notorious outlaw motorcycle gang, the Corpse Flowers. Luigi 'The Turk' Tacchini was a crazy person, without fear.

At four, needing sugar to get through the last hour, I moseyed into the staff room, where Raewyn Ross was sounding off. I dropped a coin in the charity chocolates box and took a random hit.

'... kids running away from home, missing persons. We have to find them. But they're not missing, you know? They always turn up. I don't see why we bother,' Ross was saying.

'Sometimes they really are missing,' Shanninder said, with the patience of a saint.

Late in the day, a call came requesting emergency accommodation for a family of South Sudanese refugees who had been evicted. I managed to get them one night in a motel. Tomorrow, after the inspection, they could move straight into the house left by the Sri Lankans. Human lives, bureaucracy, random chance: enough to make you drink. I turned off my PC and went out into another storm. I was picking up Brophy at seven.

17

FIRST, I ran a bath. Then I went to choose an outfit. After ten minutes, I hadn't made a decision, and went to check on the bathwater levels when I saw a message on the machine. '*It's your sister, just ringing to see how you are. Give me a call, please. ASAP.*'

Kylie rarely rang me. The call would be about the so-called Tyler business, whatever that was. I hit delete.

Now, what to wear? Something suitable for north winds, dry heat, hail storms, Armageddon. I pulled out some leggings, a vintage frock, and my good cardigan. Not that one's best was required for The Ashbrook Hotel. A clean tracksuit would suffice. Actually, so would a filthy pair of old tracky-daks. A fresh singlet with no holes, or a putrid one with holes in which you had laboured all day. Your best shoes, or your old thongs. Whatever, as long as you were well behaved and kept it nice, or went bat-shit crazy and started bashing people. The main thing was to show up with money, and then lose it all on the poker machines. That was all.

The bath was nearly full. This particular date night called for more than water and soap. In the cupboard under the sink, I found a packet of orange-scented bath salts I scored in a WORMS Kris Kringle a few years back.

As I reclined in the warm, citrusy water, fumes clearing my nasal passages, I wondered what Phuong had made of the conversation between Ricky Peck and Jeff Vanderhoek that she had recorded, then copied, then transcribed, then deleted. I couldn't ring her to ask because her calls were probably being monitored. Just the mere mention of his name on the tape had made Copeland nervous. And what of the other cop mentioned on the recording — Blyton. I would ask Phuong about Blyton tomorrow.

Dressed and clean, I headed to Paisley Street. I parked near the Narcissistic Slacker, and tooted once. Brophy appeared, clean and shaven, wearing a jacket. 'Where are you taking me?'

'Get in.'

He opened the door and I caught a whiff of what marketers call 'male fragrance': bergamot and a floral scent, rose maybe, an exotic spiciness. He loved me. 'That's a pleasant scent you're wearing.'

'Like it? Felicity gave it to me. She said if she had to sit around my studio all day, at least I could smell good.'

He loved me not.

'Well, I suppose she has the right —'

'The top notes are vetiver.'

'You don't know what that is.'

'No.' He smiled to himself, as though at a private memory. 'And the base notes are musk and cashmere wood.'

Cashmere wood? Not a material of the natural world. Felicity was a total fraud.

'And you, my darling Stella, you smell of ...' He nuzzled his nose in my hair and inhaled. 'Lemon peel?'

I sighed. 'Pine lime.' An ingredient more suited to ice-cream. Cheap bath-product remorse was a new kind of remorse. If I couldn't afford top-shelf French fragrance, then plain water and soap it would be from now on.

He buckled up. 'Where are we going?'

'The Ashbrook.'

He laughed. 'No, seriously. Where?'

'Seriously.'

He stopped laughing. 'Mate, why? There are plenty of good options around here. Have you been to The Drunken Tweet?'

I bristled. 'Been there, yes.'

'The pomegranate and cauliflower salad has cashews in it. Cashews!'

As delicious as that sounded, it was out of the question. I had a high horse to climb up on, and a sharp glare to shiv him with. 'The Ashbrook has salad. Decent, honest, proletariat salad, made with iceberg lettuce and quartered tomato.' How did I know this? I didn't; it was a guess. It was possible my assumptions were wrong. It was not inconceivable that The Ashbrook had pomegranates on the menu, next to the steak and chips. The suburb of Braybrook surprised one sometimes.

He leaned across and mashed my lips with his, until I started to black out and pushed him away.

'Ladies' choice,' he said. 'Wherever you want to go.'

'The Ashbrook it is.'

The Ashbrook was not an elegant Victorian-era pub. It was a modern-day horror with ample parking, floor to ceiling windows, wide open spaces, a gaming room, and a serve-yourself carvery from a bain-marie the length of a train carriage.

The gaming area was a barrage of noise. At every machine, punters pressed buttons, images rolled, synthetic music repeated. The cashmere wood of amusement.

Brophy grumbled through the menu and passed it across to me. He looked sad. Pasta and a glass of wine, what was so horrible about that? I told him my choice, and he sniffed.

'You seem frazzled.'

'No, not really,' he said. 'You don't want to know the details.'

'Yes, I do.'

'I'm managing; Felicity's a great help.'

'I bet.'

'She's developed a painting schedule, it's pretty intense. But if I stick to it, the work will be ready on time.'

'Does this plan include time with me?'

He coughed. 'I'm not sure that is going to help at this stage.'

'Help what?'

'Sorry, Stella. It's not personal. I'm just anxious about the exhibition.'

I touched his arm. 'It's going to be amazing.'

He smiled faintly, seeming more dismayed than encouraged, and went to order.

I studied my fellow patrons. There were families with young children, couples, and group tables of middle-aged women. But mainly there were men in singlets with shaved heads and sleeve tatts, beefy blokes drinking at the bar who seemed ready to fight. But none, as far as I could see, had *fuck yeah* tattooed on their face.

At work, regular updates on local issues had informed me that this venue alone turned over twenty million a year in poker-machine revenue. Take that much money out of the low-income economy, and see how great life is. No wonder they were angry.

Brophy returned with a number on a stick, and two glasses of wine. I sensed his mood had deteriorated. I picked up a promotional card that was on all the tables. It was an ad for a brand of beer, masquerading as a competition: give them all your details, win a hat.

'Don't you hate those competitions where the prize is hardly worth the effort?' I said.

'Like what?'

'Oh, a ticket to the movies, a stubbie holder. If I go to the trouble of entering, it has to be for something way more substantial. Like an island, or a submarine. Something cool.'

'Marigold and I once won an inflatable armchair,' Brophy admitted.

'Really?'

'The competition was on a packet of nuts. Around the time of the World Cup. Watch it from the comfort of your inflatable armchair. I won, but the chair didn't arrive until the World Cup was over.'

'Where is it now?'

'It had a puncture.'

I noticed he was hunched down in his seat, like he didn't want to be recognised. No chance of that, I thought. Unless he had another life as a factory worker. He probably did have another life. I coughed. 'How're the paintings coming along? Think you'll be ready?'

He looked into his wine. 'Don't know if I'll have twenty ready on time.'

'And the opening is Melbourne Cup Day, that night? Five days' time?'

'Yep.'

The waitress brought two plates. There was a lull in the conversation while we comprehended the consequences of our choices. Brophy bravely picked up his fork. And I took another sneaky scan of the landscape for the target. Negative. Brophy stopped skewering his penne. 'What was that you were asking me about Isaac Mortimer?'

I twirled my linguine. 'If Mortimer testifies, Copeland keeps his job. Mortimer's gone to ground, but they reckon he's still in Melbourne somewhere.'

'What's it got to do with you?'

'Phuong thinks I'm good at connecting with the kids, learning people's whereabouts.'

His laughter was not of the with-me variety. 'What do you get out of it? A reward?'

'I do it out of the goodness of my heart; also I owe her lots of favours.'

I waited for the speech — he's a dangerous, violent man, you don't know what you're getting caught up in, you don't owe Phuong something of this magnitude. If there was a time for a lecture or a caution, this was it. But he said nothing. He slathered his bread roll in butter and stuffed it in his mouth.

I sipped some wine. 'Reckon you could ask your friend Jeff Vanderhoek for me?'

'He's not my friend.'

'But he knows Mortimer.'

He shrugged. 'Does he? I wouldn't know.'

'Actually, word is, The Ashbrook is Mortimer's preferred watering hole.'

Brophy put down his fork, crestfallen. 'That explains everything.'

He took his ringing phone from his back pocket. Seeing the caller's contact details, he stood. 'Hey, you. What's up?' He walked away from the table.

I pushed remnant pasta around on my plate. Mortimer was a man in hiding. He was never going to come here, out in the open like this. That kid in the restaurant toilets sent me here for a prank. I bet she knew more than she let on. Time I revisited a certain toilet.

'That was Felicity,' Brophy said, standing beside me.

'No shit.'

'Her concert was cancelled.'

'What concert?'

'She plays the horn, didn't I tell you?'

'I bet she does.'

He ignored that. 'Anyway, she can model for me now. Can you drop me back at the studio?'

'Sure, but I'm going on a little detour to Macca's first.'

'You what?' Brophy was incredulous. 'If you're still hungry you can come back to my place; I'll make you a sandwich.'

It was a tempting offer, until I remembered Felicity would be there. 'I'm not going there for the food.'

18

THE LATE-EVENING traffic was light. I drove with the Mazda's windows up against the cold.

As I crested a hill, I saw the revolving blue lights of two cop cars, parked in the middle of the road. All traffic was being diverted into Gordon Street, left and right.

'Something's up,' I said, changing lanes. As I reached the intersection, a cop directed us left up Gordon Street. I obeyed, then took the first right into the back street that ran behind McDonald's. I parked and turned the engine off.

'So,' I said gamely. 'Coming in?'

Brophy coughed. 'I'm not getting out of the car.'

'Fine. What can I get you? A McFlurry? I believe they do sprinkles here.'

He glared at me; his sense of humour had abandoned him. 'I've eaten enough shit for one night.'

The car park was swarming with people, a sea of young, hormone-addled cola addicts. From the general air of irritation, it seemed they had been kicked out of the place. Instead of going somewhere else, the young'uns hung around, huddled in cliques. Perhaps being in the fresh air was a frightening new experience for them. A cop was standing guard, arms folded, at the entrance.

I went up to the first person I saw, a young woman in a sleeveless puffy jacket, with thumbs working on her phone, and asked what the hell had happened.

'Dunno,' she said without looking up. 'For some reason, they made us leave.'

'Some reason?'

'Who cares why? I totally hate my life. I'm freezing. Oh my god,

I'm, like, in pain it's so cold. Could my life get any worse? I want to kill myself.'

I tried another bystander, a boy of about thirteen also wearing a sleeveless puffy jacket. 'This kid came running out of the dunnies,' he said, when I asked. 'He runs outside. Next minute, there's this screech and a bang, exactly like someone chucked a sofa off a balcony.'

An oddly specific description, I thought.

'Kid got hit by a truck,' he added helpfully and pointed to a B-double, about twenty metres down the road, blocking two lanes. The rear trailer was diagonal to the front one, and long skid marks smeared the road behind it. The driver's door was open. The ambulance was parked close by, lights on and revolving like at a party in slow motion. A tent of blue plastic had already been erected around the body. I got closer. Someone had put a shoe on the nature strip. Running shoes, the gold standard of youth. I recognised the shoe — a dirty Nike with undone red, white, and blue striped laces, little bulldogs on them.

Don't let it be Cory.

An older woman was sitting on the ground, and a couple of concerned citizens were consoling her. Someone had found a blanket and draped it around her shoulders.

'Everyone went outside to look except me and me mates,' the boy was saying. 'We made a dash for the dunny to see what was so interesting. We reckoned he probably saw a massive shit. But then the manager came and kicked everyone out.'

I walked back to the restaurant. Near the door was a man in a hi-vis vest talking to a cop, who was there taking notes. Nearby was a woman in a suit, who looked like the manager, and standing with her was a posse of fast-food workers. I went closer.

'He stopped at the edge of the footpath, right there,' the man was saying. 'I thought he was waiting to cross, then all of a sudden he rushed out. But his head went back, like he got shoved in the back.' The driver demonstrated a two-handed push. 'Right in front of me.'

The cop wrote that down. 'See anyone with the boy?'

'I didn't see. The kid was there.' He pointed to a place on the footpath where the restaurant car park adjoined the apartment building next door.

The cop and the truckie noticed me, and I walked away. On my way back to the car I saw Alma leaning against the drive-through sign, tapping her phone.

'Did you know the kid, the one who got hit?'

She raised her head. 'The fuck are you?'

'Stella Hardy. I met you here last night, remember? With that youth worker, Josie.'

Surprisingly, she smiled. Or smirked. 'I remember.' Her eyes shone with malice. 'You were asking around about Mortimer. What'd you want him for?'

'It's a favour, for …' I wasn't about to tell this delinquent about my friend the cop. My mind raced — *not a cop, think of a different occupation.* '… A journalist. You know Bunny Slipper? She's doing a story on … the Corpse Flowers.'

'Bullshit.'

'Pardon?'

'Sure, sometimes journalists leave their cosy desks and go out on the street, talk to a couple of people. Mostly they make shit up, write whatever they want.'

I had to admit, the precocious upstart had a point. But not all journalists were slack. Not my friend Vince McKechnie, who was one seasoned investigator. I'd become fond of him when we were caught up in a mining-related conspiracy a couple of years ago. Sadly, his cancer had returned, and he was living out his days in a villa in Broome. As for Alma, I'd give her this: she had a cracking self-esteem and the cynicism of a politician.

'You're, um, above average, aren't you?'

She rolled her eyes. 'And you're an idiot.'

'And why's that?'

79

'You want Isaac Mortimer because you're *helping a journalist*? Come on, we both know that has *nothing* to do with it.'

'Wow, Alma. Sounds like you've got me all figured out. Why am I looking for Mortimer then?'

'Trying to jumpstart your boring life.'

I let out a laugh. 'If you say so.'

'Your life is so boring you could kill yourself, but then you read about these outlaws, these *bikies*, from the criminal *underworld*. They murder and torture people. Get too close and *death* is a real possibility, and just the thought of it makes you feel alive. The thrill and romance of violence, gets your blood flowing again like it hasn't done for years.'

'We're talking about me, right?'

She scoffed. 'Soon, you become obsessed. They have so much money, and they don't give a fuck. They're free from all the stupid social niceties.'

'Yes, Alma' I said in my driest voice. 'Thrills. That's it.'

She leaned in to whisper. 'He knows you're looking for him.'

I didn't panic — she was hardly a reliable source — but I moved away from her, backing up until I stepped on a discarded cheeseburger. I shook it off. 'Who told him?'

'Not me.' Alma pulled out a packet of cigarettes and grinned, daring me to guess.

I was losing patience with her. 'Who got hit by the truck?'

'You wouldn't know him. Kid called Cory.' She trembled slightly as she lit a smoke.

The heaviness swelled in my chest, and I feared my heart would be crushed. *Nothing you can do, miss.* I blinked. 'How?'

'I don't know.' She flicked her hair, smiled. 'But if I did, I wouldn't tell you.'

'So, you know.'

'Fuck you.' She showed me her middle finger and burped.

'Well?' I waited.

'You must have a death wish, or something.'

'Why do you say that?'

'Mortimer's gone underground for a reason, in case you didn't realise.'

'Underground where?'

'Jesus, just give up.'

'The Corpse Flowers clubhouse?'

'As if! They'd kill him.' She picked at a nail. Her villainy show had run out of steam, and I sensed a fine crack showing in the hard shell.

'What do you know, Alma?'

She brightened, bravado back in place. 'You can't touch me. I've got protection.'

'You mean Josie, the youth worker?

'She isn't a proper youth worker. Couldn't you tell?'

I acted shocked. 'No!'

Alma's lip curled. 'Think you're so clever.'

Delusions of gangsta, poor kid. 'Go to the police, Alma. Get your mum to take you. Tell them exactly what the deal is with the kids and the Corpse Flowers. Do it now, so when the whole thing blows up, you might not spend half your life in jail. You might actually get your life back on track. Get the bipolar stabilised.'

She flicked the cigarette at me, missing my eye by centimetres.

I brushed the ash from my cheek and took one of my new business cards from my bag. 'These people are violent criminals. This isn't a game you're playing, it's real life, and they couldn't care less about you. But if you're ready to get your shit together, give me a call.'

I walked back to the car, and found a grumpy Brophy. 'Are you driving me home, or do I have to walk?'

'Kid got hit by a truck and died.'

He sat up, horrified. 'A client?'

'Not officially. But he was sweet, and funny. I liked him.'

He handed me a folded handkerchief. I wiped the tears and blew my nose.

'I'll take you home,' I said. 'Felicity's waiting.'

'No rush, I called her and cancelled,' he said.

A tiny win at last. I started the car.

'Didn't know how long you'd be, and it's not fair on her to keep her hanging around.'

Followed immediately, as always, by a tiny loss. Best to call it a night before I said something I'd regret. I swung the wheel and planted my foot, cutting off a car coming up behind me. The driver leaned on the horn.

I put my hand out the window, middle finger up.

19

THERE WAS not a parking space to be found in Paisley Street, so I slotted the Mazda in a bus zone and switched the engine off. Brophy sat beside me with his fists on his knees like he was ready for the team photo. 'You don't think the rules apply to you,' he said.

'I'll move when a bus comes.'

He turned to face me. 'Stella. Can I ask you something?'

I didn't like that question. It had a bad vibe. I liked happy questions like, *what'll it be?* Or, *more cheese on that pizza?*

'That drug money, I've been wondering ...' He coughed.

The drug money. I knew what he was referring to. Several years ago, on a late-night call to some commission flats, I found a couple of dead drug dealers next to a stash of drugs and cash. In the blink of a reckless eye, I'd popped the cash in my bag. For years afterwards, I'd been haunted by guilt and fear. Guilt at the betrayal of my sense of what was right. A Catholic reflex, perhaps, to guard the future prospects of my eternal soul. And fear that the criminal owners of the cash — thirty grand, it had to belong to a king pin — might discover who had ripped them off. It wasn't until Brophy convinced me that I would never be found out that I finally felt free.

I sensed a moral reprimand coming. Perhaps I shouldn't have told him.

'What made you take it?'

I'd asked myself the same question. What happened that day was not a decision. It was an instinct. I didn't understand it myself. 'I needed the money.'

He frowned.

'You're a reformed junkie, don't judge me.'

'I'm not. I'm ... concerned.'

I laughed.

He smiled. I released my seat belt and kissed him on the mouth. I had a warm electric shock, and my mind fogged up. As I eased my torso over for full body contact, I slipped and the handbrake dug into my hip. I yelped in pain.

He looked sad. 'Go home. Get some rest. We'll see each other soon,' he said, stroking my hip. Then he went severe on me. 'And you're definitely not going after any Corpse Flowers tonight, are you?'

He was making it into a big deal. Like that over-dramatic performance from Alma. As Phuong had said, this Mortimer thing wasn't that much of a departure from my day-to-day grind: locating people who'd skipped out from their public-housing accommodation, or those who'd missed appointments with case workers. 'No, there's nothing more I can do.'

'Think I'll do more work before I turn in,' he mumbled, getting out.

I watched him go up to his studio. We were okay. Though, unfortunately, Felicity's pungent perfume still lingered in the car like rotting fruit.

I called Phuong. 'Something awful has happened.'

'Who is this?' she said.

'Oh, wrong number.' I hung up. I'd forgotten about the stupid Raw-Prawn investigators listening to her calls. I'd never get used to her being under surveillance. Every Australian citizen had their personal electronic-data retained now, and yet as bad as that was, the invasion occurred notionally, at a distance. But the tapping of Phuong's phone calls, that shit was real.

My fingers drummed the steering wheel. The wind came in gusts, strong enough to disturb the mysterious organic substance that decayed and sweated in plastic bags in a pile beside a wheelie bin. Grit came in through the open window. My childhood in Woolburn was spent powder-coated in orange dirt. In the intervening years, I'd lost my tolerance for dust, and I rolled up the window. The transcript of the Vanderhoek and Peck recording was in my bag. I read over it, circled some names while I waited. The Violent Femmes sang from my phone: number unknown.

'Go on,' Phuong said, as though nothing had happened.

'Remember that kid from the car park last night? Cory? He just got hit by a truck.'

'Oh, no. Did you witness it?'

'I got there after it happened. But the driver said Cory was standing on the footpath outside McDonald's and someone pushed him onto the road.'

'All those places have security cameras. With any luck, they'll have good vision,' Phuong said. 'Any news of Mortimer?'

'No trace as yet. I went to his usual — no luck there.'

'His usual ... wait, you mean The Ashbrook? As if he'd go *there*. Stella, he's on the run. You're supposed to be getting the word from the street, not waiting for him to show up at his favourite pub.'

'The word on the street is heard in the pub. Also, give me a break. As favours go, this is not like feeding your cat while you're on holiday. Although that is a huge responsibility.'

'I appreciate everything you're doing.'

I caught the movement of a figure in my peripheral vision. I turned to see if it was Felicity. A teenage boy was lurching his way down Paisley Street. I watched him trip over the gutter and drop to his knees on the footpath.

'You're doing your best,' Phuong was saying. 'You're a good person.'

The boy hoisted himself upright, and adjusted his pants so they hung down near his groin, showing ten centimetres of white underpants. He saw the wheelie bin on the corner and pivoted on his instep, delivering a roundhouse kick on that bad boy. It didn't move. He kicked it again, harder. It solidly refused to tip over. Bin: one; drunken *flaneur*: zero. He grabbed the handle and pulled it down, spilling refuse all over the intersection. A lad of great determination, this one, prime-minister material.

'Thing is,' I said. 'You've barely told me anything about these Corpse Flowers. You said this started with Vanderhoek, that he gave Bruce the information about Isaac Mortimer. But from the, er, package you sent, Vanderhoek doesn't seem to have much power. I doubt he has much of a say about anything.'

A pause. 'You received it?'

'Yes, it's fascinating. Tell me about the Spida Bar — why does Bruce go all the way to a bar in the Docklands for after-work drinks?'

'It's not important.'

I waited.

'Bruce drinks there sometimes because it's near Will's apartment, he's got a place in that purple tower next to the stadium.'

'Will?'

'William Blyton. A Guns and Gangs detective. Quiet, thorough. A good cop.'

I moved on. 'Ricky Peck was a nasty piece of work.'

'You don't get to be president of a motorcycle gang by being kind.'

'True. Who is Gorman? He gets a mention on the recording.'

'Lennox "The Ox" Gorman, a high-ranking Flower, the sergeant-at-arms.'

'And what does that position involve?'

'Head-kicker who kicks actual heads, a problem solver, cat herder.'

I pondered that for a second. 'He's in charge, now that Ricky Peck is dead?'

'He's been quiet in the last few months. When his girlfriend got out of prison, they said they wanted to go straight.'

'What, they had their publicist put out a press release?'

'The media followed them around the day she got out. She's famous for being in a Bangkok hellhole before she got a transfer deal and they brought her back here. Don't you remember that? It was all over the news.'

'Wait. Yes, I have a vague memory of that now you mention it, but I didn't remember the boyfriend being a bikie.'

'He made a speech about leaving the Corpse Flowers,' Phuong was saying. 'But no one believes he's going straight. If you come across him, walk away.'

'How would I know if I came across him?'

'He's lost a finger. He's been shot, stabbed.'

'I'll check the fingers of every bloke I meet. No worries.'

A bus lumbered around the corner behind me. I turned on the engine in case I had to move, but it went by, flat out like it was trying to out-run the wind. Another bus took the corner. 'I have to go.' I ended the call.

I checked my rear-view mirror. My back window filled with light. The horn blasted. In a panic, I hit the accelerator and the car lurched, side-swiping the utility pole.

I fanged down a side street and lost my bearings. I wanted Barkly Street, but I kept taking wrong turns down one-way streets. In the end, I pulled over to use the GPS on my phone, trying to figure out where I'd gone wrong. If only I could do the same with my life.

Getting home and driving into the garage felt like an unlikely triumph against the odds. I inspected the damage. The paint was scraped from front to back along one side, every panel. What surprised me was that I didn't care. The car belonged to Ben, my recidivist brother. He was the family scapegoat, mainly harmless, monumentally stupid — had been stopped on the street late at night. He was tried and convicted of *going equipped to steal*, a crime so nebulous that it was hard to believe it was still on the statute books. It was basically a catch-all for 'being dodgy'. They found gloves and a screwdriver and charged him with going equipped to steal. But according to him, he was only going for a walk. Late at night. In a wealthy suburb, far from his home. He was currently growing heirloom tomatoes in a minimum-security facility in central Victoria, awaiting sentencing. His lawyers thought he'd get about a year, but his long list of priors, and a harsh judge, could spell as much as two years. Last I spoke to him, he was radiant with joy. So much for punishment; they were letting him roast fennel and make his own labna.

I went upstairs, took out my laptop, and googled 'Corpse Flowers' and 'Gorman' and found an article on Gorman and his girlfriend. No more criminality for these two, they said. They were both going straight. There was a picture of them, outside the humble flat they lived in, above a smash-repair place in Sunshine. I studied the background. I'd driven past that mechanic's garage. I opened an online map, entered *Anderson Road, Sunshine* into the search bar, switched to street view, and zoomed in on the sign.

Talbots Body Works.

The woman in the picture with Gorman was thin, with medium-length brown hair. She was beautiful, in a wild kind of way, with her broad smile. A big happy-to-be-out-of-jail cheesy grin that offered a clear view of her broken front tooth. Caption: *Ox Gorman with Philomena Enright.* Or, as I had come to know her, Josie. Alma's so-called youth worker.

So. Josie, partner of a Corpse Flower, was a phony youth worker. Mortimer, a Corpse Flower, was a drug dealer to Footscray's youth. According to Senior Constable Raewyn Ross, Ricky Peck had been behaving weirdly with street kids.

It was tempting to begin pacing up and down, to ease the revulsion this bikie business had stirred up. Instead, I changed into my pyjamas and brushed with brutal vigour. My teeth were innocent in all this, and I eased off, spitting paste into the sink.

Institutions were set up to protect vulnerable children, those without parents — or at least competent ones. And those institutions were often inadequate, under-resourced, or did actual harm. A criminal gang could easily sweep into that responsibility vacuum, ready to recruit, or use, or abuse. What exactly did the Corpse Flowers want with homeless children?

Before I retired for the evening, there was one important bit of business to take care of. I needed a better ring tone. Something sad, and beautiful, and most of all, aggrieved. Something that conveyed my deep feeling of being tragically misunderstood. It took an hour or so, but I finally found it: Karen Carpenter's original version of 'Superstar'.

I got into bed and went over my to-do list. Number one: the Mazda needed repair. And as it happened, Ox Gorman appeared to be residing in a flat above a smash-repair place. The tired old muscle in the centre of my chest began to step up the beat.

20

ALARMS, WHAT a horrible blight on human progress they were. On the other hand, I was up, and acting like a boss in the kitchen. My scrambled eggs were totally fit for human consumption. I finished breakfast and a routine ablution, and dressed for both heat (a short-sleeved frock) and cold (a sensible cardigan). Then I was off, driving to work for the first time in my life.

I went via Buffy's on Union Road. I had a fierce loyalty to Buffy's. There were newer establishments I could go to, with better coffee. But my preferred coffee shop was run by Lucas, a pop nerd and cosplay outsider, and a man as committed to all things post-apocalyptic as me. We understood each other. We disagreed on some things, mermen mainly, but we were in complete agreement that the long-running Buffy the Vampire Slayer's lack of an Emmy was an injustice.

The transaction went like a Swiss watch. I double parked, ran in, threw coins at Lucas, who promptly handed me my double-shot flat white in a takeaway cup, and I was off, absorbing caffeine on the go.

I arrived at work early. In fact, I was first, which was a first. I turned the alarm off, and the lights on. Then I looked up the number for the Victoria Police headquarters, and dialled the number.

'Detective Blyton, please.'

Blyton and Copeland worked together. And *this* Guns and Gangs detective might be more forthcoming on Corpse Flowers information than Copeland. Plus there was the added advantage that, depending what Blyton told me, I could gauge whether the story Copeland had given me was legit. But that would have to wait.

'Who's calling?'

'Stella Hardy.'

'He's not in. Can someone else help you?'

'No, thanks,' I replied, and hung up.

Brendan Ogg-Simons announced his arrival by rattling the doors in a huff.

'Push,' I shouted from my cubicle. He ceased his ridiculous pulling.

'Forget how the door works? You've only worked here for ten years, you bloody great nuff-nuff,' I called out helpfully.

He expressed his thanks by going directly to his office and slamming the door. I waited for my fellow WORMS slaves to show, hoping to spend morning tea doing *The Age* quiz. But alas, as the morning wore on, the office remained almost empty. I knew that folk took advantage of the Melbourne Cup holiday on Tuesday by taking the Monday off and having a long weekend. It appeared my colleagues thought that such a wonderful idea was only improved by taking the previous Friday as well.

Good luck to them. I'd have done the same if I had someone to escape with.

The morning passed in a blur of emails, dull reports, and returning calls to the caller's voicemail. Some things were worthy of my attention. Like the Victorian Coroner's report shared among the migrant services sector on a house fire in which three refugees had died. The living conditions at the house had been appalling. At the time, twelve adults crowded its three bedrooms, and multiple computers and appliances piggy-backed on power boards. The owners had apparently been of the impression that only three people occupied the house.

I wrote a memo for Brendan about the need to review conditions at our clients' accommodations, suggesting we follow up on tenancy agreements, make requests for landlords to do house inspections, properly maintain smoke detectors, and assess the level of electrical safety compliance. I banged on for a bit about the need to educate migrants on fire safety. Then I raised the issue of overcrowding and the need for a solution that didn't involve vulnerable families simply being evicted.

With a creditable amount of actual work under my belt, I opened a browser and searched for *Philomena Enright*: images of a woman, jacket over her head, in handcuffs as she was bundled into a police van; exterior of a Thai jail.

I trawled on and hit a long feature article on Australians in foreign jails. Philomena Josephine Enright, AKA Josie, was included. The journalist had nicked her high-school portrait. She looked innocent, and daggy, with high side ponytails, sticking-out ears, and freckles.

In August 2005, after a tip-off from an unknown informer, Philomena was arrested in a hotel in Bangkok with five other people.

I looked up from the screen, resting my eyes for a moment. There often seemed to be a tip-off in these cases. I could only imagine the long hours sitting in a hellish prison, brooding on that colossal act of betrayal.

She had been caught with forty-five grams of heroin in her handbag. Of the others convicted with her in Thailand, three were Australians, one of whom had AIDS and later died in jail, and two were Vietnamese nationals. A fourth member of the syndicate, Jeff Vanderhoek, was arrested in Melbourne. He subsequently pleaded guilty and served eighteen months. He was, he said, a 'drone' in the gang, with limited knowledge of the deal that had gone wrong.

The judges sentenced Josie to death, that was commuted to life, then to twenty years in Lard Yao, a women's prison within Klong Prem Central Prison.

Thailand allowed transfers of prisoners between the two countries. I found some video of an interview with the journalist Bunny Slipper on ABC TV from 2008 — Josie pleading for the Australian government to facilitate a transfer.

'If I was released back to Australia,' a desperate young Josie said to the camera. 'I'd give back to the country that has given me so much. I've got so much to give back. I'll go into rehab, get my life on track.' She smiled then, showing her broken tooth.

The transfer was approved and she was sent to Fairview women's prison in Rockdale, thirty kilometres west of Melbourne. While there, Ms Enright had taken a course in community service and hoped to become a youth worker.

I opened the office copy of the Yellow Pages, and, using skills not required since the dark ages just to prove to myself I still had it, I found Talbots Body Works. I rang the number and arranged to have the Mazda inspected for a repair in the afternoon.

I was thinking of taking a tea break when I had an urge to call the police. I rang Flemington Police station and asked for Raewyn Ross.

After a brutal hold-message, Rae got on the line. 'Hardy, s'up?'

'Can an ex-prisoner do volunteer work with street kids, is there some kind of special clearance for that?'

'I doubt it. Sometimes the born-again types go rogue, do their own thing on the streets, soup and the word of Jesus. Then they get in over their heads, scumbags roll them. Then they call us to fix it up for them.'

'What can you tell me about Ox Gorman?'

'The bikie? I'm hanging up now. That's what I know.'

'Thanks.'

Around noon, Shanninder showed up. She checked in with Boss, saying she'd been giving some youth workers a two-hour training session on dealing with family violence.

'Thank Eris you're here,' I said.

'Who?'

'Some goddess — a bad one, evidently. Anyway, it's lunch time. Boss is locked in his office, and I'm dying of hunger.'

We walked to a place on Racecourse Road that made a tofu *bánh mì* with extra chilli and a strong *cà phê sữa đá*. We took our vittles to a nearby park to sit in the shade of Flemington's mature elms.

'So I was in Macca's last night, late, about three in the morning, and I came across this quasi-youth worker.'

'Is she with an agency?'

'I doubt it. I think she's a lone saviour type. One of those passionate volunteers who feed the homeless and preach Jesus. She's done time, reckons she's trying to keep at-risk young people from making the same mistakes.'

'Sounds suss.'

'Her name's Josie, nice dresser, broken tooth.'

Shanninder frowned. 'I'll ask around,' she said, making a note in her diary.

I sipped my ice coffee. 'She was with a kid called Alma. She referred to her as a "client". It's a pretty unusual name — can you ask if they know her, too?'

She wrote the name down. 'You think this Alma is at risk?'

'I don't know. I met them at the same Macca's where the boy got hit by the truck.'

'I heard about that. So sad.'

'His name was Cory. His mother was a client of mine a few years ago. Maybe you could —'

Shanninder shook her head. 'Stella, the poor boy has died. What good can it do to get information on him now?'

'It can't hurt, can it? Maybe he had contact with the bogus youth worker.'

'Oh, you're such a stickybeak. Okay, I'll look into him, too.' She scrunched up her lunch wrap. 'I'm heading back.'

We walked back to work. 'Oh, I almost forgot to tell you. Pukus is making some announcement today. Boss wants you to go with him to Parliament.'

I groaned. 'Hey, can you cover for me? I'm gonna quickly dash out and take my car to the panel beater, and I might be a bit late getting back.'

Shanninder sighed. 'How long will you be?'

'Not long. If Boss asks, I'm with a client.'

'I'm not lying for you.'

'Damn your decency, woman!'

Shanninder laughed. 'Decency has nothing to do with it. I'm covering my arse.'

'I doubt he'll ask you. He hasn't said a word to me all morning.' The blinds were still drawn on Boss's office when we got back. I logged off, sneaked out, and jumped in the Mazda.

21

TALBOTS BODY Works was an old-school mechanic's business. Wedged between a long-closed shoe factory with windows smashed, and a thriving cleaning-supply shop, the place was a quarter acre of concrete with a single covered bowser and a large mechanics workshop. An external flight of stairs led to the flat above. The enterprise was fenced off on three sides by a series of posts slung with a white chain.

A legion of grubby youths in combination overalls were swearing and wheeling car parts around on low trolleys. To the right, a small office was sectioned off. FM-radio pop, and the place reeked of the macho catnip of testosterone, motor oil, and unwashed bodies.

I sat idling in the Mazda, taking a sneaky gander at Gorman's place above the workshop. The exterior of the flat had a cosy feel, coloured leadlight in the casement windows, and to one side a rooftop patio. Fringed by a rusted railing, the terrace was decorated with large palms in concrete pots. A set of retro cane chairs was arranged under a fifties-style beach umbrella; the occupants kept serious faith with the period. There was even a Hills Hoist up there, some smalls waving in the breeze — the ex-con favoured wonder bras and frilly French knickers.

I went into the workshop area, crowded with cars in various stages of repair. None of the young men took any notice of me. Then a senior-looking mechanic came waltzing around the corner, sporting a rockabilly hairdo and carrying a fish-and-chip white-paper bundle. He'd made a hole in the paper and was throwing chips in his mouth with his filthy fingers as he approached.

'Yeah?'

'Bit of a run in with a pole.' I pointed to the damaged panels.

'That right?' He had a look. 'Yeah. Come off second best, didn't you? Won't be ready till Wednesday at the earliest.'

Damn the Cup Day long weekend. 'How much?'

'Depends.'

I gave him a look.

'Not more than … five hundred.'

I held out the keys.

'Got everything out of it?'

I held up my handbag. There was a packet of mints in the glovebox, but these lads were not going to bother with those.

'Come in the office, and I'll do the paperwork.' He wiped his hands on his overalls.

I followed him to a dingy little room lined with shelves, umpteen boxes of screws and nuts piled up everywhere, and a girlie calendar on the wall from 1968. He dropped his lunch on the work bench and picked up a stubby pencil. 'Name?'

I gave him my particulars, and he printed each word laboriously in a random combination of caps and lower case.

'Been here a while?' I asked.

He dropped the pencil and opened the chip wrappings. 'Me old man's.' He put some chips in his mouth and nodded at the wall. Stuck there among the business cards was a black-and-white photo of a man with rockabilly hair leaning on a hot-rod.

'Place belongs to you now?'

'Yeah.'

'And the flat upstairs? You live there?'

He shrugged. 'Used to. When we were kids. It was good then. Then the old man bought a bigger place out at Ardeer.'

'Anyone up there now?'

He frowned like he didn't want to say.

'You could rent it out,' I prompted him.

'Me mate's in it, he don't pay.'

'Wow. That's a sweet deal.'

He shrugged.

'What's it like inside?'

He waved a piece of steaming flake at me. 'Wouldn't go near the place I was you, 'less you wanna get shot at.' He bit the shark.

'Ah, not really. No.'

I hurried away, walking down Anderson Road. What had I achieved? I'd seen Gorman's place. What had I learned? Bikies terrified folks.

Karen Carpenter's deep vocal heartbreak crooned from inside my bag. That was more like it. I checked the caller. Shanninder: 'Got some info about those kids.'

'Shoot.'

'Alma Dunmore, fifteen. She's her own worst enemy, like a lot of them.'

'In what way?'

'The attitude. Mensa-smart, but she hangs out on the streets. Risk taker, caught riding the back of a train.'

'Tough at home,' I said, guessing.

'Not really. Upper-middle class, expelled from her private school. When she's not causing trouble, she lives in Williamstown with her mum and two sisters. Big house, apparently, amazing spot opposite the Pavilion.'

'Just a brat then?'

'Her father died in a car accident about four years ago,' she said. 'Since then, Alma's been a handful.'

There was a lot more going on with Alma than anyone knew. Her drug dealing, and her familiarity with Isaac Mortimer, for starters.

'Great. Thanks. And anything on Cory?'

'Not as much. Full name, Cory Felix Fontaine. DOB, May 2001.'

'Makes him, what, sixteen?'

'Near enough. Became a ward of the state when his mother was incarcerated. Ran away from his foster family, managed to stay on the streets, avoided Human Services, slipped through the system. But

I did get one snippet of intel, not sure if it's of any use to you. He's got hep C. The department made a couple of attempts to get him on the new antivirals, but he never showed up for appointments.'

'How did he get it?'

'Don't know. I've got to get on. I'm busy,' Shanninder said.

'One last thing. Where do kids like Alma hang out?'

'Come on, Stella, you know the hang-outs as well as me. Anywhere in central Footscray, like the kebab place on Nicholson. Or McDonald's. And there's always Funky Town, your favourite amusement parlour. I've seen actual teenagers there.'

No, not Funky Town, where bacteria thrived in the finger holes of bowling balls.

'Also, Flinders Street Station's popular, for some reason.'

'Of course, Flinders Street,' I said. Bacteria in a wind tunnel.

'By the way, you're supposed to meet Boss in the city for the Pukus meeting.'

If it wasn't for Shanninder keeping me on the ball, I would've been sacked years ago. 'What time?'

'Four. He's already left. He read your fire-safety report. He wants you to pitch a program to the minister, use your sway with him.'

'I don't have sway. I've never had sway. I don't know why he thinks that.'

'Maybe because you were the one who secured our funding for the next five years.'

'Oh, yeah. That. Where do I go?'

'Parliament. Can you make it?'

I checked the time on my phone. 'Just.'

'By the way, a man came into the office asking for you.'

'What man?'

'All muscles and tatts. Funny haircut. Orange on top. He asked for your address. We told him that's against policy and he left.'

He knows you're looking for him. What if Alma wasn't bluffing. 'Thanks, Shanninder, see you Monday.'

'Not me, honey. I'm taking Monday off for a long weekend. See you Wednesday.'

I ended the call and looked around. Spotting a man with orange hair should be an easy matter. The city train arrived, plastered in stupid tags, its interior strewn with sheets of newspapers, the floor a river of cola and other fluids, and I jumped aboard.

22

FROM THE underground station of Parliament, I ascended on a soaring, almost-vertical escalator. At ground level, I crossed Spring Street to Victoria's Parliament House, where a melange of bored journalists gathered on the steps. Boss was leaning against a pillar on the terrace. He appeared unwell, eyes set in dark hollows, a middle-distance stare.

'Boss?'

'You made it. Good. I brought your report.' He waved a bundle of papers around.

'What are you doing out here? Shouldn't you be in some briefing room?'

'Marcus isn't here yet.'

'Who?' I feigned confusion.

'The minister.'

'Not sure ...'

'Mucous Pukus.'

'Oh *him*. Yes, Boss.' I smiled.

'And don't call me Boss.'

'Yes, Mr Brendan Ogg-Simons.'

He grimaced. 'Stick with Boss.'

'Where is Pukus?'

'Held up at some urgent meeting or other. Expected any tick of the clock.' He leaned in and lowered his voice. 'Don't forget to mention that mining magnate you were friends with a while back, and go from there.'

I was never friends with any magnate. I met one once when his daughter, who was my neighbour, was murdered. My brief meeting with Clayton Brodtmann had been fraught, short-lived. Brodtmann owed me no favours. I had zero influence. I had imagined influence. I told Boss that for the umpteenth time, but he didn't believe me, or didn't want to.

A limousine entered the driveway and the journos jumped to their feet.

'As soon as he finishes his presser,' Boss was saying 'we're to wait for him in the library. He wants us to join him for drinks in his office.'

'Drinks? How did you manage that?'

He smirked. 'Connections.'

I assumed he meant my imaginary connection to the mining magnate.

A chauffeur got out and opened a rear door.

'Sorry I'm late, everyone,' The Right Honourable Marcus Pugh was saying. 'Held up.' He was glad-handing and back-slapping his way through the throng. A be-suited woman with a brutal expression began to corral the media. 'This way, the presser's in K room. Please be ready to go in a minute or two.' The journalists appeared to have expected a brisk and breezy doorstop interview, and began hurriedly gathering up their equipment. If their tweets were anything to go by, they mostly despised Pugh.

Boss and I followed the pack to what I assumed was K room. While the cameras were set up and the smart phones placed on the lectern, we took our seats at the back of the room.

At last, Pukus opened a side door and strode in. 'All set? Yes? Well, ladies and gentlemen, I wish to announce that this government is serious about homelessness. We have done more than our predecessors, more than any other government, to address this terrible issue, this blight on our beautiful city. We are announcing today a special task force to address this issue. We will be removing from the CBD anyone without a valid reason for being there. Those people will be transferred to a faculty where they will be, um, cared for by professionals from the Homeless Assembly Removal Militia, or HARM. Any questions?'

The journalists were silent. Perhaps, like me, they were stunned.

'No? Well, thank you and good day. Oh, and one more thing. The proposal to close the land-tax loopholes for multinationals has been shelved.'

Hands shot up.

'Bunny Slipper, ABC News, Minister. What changed the government's mind? Is it because large corporations making donations to your party were against the proposal?'

'No, um. I. Next question.'

'Why are you making this announcement so late on a Friday afternoon? On one of the busiest weekends in this city's calendar?'

'What? Is it Friday? I've lost track of time.'

All the journalists began firing questions at once.

'Well, if there are no further questions, I'll be off then,' Pukus declared. 'See my press secretary for our statement. Thank you, ladies and gentlemen.'

Pukus evaporated and the media packed up. Boss and I walked downstairs and into the quiet calm of the library. I picked up a newspaper and reclined in a leather Davenport. When I glanced up at Boss, he was rubbing his eye sockets with the heel of both palms.

'Boss? You okay? How's things?'

'Awful.' He took his hands away.

I was surprised at the disclosure. I went on, carefully. 'Trouble at home?'

'Michelle? No, she's not happy, but who is? She's sticking with me for now.'

Someone must've slipped a truth serum in his morning coffee, an admission of this sort was wildly out-of-character. 'Is it work?'

'This wonderful vocation? The daily shoving of shit uphill? No. We do valuable work. Truth is — this surely goes for you, too — we wouldn't do anything else.'

Did that go for me, too? Hell, no. 'Money worries then.' I was running out of causes.

'Just paid for a house at Kennett River. Weekender, three floors, all European appliances, fridge plumbed in. Delivers ice and water from the outside of the door — marvellous thing. Necessity, really, as I said to Michelle.'

That shut me up. I had no idea he had that kind of money. I assumed Boss was only one pay-level above me, but maybe not. Perhaps he was on an executive-style package of perks and incentives. Plus, his household had two incomes. Michelle was an accountant.

He went on. 'No, Hardy, it's an existential crisis that ails me. I find I stare daily into the black hole of despair.'

This crisis of his mattered less to me now that I had found out how much he earned. Money cancelled-out sympathy, in my book. Phuong had tried to point out the hypocrisy of my psychological bias, to no avail. And now my class-privilege radar was telling me to send this rich white male on his way. Especially because there was no direct threat to his safety or that of his family. It was an indulgence, a mere whimsy, this sense of dread.

He was still going on about it. 'There is no joy in my life, and what's worse, I've come to the conclusion that even art is pointless.'

'Now wait a damn minute, Ingmar Bergman. Art has a purpose. And even if it doesn't, it doesn't need one. It is a self-important thing.' I was making it worse. 'I mean it has intrinsic value, and needs no other —'

'That's one of Marcus's people in the pinstripes, he's waving us in.'

23

MARCUS PUGH'S office was furnished with worn, beige carpet and corporate-style chairs around a conference table. His large desk held a keyboard and two screens, and three telephones. On a long, half-empty bookshelf was an assortment of wood carvings, a bent figure with a long beard, possibly Confucius, a tiger with a paw raised, and a swan with wings spread. The framed photos on the wall were of Pukus with Joko 'Jokowi' Widodo, and Aung San Suu Kyi. The window had a view of a brick wall. As we entered, Pukus was sending his under-aged underlings home.

'That will do for the day, Tristan.'

Tristan nodded. He wore a brown suit with a bowtie, and his hair was parted in the middle and slicked down with goo. 'Good night, minister.' He regarded us with suspicion, and withdrew.

'Thank you, Portia.' Pugh said to another minion. 'Good night, goodbye.'

I will say this: Portia rocked a dark pantsuit. But hers was possibly the worst case of acne in recorded history, and I felt bad for her. She shook her head. 'The Prisoner Advocacy Alliance are at it again, minister. I'm preparing a statement discrediting them,' she said, then, registering our presence, darted a rueful glance at me.

'That sounds specious,' I muttered.

She was dumbfounded at something — my nerve at having an alternate opinion perhaps? My lack of political understanding? Her only reply was a haughty sniff.

'I have a brother in the system,' I explained. 'I see prisoners' rights a bit differently.'

She snorted. 'Don't be so naïve. It's not *personal*. Polling in key outer-metro electorates indicates that voters there like it when certain sections of the community are punished or harassed or at the very least humiliated.'

Pukus held up a pudgy hand. 'Portia is our most enthusiastic interpreter of polls. And we love her dearly.'

She blushed so violently I was worried the acne might rupture.

'We've done enough for today, Portia dear. Tomorrow, we will slay that dragon.'

She acquiesced with a nod, juggling a Miu Miu handbag and a briefcase as she left.

When we were alone, Pukus loosened his tie. 'Sorry to keep you.' He held a decanter of whiskey and wiggled it at us. 'Afternoon refreshment?'

'Not for me, Marcus,' Boss said.

'Got anything else?' I asked. My preference was to stay sober in this company, but it was warm and I could be persuaded by an Aperol spritz.

Pukus regarded me warily. 'No.'

My power and influence were indeed imaginary, it seemed.

Pukus poured himself a double. It was unclear whether Boss or I were invited to sit. I pulled out a chair, and Boss sat in it. I pulled out another.

'I was held up in a meeting with the OTIOSE people.' He flopped in a Chesterfield armchair. 'It's all very hush-hush at this stage, highly confidential, but they've actually caught someone doing the wrong thing.'

Boss scratched his chin, distracted; the stubble on his chin was mostly silver.

'Whistle-blower, apparently,' Pugh said.

'Sorry Marcus, back up,' Boss said. 'What are you talking about?'

Marcus and *Brendan*, was it? How had I not noticed their cosy relationship? These two went way back.

Pukus said, 'An unfortunate public servant is, they have reason to think, being blackmailed. They have her under surveillance. All I can

106

say.' He drank the contents of the glass and went to pour another. 'And something about passports.'

'Why passports?' Boss asked.

'That was what I was going to ask you, Brendan. What's the angle here?'

Boss opened his eyes fully, his attention shifting at last from whatever inner torment he was attuned to, to Pukus and I. 'The angle? No idea. It's a good thing someone had the guts to report it.'

'Very brave,' Pukus said. 'The identity of the whistle-blower is under wraps for now.'

'Have any of the passports been used?' I asked.

'They don't know, they tell me,' Pukus said with irritation. 'They're going over her work for the last three months, crosschecking. Taping her calls, all sorts of subterfuge.'

I looked out the window at the brick wall. I turned back to find Pukus had turned the discussion to the concerns of his portfolio. 'Tough times, Brendan. Every cost gets a line through it. Coffers are dry and the old boy won't hear a word.'

I groaned inwardly, assuming 'the old boy' was the treasurer. Coffers so dry the legislation to cut land-tax breaks for multinationals had just been quietly dumped. That'll create jobs, they say. Jobs for the builders of enormous private yachts.

Boss was nodding. 'The old boy reminds me of Brother Michael, remember? Saliva flying from his mouth, one eye looked the wrong way.'

Pukus cackled. 'Don't stand in the front row when Brother Michael's conducting choir, face full of spit for your trouble.'

They were school friends. How had I missed that? There'd been a whisper that Boss had gone to a top private school. We reconciled this information with his work in community services by assuming it was an act of rebellion. Or redemption. He was a complicated man.

'Enough of the nostalgia,' I said. 'Can we focus, gentlemen, please?'

Pukus was affronted, and coughed with disapproval. 'State your business, then. What's this hare-brained program?' He addressed me. 'You know, you're wasting your time; I can't get funding for diddly, let alone some socialist outfit that's beyond my ministerial scope.'

I'd encountered this pre-emptive belittling tactic before. I wondered if it was taught in management courses. 'Preventable house fires, poor immigrant families burnt to death, public liability, yadda yadda yadda, give us fifteen grand for a fire-safety education program.' An ambit bid — we'd walk away with five thousand if we were lucky.

Pukus roared laughter, turned scarlet, slapped his knee. 'I see what you mean,' he said to Boss. 'Out of touch with reality.'

'Ten grand, and we'll throw in English classes.'

'Exceeds my bailiwick.'

'Eight, and we'll assist with administering any community-based orders for anyone holding a temporary protection visa.'

'Sorry, lovey. They'd never get the visa in that case.'

I stood up, put both hands on the table and eyeballed Pukus. 'All right. How about *this*? The passports scandal, whatever it is, becomes public, which it will. The opposition says it smacks of government mismanagement. There's a great deal of hand-wringing in the press about our security. You immediately announce a fifty-thousand-dollar funding increase to public-employee background checks. Then, as a distraction, because you are so concerned with keeping the homeless off the streets, you include increased funding to get street kids into improved accommodation. And have better assessments on youth workers.'

I threw the youth worker checks in for the hell of it, thinking of Enright, and kept speaking. 'Say it like you mean it, as though it were your idea. We use our resources, working with other agencies, to identify at-risk youth and find accommodation for kids sleeping rough. That's in your purview, surely? There happens to be extra funds available, and we use it to create a fire-safety education program for recent arrivals.'

I heard tapping. Boss was beating time with a finger on the table top, a hint of a smile on the existentialist's face. 'Corrupt public servants,' Boss said. 'Looks bad.'

'Very bad,' I agreed.

Pukus pursed his thin lips. 'Pre-emptive strike? Yes, that might get through to His Nibs. I'll have a word to him, see what we can manage.' He stood, our cue to leave.

On the stairs, Boss smirked. A stark reversal of his earlier mood. 'Nice work in there, Hardy.'

He headed through the vestibule at a trot, as though he feared Pukus would change his mind and come after us.

I reflected on our success with the minister, albeit limited, and the performance we'd put on to get it. We'd circumvented all the usual channels, the painstaking application processes, the chain of public-servant command, the checks and balances. Our chances of securing funds via the official route were virtually zero. Instead, we'd taken the way of vested interests, a combination of threat and mutual benefit, and it had worked. What would this country look like if community support agencies had the clout of, say, a mining industry association, or a major bank?

Not that Pukus had actually promised us anything. In fact, the odds were that he'd take the idea, water it down, make an announcement that sounded good but offered nothing, and we'd end up with no fire-safety training money. But he had emerged so buoyant that I chose not to point that out. There was, however, one matter that remained unsettled. 'What was all that crap about art?'

'Lost its potency, for me at least. It's futile. Pointless.'

'All art? Even …' I swallowed. 'Television?'

He seemed cross. 'Be serious. I'm talking about creative works.'

I *was* being serious, and now my feelings were hurt.

We were out in the fresh air, crossing Spring Street. It felt good to be away from the recycled exhalations of exhausted power.

Cantering down Burke Street, two steps of mine to his lunging stride.

He stopped suddenly. 'My car's up there.' He pointed down an alley to a multi-level parking complex. 'When we get back to the office, we can work out the details of the program.'

'Ah, Boss, it's after five. I thought I'd hang around in the city. Do some early Christmas shopping?'

He looked at his watch. 'Monday then.' His scowl said I had better not get any ideas about taking an unauthorised day off.

'Yep,' I said cheerily. 'Bright and early.'

He hesitated. 'And I might as well tell you now, I'm thinking of resigning.'

I waited for a punchline. Surely he was not serious.

'Not thinking of. Doing. I'm leaving WORMS,' he said.

Shanninder was right. Again. That woman was Nostradamus. But even so, I felt off-kilter at the news. The earth was off its axis and was free-wheeling around the solar system. 'But why?'

Eyes on the ground. 'I can't summon the energy.'

'Okay,' I said. 'This is that crisis of yours. You need to have a break. Take some time off. You can't seriously think of leaving. I mean who can possibly replace you?'

'Interesting you should say that —'

'You know what I think the problem is? A fear of death. Well, I hate to break it to you. We can't escape it, death awaits us all.'

He glared at me; I'd touched a nerve. I continued. 'Even though those annoying health-policy bossy-pants types are constantly telling us not to die. We will. They don't like it. I know, neither do we. But humans are, well, human.'

'Nietzsche couldn't have put it better himself. But about the job —'

'We can't all die in our sleep. I mean, it's not that I *like* the idea of a fireball, or a mincer, or being eaten by some crazed sea lion —'

'I don't think sea lions eat people.'

'Maybe not eat, but they attack. Remember that girl in WA? A sea lion leapt out of the water and mauled her —'

He raised a hand, stopped me mid-sentence.

110

'What?'

'What are your career plans?'

Career plans? Did anyone's life trajectory match their plans? I reeled from one job to another, taking whatever work I could get.

'Let me put it this way,' Boss went on, sensing my confusion. 'Where do you see yourself in five years?'

In five years, I expected to be living on an island with Brophy, wearing tropical prints, making coconut cream pie, and getting together with Thurston Howell the Third for the luau on a Saturday night. I raised my shoulders. 'Dunno.'

'Apply for my job. I can't guarantee you'll get it, of course. Nothing can be guaranteed. It is a dog's arse of a job, too. Thankless, tedious, involves copious arse-kissing. Much responsibility, little thanks.'

'You make it sound so attractive.'

'It pays well, and more importantly, I know you'd do a good job.'

'Flattery won't change my relaxed attitude to working hours,' I warned him.

'Think it over,' he said, then he marched down the alley.

With his departure, a weird sensation overcame me — happiness. Not since Brophy and I had started hanging out together had I felt this kind of joy. My current job was a dead end. Being the new Boss probably had dog hairs on it, but it paid well. For those of us in the community sector, well-paid positions were rare, mythical, exotic.

I noticed that everyone else in the city seemed cheerful, too. People were chatting into their phones and to each other, and were generally being happy, and it occurred to me that I might just be getting a contact high from the people around me. It was the end of the working week, a four-day weekend was in the offing for most, and the general air of excitement in the city was almost immoderate.

I caught a passing tram heading west and stepped out near the Docklands Stadium. I did a circuit around the outside of ground, appraising the buildings that surrounded it, some built barely an arm's length from the arena. One angular glass structure, tinted mauve, was the only one that matched Phuong's description of a 'purple tower'. Inside the foyer was a bank of residents' names with buzzers. I found William Blyton's name and buzzed.

Loud sniff. 'Yes?'

'William Blyton?'

'Who is this?'

'Stella Hardy. William, sorry to bother you at home. I was told you might be able to help me. I'm a social worker with WORMS.'

A blast of nose blowing. 'You've got what?'

'I have a client, a teenage boy.' Cory was not a client in the strictest sense of the word, but I was not one to get bogged down with semantics. 'He died yesterday. I believe he was caught up in a fake charity scam, or something, with an outlaw motorcycle gang, and I wondered if —'

'Look, mate, I'd like to help, but I can't. So you tell whichever of those trainee clowns who gave you my home address that I'd like to strangle them. I've got the flu. Going back to bed. Ring the station.'

I re-entered the high-spirited atmosphere of the emptying city. I squeezed onto a packed tourist tram, and stood amid families checking maps, listening to pre-recorded commentary describing a town I didn't recognise, and headed back to Swanston Street. As I made my way towards Flinders Street Station, I encountered a human statue coated in gold. She made a grab for me as I passed, but I ducked out of her reach. I didn't know much about art, but I knew I didn't want it molesting me. Boss's crazy claim that art served no purpose was starting to seem like a carefully reasoned maxim.

The commuters at Melbourne's main train station swarmed, funnelling onto the escalators, filling out the platforms, and around them, but somehow a multitude of barely visible, lost souls gathered on the steps, or loitered in the concourse, or grazed in the burger franchise. And now they were waiting for HARM to happen.

24

I BOUGHT a falafel from a takeaway joint in the station concourse and sat on a bench. I took a hesitant bite: both dry and soggy, having no doubt languished for a day in its cling wrap. Two more bites and I binned it. I resumed searching among the teenagers congregated here for Alma Dunmore. They wandered in loose gangs, or sat on the floor in groups, or scoured the floor for dropped coins. They saw a loosely held handbag. They followed commuters too rushed to notice they'd dropped a twenty when they pulled their Myki travel card from their wallet.

Alma was not among them. Maybe she was too aloof for this place. She was not an aimless delinquent looking for any old fun. She considered herself a serious player, or that's how I read her. But she had no idea what she was getting into with Josie, AKA Philomena Josephine the drug trafficker, AKA a Corpse Flower.

Half an hour passed. The crowds rushed by, ignoring me. Ignoring the teenagers.

Another half hour. It sure was depressing watching people running towards trains, families, and fun, the holidays awaiting them. While we sat here, with nothing to do.

Another half hour. No more. Time to go. What a disheartening waste of time. I put my handbag on my shoulder. As I rose, I saw movement from the corner of my eye. A girl smoothly worked her way through the throngs and perched at the other end of the bench from me.

Her twig legs, in black leggings, were crossed, thongs flapping nervously on her feet. And her toenails were painted green. This individual might be Sleeps in the Toilet at Macca's Girl, and possibly a better information source than Alma.

I had a better look at her. Ash-white hair with green streaks through it. A grey athletic-brand hoodie. These kids with their workout clothes, all label and no fitness.

I moved closer, nonchalant, as I watched her green chipped fingernails work the screen.

After sending and receiving some texts, she glanced up at the train schedules on a bank of screens, and let out a profanity. She gathered a couple of shopping bags at her feet and dashed away. I followed her, down the ramp to Platform 5. A train was waiting. She made it on board. An announcement warned passengers to stand clear. The doors started to close. I hit the bottom of the ramp and leapt. The doors juddered shut, but I was in, face pressed against a random shoulder.

We passengers were sardines and just as smelly. I could see a white-and-green hairdo making its way to the front of the carriage and I squished my way through in pursuit. The girl found a place to stand near the disabled seats at the front. I held a strap in the middle. As the train stopped, more people got on, defying the laws of physics. All the while, I managed to keep my eye on the green streaks of hair.

As the train approached Footscray, the girl moved to the door. I followed. We alighted and I pursued her up the escalator, two paces behind. She went left, I did likewise. At the doughnut shop, she stopped. I hung around. No surprise to me that Toilet Girl lived on Macca's and doughnuts.

She walked away from the kiosk with a hefty bag of doughy-goodness, heading left around the market. I stayed back but glimpsed her heading towards the Hopkins Street Bridge and down an alley behind the old Franco Cozzo furniture shop. It was easier to stay with her now; she was dawdling, singing to herself. The houses around here were small and close together. Patches of concrete in the front, peeling paint, bins full of beer cans. At a house with high weeds and boarded-up windows, she banged a two-handed flam on the door. It was a code no one could remember, let alone repeat. The door opened and she was admitted.

I hung around for a while, not sure what to do next. There was a rusted letter box hanging off the fence. Weathered envelopes protruded. I took a quick look around, no one was about. I casually pulled the letters out and flipped through them. Junk mail, and *To The Owner* newsletters from a real estate agent. Three were properly addressed mail — to *Mr Richard Peck* and *Mr Richard Turner*. I stuffed those in my bag, and the junk back in the letterbox.

I tapped lightly on the door and waited. The door opened a crack, dark interior, a pair of eyes.

'What?'

'Yes, hi, I'm looking for Alma. I was told she'd be here.'

The eyes narrowed. 'Who's asking?'

'Friend of Isaac Mortimer's.'

'The fuck didn't you say so?'

'I … I just did.'

Something heavy was moved from behind the door, it opened and an adolescent boy stood staring at me. Floppy hair, short shorts, a bum bag slung over one shoulder. I'd noticed the kids I worked with wearing the same bags in the same way lately. Usual contents: spray-paint, or a thick Texta, a boxie, for those hard-to-open boxes, and a packet of smokes. He grinned at me, mouth full of doughnut. 'She's a pain, isn't she?' He turned to the house. 'Brook, some lady's here, says she's a friend of Isaac's.'

'Who?' Toilet Girl popped her head into the hall. 'Who told you about this place?'

'Isaac,' I said, clearly first names the way to go.

'She wants to know where Alma is, heard from her lately?' said the boy.

'Get fucked.'

He turned back to me with a smile. 'Sorry.'

'Truth is, I needed to make sure she *wasn't* here. She's —'

'We know!' The boy was saying, 'A big pain in the arse.'

'Er, yes.'

He stood back and allowed me inside. 'So Isaac sent you? Cool.' He led me through the house. At the rear, one step down, was a dodgy extension, aluminium, roof and walls, with a concrete floor covered in worn and blackened sea-grass matting. Graffiti on the walls. Despite it still being daylight outside, the room was dingy. I wondered if the lights worked. Maybe the electricity was off. Tinny music came from a portable speaker on an upturned crate.

Brook was sprawled on a mattress on the floor, flicking her thumb on her phone with one hand, twirling her green hair with the other. Cans of spray-paint were strewn about. I thought of Phuong's car. It was possible, but not probable. I doubted they knew who she was, let alone which car she drove.

Without looking up, she sighed and hit a button on her phone. The speaker became silent. 'Well, come in then,' Brook said. 'Make yourself at home. Have a doughnut.'

There was nowhere to sit except a couple of filthy mattresses and an esky. I sat on the esky. 'So this place was Ricky's?'

'Was. Now it's mine. Me and me graff crew.' The boy crossed his arms.

Brook rolled her eyes. 'You wish.'

I helped myself to a doughnut. 'So you haven't seen Alma around? What's she up to, you reckon?'

'Who knows?' the boy said. 'Kids these days. Am I right, Angie?'

The girl was sitting in the shadows, staring at a white card, knees up to her chin, her black hair in a top-knot bun. My guess was South Pacific background, one parent at least. Currently a resident of the streets. I realised the card was a photo, which she folded and left on the floor. Then she sniffed loudly and wiped her eyes on her sleeve.

'Is she okay?'

'She's cut up about Cory.'

I knew the feeling.

Brook stood up, impatient. 'Come on, Angie, get the gear out.'

The girl, Angie, moved into the centre of the room and pulled a jumbo pack of chem-brand ParaCode from a paper bag. Now I had a proper look at her, she was the girl we saw with Cory and Razz in the car park waiting for Alma. The night Copeland showed up and sent them scattering.

'What happened to Cory?' Her version would be good to know.

Angie shrugged. 'He died.'

Brook emptied her bags on the floor: glass measuring jug with lid, and a spoon.

'Gave an old guy near the funeral parlour a twenty,' Angie said. 'He got a forty-pack with paracetamol, so we have to CWE it.'

'Um, so, Cory. You think it was an accident?' I addressed the room generally.

'Oh, my God.' Angie shook her head. 'I miss him.' She measured out water from a bottle into the jug. When she was satisfied, she took out the blister packs, started popping out pills, sheet after sheet, dropping them in the water.

'Has to be distilled water,' the boy said.

'Nah,' Angie said. 'I've used tap before, works fine. If you've had problems, there's lots of other reasons why yours might not work.'

'Mine works. I don't have problems.'

'It just seemed really, like, weird, the way Cory died,' I said.

'Maybe it's your metabolism,' Angie said, stirring the mixture. 'Also, don't have any Phenergan with it because that inhibits the shit out of codeine.'

He made a face. 'I'm the one who told you that.' He flicked his hair back. 'Been extracting codeine since before you were born.'

'Calm the farm, sunshine,' Brook said, picking at a nail.

'You need to filter it three times.' He sighed. 'Coffee filters.'

'T-shirt's fine,' Angie said.

'Comes out cloudy.' He groaned, turned to me. 'They're going to mess it up.' He turned to the wall, found a mark like a bullet hole and started scratching at it with a pen.

117

I was struggling to think of a way to get the conversation back to Cory.

'He thinks he knows everything because his dad's a scientist,' Brook said.

'Was. He mows lawns now,' he said.

'Did you know Cory?' Angie asked. She gestured for me to stand.

'Yeah. I knew him,' I said, getting up from the esky. 'He was funny.'

When I moved, she opened the lid of the esky; it was half-full of ice.

I walked around to where Angie had left the photos. Four small passport-sized portraits. Big cheeky grin. The passport types don't like smiling. It would have been rejected. I turned to see Angie watching me.

'Did he sit the exam?' I asked.

'What exam?' Brook stopped picking at her nails and looked at me.

'The test, I mean. Did any of you take the test? Isaac told me the Corpse Flowers wanted some kids to take a test.'

Angie laughed. 'He means the *blood* test. You need your blood type to get your passport.'

Not true, I thought. I didn't contradict her.

She put the lid on the jug, placed it down into the ice and closed the lid on the esky.

I could contain my curiosity no longer. 'What's CWE?'

'Cold water extraction,' the boy said, lighting a cigarette. 'Get the codeine, but leave out the paracetamol. That shit will kill ya.'

'Why are you here again?' Angie asked.

The boy sucked on the cigarette. 'She reckons Isaac sent her.'

'That's right.' I acted solemn and official, like I was on a serious mission. 'Isaac's very concerned. Since Cory died.'

'What'd he say?' Brook said, getting to her feet.

'Um, he's concerned.'

She appeared to accept that. 'Isaac goes, *stop using their shit, and stay away from them*. But they were giving us wads of cash, buying us drinks. We were having a great time.'

'Yeah, haircuts,' Angie said. 'Tried to.'

'Wait, haircuts?'

'They made appointments, but we didn't go,' Angie was saying. 'One time, Brook did show up, but they went bat-shit about her green hair.'

Brook shrugged. 'I started getting suss, then. Isaac goes, "Yeah, stay away."'

The boy agreed. 'Don't even *talk* to them, he reckons.'

'Who's *them*? Can you be more specific? Was it Josie?'

Brook smirked. 'Some old lady came in Macca's toilets asking Alma where Isaac was. After Alma left, I fed her some bullshit about The Ashbrook.'

'Good one, Brook.' The boy laughed. 'As if he'd go there.'

I nodded furiously. 'Yeah. Good move, Brook, sending her to The Ashbrook, which she probably would have hated because, like, the food there isn't that nice, and her boyfriend too, if she had one, I bet he hated it. Probably created all kinds of tension between them.' I hooted. 'Too funny.'

'I don't think one bad meal would create tension.' The boy was pensive. 'Only if things were already a bit rocky, like if there was another underlying issue.'

'Like what?' I asked.

'Well, maybe he's got pressures in his life. Conflicting priorities.'

'What the fuck, you guys,' Brook said.

'This boyfriend, say he just got retrenched, and he's finding it hard to adjust, and he doesn't feel supported by her …' the boy was saying.

'Alma thinks she's so smart, but they're using her,' Angie said. 'It's like Amway. My mum was into that for a while. You have to get your friends to buy. It's horrible.'

'What's Alma selling?'

'Kengtung, and the money everyone's gonna make.'

Brook laughed. 'Yeah, but they didn't realise we hate Alma.' She stood in front of me. 'That's why we'd never bring her here. We're not supposed to be here, no one is. If you're friends with Isaac, you'd know that.'

We faced each other. My heart rate rising, but my gaze steady.

'He's skipped town,' she said. 'He's not talking to anyone.'

'He's still in Melbourne.' I kept my voice low and flat.

She put both hands in her back pockets. I exhaled, my fear easing. She was mere bones. I could lift her off the ground with one hand.

Then her hand came out holding a blade. My legs went to water. She darted forward and pressed the edge into my flab, looking for a rib, twisting. 'Where?'

I found myself against the wall, no room to move. 'I spoke to him today.' Calm as I could, as blood trickled down my side.

'Who *are* you?'

'Me? I'm the one with the cool drugs Isaac wanted you to have.'

She lowered the blade.

'That's right.' I was speaking, and moving sideways. 'They're in my car. Which is parked. Near. The Footscray market.'

The three of them were watching me. 'Thank God,' said Angie. 'This CWE is shit.'

'I'm going to get the stuff from my car, and I'll bring it back here.'

They stared at me with heartbreaking optimism.

'Be right back.' I gave them a thumbs up.

I darted down the hall and slammed the front door behind me. I hit the footpath at a canter. It had been a very long time since I'd run flat-out. Soon I was puffing, struggling to get air in my lungs. Like a middle-aged fool, I worried I might trip, maybe break something. On the other hand, if Brook or Angie caught me, they'd go the bash. Or the slash. The boy, not so much.

I ran alongside the market, in the shadow of the awnings, and turned into Leeds Street. The passers-by went about their business, shopping, and chatting. Some looking to score. No one seemed concerned by the desperate life-or-death expression on my face, or the blood stain spreading on my t-shirt. At last, I thought, I was fitting in.

25

I ASSESSED each shop for hiding potential: immigration agent, no; gold and jade merchant, no; mobile phones and sim cards, no. Indian grocery shop, yes.

Inside, the air was cool and heavy with fragrance. Rows of lentils, bags of spices, bottles of rose water and soap and henna, and packets of incense. I walked straight to the back of the shop and, obscured by a pile of atta-flour bags, I dabbed my injury with a tissue. It wasn't bad; the bleeding had stopped. I rolled up my t-shirt in the front and tied a knot, exposing some skin but concealing the bloody stain. Then, to avoid attracting attention, I occupied myself reading the contents of the fridge. Time passed. I moved past a display of five-litre ghee tins, and casually peered over a pile of forty-kilo sacks of basmati. The streets were delinquent-free, as far as I could tell. Had they followed me, they'd have come in and clobbered me by now. I relaxed a little, though I waited a bit longer to be sure. I walked along the aisles, past shelves of neatly arranged kilo bags of whole spices. Who, I wondered, used that many cloves?

A man wearing a shirt that reached down to his knees, and baggy long pants, came down the aisle carrying some boxes from the back of the shop. He ripped the tape from a box. It would seem suspicious if I simply stood here, so I moved down to the next shelf and picked up a bag of cardamom pods.

The man smiled at me. 'Not that one.'

'Pardon?'

'The black, not the green. The green are not as good. Madagascan is the best, but here we have only black and green. Take the black.' He looked on the shelves and found a packet of black cardamom and offered it to me. A one-kilo bag. 'What are you making?'

'Oh, a delicious … food thing … that you eat.'

'Cookies? Iraqi cookies with almonds and cardamom, they are very nice. Or maybe you put it in coffee? That is good also.'

'Yes, cookies … and coffee. Coffee-flavoured cookies.'

I took my cardamom to the counter.

He ran the scanner over the bag. 'Fifty dollars, please.'

A pineapple? A whole *pineapple* for a spice I didn't want or need? If I cooked at home for the rest of my life, I'd never use a kilo of cardamom. 'Do you have a smaller bag?'

The man went to the back of the shop. I glanced out the front, crowds bustled to and from the station, people with trollies doing last-minute food shopping, families out to dinner. A bone-thin man with a maniac stare tried to run through the crowd, he turned to yell at the woman following behind him. Her expression was grim and hostile. He stuck out a hand, she grabbed it and they ran on together. Romance was not dead for some.

On the counter was a stack of brochures for a brand of lentil, the world's best lentil, it said. On the back was a recipe. Curiously, the recipe did not include lentils. But I liked the sound of it, *kaddu bharta,* and it had palm sugar in it. That had to be a good thing.

A plan was forming. A romantic dinner for two, at the triumphant close of Brophy's exhibition. Reading the ingredients: cardamom seeds, crushed, was taken care of; pumpkin, easy. Unsalted butter, fennel seeds, green chillies, palm sugar, chopped toasted hazelnuts, and lime juice. The salt, I had already.

All this spice was going to my head. I imagined myself pounding them with a mortar and pestle, guiding these flavours into a seductive unity. I'd create my own *garam masala*, a secret blend with potent seduction properties.

The man put a smaller packet of cardamom on the counter. 'Anything else?'

I rattled off the list on the recipe card.

'Ah, *kaddu bharta*. Very good.' He pointed to a stack of plastic hand baskets. 'You will find all of those items here.' He smiled.

I went hunting around the shop. On a high shelf, I spotted a box of Turkish delight from Iran, for which I had a sudden hankering. I was counting out the green chillies when my phone rang. It was Afshan. 'Hello, Stella!'

I could hear a rumble in the background and then a crashing sound. 'Where are you?'

'Funky Town.'

'Are you kidding?'

'No. Shahid wanted to try bowling. Like The Dude.'

'The Dude abides, man,' I said solemnly.

'Stella, join us, come to bowling with Shahid and me. If you're free?' He was shouting over the noise.

It was a lovely offer. Trouble was, I now categorically hated bowling. 'Another time.'

'What?'

'No thanks,' I yelled. I put my phone away and took my basket to the counter. The butter and the pumpkin, I would get at the supermarket.

'Rice?' The man asked. 'I'd serve *kaddu bharta* with rice or chapati.'

'Rice,' I agreed. 'But your smallest bag is five kilos. I'll never manage it on the tram.'

His response was a subtle tilting motion of the head. At once enigmatic and full of meaning. A gesture that I understood to mean: *we are all one, creation exists in the mind, beyond all thought is the ultimate bliss of consciousness.* But he may also have meant: *that is the amount of rice we have; the decision is up to you.*

I bought the rice. Outside, seeing no one with green hair, I slipped into the shadows and moseyed down the street to a waiting tram. I hauled my rice aboard and sat near a window, where I had a view of anyone coming from Hopkins Street. My fellow passengers seemed harmless, no orange-topped heavies, and no scary teenage combatants.

On the way home, I sifted through the mail I'd lifted from the letterbox at the squat. Some catalogues from a local supermarket, a generic message from the local member of state parliament, and two window envelopes, each addressed to a different Richard. Richard Peck had a summons for an altercation with a driver in a car park in Norlane. The incident happened in June, the letter was dated three weeks ago.

And a Richard Turner had an itemised account from Rising Star Glamour Photography. They were based in Werribee. Company slogan: *We put you in the picture.* Listed on the bill were forty high-definition colour photographs, files supplied.

It was after nine on a Friday night. Some places worked late on Fridays though. I glanced up; a handful of passengers were mostly at the front of the tram, out of earshot. I searched on my phone and hit the number.

'Rising Star Glamour, this is Travis.'

'Travis, I'm Emily Turner, sister of Richard Turner and executor of his will. Richard passed away and I'm paying his accounts. I'm ringing about some shots you did for him?'

'Honey, you have my condolences, but that job was a nightmare from start to finish and I still haven't been paid. Would you mind telling me when I'm going to get my money? What's the hold-up?'

Jeez, what an arsehole. 'Just a small issue. I need to know the purpose of the photos, if they were personal or —'

'Business. Nasty business.'

'Why nasty?'

'One of those fucking kids had head lice. I had to fumigate the studio after that.'

'Sorry, would you mind giving me more detail?'

'First, the assistant came in, she gets some sexy portraits — impress the boyfriend. Tasteful lingerie, you know? Beautiful. She took the full package. Then she asks about shooting kids, says she's asking on behalf of her boss, this guy who runs a kids' charity. He wants glamour shots. Hair, make-up, the whole shebang. He wants passport head shots and these ghastly full-body poses. Says he'll pay extra, for discretion.'

'Full-body? Like frontals? As in … nude?'

'Clothed. This is a legit business, lovey. Full, as in you can see the feet. Afterwards, I see all these fucking bugs in the basin and I rang her, I said head lice is going to cost you extra, sweetie, and no more kiddie shots. Nada, zero, zip, that's it for me.'

I thanked him, said I'd send a cheque, and ended the call.

What drug-dealing thug wanted to take disadvantaged children to get glamour portraits? I recalled Josie in Macca's, talking to Alma about hair appointments for the kids, and something about a test. According to Raewyn Ross, some kids had called Ricky Peck a paedophile. Maybe he was. But he was working with Enright. Was she a sex offender, too? Or was she genuinely volunteering to save street kids from her fate?

At my stop, a kind soul helped me off the tram with my bags. I struggled up the hill, glancing behind me to see if I was being followed. There was no one around, but instead of entering my building, I crossed to the street and slumped down in a dark position between street lights and waited. It felt like an age since I'd last been home, in my sanctuary from life's knockage, and I was dying to get inside, pour a glass of wine, and watch a movie, preferably a soothing old favourite. The minutes passed. I put on my cardigan.

The street was quiet, and apart from the occasional car going by, no one stirred.

This was silly, I told myself, no goons were coming for me. Least of all Mortimer, who was supposedly in hiding. I started to cross the street.

A light-coloured SUV turned the corner and crawled down Roxburgh Street, and paused outside my building.

Panic froze me to the spot. A startled rabbit had more self-control. *Think*, I thought. Run? They'd follow me. Weapons — what did I have? A five-kilo bag of rice. Not very helpful. There was nothing for it, death had arrived at last. Sorry, Hardy, you've had a few lucky escapes in your time, but your hour has come. I crossed the road, went to the car, and looked in at the driver. A woman in her late thirties, blonde, similar facial structure to mine, only a lot more attractive. '*Kylie?*'

'Stella, at bloody last,' she said, getting out. Two boys of about ten jumped from the car and immediately started to rumble on the nature strip.

I wrapped my cardigan around me to conceal the blood stain on my t-shirt. 'This is a surprise,' I said.

'Where've you been? We've been waiting for *ages.*'

My sister still lived in the same town we grew up in, and assumed a city of five million functioned much the same as Woolburn, a town of two hundred and seventy people. In Woolburn, you could rock up unannounced to your sister's house, and if she wasn't home, let yourself in. In Woolburn, you could ask a neighbour where your sister was and they'd know. In Woolburn, you could expect someone to be home on a Friday night. She'd driven for four hours on the off-chance I'd be here, ready to receive visitors. 'Why didn't you ring me first?'

'I left about five messages,' she said. 'You never return my calls.'

'Aunty Stella, we're starving!' one of her boys moaned. Chad? Blair? I could never tell them apart.

'You've just had cheeseburgers,' Kylie said, and then to me, 'We were driving around for something to do. I let them have McDonald's, Stella. *That's* how drained I was.'

The only diet-conscious parent in the Mallee.

'But we're *starving!*'

She seemed on the verge of tears.

'Come on, everyone upstairs,' I said. 'How's Vegemite on toast?'

The flat was hot and stuffy. I opened a window, whacked the kettle on and threw some bread in the toaster. Kylie's judging eye roved, appraising every detail. 'Nice place.'

Nothing about my lifestyle fitted her idea of 'nice'. 'Thanks. What brings you here?'

She pulled out a chair and gave it a quick brush, and sat. 'We need to halt the sale.'

Our mother's farm, she meant. My mother, Delia, and her partner, Ted, made plans to move to a unit in Ouyen. The Hardy matriarch was as tough as granite, and a farmer in her own right, but getting on in years. Semi-retired, they'd sold off stock, and half the land in acreage lots. The sale of the rest of the land with the family home, had stalled for some reason. I suspected the delay was emotional rather than a simple matter of red tape. My father had worked the place for twenty years, sheep and wheat. In the late eighties, when he was crop-dusting, his light plane had crashed. Thirty years had passed, yet I suspected my mother still quietly grieved for him, and was still attached to the house they had made into a home together.

To make matters even more complicated, Shane Farquhar, the Woolburn farmer who wanted to buy the land, was my former high-school tormenter. He'd bullied me, spread rumours about me, and generally made my life hell. His place bordered the Hardy farm. When he first tried to contact my mother to discuss the purchase, he couldn't get her on the phone. This was sufficient grounds to accuse me — *me* — of blocking his progress as payback for high school. The truth was, my mother had not sought my opinion on the matter, let alone my counsel. He was just paranoid and feeling guilty.

Since then, both parties had come to the table and seemed on the verge of reaching an agreement. I was pretty sure there'd been a handshake. 'It's a done deal, isn't it?'

'It's not done until the paperwork is signed.'

'I see. And you want to halt the sale because?'

'We've been talking it over.'

'We?'

'Mum and I.'

127

The kettle boiled. I made two mugs of tea, and passed one to Kylie.

'We think it should stay in the family.'

Our family was Kylie — who'd never shown any interest in the farm, ditto me — and our brother, Ben. 'If you mean Ben, forget it. He's about to do another stretch.'

Kylie nodded. '*Going equipped to steal* is a level-seven offence; based on his previous record, he'll get the full two years. With parole, eighteen months.'

I raised my eyebrows. Ordinarily, she took no interest in the details of Ben's legal circumstances. In fact, she would rarely admit she had a brother. A duck quacked; she ripped her phone from her pocket, frowned at the screen, and commenced thumbing.

The toast popped, and I slapped on the butter. 'Then I hope you don't mean *me*. I'd rather stick a knife in this toaster than return to Woolburn, that lifeless dustbowl.' I looked up. 'No offence.'

Kylie put her phone down, turned her head. 'Pardon?'

I spread a thin layer of Vegemite over the toast. 'Who is going to be the farmer in the family?'

'Tyler.'

'Your husband, Tyler?' The man couldn't grow a beard. He called horses 'ponies'. Chickens scared him.

'He did a course. Correspondence. We're going to breed Dexters. They're small cattle, very cute actually. From Ireland.'

'Hmm. Miniature Irish cows. How do they get on in the desert?'

'Woolburn isn't the desert, it's semi-arid. There's a *big* difference.'

'What about capital?'

'We'll borrow, like everyone else does. He'll make it work.'

I formed a noncommittal smile. He'd make it work like the Betamax tape recorder. I called the boys, who ran in from my room, where they'd been suspiciously quiet. While they scoffed the toast, Kylie pursed her lips to sip her tea.

'Did you want to stay here tonight?' I asked.

She seemed amused by the question. 'No. We're staying with friends.'

Another long pause.

'Is there something you want me to do?' I asked.

'Talk to Mum. Get her to wait until Tyler can put together a proper offer.'

'You said she'd already changed her mind.'

Kylie went coy. 'She's wavering. I need you to clinch the deal. Can you do that much for me?' She patted one of the boys on the head. He flinched and pulled away. 'For the sake of their future.'

'And what about Shane Farquhar? He's been in negotiations with Mum for months.'

I couldn't believe I was sticking up for that man. Especially after he'd falsely accused me of having stymied the deal. Now, by some weird twist of fate, here I was being asked to meddle for real.

'He's not *family*. Don't you want to keep it in the family?' Kylie asked.

'I don't care who owns it.'

She acted wounded. It was a good performance.

'But I like the sound of those Dexters. Fine. I'll speak to Delia.'

When they left, I went to the bathroom and lifted my t-shirt. A short, shallow cut throbbed faintly on my side. I dabbed at it with a tissue. Brook had pressed the blade into my skin enough to draw blood, but it wasn't deep.

I showered and applied a Band-Aid. Then I put on a pair of shorts and an old t-shirt and stretched out on the couch. I turned on my old TV, and flicked around. There was going to be a Paul Newman movie marathon on over the weekend, starting tonight. That would be worth staying in for. I made my usual eat-in meal of cheese and crackers, washed it down with the last glass of white I could squeeze from the cask.

First up, *Sweet Bird of Youth*. It was good, but my eyes drooped. I closed them for a minute. *Keng* something. *Kengtung*, was that the word? Angie had said it was part of the lure Alma had dangled at them. Kengtung, drugs, and lots of money. Who was Kengtung? Or maybe Kengtung was a company?

Angie and green-toenails Brook, living in a squat once used by Ricky Peck. Brook was handy with a blade. Angie loved Cory, and kept his discarded passport photo in her wallet. They were all in the orbit of the Corpse Flowers, locked in their evil tractor beam.

Nothing you can do, miss. Why did someone push Cory Fontaine in front of a truck?

Isaac Mortimer had warned the kids to *avoid* them. Presumably, he meant Josie and her bikie boyfriend, Ox Gorman. Maybe the Turk, too. Even Alma. Brook said the Turk was with 'them' and was looking for Mortimer. If Gorman found out Mortimer was tipping off the street kids that he planned to enlist, that was reason enough for Mortimer to skip town.

Mortimer's testimony was crucial to Copeland, to saving his reputation, his job. I'd promised Phuong I would help find him, for her. Because, for whatever silly reason, Copeland mattered to her. I liked to think that if something silly mattered to me, she would support me. I hoped so, because I'd arrived at mission creep. The state of affairs was in flux, and disturbing information had broadened the focus beyond Mortimer. The Corpse Flowers's gambit appeared to involve a program to groom children, in the literal sense. That was suspect in the extreme. And, in my view, a much bigger problem.

I fired up my laptop and opened a browser.

Burma. Kengtung, it turned out, was a town on the Chinese border. What kind of money, I wondered, was to be made in Burma? Something legal and completely above board?

My dark thoughts were interrupted by a Shih tzu yapping inside Brown Cardigan's adjoining flat. And a moment later, insistent pounding on my front door.

26

'COMING.' I slid the chain, but my hand paused on the deadbolt. There'd been a lot of talk of danger lately, some of it concerning me as the target. Odd women in suits threatening me, teens with box cutters and auxiliary sharp objects, and other general unpleasantness. I secured the chain and backed away to the kitchen.

'Who is it?' I said.

'Stella?' Phuong called.

'Oh, thank Christ. You scared the crap out of me.'

'Sorry to wake you.'

'I'm awake, what's happened?'

She strode in, her sequined top shimmering over skinny jeans and stiletto-heeled leopard-skin ankle boots. I invited her to sit, and relax. I demonstrated the technique.

'Cuong. The bastard's in deep shit this time.'

'What's he done?'

Her groan was almost violent. 'I went to pick up my car from his place, like we arranged. He's not there. He's not answering his phone. Something's going on with him. I'm sure of it. He's going to look me in the eye and tell me exactly what he's involved in.'

'Do you know where he is?'

She shrugged. 'Crown. Where else?'

'You're pretty upset. I better come with you.' I tapped her bag. The Glock was ever within reach and loaded. 'In case you shoot him.'

She moved her bag away from me. 'I was hoping you'd say that.'

I quickly threw on some clothes more suited to Melbourne's casino. Then we went downstairs and into the night. My street was silent. Ascot Vale people were decent, hardworking types; young families or the elderly. We kept civilised hours. The odd ice fiend from time to time, but not tonight.

I looked around. 'Where's your car?'

'Still at Cuong's. I took a cab here. Where's yours?'

'In the shop. I had an altercation with a power pole.'

Phuong paused, seemed about to speak, but then didn't.

We walked down to Union Road to hail a passing cab. Ever since the Uber disruption, cabs were plentiful. One pulled up and soon we were speeding towards Crown. I lowered my window, let the warm wind caress my hand. The only caressing I'd had for a while. I breathed in and hit the button, watched the window slowly rise.

'How's the investigation going into Cory Fontaine's death?' I asked Phuong.

'Who?'

I sighed. 'The boy hit by a truck at the Footscray McDonald's. I think he was mixed up in something the Corpse Flowers are doing. I think they're coaching homeless kids.'

'Coaching?'

'I don't know. Favours, paying for haircuts, photographs, other unusual activities. Who do I talk to at VicPol about it?'

She looked at me. 'Bikies use kids to sell drugs to other kids. They all do it. They've been doing it for years. For now, Stella, please don't go to HQ with this. Keep it under wraps until we get Mortimer? Then Bruce will smash the whole Corpse Flowers enterprise, get them out of business.'

That was straight from Copeland, he was making her act against her better judgement. I wished Phuong would stand up to him. I looked out the window. I would not keep my concerns under wraps. I'd try Blyton one more time.

'I'm surprised at Cuong,' I said. 'He doesn't seem the type. He seems very straight.'

'The signs were there, early on,' Phuong was saying. 'He was trouble as a kid. My poor aunt and uncle, they didn't know what to do with him. They used to come over and have long conversations

132

with my parents. They suggested he go back to Vietnam. Get himself sorted out. So they sent him back to live with a relative. Boy, was that a mistake.'

'Why?'

'He came back full of stories. Bad magic, ghosts, curses, hauntings.'

'Maybe the ghost thing is real,' I said. I'd lost count of mine. I'd been haunted by people fixations, good and bad, or sometimes a spectre from the past. I'd want them gone, and later suffer pangs of regret when they went. The daily presence of my deceased father was a scaffold of affection, in the process of slow dismantling.

Phuong tossed her silky hair. 'Who knows. Dad always said Cuong got off to a bad start because he was born in *năm của dê*, the Year of the Goat. Dad said that's where the trouble started. Goat babies are calm, gentle, and honest. In the Goat year, you avoid the word '*cường*'. As in, *cường độ*, meaning intensity. You see the problem.'

I really didn't. 'You're saying the trouble is all in Cuong's name? Or is it because he went to Vietnam and developed a fear of ghosts?'

She shrugged. 'Rich tapestry.'

I looked out the window, wondering at my fate. Considering how much I loathed the place, it was weird that I often found myself at Crown. A place untroubled by conscience. Gambling, my father used to say, was a tax on fools. Nowadays it was referred to as 'gaming', a euphemism for a legal swindle, a theft from those least able to afford it.

27

PHUONG MARCHED into the gaming room, eschewing the roulette, and making directly for the blackjack tables. I supposed she'd done this kind of thing before. She took her responsibilities to Cuong seriously, in the Phuong way. It made me feel guilty about the way I treated my brother, Ben. Perhaps if I'd taken a more involved role in his life, prying and meddling in his affairs occasionally, he may not have ended up in jail. Or perhaps so. Hard to say.

After a circuit of the floor and no Cuong, we went to a bar, and positioned ourselves with a reasonable view of the blackjack tables on one side and the roulette tables on the other. A baccarat table near the entrance to a sports bar at the other end of the room was the only table not occupied with a punter. I ordered a couple of Aperol spritzes, figuring we might as well enjoy ourselves.

'I have news.'

Phuong moved her chin towards me, a sign she was listening, but her eyes were on the crowds moving around the tables. 'About Mortimer?'

'Sort of. Before he died, Ricky Peck was trying to get access to wards of the state. He'd applied to work for a child protection agency but they got him on the background checks. Can you imagine? A bikie working for a charity?'

Phuong shrugged. 'It has happened. I heard about this drug dealer who found religion and now he runs a rehab.'

'I doubt Ricky Peck found religion,' I said, tartly. 'And the thing is, there's a pattern here. You know that Ox Gorman's girlfriend is a convicted drug dealer called Philomena Josephine Enright, right? Well now she's calling herself Josie and she's acting like she has a saviour complex, making friends with all the kids who deal drugs in Footscray.

Then there's her client, Alma. She's a damaged, vulnerable child with a massive IQ and an equally massive chip on her shoulder. Some street kids told me Enright recruited Alma to co-opt them into some scheme. She told them that everyone stood to make lots of money.'

Phuong stopped scanning the crowds and stared at me. 'Doing what exactly?'

'I don't *know*, but it involves a place in Burma. Kengtung. Drug smuggling is my best guess.'

'Probably,' she said, and turned back to the blackjack tables.

'They also told me that your friend, Isaac Mortimer, warned them to keep away from Alma and not be sucked in by all the cash she was throwing around.'

Phuong was nodding. 'Did they say where he is?'

'No.' I took a sip of spritz. 'They reckon Mortimer comes to Crown.'

Phuong rolled her eyes. 'Cameras all over this place. He's not silly.'

'I suppose so.' No doubt about it, I was useless at finding people. I had to wonder why she'd asked me to do it in the first place. I had no idea what I was doing. I glanced around the gaming room, wondering if I would even recognise Mortimer if he did show up. The punters were leisurely, watching tables, or waiting for a chair to become available. Except for one woman, who was making her way through the room. Late fifties, dressed like a primary-school teacher, holding a plastic shopping bag up to her chest. It was as if her efforts to avoid notice — head down, shifty glances to security — were what drew my attention to her. That and the look of raw panic on her face.

'Look at her. What's she up to?' Phuong pointed out the same woman.

The woman was heading for the baccarat table, where a patron in a dark suit was now playing. 'Isn't that ...'

'Cuong,' Phuong said flatly, and moved off her stool. How had we missed him?

'Wait.' I grabbed her by the arm. 'Just, wait a second.'

Cuong checked his watch, then turned around, looking behind him — directly at the woman with the shopping bag. He was nodding and smiling. I turned to see her response. She smiled faintly back at him. She was about five metres away from him when, from out of the crowd, a man in a suit came and stood in front of her. He touched her arm and spoke to her, leaning into her ear.

Another man and a woman joined him.

'Security?' I asked.

'Cops,' said Phuong.

The two men took an arm each, the woman offering no resistance. From my reading, she appeared resigned, almost relieved, as if she had been expecting to be detained. The female officer took the bag from her, and with little fuss, they all walked out.

Phuong pursed her lips.

Cuong didn't react. The only sign something had happened was a wrinkling of his nose, like he was about to sneeze. He watched the police lead the woman away. In a moment, Phuong was upon him and gave him a burst of vehement Vietnamese. From what I could tell, he wasn't defending himself — he seemed to be agreeing with her.

She finished her harangue, took a breath, and said in English, 'You're leaving with us. Get going!'

He glanced around, and caught me watching. My immediate reflex was a friendly wave, but I hesitated. He put his hands in his pockets, looked down with a resigned sigh, and started to the exit, Phuong keeping close behind him.

We went down the escalators, past all that gleaming gold and the mirrors and water features and ominously placed yin and yang symbols. Other Feng Shui luck remedies and gambling inducements were suspended from the ceilings. And every five metres or so, an enormous poster advertised *Cup Day at Crown* festivities in the grand ballroom. We passed the cardboard cut-out of a racehorse in the foyer, and went out into the roar of Friday-night city traffic.

Cuong kept walking, heading to Flinders Street, but Phuong stopped him. 'What the hell was that?' she said in English.

'I can't tell you that.'

'Like hell.'

'Believe me, I want to tell you.'

She laughed, shook her head. 'Can you believe him?' she said to me.

'This is a family matter,' I said. 'I'd rather not get —'

'Right,' she said to him. 'I'm taking you home.'

She hailed a passing cab. 'Sunshine.' The driver nodded. When she was like this, even strangers instinctively knew not to question her.

The *La Fonderie* building was in darkness, except for two lights: the red candles on Cuong's balcony shrine, and one flat over, where blue cathode rays flickered. There was a brief exchange in Vietnamese. I gathered we were coming up. Cuong waved a card at the panel near the door; it clicked and he pushed it open. The lift was operational, praise Jesus. We hadn't made it inside the flat when she started on him again.

'Tell me the truth for once,' Phuong said. 'What was that?'

He flinched. 'Keep your voice down. You'll wake the neighbours.'

What neighbours, I wondered.

He ushered us inside.

Phuong walked around, clacking her high heels on the tiles. 'I come to your rescue in a storm. I hold your hand when you think ghosts are coming for you. I cover for you, turn a blind eye.'

Cuong shook his head, bewildered, or pretending to be. 'I already said thank you.'

'But with you, there's always something worse. The betting rings in Chinatown.'

'What?' It was me talking now. 'Betting rings?'

'Private games, invitation only,' Phuong said, exasperated that she had to stop haranguing Cuong to fill me in.

'Games like what?'

'Baccarat and mahjong.'

I wasn't familiar with baccarat, but mahjong was basically pairs, wasn't it? 'Really, Cuong, you gamble on mahjong?'

He shrugged. 'I have to get up early tomorrow. Derby Day at Flemington.'

I'd never been to the races. 'Who are you going with?'

'Just me. You can come if you want.'

Before I could answer, Phuong cut him off. 'Stella is not going to the races with you.' She started pacing again. 'You told me you avoid Crown.'

'It's not illegal to go to Crown,' he said.

'That woman, who was she?'

'*Tâm kinh doanh của riêng bạn.*'

'This *is* my business. I wish it wasn't. Detectives took her away. Everyone in the room could see she was about to approach you. Now tell me, who is she? And what were you doing?'

'You can't help me. You said so.' He held the door open. 'Now can you please leave? I have to get up early in the morning.'

She didn't move. 'How do you know her? Who introduced you to her?'

'No one.'

This was going to take a while. I parked myself on the sofa. I moved a pile of books and magazines, put my feet up on his coffee table.

'Are you in debt, Cuong?' Phuong asked.

He shook his head, turned away.

Phuong picked up a book from a pile, turned it around to show me the title. The title was in both Vietnamese and English: *Mastering the Art of Hypnotism: control others and get all you want.*

'This is yours, I suppose?' she asked Cuong. 'Who do you want to control?'

'Nobody. It's for fun.'

Phuong threw it on the floor. 'What am I going to do with you?'

'Nothing. There's nothing going on, stop worrying. Anyway, I cleaned your car. You can take it now. Go home, get an early night.'

She let out a groan and announced that she was going to the bathroom.

Cuong scratched the back of his head. 'Want a beer?'

I glanced at the bathroom door. 'One wouldn't hurt.'

He went to the fridge, flipped off the caps. 'Japanese beer. On Special.'

'Canny shopper.'

He handed me a bottle and sat on the armchair, clearly exhausted.

I had a sip. 'So,' I said. 'How's your day been?'

'Had better.' Cuong rubbed his nose. 'Want to give me your number?'

'What for?'

'We can go to the races tomorrow.'

'I can't.' My weekend was full, mainly with digging up a bikie. Possibly, literally.

'Another time.'

'Sure.'

In the pause that followed, we listened to Phuong shouting on the phone in the bathroom.

'Can you really hypnotise people?' I asked Cuong.

He peered intently into my eyes. 'Relax, let go now, and totally relax.'

I did as he said and tried to relax; my whole body sank into the cushions. The velvety throw was luxurious.

'Look in my eyes,' he was saying.

I stared; they seemed to have their own light in the dim room.

'You are surrendering to my voice ... you are under my complete control ... now you will answer my questions.'

'Go ahead, ask away.'

'Have you found Isaac Mortimer yet?'

'No. You ask me, the man cannot be found.'

He sat back and regarded me with curiosity. 'And when I snap my fingers you are back and refreshed. And also, you will not want a cigarette ever again. And ...' He snapped his fingers.

'Wow, thanks. I ... *I don't smoke now.* I didn't smoke before, but thanks.'

He flicked his hand, like it was nothing. Which it was.

'Let me try,' I said. 'You are getting very relaxed.'

Cuong eased back in the chair.

'Now you will answer my questions,' I said.

'Yes,' he said. 'Yes, I will.'

'Whose ghost are you afraid of?'

'What the hell are you two doing?' Phuong stood ridged in the doorway.

'And when I snap my fingers, you no longer smoke,' I said, and snapped.

Cuong seemed momentarily confused, then he beamed. 'Cigarettes are bad. I don't want to smoke.'

'Well?' She pointed her phone at Cuong.

I hunkered down in the sofa.

'Just a bit of fun.' Cuong said, unconcerned.

'If you're quite *finished,* I have information. The detectives we saw at Crown are with OTIOSE.'

I sat up. 'Really? The public-sector corruption thingy?'

'Yes. And the woman my cousin knows *nothing about* is a passport-office employee.'

'Marcus Pugh said something about a passport scam.' I recalled him saying so earlier that afternoon, a lifetime ago.

Phuong raised her eyebrows. 'That blabbermouth? Well, he's right. She'd been certifying unauthorised passports.'

'How'd they find out?'

'A whistle-blower.'

'Two careers burned then.'

Cuong had been quiet.

'Last chance,' Phuong said to him. 'What are you caught up in?'

'I can't say.'

She lowered her eyes to the floor. Nodded once. 'Where are my keys?'

He tossed them to her. She snatched them out of the air and went out without a word.

'Bye, Cuong,' I said.

He took my hands in his. 'Don't worry. Everything is under control.'

Cuong was exasperating. No wonder Phuong was at her wit's end. I said good night and found Phuong in her hatchback in the car park. The graffiti had been removed.

As we hit the street, I glanced back at Cuong's flat. The altar lights were off.

28

'CAN YOU believe that stupid book?' Phuong drove one-handed, glaring at me, as though I was the problem.

'I don't know what to think of it.'

'This is how he solves his problems. He *hypnotises* his way out of trouble.'

She swerved to avoid a dead animal on the road, oversteered, tyres squealing.

'Are you sure that's his plan, because I didn't —'

'That's how desperate he is,' she said. 'No wonder Dad asked me to watch him.'

This was high-horse Phuong. I looked out the window.

'What were you up to with him?'

'Me?' Irritated now, a red mist on my vision. 'I wasn't *up to* anything.'

'Whispering together.'

I undid my seat belt. 'Let me out.'

'What? Don't be stupid.'

'Stop the car.'

'I'm not leaving you here in the middle of the night.'

'You will, or so help me I'll jump out of the car.'

'Stella.'

I opened the door. She hit the brakes and we skidded to a halt. I started down Ballarat Road on foot. She caught me as I was nearing a McDonald's. Those places were everywhere.

'Stella, wait.' She pulled on my shoulder. 'You'd rather kill yourself than sit in a car with me for five minutes?'

I yanked out of her grip. 'I'm walking. It's not far.'

'But that's stupid.' She made another grab for me.

'Don't call me stupid.' Like a teenager yelling at her parents. My voice was cracked.

She paused, then used her calmest voice. 'Come on. Let me drive you home.'

'You say I *whisper* with your cousin, meanwhile you're a love-struck schoolgirl over Copeland — you're obsessed with him!'

'He's my fiancé.'

'He's *all* you care about. Not your career, not your friends. He's got you breaking half the laws in the state. And I can't speak to the police, only Copeland. I mean, come on. How suss is that?'

'That's for your own protection. There's cops in Gorman's pocket.'

'It's for your convenience.'

She sighed and walked away, turned back. 'Is this about the wedding?'

'What? Jesus, Phuong, have a look at yourself.'

'It must be about the wedding, otherwise I don't understand why you're so angry.'

'You *played* me. I thought, *nah, Phuong is my friend, she wouldn't do that.*'

'Played you how?'

'He's guilty. You know it. But you'd do anything to protect him.'

'Yes. I am terrified Bruce will go to jail. I'm frightened of *everything*, of being alone, of strangers, of what I might find in my letterbox. But I'm not as conniving as you obviously think. Bruce was in trouble and I turned to the only person I trust.'

That was the story I'd been telling myself, that she turned to me because we were friends. But I didn't know how much she was under Copeland's sway. 'I declined, remember? I thought he should face the inquiry.'

'You were wise to say no the first time.'

'And why did I change my mind? The bullet. Wow, that was a master stroke. Pure genius.'

143

'Stella!'

'You're basically his hostage.'

She gasped, put her hand over her mouth.

I walked away, and this time she made no attempt to stop me. I was seething inside, barely containing my distress. Tomorrow, when the righteousness wore off, I'd be bereft. I continued on my march of offence, trying to forestall that moment. Mist rose from the road. I watched it curl. I'd gone two blocks when the regret hit.

I waved down a taxi. Walking alone around here at night wasn't worth the risk.

29

ANOTHER DAWN. I was getting sick of mornings, and existence in general. I was seedy and raw and broken-hearted. Rather than face the day, I listened to the radio in bed. An ecstatic voice announced that this was the first day of the Victorian Racing Club's annual Spring Racing Carnival, and therefore, Derby Day. The carnival revolved around the Melbourne Cup, always scheduled for the first Tuesday in November. Derby Day kicked off the party on the Saturday, with ladies in black and white; morning suits for the men, with the traditional cornflower in the lapel. I wanted to vomit. The announcer read the weather: another warm day on the way, with higher temperatures expected in the coming days. Cup Day was predicted to be in the forties. A glass of warm spumante would console some, I imagined.

I breakfasted on toast. Then, in need of proper coffee and some supermarket essentials, I dressed in jeans, a clean white shirt, and flats. I was going to make *kaddu bharta*.

The traders in my part of town were deeply invested in the racing carnival, positioned as we were between the race tracks of Flemington and Moonee Valley. The very path beneath our feet was emblazoned with the names of former Cup winners. Being mid-carnival, the place was busier than usual, the street was as hyped as a toddler on red cordial. A lot of people were out buying last-minute party supplies, and the warm weather had stirred a vigorous trade in hair removal.

Despite my low mood, I skipped into Buffy's with faux élan. 'The usual, my good man.'

It was not Lucas beside the machine but a clear-faced new girl. A stranger. I hesitated.

'What's your usual?' she asked pleasantly.

I went blank.

'Strong flat-white,' said a voice behind me.

'Lucas, thank Christ.'

'I'll make it, Delores,' he said, with a wink at me.

I picked up the paper and held it up to him. 'And this.'

He frowned. 'You alright, Stella? You look wasted.'

'I feel fantastic, never better.'

'What's your secret?'

'Hypnotism,' I said, without hesitation. 'Special *Vietnamese* hypnotism.'

The person he called Delores guffawed. 'For real? Sorry, it's a con.'

I turned to Lucas, one eyebrow raised.

'Delores lived in Hanoi for a while,' he explained. 'Teaching English.'

My other eyebrow joined the first. 'Is that so? Did you come across any hypnotism?'

'You read about it in the English-language papers,' she was saying. 'Someone calling themselves Doctor So-and-So sets up a school of hypnotism, making outrageous claims. People pay a fortune to learn this stuff, but it doesn't work of course, and then they're angry so the doctor says it's their fault and they have to take another class. Usually, people want their money back — but when the authorities get involved, the good doctor skips town.'

'So it's complete bunkum?'

'Well, it is to us. But it goes back a long way there. I think it has links to kungfu. There's reports sometimes of hypnotism-related crimes, people are completely convinced they've been hypnotised by a random stranger. He looks into their eyes and they give the guy their wallet or whatever. Or the robber walks right into a shop and starts hypnotising the salesperson, who then hands over the cash.'

I thought about Cuong. I pictured him at the races, in a morning suit with a cornflower in the label, adorably gloomy. But I couldn't help wondering, too, about the strange goings-on of last night. For instance, why the cops approached only the woman and not Cuong. I hated to admit it, but on reflection Phuong was right — Cuong and the woman clearly knew each other. They were about to speak when the cops moved in. But they left Cuong alone. Almost as if he wasn't even there.

But why did he refuse to speak about it? Phuong knew about his gambling; what was so bad he had to keep from her? If he was involved somehow with the passport thing, then how bizarre was that?

Lucas was laughing. 'No hypnotic tricks, Hardy.'

'Tricks, *ha ha*. No.' I placed some shrapnel on the counter, hoped it was right, and started to walk out.

Lucas came around and placed a takeaway cup in my hand. 'Mate, take it easy.'

'I'm fine,' I lied.

I walked up the street, drinking my coffee, and paused at the entrance to the supermarket. The entire Cuong episode was none of my business. Phuong, on the other hand, was my bestie. I needed to clear the air with her. Then I thought about how she'd discouraged me from raising the Corpse Flowers's behaviour towards homeless children with the police. Other than her. Usually, I'd trust her judgement, but not this time. A cab ejected a gaggle of women outside a hairdresser, and I leapt in. I gave directions to the purple tower in the Docklands.

I asked the driver to wait a few minutes while I ran into the foyer. No one answered the buzzer this time. Perhaps he was still unwell. I took out one of my WORMS business cards and scribbled a hasty note on an old receipt at the bottom of my bag:

Dear Detective Blyton,
Have information that Corpse Flowers are training homeless children in criminal activity. Contact me to discuss.
Regards, Stella Hardy.

A bank of numbered mail boxes lined one wall of the foyer. I located the numbered slot that matched Blyton's apartment number, then folded my card in with the note and slotted it.

The cab was waiting, metre running. In less than ten minutes, I was returned to Ascot Vale and had re-joined the masses on Union Road. All up, my detour to Blyton's cost me thirty bucks. When the time came, I'd bill Copeland.

Now, my attention returned to the matter at hand: pumpkin curry. I shopped for groceries like a pro. After choosing a fresh lime, I made a study of the pumpkins, knowledgeably flicking specimens with my finger, smelling the skin, shaking them next to my ear. The results were mixed, and a lot of shaken-up pumpkins. Then I saw one with grey-blue skin, cut in sections along deep ribs, showing golden-orange flesh. The magnificent Queensland Blue it would be. I shoved half a dozen pieces in a plastic bag and grabbed a packet of unsalted butter on my way out.

I made like a Sherpa up the Roxburgh Street incline, carrying two bags of shopping, my coffee, and an entire pumpkin, cut into pieces, in a plastic bag. Remonstrating with myself all the way home. As if Phuong would place a bullet in her own letterbox. What kind of person accused their friend of faking a death threat? Answer: the most horrible person possible, a complete monster. Was that who I was? I didn't know *who* I was anymore.

My progress was stopped by a block of granite. A chap, more refrigerator than man, obstructed my path. He wore a cut-off leather vest, over a black t-shirt. I spotted a couple of fabric badges sewn on the vest: a skull, two crossed rifles, a bent flower with 'CF' in gothic script. His biceps bulged out of the t-shirt, tatt-sleeve arms. His head was shaved save for a tuft of orange fluff on top, wafting in the breeze. His do put me in mind of those Troll Dolls.

'Stella Hardy?'

'No.'

He sighed. 'But she lives here, right?'

'I know of no such person,' I announced, and tried to step around him.

He stepped in front of me, face right up to my mine. 'You *sure?*'

I reeled back, one arm cartwheeling. The pumpkin bag slipped from my hand, and sailed up into the air. We watched the pumpkin pieces fly from the bag, spin upwards, pause, and descend. Falling, falling, and hitting the ground. I stood there like a dummy, and all the emotion of recent events got the better of me. Tears spilled onto my cheeks.

The giant troll looked horrified. 'Sorry,' he muttered. 'I'm a bit clumsy.'

'It's not your fault,' I said idiotically. 'It's the bags they give you.'

'I know, right? I usually take me own,' he said. 'Not that I'm judging you; I don't trust their bags. Give us some sheets of that paper.'

I put down the shopping and pulled out the real-estate section of the newspaper. At the same time, Brown Cardigan's Shih tzu came trotting out of the foyer of my building. It approached and stopped to sniff the bikie's bottom as he crouched near the pumpkin pieces. Following behind him was Brown, holding a red leather lead studded with diamantes. I was tempted to make a Paris Hilton joke. Then I realised that if Brown addressed me by name, the jig would be up. I made fierce eye-contact, telepathically imploring him to keep moving.

'Trotsky likes his morning walk,' he said, completely failing to catch on.

'You named your dog after a *communist?*' I said, despite myself. Brown was a dyed-in-the-wool conservative.

'He's not mine. One of the ladies from bowls died, and I said I'd take him. The name isn't ideal, but I wasn't going to grandstand about ideology,' he said, pointedly.

Brown thought I was a virtue-signalling bolshie. At least, I presumed he did. We represented a microcosm of the country, he

149

and I. Two halves, each deaf to the other, entrenched in our camps, belittling the other, with no consideration of the other person's reasoning or concerns. Maybe, for the sake of the country, I should make a gesture of conciliation. If he could have a dog called Trotsky, maybe I could get a rodent and call it Dutton.

'Besides, I like him,' Brown was saying. 'He's quite a cheery fellow.' Then he tapped his forehead in salute, and went down the path after Trotsky, who'd gone as far as his glamourous lead would allow.

The goon had placed the pumpkin pieces in the newspaper. 'It's still good,' he said. 'Just give it a wash.'

'I like your tatts. What's that on your knuckles?'

I took the paper from him, and he held two fists in front of my face. One hand said *BUST* and the other said *FACE*.

'Very nice,' I said. 'I like the lettering.'

'Thanks,' he said with a sniff of pride. 'Better boot. Finding fuckers isn't easy.'

'Tell me about it. Thanks for your help.' My nonchalance act was top-notch.

'Yeah.' He coughed. 'S'alright.'

I retreated to my apartment and paced. He knew my building, but not my flat number. And he didn't know *me*. These were difficult times. I lifted the lid on the takeaway cup, swirled the froth, drank the tepid coffee. Alma said: *he knows you're after him*. That bikie was not Isaac Mortimer, a man easily identified by the *fuck yeah* on his face.

So, who was that man? Who was *Bust Face*, and who had sent him to look for me? Did the 'CF' signify a Corpse Flower?

Was I a threat to the Corpse Flowers? I didn't see how. All I had done was enquire after Mortimer. Why would they care? Why send a goon, some low-level Flower?

It was Copeland's stupid fault I was in this mess. When this was over, he'd owe me an explanation — a better one than needing

Mortimer to testify. And he'd owe me a new pumpkin.

In the meantime, the goon was gone, and I still had one more lead to follow up in the search for Mortimer. I sat down, deflated. What to do?

My flat was a bombsite. I hadn't been keeping up with domestic affairs. First, I'd tidy up, then I'd make the damn curry.

Then I'd pay a visit to the Talbots Body Works.

30

BEFORE I could start cooking, I had to clean my kitchen. I set to work on the clutter, the old newspapers, the bills piled up, the plate I used for a fruit bowl with the two brown bananas. I shoved things in garbage bags, wiping down surfaces; gathered dishes from around the flat and piled them in the sink, and then launched into a frenzy of washing and drying.

With the shopping put away, and the table cleared, I had a decent sized area in which to work, ready to begin stage one of the *kaddu bharta*. I took out the broken pieces of pumpkin, which I peeled and cut into smaller pieces, and put them in a steamer on the stove.

The apartment was steamy and smelled of pumpkin. I tested a piece, and they were soft. A potato masher pulped them in seconds. I put the pumpkin mash to one side.

I paced the flat again, it seemed to help my thinking. All I needed was one person who knew Mortimer. He associated with street kids, and the kids seemed to like him. Those teenagers in the Footscray flophouse — Brook, that boy with the hair, and Angie — they knew Mortimer. But I'd burnt my bridges with those three. I could try to find Cory's friend, Razz, the boy who was with him that night in the car park. But that was probably going to be as difficult as finding Isaac Mortimer. All the young people who were in contact with the Corpse Flowers were homeless and hard to locate in a hurry.

Except for Alma Dunmore, who slept each night in a warm bed in a well-to-do part of Williamstown. I disliked her, but that wasn't relevant. I had some serious questions for the little Mensa mobster, but she would be unlikely to oblige.

Hopefully, Blyton was as good a cop as Phuong said he was, and would find my note and ring me. While I waited, my pumpkin creation put aside for now, I had another go at looking for Corpse Flower information online.

> Gorman, high-level member of motorcycle gang, the Corpse Flowers, publicly announcing his departure from the club following the release of his partner Philomena Enright from jail last year.

In an *Age* article titled, *BIKIE CLUB IN MEMBERSHIP SHAKE-UP*:

> The Corpse Flowers outlaw motorcycle gang members are handing in their club colours, police say, due to a leadership vacuum left by the departure of Sargeant-at-arms Ox Gorman and the death of president, Ricky Peck. All major positions within the Corpse Flowers remain vacant.
>
> Police Minister Marcus Pugh confirmed officers are investigating a number of serious criminal activities, including assaults and kidnappings. Notorious convicted criminal, Luigi 'The Turk' Tacchini, has been under suspicion for some time, even after declaring he'd left the Corpse Flowers.
>
> Minister Pugh said the power and influence of gangs were 'weakening' and their ranks had thinned.

Was there no police-related news story that Pukus would not comment on?

I was getting nowhere. It was time to go straight to the source, to the aspiring do-gooder, Josie. She was like the Hindenburg, I decided: volatile, clumsy, hard to manoeuvre, and ready to crash and burn. Or was that me?

My mobile buzzed. ID: Delia. I answered.

'Shane Farquhar,' my mother said, without preamble. 'I haven't sold the farm yet. I've spoken to your sister. I'm not sure which way to go.'

'What?'

'I've told Shane I need time to think. Kylie's that keen. Between you, me, and the lamppost, I don't know if Tyler's up to it. New breed of cattle, never heard of them — the Dexterous? — small, like a child's pet. Shane's not happy, of course. Once upon a time, he couldn't pluck up the courage to call me. Now he rings me twice a day: "Have you decided yet, Mrs Hardy?" Thing is, I'd like to give Kylie and Tyler a chance, but they've got no money, and we can't afford to just *give* it to them. Ted and I have made plans; the proceeds from the farm were supposed to be our retirement.' She drew breath at last.

I wasn't close to my sister, but I wanted to see her and Tyler settled. As for Farquhar, I had zero good will. 'Mum, what can I do to help?'

'Help?' she scoffed. 'Honestly, I don't know. What can you do?'

She had a point, and made it with her usual sprinkle of disapproval. I imagined she only wanted to vent. Now wasn't a good time. 'Sounds like you've got it sorted,' I said.

'It's not sorted. Nothing like sorted. Kylie's broke; going into more debt won't help.'

'Something's on the stove, better go.'

'You've never had anything on the stove in your life.'

'Yes, I have. Sporadically. Something is *categorically* on my stove.'

'When are you coming up to Woolburn? Bring that boyfriend of yours we never see.'

'Must go. Bye, Mum.'

Families were a trial for everyone. Mine seemed unable to share any form of direct, simple communication. All interaction was oblique, through hints, or via third parties. Somehow, I had materialised from such an environment comparatively sane.

I was grinding spices and my teeth when I heard someone in the stairwell. Dejected thongs slapped up the steps. Brown Cardigan would never wear thongs. The other flats on my floor were unoccupied. If it was a thug sent to murder me, he sounded very reluctant about it. I put an anxious eye to the peephole. Brophy! On my doorstep. This spectacular situation was so utterly unexpected, that I hardly knew what to do.

I ripped off the chain and flung back the door, grinning at him. 'S'up, yo.'

'Can I come in?' he asked, like a vampire. He had a bearer-of-bad-news expression that made me hesitate. A hollowness grew in the pit of my stomach.

'Stella?'

'Yes. *Of course*, come in.'

He spotted the doings in the kitchen. The cooked pumpkin smelled wonderfully domestic. 'What's all this?'

'Oh, nothing, just cooking, like I often do.'

'That sounds wholesome. I'm glad to hear it. Do you good.'

'And that is possibly the most patronising thing I have ever heard anyone say. Ever.'

'Don't get defensive, I'm here to talk. You always want to talk, don't you?'

I looked him up and down. 'You insult me, then tell me not to get defensive. And now this, whatever *this* is, this putdown manoeuvre, it's awful. I don't *always* want to talk.'

At least he had the decency to look chastened. 'Sorry. I haven't been myself lately. Under pressure. The exhibition.'

I accepted that with a sigh, and led him to the sofa. I sat beside him and held one of his paint-stained hands. 'Is it my imagination or is what you are about to say something terrible? Better get it over with so I can go back to crushing the cardamom.'

He coughed. 'It's about Felicity.'

Naturally. 'What about her?'

'I know you don't like her.'

My scoff came out as a yelp. 'You know nothing, Peter Brophy.'

'I know that since the day I met her, my creative process changed. It shows in my work. She's introduced me to new concepts, and my paintings are considered, more intense. She's more than a life model, she's a source of inspiration. She understands —'

'That's enough.'

'You need to know this.'

'Why?'

'So you'll … help me.'

'Help you how? Make her sit still?'

He shook his head.

'What's the problem? You're nearly finished, aren't you?' The exhibition opened on Tuesday night. He was cutting it fine.

'It's done. Twenty works, packed and ready.'

Why had he not told me? Why were we not naked? 'So what is it?'

He stared at a spot on my floor. 'I think she has a problem …'

A rich, white girl problem, no doubt. Drugs? Only in a whimsical way. Gambling, probably not. 'Like what? She's too pretty? No one takes her seriously?'

'It was little things at first. Then money, some cash I had in a drawer.'

'She's *stealing* from you?' But this was wonderful. I wanted to leap about, to sing, to dance. I held off. 'What little things?'

He cringed. 'A photo of us, in a frame.'

'*Us?* As in, you and me?'

He nodded.

'Right.' I punched a fist into my palm. 'Let's go pay her a visit.'

'I don't want you to *confront* her.'

I threw up my hands in despair. 'What are you asking me to do, then?'

'Find out if she's okay.'

'Ask her yourself, next time you see her.'

He closed his eyes, deep lines in his face. Since embarking on his blockbuster exhibition, he'd been plagued by doubts that were not natural to him. He questioned his skill, the relevance of his work. He'd succumbed to some vague quest for success — whatever that was, and whoever decided it — until the joy of painting was gone, weighed down with concerns about critics and 'established schools'.

'What happened to the old Brophy, the contented one who hummed sappy tunes while he painted?'

'I'm not playing around. This is serious work I'm trying to create. It takes time and effort and attention.'

A scold, of sorts. I didn't respond.

I had an urge to call off my entire day, to spend it in bed with this man. We could feed each other spring rolls and watch *The Lord of the Rings* like we used to. I knew I should tell him about the promotion I'd been offered at WORMS. Imagine, me, the director of such an organisation, with an executive salary and a company car. Soon, *I* might have a holiday house and a fancy-arse fridge that makes Margarita slushies at the push of a button. And maybe this lovely man might like to stay there with me. If he would stay.

I resisted that urge because I, too, had serious work to do. 'I have urgent business in Sunshine,' I said. 'I'm late as it is.'

A slow nod, then Brophy frowned. 'I think Felicity's in some kind of trouble.'

I sighed, long and loud. 'What's her name and where does she live?'

'Sparks. Felicity Sparks.'

'*Flicky Sparks?* She couldn't be more ridiculous.'

'She prefers "Felicity".'

'And where does Flicky live?'

He scribbled the address on a corner of newspaper. 'Williamstown. With her parents.'

'I'm busy, but I'll see what I can do,' I said, ignoring her address and picking up my handbag.

'Something else I had to tell you. Jeff Vanderhoek is missing.'

I winced. 'Missing?'

'Talking to a bloke at the market this morning, said he hadn't seen Jeff for days.'

'A short break? Trip to Sydney?'

'If you're a drug dealer and an informer and you go missing without a word to anyone, that's not good.'

'No,' I admitted. 'It isn't.'

Brophy was right, it was bad for informers to disappear. That thought, and the visit from the bikie, was having a negative impact on my mental health. Time to get this Corpse Flower mess over with.

He gave me a stern look. 'Tell me you're not still trying to find that bikie for Phuong.'

'Phuong and I aren't speaking.' It was both true and a diversion.

He was astonished.

I took his arm and led him outside. 'Tell you what, if you drop me off in Sunshine, I'll check in on poor Flicky, maybe even later today.' Or tomorrow. Or maybe never.

31

AFTER A short drive through the mostly deserted streets, we arrived at Talbots. It was closed and the garage doors were down. I imagined that cars I'd seen outside were secured within, my Mazda among them. I lifted my gaze to the flat, and weathered a wave of panic. I stopped. There was still time to back out. Brophy did a U-turn and parked across the street.

I was about to jump out when he turned off the engine and sighed like a condemned man. 'She refuses to read *The Lord of the Rings*.'

Felicity again, always Felicity. 'Why, because it's unfair to orcs?'

'Because there's no decent female characters.'

'That'll show Tolkien. What a misogynist. He'll change his ways now.'

He stared straight ahead. 'Saruman's shadow defeated him.'

This, I knew. 'And Gandalf defeated his.'

He grimaced like he doubted it was possible for *anyone* to defeat their dark side. For myself, I chose an uneasy cohabitation. Darkness and I split the bills, had a roster for the dishes. It seemed to work. I didn't pretend to be a good person.

Brophy rubbed his forehead. What was he so afraid of? That he'd drift back to heroin? Or was there another darkness he grappled with?

He's finding it hard to adjust, and he doesn't feel supported by her. That bloody street kid was now the voice of my conscience. How the heck did that happen? 'Don't worry about Felicity. I'll speak to her.' It would be a lightning visit. I'd hear her confession: theft, of cash, boyfriend, and photos; then I'd bolt home to enjoy a quiet evening eating pumpkin mash and watching the rest of *Blood Diamond*. 'If I see her, I'll report back. Is that helpful enough?'

159

He smiled. 'I don't know what you're doing out here, but be careful.'

We said our goodbyes and I tore myself away.

I walked towards Talbots Body Works thinking about Enright. A woman on parole was likely to stay clean, keep within the law. Nothing to fear from her, I told myself, get this done.

Onward, upward.

I was halfway up the stairs when Enright came out wearing a lime-green velour tracksuit, hair down in curls that didn't move in the breeze. She gave me a quizzical look. Either she took a moment to recognise me or she was amazed I had the guts to approach her.

'Stella, what the fuck are you doing here?' Her tongue behind her top teeth, happy smile.

'Well, if it isn't Josie ... then it must Philomena Enright.' I smiled, too.

She closed her mouth with a shake of the head, like she was sorry to have to kill me. 'So you know about me, hey? So what? It's my name, either way. What's your point?'

'Hey, that's cool. Don't take me the wrong way. I'm not hassling you, promise. Truth is, I read your story. I see you want to get into community work. I thought I'd help you out, as a mentor sort of thing.'

'How the fuck did you find me?'

'Funny story. My car's booked in here and I happened to see you coming out of the flat when I was dropping off my car. And I asked the mechanic, just to be sure it was you.'

'Jim?'

'Is that his name? Anyway, I thought I'd let you know — that volunteering you do will get you into hot water. There's so many laws about working with kids now. If you want a career, you don't want to get off on the wrong foot.'

She scratched her hairline. 'That so?'

'Yes. But if you want a job in the community sector, I can help you. Despite your record, there's legit work you can do.' I paused. 'If you want.'

Her face broke into a smile. 'Come on up, mate, I'll put the kettle on.'

I trotted up the last few steps.

'Nobody lets you forget your past, do they?' she asked. I would have agreed with her, but she didn't wait for an answer. 'If I'm *Josie*, I can move on with my life.'

'Fair enough. Alma spoken to you lately?'

'That kid, I tell you. Too smart for her own good.' A burst of laughter. 'How you been, mate?'

'Not bad,' I followed her into the flat. It was fitted out in fifties retro, or maybe it was all original. An engine in pieces on the floor.

'Don't mind Ox's shit. Messy bastard. Men, eh?'

'Yeah.' I thought of Brophy. He was neater than me.

'Take a seat, mate. Cuppa? Earl Grey?'

A canary-yellow kitchen, a circular glass-top table, four yellow vinyl chairs. Checkerboard lino and lace curtains on the window, drawn back fifties-style. She took some tea bags from a yellow canister. I pulled out a cane stool, cushion upholstered in yellow floral.

It was hot in the flat, and she stripped off her tracksuit top to the tank top beneath. She had thin, muscular arms, a couple of smudges of blue ink — definite prison tatts — and across each wrist a long white scar. 'Sugar?'

'Two,' I said.

She grinned. 'Yeah, me too. Didn't have a sweet-tooth until Thailand. They put sugar in everything. Pretty soon I'm on board. Five years is a long time. A hit of sugar helps.'

'Five years,' I muttered, mechanically.

'Death sentence first, then life, then twenty. Then busted down to

161

nine. I did five in Klong Prem, women's unit, packed to the shithouse. We were in each other's armpits.'

'Sounds like hell.'

'You get used to it. They reckon for the same amount here I would've walked. But after the transfer, to make the Thais happy, they had to keep me locked up.'

'Smuggling heroin out of Thailand — pretty dicey,' I said, trying not to sound judgemental. 'You must have been young at the time, who put you up to it?'

'No one put me up to it.' She turned her back, busy at the sink. 'We knew the risks.'

I glanced around the flat. Leftovers on the kitchen table. A takeaway bag labelled *Madame Mao's Handmade Dumplings*. 'What went wrong?' I asked. 'Sniffer dogs at the airport?'

'Someone talked.' She faced me, ferociously eyeballing me, like it might have been me she was talking about.

'Who?'

She shrugged, gave the bench a breezy wipe-down. 'Dunno. But I'd like to punch him in the face — but then I'd be up for assault, right?'

'Hire someone else to punch them for you?'

She cracked up. 'You offering?'

'Nah,' I said. 'I'm making a living, thank you. Just.'

She cocked her head. 'So, social work. Good fun?'

'Sometimes. I went bowling recently.'

She laughed her deep cackle.

'Mostly we settle for a minor gain against the tides of shit.'

She shrugged. 'World's fucked up. What are you going to do?'

'And you're trying to get through to the kids on the street because of what you went through, is that right? Keep them out of trouble, off the drugs and out of the jails?'

Her eyes wide, big nod. 'Yep. I'm getting through to them, too.'

'Awesome.'

The water boiled and she jiggled teabags in the mugs, an image of a woman on each one. They were dressed in black, in a silly pose, back to the camera, turning and blowing a kiss behind them.

'So you're trying to keep them out of places like Thailand?'

'For sure.'

'And Burma?'

Josie paused the teabag-jiggling for a beat, and then glanced up, smiling. 'Wherever, mate! Keep 'em out of anywhere you like.'

She placed a mug in front of me and waited behind the counter. I picked it up. The hot water had changed the pictures, erasing the black clothes. The women were naked. 'Pisser, isn't it? Had to buy 'em.'

'Wow. How about that.'

'Now, Stella, what's this really about?'

'Um. Your career.' I made a note of the exits. It looked like the main door, down to the workshop, was the only one.

'Alma reckons you're looking for Mortimer. I said she's dreaming. You're too smart to get involved with that crowd.'

I leaned on the counter. 'The Corpse Flowers, you mean? Like your boyfriend?'

Her head tipped to the side. 'Ox isn't a Corpse Flower, that's all behind him.'

'Right. I heard that. Good for him.'

'As for Mortimer, he's still with them, as far as I know. Don't really care. Bikies are a bunch of dicks. There's no honour. It's money and hurting people for fun.'

'I have an address in Norlane, his old place. Would he still be there?'

She shrugged. 'What do you care? I don't get it, what's a nice girl like you want with a thug like Mortimer?'

'He owes me money.'

She raised her eyebrows. 'That'd be right,' she said eventually.

'What about his friends, like the Turk? Would he help Mortimer?

Hide him maybe?'

She glanced out the kitchen window. 'Who?'

I turned the mug around; the other side was a full frontal. I sipped the tea. 'I've wasted your time. I'm sorry.'

She rinsed her cup. 'I bet he's crawled back to Norlane.'

'The cops have been there.'

She turned the tap off, turned around slowly. 'How do you know?'

'It was on the news.'

'Is that right?' A broad smile on her face, but not reaching to her unblinking eyes.

'Yeah, the cops went there to arrest him, but he'd cleared out.'

'I'm not surprised the jacks haven't found him. Not looking too hard. Certain people up high don't want Mortimer found. Rather kill him than arrest him.'

'Like who?' I asked. 'Which cops might want to kill him?'

'They're all bastards.'

The girl on my mug had her clothes back on. Another dead end. 'I better get going.'

'Wait, have another cup of tea. Ox is on his way home, he'd love to meet you.'

'I'd love to meet him too, but I've got stuff to do.'

A long pause. We locked eyes. I would not've been surprised if a harmonica played a Morricone riff.

She blinked first. 'I shouldn't tell you this …' She leaned over the counter and gripped my arm, hard. 'And don't breathe a word to anyone.' She tapped a finger on her lips.

I crossed my heart.

'Norlane. Really. He's back there.'

32

I WALKED to Sunshine station. It was time to ring Phuong, give her this unsubstantiated report of Mortimer's whereabouts, and go home.

I could do that ...

Or better yet, as a peace-offering, go to Norlane, confirm if Mortimer was there, ring Phuong, and go home.

I made up a song about taking the last train to Norlane; it was pretty catchy. To get to Geelong, I had to take a V/Line service, and I had to buy a separate ticket. I should keep better track of my expenses, I thought. When this was over, I'd hand Copeland my bill. A train approached, but didn't stop. I sat down.

Ox Gorman — boy, I was glad I didn't cross paths with him. If he wasn't an actual Flower, he was part of the arrangement, a decorative branch perhaps.

Another train came and went without stopping. I was getting sick of this. I pulled out my phone. 'Hey, Afshan. Where are you? It's so noisy.'

'Guess!'

The rumble of balls rolling on the boards, the ping of scattering pins, the tinny blare of Shania Twain on the PA. 'Funky Town?'

'Correct!'

'Sorry to interrupt your game, but I need your transport services.'

'Not now, Stella. Shahid missed two easy spares, he's so bad at this.'

'I need to get to Geelong. I'll pay you.'

A pause.

'One hundred,' I said. 'Cash.'

'On our way.'

It was a short drive from Funky Town to the Sunshine train

station; it wouldn't take them long. I hurried to a nearby ATM and withdrew the cash. Sure, I was over-paying, but I needed the ride. Also, people on temporary protection visas were not allowed to work. I didn't know how Shahid and Afshan could possibly survive without some help. As I walked back to the station to wait for them, I made up a song about Afshan and Shahid bowling at Funky Town. It was pretty catchy, too.

A wreck of a van appeared in a puff of exhaust smoke. Afshan saw me and waved. He'd had a haircut; the fringe was ruler-straight. 'Stella, would you like a hotdog?'

'No, thank you,' I said, shocked. 'I'm pretty sure they're not halal.'

'Not for me, for you.'

'I'm a vegetarian.'

'Oh, yes. As you said.' He and Shahid enjoyed a good laugh. Then he handed the hotdog out the window to a startled passer-by.

'How did you go?' I asked, getting in the van.

Afshan beamed. 'Hundred and fifty-three. Personal best! In this game, five strikes.'

Shahid clapped him on the shoulder. 'Sweet bowling, man.'

I had to laugh. 'Yeah, man. Sweet.'

'Now, where to, lady?'

'You guys know where Norlane is?'

'You can direct us.'

And with a backfire that could break a window, we were off. I have always liked an old-fashioned bench seat. They were friendlier than bucket seats. With Shahid driving and Afshan hanging his elbow out the passenger side window, and me in the middle, I was feeling pretty content. On the other hand, the van was less roadworthy than Brophy's. Shahid struggled with the wheel. He battled a sideways drift, and we pitched forward. The experience was like sitting in a tin can, balanced on a ride-on mower … that was doing ninety. Ricocheting rather than driving. We were gestured at, abused, and often cut off.

I checked the glove box and found a cassette of Dave Dudley singing *your truck-drivin' favourites*. Before long, we were singing along, to the kiss-stealin', wheelin-dealin', truck-drivin' son of a gun.

They didn't ask my business in Geelong, and I didn't tell them.

Around the You Yangs, when the tape ran out, Afshan turned to me.

'You know what whippy is?'

I shrugged. 'Ice-cream?'

'Whippy is the money the police take from you. If they find money while they search your place, they keep it.'

'Did they search your place?'

He waved his hand. 'There was trouble with that boy in our street, the weird one who burned the cat? Last year, he broke some car windows. The police came, talked to everyone in the street. We all knew who was responsible. When they came to our house, they asked for papers. They saw we are on temporary visas, everything changed. They pushed us, asked for money. And every few months, they come back. Each time, the same two cops, and they always search.'

In the scheme of things, it was probably small Tim Tams. 'What did they take?'

'We had some cash. A gold watch. Some precious things. Things we sold for money to live on, because we can't work. We'll never get those things back.'

He was right. The powerless seeking justice was a time-consuming, soul-destroying business. Victories were rare, often pyrrhic. 'How much money are we talking about?'

He lowered his voice. 'Ten thousand.'

I coughed.

'You think I'm making it up?'

'No.' He had my attention now. 'What are their names? We'll contact the multicultural legal agencies, make a fuss, protest to police-integrity people. Make them investigate.'

He shook his head. 'If we go to the authorities, first they won't believe us, then they will stall, it will go to court. It might take years. Even then, the money is gone.'

That was a pretty accurate description of the process.

We hit the suburb of Corio, and I used a phone app to direct Shahid to a grid of narrow streets on the coast-side of the highway. We found Marsden Avenue, and I asked him to stop the van on the corner.

'Now, you two, please don't go doing anything stupid. That money's gone now. I'll help you with legal channels. Legal. Not vigilante.'

Afshan shook his head. 'What do you think, Shahid?'

'The Dude abides,' he said.

I took that to mean they would take my advice, and I hopped out of the van.

'You want us to wait?'

'No. I'll take the train back.'

'Sweet. *Abyssinia.*'

'*Salada.*' I waved, and hurried away from the fumes.

33

I CROSSED the road and walked, acting nonchalant. Cars lined the street: Falcon, Commodore, Commodore, Falcon, beaten-up Hyundai, Falcon. No one was in them that I could see. The place had a dead feel, not a ghost town exactly, because there were people about. On a porch, an old guy with one leg was smoking and listening to the races. A kid on a bike wobbled by. A lady held a hose on a rose bush. The afternoon had a dry, lazy heat. I passed Isaac Mortimer's house, no visible signs of people, neither cop nor crim. It was neat, the lawn cut. A carpet of dead flowers beneath an old camellia. Empty letter box.

I crossed again and walked back.

I went up the driveway. A high fence from the back of the house to the garage blocked access to the backyard. Between the garage and the house next door was a narrow gap. I squeezed through. Just. The back was sparse but well maintained, the Hills hoist had a token towel. The bungalow was a sad fibro box with louvre windows. One set of louvres was ajar. I stood on tiptoes and peered in. It was dim, but I could see the double bed with a candlewick bedspread, and a vinyl armchair. On the coffee table, piles of motorcycle magazines and a full ashtray. Smoke rose from one of the cigarettes. I swore, and a gut feeling hit me with a flood of cold adrenalin. *Go, now, time to leave.* I spun in a panic, and smacked into a brick wall that wasn't there before. I stepped back. He was in leathers, head freshly shaved and shining, the cheerful tangerine tuft atop. Mr Bust Face.

The fist blocked out the sun, force of a machine, smacked into cheek, jaw, eye. Head snapped back, and staggering, falling, and bright light, lights out.

34

MY FEET together, on my side. Engine drone. Jostled up and down, rolling. Green-apple fresh and oily odours and the sour smell of my fear. My abject terror. My forthcoming death, though not yet. Alive for now in this lurching car or van or something, something that moved down a second-rate stretch of road. Possibly dirt — the tyres didn't hum, they crunched on the corrugations and pot holes.

Sudden breaking, waiting, and sharp turns sent me sliding across the seat. Fabric against my mouth and nose, a hood of some kind. I pushed my legs back and found the door, my feet were bare. I moved my hands, tried to, they were bound behind me. My eye adjusted and bits of light filtered in. I attempted a roll and lift to get myself upright, but my head hurt, enough pain to give up on that idea.

If I put my head at an angle, right on up the fabric, there was a narrow gap, a stitch hole, and I could see the back of his head. 'Buster?' I called.

Buster twisted in the seat. 'What'd you call me?'

'*Bust Face*, from the tattoo on your knuckles. *Buster*.'

No response.

'What do *they* call you?'

He hesitated. 'It doesn't matter.'

'Where're we headed, Buster?'

'Fucking Woop Woop. They give me directions.'

I had dealt with unpredictable people. An aggressive, or drunk, client, who had to be cajoled. Any public transport user, any public library patron, anyone who'd ever left the safety of their home had had to deal with a wildling — free folk, who screamed *'you bastards'* at a fire hydrant or sat staring at you while they wet their pants. And what had all that experience taught me? Stay calm, or try to.

Minimal eye contact? *Check*. Keep the conversation friendly. Deep breaths, slow in, slow out. Eyes closed. 'So,' I said. 'How's your day been?'

He sniggered.

'Mine's been grand. Impromptu trip to the county. I often say I should get out of Melbourne more often. Get among nature.'

'Got that right.'

'Ha! You mean buried in it, right?'

Another snigger.

Heart rate soaring; sweating. Don't panic, I repeated in my head. Calm. Slow and calm. Breathe.

'Hey mate, can you take the hood off? If I suffocate, no fun of killing me, or whatever.'

For a moment nothing, then he hit the brakes and we skidded to a stop. I felt the car mount an embankment. A hand grabbed the hood from the back of my head, a handful of hair with it, and pulled. I was free and gasping. Plastic cable ties held my ankles, impossible to walk, let alone run. Only Buster and I in the car.

'Thanks. Much better.'

'No worries.' He gunned it.

'Whereabouts are we going, Buster? Is it someone's house? I promise I won't tell.'

He sighed, almost wistfully.

I lifted my head, and checked out the scenery. The volcanic plains of the outer western precincts. Low clouds rolled in over the developer's dreams, the first-home-buyers' only hope. I saw a multiple powerline, tall transmission towers. The edge of Tarneit, perhaps, between Werribee and Rockbank. My guess, we were heading towards Luigi Tacchini. The Turk.

At a lonely crossroad, Buster turned onto a road with open paddocks on either side that gave way to five-acre blocks with generic brick-veneer houses surrounded by rusted car bodies, half-arsed shedding, and derelict farm equipment. A pastoral ghetto, which would soon be sacrificed to the medium-density lifestyle, only thirty kilometres from the CBD.

Buster reduced his speed and lowered the window, anxiously checking each letterbox. I was glad of the fresh air. If my hands were free, I'd grab that cheap apple-scented air freshener that dangled from the rear-vision mirror and throw it out the window. He slammed on the brakes, checked his phone, sighed, made a call. 'Yeah, I fucking am … It's not here. But you said … Calm down? You fucking calm down … Fuck you, too.'

He drove on and stopped at a cream-brick place. A letterbox mounted on the fence said *L. Tacchini*. The not-so-secret hideout. In the middle of the driveway was a rusted kitchen chair, and a broken chest of drawers, particleboard festering in the elements.

Buster drove onto the lawn. I struggled when the door opened, but he dragged me out by my feet without fuss. A meaty arm lugged me upwards. My view as he carried me to the house was of several barking dogs in a miserable fenced-off side-yard. And the sun melting into the orange-mauve horizon.

He dropped me on the concrete porch and knocked.

The screen door flung open. A man stood, grinning at the sight of me. Trim, but small, he had a lot of forehead, and dark hair sprouted from his ears. No battle jacket for him, not the leather cut-off with the insignia of the Corpse Flowers. This killer was all for mingling with the normal folk, in the grey, zip-up jacket with a couple of biros in the sleeve pocket.

'Turk. Lookee here.'

He nodded with gratification. 'Round the back,' he said. 'That way.'

Buster grunted and shifted me to his shoulder in a firefighter's lift. We followed the Turk as he waddled down a path beside the house, cluttered with white Styrofoam boxes with weeds growing out of them and rusting white goods. Behind the house was an American-style barn — not a tin shed, but a sturdy wooden building. Over the door was a sign: *DUE TO THE RISING COST OF AMMO*

172

THERE WILL BE NO WARNING SHOT.

Security cameras, high windows, with bars on them. In my agrarian childhood, with all the visits to other people's farms, I'd never seen a shed like it.

The Turk turned a key in the lock, reached in and flicked a switch. A row of lights blinked. This workspace would be a mechanic's dream; it was spacious, and well-equipped. Except it looked like a teenager's bedroom, an unholy jumble of junk. Three motorbikes, rested on their stands. Piles of sacks, stacks of crates, boxes scattered everywhere.

A nasty smell hung in the air — a mix of sump oil, mould, urine. And some other rotten substance.

Benches piled with open packaging. Tools, takeaway pizza boxes, newspapers, buckets, books, a stack of speakers. Dirty mugs and plates and glasses. Gym equipment lay in odd places, weights here, a pulley there. A tread mill was covered in boxes labelled *Power Fitness Blaster* and *Killer Abs Twister*. There was even a cappuccino machine, but it was broken and dirty. A double door, big enough for a tractor to pass through, was at the other end of the barn near a freezer and a pile of plumbing supplies: sinks, toilets, tapware.

'Dump her there.'

'There' was a vinyl-covered kitchen stool.

Buster let me slide from his grip onto the stool, and I steadied myself upright. I took in the welding equipment, the block-and-tackle that dangled above me.

'Off you fuck,' he said to Buster.

'I got me patch, right? I'm in now, right?'

'Gorman handles that shit, mate, talk to him. Now piss off.'

Buster left and the Turk locked the barn door. Then he pulled out a phone and tapped. Soft music played somewhere. He adjusted the volume. A Human League dirge surrounded us from the speakers mounted on the wall. So, I thought, the torture begins.

35

THE TURK walked about picking up, inspecting, and rejecting items as he went. From a pile of junk and sundry mechanical spare parts, he picked up a chain. 'Are you *au fait* with the laws of physics?' The Turk juggled the weight of the chain between his hands. 'For every action there is a reaction. Consequences.'

I wasn't well versed in the laws of physics. But I was *au fait* with other subjects. The facts before me — being kidnapped, imprisoned — meant I was about to be terminated. But some part of me considered this preposterous. It was inconceivable that criminal bikie gangs would kill a nobody like me. Let alone risk the investigation, the scrutiny that would surely follow.

But this man didn't care about being investigated.

I didn't speak, in case he put a gag on me, but I had a few thoughts on the way he was wielding the chain. So far, I was holding up well. I breathed in shallow puffs. I hadn't screamed at him to turn off the Human League. I was saving my energy.

He came close and held up his fist. I flinched, and he sniggered. 'Bit jumpy. I was only going to show you me watch.'

'Oh,' I said. 'Let's see.'

The sleeve pulled back and jangled a chunky monstrosity. 'Eighteen-carat pink gold.'

'It's very nice.'

'Cartier. Got it in the States. Worth ten grand.'

It was ugly and a stupid waste of money. What kind of psychopath tells you how much their watch is worth? He grinned in my face. He had what romance books called a generous mouth, gaps between his teeth. Flossing should have been a breeze, but he had bits of meat in there. That foul maw had halitosis that could strip paint.

'You blithely enter a bikie's house.' He grinned, as though he was in fact delighted that I had.

Blithely? The man had an interesting turn of phrase; a well-read psychopath. I turned away to avoid his breath, noted the discarded boxes near my feet, Detroit Ammunition Company, 9mm cartridges. A gun must be somewhere around here. More than one.

'What did you *think* would happen?'

'It's all an innocent mistake. I was selling Avon. Got the address wrong,' I said.

The Turk chortled. 'Josie tells a different story.'

Enright. She'd set me up.

'We're violent people. Didn't you know that? We trade in genuine harm.'

'I ... you do? Okay. Sorry to bother you. I'll just go now.'

'What's the problem? You like violence, don't you? On TV?'

'Sometimes I do.'

'Of course you do. Everyone does. But real life is different. You act like violence doesn't exist.' He was getting annoyed. 'Here's a news flash. This country's built on it. Violence gets the job done, gets the juices flowing. We love to hurt cunts.'

He tossed the chain away, took off the jacket, unbuttoned his cuffs, and rolled up his sleeves. Forearm muscles like undersea cable. The man found the time to work out. And to read. Pina Coladas? Walking in the rain? Look out, ladies.

'We lost a great man, recently.'

This caught me off-guard. 'Who?'

'Ricky-fucking-Peck. Sick cunt, full of ideas, loved life. A true Corpse Flower.'

'Yes. His funeral was on TV, lots of people. He was a popular man.'

'He was. Sent off with full honours.' He opened a drawer and rummaged through the contents. He returned with a police-issue extendable baton and extended it.

'Now.' He tapped the palm of his hand with the baton. 'The jacks say it was an accident. But I don't believe it. I'll tell you why. That house, where Ricky died, that was a hydroponic set up. Full of dope, right? The man loved life, but for some reason he gets pissed and takes a bath in a house full of hippy lettuce?'

'That sounds ... unlikely.'

'Good answer.' He pointed at me 'Now, what I want to know is, who killed him.'

'Please don't hurt me. I don't know,' I said. 'Why would I?'

He ran the baton over his chin stubble. 'Because of your interest in Mortimer. Guess who didn't go to the funeral?'

'Um ... Mortimer?'

'Give the girl a lollypop.' Tap, tap, tap. 'Ricky gets done, Mortimer runs off the next day. It might be a coincidence. But I need to know. You're his mate, you know he's connected.'

'I've never even met Mortimer!'

'You told Josie Enright he owes you money. So you're cosy.'

'I lied to her.' I couldn't have been more stupid in my approach to Enright.

'Who killed Ricky?' This time, he whipped the baton into his hand.

'I don't know! He was drunk, maybe it *was* an accident. More accidents happen —'

The crack, like lightning across my cheek, knocked me off the stool. My bound hands and feet couldn't cushion my fall, I landed hard on my shoulder.

'Ricky never got *drunk*,' he said. 'No accident.'

'No way,' I said, gasping, trying to get up. 'He was murdered.'

'By?'

I struggled to my knees. 'By that bastard Mortimer.'

'Well done. And where is he now?'

'I don't know, and I wish I'd never heard of him. Please, can I go home? Please?'

'Nah, not yet.'

He took hold of the cable-tie at my wrists and dragged me to the wall. There was a chain attached to a bracket about a metre off the ground. He dragged my arms back, hooked the chain through my wrists. I had to kneel to relieve the pull of my weight on my arms. The floor around me was smeared with brown stains.

The Turk snapped a padlock over the chain and tossed the key on the bench. He touched his phone and the Human League stopped.

'Got a few things to take care of. Take it easy, and I'll see you in a bit.'

To my surprise and relief, he headed for the door. He hit the light on the way out, and I was in total darkness. The bolt slid shut outside.

I shifted, trying to get the pressure off my wrists. I found if I twisted my body to the side, my shoulder against the wall, I could let my weight fall. It was an improvement. My head dropped forward to rest on a wall bracket that jutted beside me. I tried to breathe, to think, but I was filled with too much angry static to think. One thing was clear — I was doomed.

At least the Human League had ceased. The place was quiet.

Then somewhere in the darkness, I heard a low groan.

36

'WHO'S THERE?' I hissed.

I heard panting, then another pitiful, agonised groan.

'Jeff Vanderhoek?'

'Yes?' His voice was thin, an exhale.

'Are you okay?'

'You have to get out. He'll be back. He always comes back.'

'I'm stuck, locked in,' I said. 'The key's on the bench. Can you get to it?'

'I can't *get* anywhere.'

I took that in. 'This is bad.'

Hollow laughter. 'You think?'

Then the fear receded and I went low, into deep despair. Dead soon. Last thoughts turned to Brophy: that had been good. It had been a fine thing to know that man.

'Jeff? Peter Brophy told me you saved his life.'

Nothing but rasping groans.

'He ODd and you called the ambulance.'

Soft murmuring now. 'Peter. Yeah. Peter. We hit up in the park, on the grass, drifting off. I seen his lips go blue. A lady's walking her dog and I go ring the ambos or he'll die.'

I realised I was crying; tears were streaming down my face at any rate.

'Woman on the phone talked me through it. Mouth-to-mouth, till the ambos got there.'

'Thank you.'

The outside bolt slid back.

'Oh, Christ,' Vanderhoek said.

The door swung open and the lights blinked on. The Turk was

standing in the doorway holding my handbag. 'Your phone's been ringing. Every time I answer, it's some *ching-chong* voice.'

I didn't know what to say.

'A messy bitch, aren't you? I found a fucking apple core in here. Who the fuck puts an old apple core in their handbag?'

'I couldn't find a bin.'

He laughed, a mouth so wide I could shove a softball in there.

With the lights on, I scanned the room for Jeff. A pile of canvas drop-sheets was shoved into a space behind the row of motorbikes. It moved.

Karen Carpenter's sad singing started to echo through the shed. He held up my phone and winked at me, listened until it rang out. 'No ID. Who could it be?'

Not Brophy then. Maybe Phuong. It started up again.

'Persistent fucker,' he said, swiping the screen. 'Stella Hardy's boyfriend speaking.'

A pause then he frowned. 'Wrong number, mate. Can't understand you.' He shook his head. 'That's a pity — I was going to have a bit of fun. Put out the idea that you and I had run off together.' He tossed the phone over his shoulder.

'They use mobiles to track people. They'll track that call, see it was answered here.'

He upended a milk crate, spilling its contents on the floor, and straddled it. 'Who's going to do that? The jacks? I *own* half of them.'

The detritus from the crate: a wallet, a broad-blade knife in a leather sheath, some keys, a stubby Phillips-head screwdriver, a packet of Tic Tacs, a paperback. I tilted my head, trying to see the title. 'Is that yours?' I asked, nodding at the book.

He picked up the knife and pulled it from the sheath. 'This? A good one, isn't it? A Bowie knife from the States. There are more regulations in Texas on carrying one of these knives than there are on carrying guns. So that's a fun place. No doubt about it.'

I'd meant the book, but I let it go.

179

'You read shit about gun laws,' the Turk was saying. 'Some journalist having a go. Reckons guns are bad. But journalists are worse. Someone's lost their kid and they shove a camera in their face.'

He went back to my bag and started to pull things out. 'Old receipts, about ten fucking ballpoint pens, and some lip balm. Why do chicks always have lip balm?' His face close to mine, liquor on his breath.

'We don't like chapped lips, it's not a mystery.'

'Got your phone, and some nail clippers, in here.'

I stared at a patch of dried blood at my feet, my eye followed the long smear to the drop-sheets covering Jeff. The movement had stopped for now.

'So much *rubbish*.'

What was he looking for? There was nothing … Wait, did I still have Ricky Peck's letters? Why did I leave them in there? Because I was an idiot.

I heard myself blabbering. 'Yes, it's all rubbish, debris, litter basically. Mouldy, rotting biological matter. Probably toxic, probably noxious, poisonous …'

'Look what I found.' He held up the letters, acted shocked. 'Uh oh, these aren't yours, are they?'

'I don't know how they —'

'You *opened* them. You always open other people's mail?'

'I was going to give them —'

'Shut up.' He went to the bench, opened up a box in one furious rip, and went through it. He stopped and lifted his head. I heard it, too, the low whimpering. I glanced at the tarp. The thing was shaking, and then it seemed to fold in on itself.

'Jeffy. Forgot all about you, mate.' The Turk rubbed his nose, sniffed. Scratched the back of his neck, seemed to be trying to make up his mind. 'Yeah. Rightio.'

He opened a draw and took out a pistol, pulled the slide, released it. He went to the bundle of tarp on the floor and kicked the sheet away, exposing Vanderhoek's bloodied face, bruised torso. 'Do it,' Vanderhoek said.

'Check this out,' The Turk said to me.

He dropped to one knee and put the gun under Vanderhoek's chin. 'This is for Thailand.'

I shut my eyes. The blast rang in my ears. I couldn't breathe, forgot how. I opened my eyes, and stared resolutely ahead.

The Turk tossed the pistol on the bench. 'Only nine mil, makes a decent mess but.'

He resumed his rummaging in the box. He held up what looked like an old-fashioned tin of hairspray. In the other hand was a nozzle of some kind. It wasn't hairspray; it was a butane blowtorch. He tested the firing mechanism on the nozzle. Then he unscrewed the cap on the can and slotted the nozzle over the opening. It hissed, until he twisted the thing and it clicked into place. He adjusted a regulator knob on the back of the nozzle, and I heard more hissing. He pulled the trigger mechanism like a gun and a blue flame jetted out.

'Oh dear.' I heard myself say.

He adjusted the flame as he came towards me.

'Ricky was a serious man. He wasn't your average criminal. He had ambition. We were going to go big. He was strategic, crunched the numbers. Big numbers. Data sets.'

'Um. I suppose so.'

'That's what he said. Supply and demand. Simple economics.'

'What are you going to do?' I nodded to the blowtorch.

He brought the torch to my knee until the denim was smoking.

I breathed hard through clenched teeth, as the tears ran down my face. 'Please, stop.'

'What's that? Does it hurt?'

'Yes.'

'Okay, have a rest, we got all night.' He moved the flame to the side.

Deep breaths now, a reprieve. Didn't last long. He directed the heat to the other knee.

Shallow panting as I counted down in my head. It felt like a long time before he turned the flame away. 'There, holes in your jeans. Now you're cool.' He waited for me to recover myself. 'Brings a whole new meaning to the term "fashion victim", doesn't it?' he said, chuckling.

I started sobbing.

He frowned and cocked his head. A car coming up the drive. It stopped, right outside the barn. Doors slammed. A man's low voice, then a woman swearing. I recognised that deep voice, that unique style of cursing. Philomena Enright.

'Lord and Lady Fuckhead can't hold their horses.' The Turk sighed, getting up. 'Hold this for me.' He picked up the screwdriver and stabbed my thigh. I screamed as the pain hit. 'Keep it down, will ya? You'll upset the neighbours.' He hurried out, leaving the light on. A second later, the bolt slid shut.

37

BLOOD SEEPED around the screwdriver in my leg. The sharp pain replaced by an enervating ache arriving in waves like light through fog. I knew I had to get out, but mentally I was a mess, I couldn't think. The gun on the bench? Impossible to get to.

Outside, The Turk, Enright, and another male voice — hostile, shouting.

Male: 'Don't fuck me around.'

The Turk, soothing: 'Forget it, mate. The plan's dead. It died with Ricky.'

Male: 'No fucking way. We go on. I didn't come this far —'

Turk: 'Mate, we don't even know where he stashed it all.'

Male: 'It's in the house.'

Turk: 'Cops didn't find shit. Ergo, shit ain't there.'

Josie Enright: 'Jacks don't know where to look. It's there.'

Turk: 'Mate, okay. Say it's there. We can't just rock up, cops all over the joint.'

Male: 'We thought so too, but I went up there, had a look around. Cops've gone.'

Turk: 'Maybe not. Plain clothes in an unmarked car. Just a few days. Two days.'

The other voice was probably Ox Gorman.

Josie: 'What about that *problem*?'

Turk: 'Sorted. She's in there and she's not coming out. Relax, both of youse. Jeez, youse are uptight. Have a drink. I've got bourbon, vodka. Come in and calm down.'

Not coming out.

I sat there, dumbfounded. For how long, I don't know. I just stared at nothing. Then I realised I was actually looking at the blowtorch. It took me another moment to comprehend that, possibly, it was within reach. I got low to the ground and extended both feet. Searing pain up my leg for my trouble. I tried again, sliding both legs out until I could hook the top of it with a big toe. I pulled it in but lost purchase. Legs out, my toe hooked the nozzle. Again I drew the can closer and again it slipped. But it was closer. My toe hooked it, and I drew my legs in. Close enough. I twisted around and felt behind me with my bound hands. Something smooth and cold, wrong end. I ran my hand to the top, but I was slippery with sweat. A finger touched the nozzle. I had it. I couldn't see what I was doing, but I had it.

I felt around the mechanism, trying to find the regulator handle. The cable ties were tight around my wrists, and my fingers struggled to grip the nozzle. I manoeuvred it around until I could put my thumb and index finger on the regulator. Griping, turning, until I heard the magnificent hiss of gas. I moved to the handle and put a finger to the trigger. A click and the gas ignited.

I attempted to keep the trigger down, while holding the torch in the general area of the cable tie around my wrists. Without seeing what I was doing I couldn't aim with any control. I was frying my own hands and after a short burst I had to have a break. I released the trigger but the torch stayed on, the mechanism was stuck. Now I could hold the nozzle at the top and direct the flame at the small gap between my wrists. Something burned — mostly me — and I stopped several times when the scorching became intolerable, but I smelled burning plastic, too. I held it there for as long as I could stand it. Then I dropped the can, pulled my arms hard apart, stretching the cable tie until it broke.

My hands were free. I wrapped my fingers tightly around the screwdriver handle, took a deep breath and dragged the thing out of my thigh. I took off my shirt and wrapped it round the wound.

Then I picked up the knife and cut the tie around my ankles.

The still-burning blowtorch had rolled to the side, and flame now lapped the concrete floor near the paperback book. I tried to kick the blowtorch away with my good leg, and sent it skittering away towards the motorbikes.

I stood, fell over, and hauled myself up against the stool. I searched the floor for my phone. It was lying near Jeff Vanderhoek's body. I hobbled over, pulled the coverings over him, my head turned away. The phone screen was mostly intact, but the battery was low. I hit the keypad to call triple zero. It vibrated, a death rattle, and died trying.

I shoved it in my pocket and saw the blowtorch was burning close to an oil stain on the concrete. A second later the oil ignited into hot orange vapour. The flames spread along the floor to the motorbikes.

I wanted to run, but my right leg could take no weight. I hopped to the wall and used it for support.

Smoke poured from the nearest bike. There was no boom — more of a *woof* — as it was consumed. Rivers of flame were running on the oil leaks and petrol spills that covered the barn floor. I hauled myself along with the posts on the wall, headed for the double doors at the freezer end of the barn. These doors faced away from the Turk's house, and if I could get them open I might be able to sneak away before they saw the fire and came looking for me.

I heard another *woof* and turned to see the other motorbike engulfed. Then it exploded. Pieces of metal flew, a cloud of heat followed. The air was now thick with smoke.

I made it to the doors. The deadbolt was locked. I tried to remember if he'd left the keys on the bench. I slumped to the floor, intending to crawl there. I was better off on the ground anyway. Fire had consumed the last of the motorbikes, and to my horror, it crept towards Jeff's body. I limped to the bench, and hunted through the mess for a weapon. I had the knife, but I needed more. Then I heard the outside bolt slide back once more.

38

I MADE a lumbering dash for cover behind the freezer just as the door opened. The barn inhaled and the flames roared up.

'Stella? Are you in here?' A Vietnamese accent.

Cuong? What the actual heck? I bobbed up to get a visual through the smoke. 'Over here.'

I hobbled over to him. He looked doubtful. 'Can you run?'

'I can move, sort of.'

He put an arm around my waist, half lifted me. I leaned some of my weight on his shoulder and we started towards the exit. Outside, a man's voice cursed. We immediately changed direction, heading behind the door. I planted myself against the wall.

Other voices outside. Enright screeching: 'Get the hose.'

'I can't see shit in this smoke,' said a male voice.

'How'd the door get open is my question,' the Turk slurred. 'Shit. The bikes.'

'Got a fire extinguisher?' The other man was taking charge.

'No, I haven't got a fucking fire extinguisher.'

'Is she even in here?'

In our favour, they couldn't see. Against us was not being able to breathe. 'She's not exactly fucking free to roam around,' the Turk shouted.

'Let it burn then. Unless you got flammable shit we should worry about?'

'Nah. Oh, but there's a tin of two-stroke somewhere,' the Turk said.

A loud explosion followed by a metallic *ting* as the can hit the ceiling. We were shielded from the flash and the heat, but the smoke was becoming intolerable. Then the barn lights flickered and went off. Now there was only flames and smoke.

The two men were outside and screaming. 'Stand still and I'll hose you both.' Enright's voice — she was taking charge. 'What a couple of babies. Singed hair, no biggie.' A blast of water spray.

I felt Cuong's hand grip mine hard, and pull me along. I followed his trajectory, and we rushed out in a swift circle, staying close to the wall. The exterior light was out and the yard was now in darkness. Josie and the Turk were arguing about putting out the fire.

We crawled alongside the barn, away from the house.

I gasped, drawing cool air into my lungs.

Behind the barn, it was a short distance to the line of trees that marked the rear boundary, then open land. Crossing it seemed to take forever. The chained dogs were in a frenzy of barking.

We came to a wire fence. Cuong held open a gap in the wire, and I crawled through. This property was a tangle of straggly eucalypts and thick bracken undergrowth. We went on for a few more metres then stopped. I lay down on the cold ground and watched the barn burn.

'Rest later,' Cuong was saying. 'Car's that way. Let's go.'

I struggled up on my good foot. He helped me through the vegetation and on to a narrow track. We came to a house. The Turk's rear neighbour. We passed silently by. Lights on in the sitting room window. A family were eating dinner, plates balanced on their laps, eyes glued to the TV.

We made it to the road, a narrow line of bitumen with a solitary street light. Distant sirens screamed.

Cuong's small Peugeot was about fifty metres away. I was hobbling as fast as I could. A series of cracking booms, like combat, like we were in a war, echoed in the night. He hit his keys, the lights flashed, and I fell in. Then we were flying down the empty road.

187

39

WE HEARD more sirens but didn't see any other vehicles. The roads were dark but for the odd street light. After a few kilometres, Cuong slowed and drove steadily. We passed a shiny new train station in the middle of the windswept plains, near the edge of a new housing estate. Rows and rows of brand-new houses, in various stages of construction, stretching out to the horizon. He pulled over near to a hulking wooden skeleton. 'Are you alright?' he asked.

'You rang my phone.'

'Yes.'

'The Turk answered.'

He nodded. 'That's how I guessed where you were. I drove straight there. Kept calling your phone.'

'How is that possible? How is it that you *know* the Turk, let alone where he fucking lives?'

He didn't answer.

'I'm not unappreciative. I'm grateful you showed up. But I can't figure it out. How do you, a decent person, a cousin to a cop, know the Turk?'

A slow shake of his head told me nothing.

Reality was so messed up right now, I genuinely wondered if he'd hypnotised me. But I was losing patience with his reserve. And I was fed up with Copeland, Phuong, and everyone telling me not to go to the police. 'You're driving to the nearest police station, right?'

'How's the leg?'

'It hurts. So now we're going to the police.'

'No.'

I let out a howl. 'Why? What the hell is going on?'

'Fair enough. I'll tell you.' He hit the indicator and pulled out.

'But first we have to hide the car.'

We drove until we hit wide roads and darkened factories. He took a series of turns and came to a dead-end street that ended at an industrial precinct. Concrete partitions of warehouses, workshops, and manufacturing works, all closed for the weekend. Cuong drove up to a building marked *Pham's Car Care and Auto Works*. The roller door was up, and the interior was a cold cavern of darkness. A light was on in an office. A man in mechanic's overalls was reading a paperback. Seeing us approach, he closed the book.

'Come in,' Cuong said to me. 'You can use the restroom.'

I found a stinky staff toilet and sink. I used a damp paper towel to clean my face, and let the water run over my blackened hands. Under the dirt were the burns, and lesions where the cable ties had dug into my skin. I took the knife from my back pocket and cut the legs off my jeans. More paper towel, and I cleaned the stab wound.

Cuong was outside, sitting on the footpath. 'I'm leaving my car with Mr Pham.'

I sat next to him and didn't say anything.

He held out a can of Coke. 'Taxi's coming,' he said.

I drank half the can in one go. 'He shot Jeff Vanderhoek. I saw him. The Turk goes, "This is for Thailand," and then he just ... shot him.'

He pulled out a pack of cigarettes and lit one. 'Try to forget it.'

Not a chance. I looked at him. 'You've been to the Turk's place before?'

'I have. Yes.' Cuong leaned forward, his fringe fell over his eyes. 'I knew the back way is not secured, only plain wire.'

He hadn't answered the question, but he was saying such a large number of words that I didn't want to interrupt.

He paused.

I said, 'I'm gonna ask that nice mechanic if I can use his phone to call the cops.'

'I'm telling you.' He took a drag, sighed. 'They got me at Crown.

189

I was playing baccarat. Losing. Two of them came up, very friendly, bought me a drink, and said they had a deal. They pay my debts if I gamble for them, launder their money — I keep some.'

Cuong and the Corpse Flowers. I pictured Phuong's face hearing that. 'When?'

'Maybe six months. They control you. Your whole life. You can't trust anyone, can't go to the cops, can't tell anyone. I'm trapped.'

Yeah, he looked like he'd been in hell. 'You've met the Turk, you know his place.'

'I went there. Once. They wanted my help with their finances, for their businesses.'

I waited for him to say more, but he disappeared in his thoughts. I finished the Coke and crushed the can. I decided to take a different approach with him. 'Why was I in there, your best guess.'

A face like the sphinx.

'No theories? My initial thought was Mortimer. Because of my cack-handed enquiries. But, no, the Turk wanted info on Ricky Peck. Like I know anything about that guy.'

A flick of his wrist shook the ash from his cigarette. That was the extent of his reply.

'Ricky Peck,' I said again. 'Any thoughts?'

The stone heads of Rapa Nui had more to say.

I blew on the sore spot on my leg. My face hurt where I'd been punched. *Bust face,* manifestly. I touched my cheek: a fat lump. There'd be an eye-catching shiner tomorrow, one of those colourful bruises that go from blue to green to yellow.

He took my hand away to inspect my face. Then he checked my wrists, holding both hands and turning them over. He looked at me. 'So,' he said. 'How's your day been?'

I laughed, or maybe I cried, it was hard to tell the difference, there were tears and shaking and noises.

'Mine's been great. Went to Derby Day. That's why I rang, to tell you about it.'

I was genuinely touched. 'Who won?'

'Ghostbuster.'

'Was that your horse?'

He shook his head. 'Bad name.'

'Of course.'

The cab arrived. 'Sunshine hospital,' Cuong said.

The driver drove without a word. Speech was at serious risk of becoming redundant.

40

AS CUONG and I were leaving the hospital, I asked a nurse for the time. He said it was coming up to three. That sounded about right. We made our way to the taxi rank. A warm night, my pain killers kicking in, and the world was a little less threatening.

The tired-looking doctor who'd treated me had appraised my injuries impassively. The burns were superficial, she told me, easily seen to with cream and a plaster. Well, fancy that, because they hurt like all get out. I expected some awkward questions about the stab wound. Instead, she talked about sutures, and like a sadistic monster, injected a local anaesthetic directly in the cut. Three stitches and a tetanus injection later, I was handed a prescription for antibiotics and a brochure about domestic violence.

I touched my pocket to make sure the knife and the screwdriver were still there. Now would be a bad time for a cop to decide to frisk me. I might be up on charges of going equipped to steal.

Cuong leaned against the railing, pulled out the ubiquitous packet of cigarettes, and looked down the road for a taxi. He lit the smoke with shaking hands. 'I can't go home.'

'They didn't see you.'

'I don't know. Maybe.'

He reminded me of a skittish wild animal. I could chat with him, but ask a tricky question or get too close and an exotic defence system would spring up, like a frill of neck skin or a jet of ink in my eye, before he flapped his tentacles and fled. I decided to have one more shot at him — from the side, an oblique attack: 'Ever been to Burma?'

Cuong brushed his fringe back, didn't answer.

'Kengtung — what does that mean to you?'

'Opium.'

Good Lord! A proper answer. 'I thought the Burmese opium trade was finished.'

'Poppies are in the hills again. In Shan, many places.'

I had a bite. A nibble. 'What's your part in that?'

He dragged on the smoke.

'You're silent like the 'b' in 'tomb', you're silent like a holy night, but Cuong, you have vocal chords, a voice box, other anatomy things that might shrivel up if you don't use them. Not to mention there's a section of your brain just for language, it's a shame not to use a perfectly good part of your brain. And —'

'Nineteen hours by car from Hà Nội to Kengtung. Across Laos. Slow driving. Mountain roads. Gorman has business in Kengtung.'

I shuddered. How deeply involved was Cuong? 'Why would you do that?'

He turned away. 'To pay back the money I owe him.'

Not far away, a B-double on the ring road used its air brakes, shuddering groans.

'Aren't you scared?'

'I'll have bribes for anyone who stops me: army, gangs, police, rebel groups.'

'The Corpse Flowers trust you on your own?'

'The orange-hair one, he comes with me.'

Bust Face would make a terrible travelling companion. Poor Cuong. 'They've got you, haven't they? One minute you're a humble economist, and the next you're the middle man in the opium trade.'

'Not only opium. Heroin and meth.'

'Let's just say "drugs", I think that covers most things.' It was like talking to Brophy's daughter, Marigold, the primary-school student with the literalism of an Evangelical pastor.

'Gorman's Asian syndicate has the connections. He wants me to buy, maybe, a couple of hundred kilos.'

I looked up, a sky the colour of rust. Soft rain beginning to fall.

'Not a word, Stella. Not Phuong or anyone.'

'No cops. That's a threat from Gorman, isn't it? What did he say?'

'He didn't say anything, just showed photos of my parent's house in Melbourne.'

'But right now, they're in Vietnam.'

Cuong had closed his eyes. Subject closed.

I felt woozy, maybe it was the passive smoke. Something passive was getting to me.

A taxi entered the driveway and pulled up at the rank. A bloke got out with a bloody hanky wrapped around his hand. Snap, bro. I'd have high-fived him, but it would have hurt us both. I looked at the driver through the opened door. He glared at me as though I was trouble. I turned back to Cuong. 'Where're we going?'

'Not your place. And we can't go to mine.'

'Make up your mind,' the driver demanded. It was time he explored other employment options, for the sake of his mental health.

In my exhaustion, I struggled to think of somewhere to go. Then I thought of a place that was safe, and quite close by. 'St Albans,' I said, and we climbed in the cab.

41

I KNOCKED. The door was unlocked, and opened the width of a fearful eye. 'Who is it?'

'Stella. And my friend, Cuong.'

'It's late. What do you want?'

'A bed for the night?'

The gap widened, Afshan's eyes darted from Cuong to me.

Cuong bowed his head, his expression serious. 'Please, help us.'

'How did you get here?'

'What?' I asked, incredulous. 'Let us in. I've been tortured, for heaven's sake. There's people who want us dead.'

'Did you come by *boat*?'

Cuong sniggered, but I was appalled. 'Afshan, for God's sake.'

'I've been dying to use that one,' he hooted, wiping a tear from his eye.

'Look, see for yourself.'

The porch light came on. He took in my bruised face, my bloodstained clothes, the bandages. 'Stella, this is bad,' Afshan said. 'Quickly, come inside.'

Shahid was standing in the hall wearing a towelling robe and slippers; he looked shocked. 'Are you alright?'

'Cuts and burns. I've had stitches. How are you?'

'But what happened?

'They can tell us in the morning,' Afshan said. 'Make them a place to sleep.'

'She can have my mattress,' Shahid said immediately. 'And we have a spare for him.'

'No,' I said. 'I can't take your bed, the couch is fine.'

'I was not sleeping. Please, take the bed.'

'I don't think I can sleep either,' I said. 'But I could murder a cup of tea.'

The three men did a simultaneous inhale.

'It's a figure of speech, you guys.'

Afshan said, 'Of course.' And he went to the kitchen.

I made my way to the bathroom at the rear of the house, soft snores coming from the other bedrooms on the way. I passed the main room where *Cool Hand Luke* was on the TV.

The bathroom was mildly disgusting, as any men-only household tended to be. Multiple double-adaptors piggy-backed on the one power point in the room, and several appliances were charging. There was a dangerous-looking bar-heater on the wall, an electric shaver, a tablet, and someone's phone. What a death trap this place was. These guys would be first on my list for fire-safety training.

The painkillers were wearing off. I closed the lid of the toilet and sat down, trembling. The burns stung and the stab wound throbbed. I took the screwdriver from my pocket. Could I jam that thing in the Turk's neck, or maybe his eye?

Who was I kidding? Revenge was stupid.

One of the chargers matched my phone; I plugged it in, hoped like hell my phone was salvageable, and went to join Cuong. He was discussing the movie with Shahid, who was cross-legged on the carpet.

'Do either of you have a Panadol by any chance?'

'A what?' Shahid asked.

'Never mind.'

Afshan came in with mugs of black tea, two in each hand. In his serious way, he handed them out. Then he sat on the floor, waiting, I thought, for me to say something.

I sipped my tea, so sweet I flinched. I had nothing to say.

'Have you seen this one, Stella?' Cuong asked, pointing to the TV. 'Great movie.'

'Yeah, couple of times. He eats lots of eggs,' I said.

Cuong shook his head. 'For a punishment, Luke must go in "the box", and the guard says, "*Sorry, Luke, just doing my job.*" And Luke says, "*Calling it your job don't make it right, boss.*"'

'Spoiler alert,' I said. 'You going to watch this movie or just ruin it for everyone?'

'You look tired. Do you want to sleep?' Shahid asked.

'Not right now. I'm going to the bathroom.' I went to check if my phone was functional. Small merciful goddesses: it was charging. I tried Phuong's secure number.

'Stella? It's the middle of the night. What's happened?'

'First, let me apologise.' I cleared my throat, ready to continue with a full and frank self-analysis, exploring the extent of what I did, what I could have done, owning my faults.

'Stella, none of it matters. That conversation was probably overdue.' No one at fault, air cleared, now we could continue. At least, that's how I interpreted it.

I gave her the whole story, starting with the cup of tea at Enright's flat above the mechanic's shop in Sunshine, and the trip to Mortimer's last known address in Norlane.

'On your own?'

'I wanted to check the house before I spoke to you. A waste of everyone's time if he wasn't there.' I paused, reluctant to give her the rest.

'So foolish. I told you *not* to take risks like that.'

'It's done now. Anyway, funny story, Bust Face lives up to his name.'

'Who?'

'A low-level Flower. He … um … brought me to the Turk.'

'Are you alright?'

'Can you shoot the bastard for me? That's allowed, isn't it? Cops can shoot thugs. It's in the rules somewhere.'

'The Turk's place is all over the news. Huge fire there. Did you see that?'

I looked at my hands. 'Hmm. Yeah, I saw it.' I told her that the Turk and Gorman had been burned, and I had run out.

'Very lucky.'

'I'm alive. Which is more than I can say for Jeff Vanderhoek. Did they find his body?'

'Vanderhoek? No one's saying that yet. Was he there?'

'If it's okay with you, I'd rather not go into detail.'

I could hear her breathing. 'No. Don't.'

'The Turk is convinced Mortimer killed Ricky Peck.'

'Not possible.'

'I'm not sure, he might be right. It's all about the timing. That day of your dinner party, Copeland put Mortimer in the lock-up. Then he and Blyton went drinking in the Spida Bar. That's when he got the call that Peck's body had been found. If Peck died in the afternoon, it could have been Mortimer. There would have been time.'

'Time of death for a body in a bath is complicated — temperatures matter, wide time range.' The Phuong calculator was at full whir. She changed to a softer tone. 'You were lucky to get out of there. Want me to come and get you?'

'No, I'm okay now. I'm here with Cuong.'

A long pause. 'Who?'

'Um. Cuong.'

'I think the line is faulty, sounded like you said "Cuong".'

'Cuong owes Gorman money for his gambling debts. That's how he blackmailed Cuong into helping them — he's supposed to travel to Kengtung. Actually, he helped me get out of there. Your cousin is full of surprises.'

'I don't like surprises.'

'I know,' I said.

'Give me the address. I'll see you soon. And he'd better have some answers.'

I rattled off the address.

'I'll be there in an hour.'

An hour? She was with Copeland, at his father's place in Somerville.

'For now, just until I can work out what to do, can we keep this between us?'

'You mean ... Sure.'

'Oh, and one more thing,' Phuong said. 'OTIOSE think they've traced all the dodgy passports. They've all been for minors, kids under fifteen.'

My brain was a slow-motion car crash of disparate mental notes. The passport photos of Cory I found at the squat in Footscray. Mortimer warning the kids to stay away from Gorman. Cuong in debt to Gorman. Cuong meeting that woman at Crown.

42

'COME,' SHAHID said. 'I'll show you where you can sleep.'

His bedroom was a covered veranda at the back of the house. Blankets had been hung over the louvre windows, attached to the walls with tacks. An old wardrobe against one wall had a massive crack in the door. There was a single mattress on the floor and another mattress propped up on its side against the wall. He dropped it to the floor. From the wardrobe, he took out blankets and pillows. 'Sleep well,' he said, and left.

Cuong reclined, not bothering with the blankets and pillow, and pulled out a cigarette.

'So my hypnotism didn't work.'

'Huh?' He lit the smoke.

'Still smoking.'

He did a half smile; it must've been in the DNA.

Could the Flowers have orchestrated passport fraud for street kids? A ready supply of drug couriers with no families to agitate for them, no strings. The invisible strays of the fast food joints and train stations, those kids had no radar for exploitation. Offer them drugs, money, adventure, and they'd jump on board without a moment's hesitation. They would be up for anything, any crime, to turn a dollar.

On the other hand, those kids had the kind of entrepreneurial spirit that was sorely lacking in this country, I'd give them that.

'So Kengtung,' I said. 'Quite an adventure for those kids. Beats the school bus trip to Uluru.'

'No kids.'

'But the passports your friend was forging, they were for teenagers.' I watched him for signs of guilt. The man had a terrific poker face, probably had a lot of practice with all the gambling.

'You spoke to Phuong?'

'I'm sorry, Cuong, I had to. But not as a cop, as my friend, and your cousin. She's on her way.'

He frowned.

'I understand you're upset, but it's better to have her help, don't you think?'

Cuong rubbed his eye with the heel of his palm.

I stretched out my legs to ease the ache. 'Tell her everything. The trip to Burma and about how the Corpse Flowers are grooming kids as would-be couriers.'

'I don't know about that.'

'Like hell you don't.'

He took a long drag and then stubbed the cigarette out in an overflowing saucer. 'Alright, when Phuong gets here, I'll tell her everything.'

I pulled up the blanket and settled into a sideways foetal, thinking I'd have a short nap before Phuong arrived. I closed my eyes, but just saw Jeff Vanderhoek's corpse.

Outside the room, the sound of low voices arguing. I opened an eye. 'Phuong?'

'Visitors,' Cuong whispered.

I sat up gingerly. 'Ghosts, you mean?'

'Don't say that,' he said firmly.

'Oh right, sorry. *Friends*. That's some serious phobia you got there.'

'It's not a phobia, it's my culture.'

'Right. But I'm just saying, if the dudes behind the DSM-5 ever got wind of this, your whole culture would be branded bizarre.'

'Shows how worthless it is.'

'Ssh. Listen.'

The voices stopped. Cuong put his ear to the door. I gripped the knife. Afshan, sounding angry, and a man, a deeper voice. Cuong and I locked eyes for a second. 'The Turk?'

'No,' he said. 'We would be dead already.'

'Then —'

'In the wardrobe. Quick!'

I dived in and pulled the door shut behind me. The mechanism was dodgy and the door wanted to swing open. I held the tiny screw on the inside, holding the door in place.

A soft tap outside the room, then Shahid's voice, anxious, apologetic. 'Excuse me.'

The crack in the door offered a segment of room and I saw Shahid shoved aside.

'Make yourself scarce, mate, if you know what's good for you.'

Shahid reluctantly withdrew.

I exhaled silently, shallow breaths. Cuong moved to the mattress, perhaps to draw attention away from the wardrobe. But I couldn't see him now. What I could see was the spruce dude, fifties, healthy tan, trim beard, and collar-length grey hair striding into the room. I thought he was a cop, but he was bone thin, his white t-shirt hung off him, and the jeans were pulled in with a belt. A half-full green garbage bag over his shoulder. But it was the shoulder holster and gun that caught my attention. He dropped the bag and leaned against the wall.

'Where's Stella Hardy?'

I stood perfectly still, but my wounded leg protested.

'Who are you?' Cuong said.

'Detective Senior Sergeant Blyton.'

William Blyton? Phuong's good cop, the one I'd left my card with? I didn't know how he'd found me, but I was greatly relieved. At last, *proper* police were involved. I was all set to leap out of the wardrobe and demand he take action. That he arrange protection for Cuong until he could testify. That he round up everyone. But something about the way he was behaving held me back.

He sniffed. 'You the boyfriend?'

Cuong said nothing.

'Hang on, don't I know you? You're Peck's flunky.'

Static electricity buzzed in my ears. Blyton had met Cuong?

'Where is she?' Blyton demanded so aggressively I wondered if Phuong might have been wrong about him.

'She left.'

A long pause. My leg ached to move.

'How's her leg? A stab wound, the hospital tells me.'

'The hospital told you?'

He pulled my handbag from the garbage bag. 'Found this at the fire in Tarneit. My brilliant deduction is, if she was there, then odds on she's not healthy. Basic detective work, really, check the hospitals, taxi companies. You bozos didn't even try to cover your tracks.'

Phuong had been wrong — very, very wrong — about bloody William Blyton.

He dropped my handbag in disgust. 'Stella-fucking-Hardy. Never heard of her, then the next minute, she's ringing me at work, coming to my place. Says she's a social worker all upset about some dead kid. I don't know if he was wasted or if it was natural causes, but I'll tell you this for free, if the Flowers give two shits about some homeless kid, I'll turn in my gun.'

Blyton put his hands on his hips, big patch of sweat under his arms.

'Detective, is there something I can help you with?' Cuong asked.

'Yes.' He paused.

I watched his face contort as he fought to compose himself. It seemed Blyton was straining not to weep. 'When I didn't hear from him ...' He broke off, took a big breath. 'I thought they wouldn't touch him. We both did. But they crossed that line. And that was a big fucking mistake.'

Perhaps Blyton was unhinged. I kept my eye on the gun.

'Who are we talking about?' Cuong asked.

He let out a breath. 'Emergency services get called to a property in Tarneit last night. The Turk's little set-up. For days, I had a bad feeling. Waiting to hear from him. So I go up there.' He put his hand over his mouth, his face momentarily frozen in anguish. Deep breath through the nose, blinking back tears. 'Ambos are carrying him out.'

'Jeff Vanderhoek,' Cuong said, softly.

Blyton nodded; he seemed relieved that he didn't have to say the name.

'Were you there? With Hardy?'

'Briefly, yes,' Cuong said. 'The fire had already started.'

'Did you talk to him before he died?'

'No,' Cuong said. 'He was dead when I got there.'

Blyton let out a howl, then closed his eyes and gritted his teeth. 'Someone talked.'

Cuong coughed.

Beads of sweat on Blyton's face. 'Now the scum've gone to ground. Turk's absconded. The only possible witness is this mad social worker who's trying to save all the little kiddies. This Hardy and her fucking handbag.'

The Turk was on the lam?

'Detective,' Cuong said, respectfully. 'As I said, Stella's not here. I'm very sorry about Jeff. But there's nothing more I can tell you.'

I couldn't see Cuong, but I could hear the calm in his voice. I imagined his sangfroid came in handy at poker.

'Why did they snatch Hardy?'

'They think she knows where Mortimer is, they think Mortimer killed Peck.'

'Bastard drowned,' Blyton snarled.

'I believe you,' Cuong said. 'But they're paranoid, they suspect everyone. Maybe they thought it was Jeff?'

'It wasn't Jeff. He didn't have a violent bone in his body.'

'Of course not,' Cuong said.

'Doesn't mean he wasn't brave. I've met some hard men in my time,' Blyton was saying. 'Lean on them and they crumble. But Jeff Vanderhoek was the bravest human being I've ever met. The Flowers stopped supplying me, and I had the Raw-bloody-Prawn enquiry breathing down my neck. So Jeff offers to turn against Gorman. Make it look like I'm doing my job. He did it for me. We were in love. That's something you wouldn't understand.'

'I understand,' said Cuong in a soothing voice. 'Jeff was very brave.'

Blyton was shaking his head, seemed unable to concentrate. 'Get Mortimer arrested, take smack. That was the plan.' He wiped his nose with the back of his hand. 'The gear was for Jeff and me,' he muttered.

'Right,' Cuong said. 'For Jeff.'

Cuong was humouring him, even though he didn't have a clue what Blyton was talking about. But I did. It was Blyton who stole the evidence Bruce Copeland had put in the Guns and Gangs safe. Blyton was the other detective under investigation.

'We were going to get clean, get the hell out of Melbourne.'

'You think someone told Gorman?' Cuong asked.

'Someone? It was bloody Mortimer. I'd bet my life on it.'

'Wait,' Cuong said. 'I just remembered something Stella said. Before he shot Jeff, the Turk said, *"This is for Thailand."*'

'Thailand?' Blyton frowned. 'Enright?'

'I don't know,' Cuong said.

'You're wrong!' Blyton thundered at him. 'Jeff didn't do it. How the fuck did she even *get* that idea? The feds knew about it before that Enright bitch left the fucking country.'

Cuong shrugged. 'I don't know.'

Blyton pulled the gun from the holster and put it to Cuong's temple. 'Where is Mortimer?'

I had to stop myself from leaping out of the wardrobe and screaming *Don't shoot!*

Cuong spoke, icy calm. 'I don't know.'

'I'm not playing games, sonny.'

A pause.

'Nothing to say? Then you will be dead in five, four, three —'

A sigh. 'Sunshine,' Cuong said. 'A squat. I'll take you. It's not far.'

Blyton thought this over. 'Okay. Yes.' He threw a pair of handcuffs at him.

Cuong started attaching the cuffs. 'Maybe we can help each other,' he said in that low soothing voice. 'You want Mortimer to testify at the enquiry, is that it? Help out Copeland?'

'I'd rather eat dog shit than help Copeland.'

I knew the feeling.

'This isn't about Copeland, with his money problems, the ex-wife, the fucking wedding. He's not my concern.' Blyton turned away, used the hanky to pat his sweaty face. Flu, he'd said on Friday. Yeah, right.

He grabbed Cuong by the shoulder, put the gun to his back, and ordered him outside.

I waited a moment then climbed out of the wardrobe. I picked up my bag from where Blyton had thrown it; it smelled of smoke. Still in shock, I unplugged my phone in the bathroom and rang Phuong. She was in her car, she said, only five minutes from St Albans. The sun hadn't risen and yet the household was up and about. Blyton's visit had disturbed everyone. Afshan was in the kitchen, buttering a piece of toast.

'I'm sorry,' I said. 'You offer me sanctuary and I've brought danger to you and your friends.'

He opened a jar of Vegemite. 'We're used to the police bullying us.'

The grubby kitchen window looked out onto the neighbour's weatherboards, pink undercoat, a project trapped in perpetual stasis. I stared out, bewildered. *Used to the police bullying.* Wait, what? 'Afshan, who *are* these bullies?'

'Their names, I don't know. Who asks names when they are ransacking your house?'

'Can you describe them?'

He smudged the Vegemite. 'One is young, light-brown skin and thick black eyebrows. The other is older, a white man. An Australian man.'

'That narrows it down.'

'Here,' he said. 'Some breakfast.'

I took the toast to the front steps to wait for Phuong, hoping Cuong was safe. Blyton was a dangerous addict, armed and desperate for someone to blame for Jeff Vanderhoek's death. And Cuong — what was he thinking? — giving him a crazy brave line about knowing where Mortimer was. He was a good liar, I'd give him that. He even had me going with that quick-as-a-flash response. Sunshine. He was probably going to take Blyton to *La Fonderie*. But what would he do once they got there?

Phuong's little blue car pulled into the driveway. I went down the steps to meet her. She looked at my dirty feet, cut-off jeans and blood-stained t-shirt, knees and hands covered in bandages, half my face blue.

'Stella, look at you.'

'Blyton. He's the detective caught on the phone, the one who had been demanding money from the Corpse Flowers. But it wasn't money he wanted, it was heroin. He and Vanderhoek were lovers. Blyton stole the evidence that Bruce had put in the safe so that he and Vanderhoek could use.'

She blinked. 'I didn't know …'

'You don't need Mortimer to clear Bruce now. Blyton admitted everything. I heard him.'

An inscrutable movement of her head.

'Call the squad cars, the helicopter. Call the fucking army. He's the guy everyone wants.'

Her face broke into the saddest Phuong-smile I ever saw. 'I can't.'

I didn't understand. And then I did. Copeland. An involuntary gasp escaped.

'Friday night, you put it so bluntly, like a slap,' Phuong said. 'His behaviour, the explanations, the secrecy.'

I blinked at her. 'And getting you to delete the recording.'

'Yes. I had my doubts, nagging away at the back of my mind. After you went off, I sat in my car thinking … and I had to admit you might be right.'

I nodded. 'What he's involved in? Is he in the Flowers's pocket?'

She shook her head. 'I don't know. I've tried to contact him. He hasn't got back.'

'You can't protect him, Phuong. Not now. Your career. Your reputation.'

'I'm not doing that. All I'll do is … delay things. He just needs more time.'

'Oh, Phuong.' Tears stung my eyes. I felt caught between triumphal glee that she'd seen through Copeland's bullshit at last, and horror at her passive response. Sticking by him was stupid. I wanted her to get angry, to rid herself of his taint.

We hugged.

I wiped my eyes. 'Shit. Cuong. He's pretending he knows where Mortimer is. Blyton's dangerous, he's withdrawing. My guess is they went to *La Fonderie*. We better hurry.'

'*I* better hurry. You've done enough, Stella. Go home.'

43

I WATCHED Phuong drive away. Afshan brought me a glass of his crazy sweet tea and sat beside me on the steps. 'What will you do now, Stella?'

I didn't have a clue.

We stayed on the steps, watching the sun come up. 'I will drive you home, I think that is best.'

I could not be more indebted to that man. He dropped me off at the supermarket and left me to my misery.

I took a fifty from my wallet that smelled of barbeque, and bought a bottle of vodka. I was done. I'd nearly died. I walked home unconcerned. Everyone at the Turk's place had run off. None of them, not Josie or Bust Face, had seen me escape. As far as the Corpse Flowers were concerned, I was dead.

My street was quiet, as per usual on a Sunday morning. Out of habit, I did a perfunctory scan of the area for bikies, and, finding none, plodded up the stairs. The kitchen was as I'd left it, with day-old cooked pumpkin in a saucepan, and all the ingredients ready for stage two of the *kaddu bharta*. That meal was never going to happen. I didn't have it in me to clean it away. Instead, I ran a bath. Then I rang Flemington police and asked for Raewyn Ross.

'Hardy, you working today, too?'

'No, I'm ... this is a personal call.'

'Not another favour.'

'This is different. It's for romance's sake. And it's not for me, it's for a friend. She fancies this cop.'

'My advice, stay away. Cops are trouble.'

'Probably wise, but she's obsessed. Do you know the cops at St Albans?'

'Her funeral. Name?'

'Ah. Well. She's not sure. She met him while he was attending a burg and being, you know, a spunk.'

'Gawd. What a loser.' Ross was chuckling. 'So it's basically stalking?'

'Um, yeah. Kinda.'

'Cool. Got a description?'

'He's young; nice big, bushy eyebrows. Not my thing, but there you go.'

'That's it? The eyebrows?'

'She said he was with his partner. He's older, sort of old-school Aussie white male. If you get a name for eyebrows, maybe an address, she's gonna ask him out.'

She giggled. 'Roger that. I'll get back to you.'

I took the screwdriver and the knife from my pocket and placed them on the bathroom sink. They looked out of place on the laminex, so I put a towel over them. Then I stripped everything off and assessed the damage. A square sticking-plaster over the screwdriver wound, the burns were healing. I slid into the hot water, leaving one leg hanging over the side, sipping a double vodka. The water was cold when I staggered out. I put my phone on silent and crawled into bed, falling into dreamless oblivion.

Some disturbance of mind woke me a few hours later. Pain was everywhere. I washed down a couple of Panadol and made a mug of tea.

Trotsky started barking next door. I put on a robe and checked the peephole. Phuong.

'You didn't answer your phone,' she said. 'I was ready to call the cops.'

I was horrified. 'Are you crazy? You're the one telling me not to.'

'I'm joking.'

'Oh, right. Hilarious.' I checked my phone: three missed calls, all from Phuong. Nothing from Brophy. I threw it on the sofa with a heavy sigh.

'You're stressed.'

'You think?'

'You haven't debriefed. You need to slow down and you need to talk to someone.'

'I'm fine.'

'When you're under stress, you fall into bad habits, like binge-eating.'

'Binge-eating, nope. Binge-watching, hell yes.'

'Or drinking.'

I had to laugh at that.

'And there's the flashes of uncharacteristic anger.' She met my eye.

'Look, I said I was sorry.'

'And the obsessive need to solve problems. Leading to guilt and exhaustion.'

I put my hands to my face, acted shocked. 'You've been reading my diary.'

'I've been reading psychology texts.'

This was Phuong's way of saying she cared. But analysis was not understanding and the road to hell was paved with second guesses. She lifted a saucepan lid, inspecting the day-old pumpkin fiasco. Her concern was hard to take sometimes, and I moved the conversation along. 'Come away from there. Tell me, did you find Cuong?'

She parked her skinny arse on the edge of my coffee table. 'Yes.' A sheepish, almost contrite Phuong put her hand on mine. 'Mortimer was squatting in the empty flat next to Cuong's. Well, he had been. When they got to the flat, Mortimer wasn't there. So, Blyton went off and left Cuong behind.'

I took my hand away, not in anger; I wanted both hands in the air to express my incredulity. 'Mortimer was there the whole time?'

Phuong sighed. 'I think so.'

'I'm running around the state, getting abducted, beaten, and Mortimer was hiding in *La Fonderie* the whole time.'

'I know.' Phuong was more pale than usual. 'Every time I look at your face I feel sick.'

'What am I, hideous?'

'I should never have got you involved.'

'Yes, you should've asked your cousin. He knows where everyone is.'

'Are you sure you're alright here? You can come and stay with me, if you like, let me take care of you.'

Tempting — she may have had poor judgement with men, but the woman could cook. 'That's a nice offer … but I'm fine, really.'

'Then come for dinner.' She glanced around my flat like she expected to see listening devices. 'We have things to discuss.'

'True that. Phuong, we have to report this.'

'No.'

'And what about Bruce? You've been keeping him informed about Cuong?'

The Phuong-smile came tinged with sadness. 'Not yet.'

I raised my eyebrows. 'What? Not even Bruce?'

'He's my cousin.'

'Your cousin is up to his neck in Corpse Flower doings. Did he finally confess everything to you?'

She shrugged. 'Some things. But I feel like there's still a lot he's not telling me.'

She probably had that right. Still waters ran to the Mariana Trench with that one.

'I need to talk to him.'

She nodded, like that was fair. 'He said he's going to the temple in Braybrook. He's going to make offerings, say a million prayers. He's freaking out again. Worried about appeasing the "friend". Says he sees it in his sleep.'

'The friend is your departed loved ones, right? Family?'

'Not necessarily. Anyway, he's convinced Gorman knows he helped you. He's going to ask the monks if he can stay at the temple.'

'I didn't know you could do that.'

'You should stay at my place, just for a few days.'

'Not necessary. Gorman thinks I'm dead.'

She gave me a hug. 'Come for dinner, let me feed you proper food at least.'

I said I would. When she passed Brown Cardigan's door, Trotsky burst into frenzied yapping. Tough revolutionary he was, barking a rallying call to the workers to bring down the government.

I stood in my kitchen, feeling overtired and overwhelmed. I scraped the half-finished *kaddu bharta* pumpkin mess into the bin. Then I took a couple of aspirin to help the Panadol along. If I had another nap, I'd probably sleep all day and wake up feeling like crap. Instead, I put the dishes in the sink, hit the hot tap and squirted a shot of green liquid. Foam rose. I stared into the bubbles. It was not over. Gorman had said so. I put on some washing-up gloves. *Jacks don't know where to look.*

I took off the gloves and opened my laptop.

There were plenty of articles on Ricky Peck's death, but not many featuring photos of the house. After a bit of trawling, I found a suburban paper with a short piece, and a large picture of the location. *Peck was recently found dead in a house in Sullivan Street, North Sunshine. The unoccupied house was used to grow cannabis.*

Ricky Peck died in a fifties cream brick-veneer, double-fronted place with a high iron fence, and large, slightly rusty wrought-iron gates across the driveway. The house appeared to be adjacent to open land, or a park of some kind. A quick search on a map showed Sullivan Street was a cul-de-sac, which ended at the Kororoit Creek reserve.

I had a brief debate with myself about this idea. Ethically, I was on shaky ground. Legally, I was on no ground at all. But my considerations were of a different order. I turned my hands around, seeing the burns and cuts. I had a reason to go. I wanted those bastards crushed. And I had plenty more reasons to go. This was for Cory. And it was for the girl I saw him with, and Razz and Brook and Angie, and for all the ones who slip through the cracks and were cheerfully preyed upon. It was politics. It was personal.

It was not for Copeland.

I dressed in long pants to cover the bandages, a t-shirt, and put on a pair of runners. Then I ran around the flat gathering my washing-up gloves, the knife, and the screwdriver, and threw them in my handbag. I was going to break in, maybe steal, and I was *equipped*. I went down to Union Road and hailed a cab, telling the driver to head to North Sunshine.

Fifteen minutes later, I was at the corner of Sullivan and Wright. I paid the driver and walked to the end of the street. The house looked the same as the photo, a respectable-looking family home. That surprised me. I foolishly imagined that perhaps the hostility of its owners, the drowning, or even this ridiculous weather might cause some deterioration. I expected police tape or some crime scene barriers, but nothing about the place indicated a criminality had been committed there or that it was off-limits. It was plain and tidy. The tall, ironwork fence and closed gates were the only clues to the owner's need for privacy. One side of the property bordered the reserve. A pathway between Ricky Peck's place and the adjoining property led into it, and I follow it through to a stretch of rolling green crown land with a bike path flanking the creek. Along the length of the dope-house property, ran a high paling fence.

I sat under a tree in the park and considered my options.

A young child on a bike with training wheels rocketed along the path, followed by a mature woman on a dragster, awkwardly perched on the banana seat, helmet sliding off her head, yelling 'Slow down!'

Last time I'd gone into a Corpse Flower house it had ended badly. I stretched my leg. I had been lucky. Luckier than Jeff Vanderhoek.

I turned back to look at the Ricky Peck house. There would

have been cameras. But not now. Padlocks and deadlocks. Burglary required skill, the right tools, and the knowhow.

I walked back towards Wright Street, thinking of catching a bus to Phuong's. At a small strip of shops, most of them closed, I walked into a convenience store. Baked beans, dog food, toilet brushes. A woman sold me a chocolate milk and a Mars Bar, the tradie lunch.

I sat on a bench outside and downed the food. After some deliberation — in which I talked myself out of, and then back into, my next move — I wandered up the street to Ricky Peck's house.

The front gates had a simple latch mechanism. I went up the steps to the house. A dead pot plant on the concrete porch. The bamboo curtain over the door slapped in the wind. I looked in the front windows: a mess of plastic bags, takeaway food boxes, and more industrial-type waste, hoses and metal scraps. I pressed a hand to the sliding aluminium window to shove it sideways, but it was locked.

Time to go.

I hesitated.

I'd broken into buildings before, but I'd always had help. My brother, the petty criminal, could jimmy open a window on the third floor of my building before you could say 'Magistrates' Court appearance'. Even Phuong had a nifty multi-purpose tool and a no-nonsense approach that got us inside a Sunbury meth lab in about five seconds flat.

Today, I was on my own, but feeling upbeat. I could do this.

I walked around the back; the backyard was bare concrete, a few concrete planters with dead plants in them, and big, ugly fish pond full of green water. Other than that, there was no garden, not even a tree. Against the back fence, a pile of household rubbish rotted in the sun. A haven for rats. I checked the house for points of entry. The windows were small and too high to climb in. The back door was locked. I walked down the side of the house and put on the gloves. The side windows were about waist-high. I peered through them, and saw empty rooms strewn with rubbish, boxes, lengths of pipe, a mixer tap that might inflict harm if used with sufficient force. Rolls of plastic, bags of rocks, lights, cords piled in a heap.

I put my gloved hand flat on the window and tried to slide it. The catch snapped and the window moved about three centimetres and stopped, held up by a length of thin dowel in the runner. The cold stink of fusty organic matter drifted out. I tried to use the screwdriver but the handle was bulky and couldn't get through the gap. The knife slipped through, held by two fingers. I bent my hand around, fingers extended, and edged the point of the knife under the dowel. Out it popped. The window slid open. I put one foot on the fence behind me and lifted my weight to the sill, leaned in, and fell the rest of the way. I landed on a pedestal electric fan, hitting my leg. I suppressed a shriek of pain and waited for the worst to pass. I breathed, did a few stretches, and got to my feet.

Internal glass double doors separating the room from the next were propped open. A lighting rig on the ceiling ran the length of both rooms, and a series of extension cords dangled from it. Wide strips of black plastic were piled up on the floor, a few strips were still taped to a window. A row of large plastic tubs, with taps on the side, were hooked up to hoses that went nowhere. Cut by the cops, presumably, who'd hauled the dope out of here.

I sifted through the contents of the boxes. Seed trays, sundry horticultural items.

The two bedrooms were a mess of junk-food detritus, takeaway bag's from Madame Mao's Handmade Dumplings, empty beer cartons, numerous bottles, a couple of camp chairs. Neither room had a bed, and the built-in robes were bare.

I checked the bathroom. A compact space, shower head over the bath where Peck's body had been. A mouldy shower curtain. Pink fifties' porcelain. The matching basin built in a cupboard, both doors open, and overflowing with plastic supermarket bags. The mirrored cabinet above was open and bare.

I went through the house again, checking for secret doors, or fake panels. That was fruitless. Then I went scanning the ceiling for the manhole into the roof. It was in the hallway, but the cover had been removed. The police had probably been through it, but I dragged a crate over from the main room, and shone my phone up there. Nothing. I put the crate back and noticed the drop-sheet that had been scrunched up behind it.

I held it up — it was about the size of a single bed sheet. Dirty and mouldy, and smeared with mud. I was about to toss it aside. In the dirty smudges were patterns. I spread the sheet out on the floor. There was a mark on it, a foot print. It was a clear distinctive sole, with a unique ripple pattern. The print was a Dunlop Volley. The preferred casual sneaker of Ricky Peck.

I stood there, thinking. One clear shoe print and a mess of mud. Brown clay. I got down on the carpet. It was soiled, but not muddy. I walked around the house. The floors were filthy with dust and dirt, but not the same type of mud.

I stood in the narrow hall leading from the front door, past the bathroom, to the back door. No muddy tracks.

I went back to the room where the hydroponic set-up had been. Water had been stored in the tubs, which the crims had kept tidy, and which were now emptied and stacked. Even if the water had leaked, there was not enough dirt there to make mud. I scrutinised the rear yard, just a square of dry grass. Mud was inside the house, and had been hastily wiped up with a drop-sheet. But it hadn't been walked in from the backyard.

I walked slowly, from room to room, scrutinising the floor.

Halfway down the hall, I clocked a streak of brown dirt on the linoleum. The same brown as on the drop-sheet. But someone had tried to wipe it up and done a crappy job. I got down on the floor. There was a small smudge on the skirting board. I inspected the pattern in the lino, looking for a break. There was a join, but it was a neat line and easy to miss. I couldn't lift the corner. I dug the knife under there and a piece nearly a metre-square came away.

A small rectangular hatch was built into the floorboards. The knife slid into the edge and the boards lifted out. Too dark down there to see anything, but I did manage to inhale the fetid air, and probably air-borne diseases. They had a dampness problem. Water leaking under the house, a blocked downpipe maybe.

I shone my phone down, saw the problem. No ventilation, all the vents were obstructed by stacks of plastic containers. The space was small, and cramped, but there was enough room down there to also store a large packing crate and a big metal toolbox.

A car drove by outside. I froze. A door slammed, some people said goodbye, and it drove away. I should leave now.

I took off my runners and lowered myself down. The ground was cold and soft and squished through my toes. I lifted the lid of the nearest container, aimed my phone inside. Files. I opened one marked *inventory*: statements, customs information, quarantine periods, lists of units in a shipping container.

Another container held more files. I flipped one open. Photos of Brook, some in a t-shirt and shorts, measuring one hundred and sixty-eight centimetres against a height chart; another, a simple headshot, blonde with a slick make-up job, almost unrecognisable, smiling at the camera. Under it, a statement of medical history, with blood type, boxes ticked *normal* for all tests, screened and all clear for viruses, including HIV.

The toolbox was new-looking. A padlock dangled from the catch. Someone was careless, or maybe in a hurry.

I lifted the lid, shone the phone on neat rows of fifties and hundreds bound with elastic. It was a deep toolbox. My guess, over a hundred-thousand dollars' worth.

I touched nothing, closed the lid and moved on.

Another plastic container held more paperwork. Correspondence. More documents. They would be worth proper inspection. I looked for something to hold all the paperwork, and found a large manila envelope. It had weight, something bulky inside. I held the phone up higher and tipped out the contents. Five Australian passports. I opened one and checked the photo. A serious boy, staring. Razz, Cory's friend from the car park. I opened another: the girl I'd seen with Cory, outside Brophy's studio. I put all the passports back in the envelope, thrust in the other documents, and threw it up through the hatch on the floor.

Best be on my way.

Maybe one more container. Or maybe the crate. The lid had been removed. I held my phone up. It was full of white spongy packing beads. I shifted them around, saw a grapefruit-sized olive-green casing, pin still attached.

Another car, right outside. A door slammed and I nearly fainted. I moved a container away from an air vent and looked out. A beaten-up old station wagon was parked in the driveway — not the usual bikie transport. A man of about sixty in overalls, and another much younger man, for whom 'Stretch' or 'Beanpole' would be a good nickname, also in overalls, came sauntering up the drive, conversing loudly in a language that sounded Eastern Europe. The younger one was holding a wrench. Run or hide? I climbed out from under the house, wiping the mud off my feet on the drop-sheet. They were at the back door, talking something over. I pulled off the gloves and slipped my feet into my runners, just as a rock came through the glass in the back door. I picked up the manila envelope and covered the hole in the floor with the sheet of lino.

A hand came through the broken window and tried to turn the deadlock. Amateurs.

I went to the back door, shoulders squared, holding the envelope in an officious manner. 'Can I help you?' I asked through the broken window.

'Dad, someone here.'

'Marion Cunningham, Cunningham Real Estate.'

The boy stepped back. The older man stood behind him, his legs planted. 'What's this?' he demanded.

'I should ask you that.'

'This place is abandoned,' said the boy.

'I'm afraid not. The house is the legal property of my client.'

'We take only metal,' his father said.

'I can't allow that. I have instructions from the owners to make an evaluation for the future sale of the property. Including all fittings, fixtures, taps, pipes, and decorations.'

'You don't look like real estate,' the boy said. 'You have a bruise on your face.'

'I'm aware of that. If you leave now, I'll forget about the window.'

The father hooked his thumbs in the bib of his overalls, and spat at his feet. 'This is bullshit.'

'I must ask you to leave or I'm calling the police.'

He said something in his own language, and they walked back the way they'd come. I put the passports in my handbag and waited while they climbed, swearing, into the car and slammed the doors. When they drove away, I kicked off my shoes again and, once more pulling back the lino, jumped down. I opened the boxes and started to stuff files into my bag.

44

I HAD files, passports, correspondence. That should be plenty. I hauled myself out. I replaced the hatch, and lined up the lino. Then I used the drop sheet to wipe my feet a second time, and to clean mud from the floor. I got as far as the window I'd climbed in through, and stopped.

One stiflingly hot afternoon, in my sixth year at Woolburn Primary school, my teacher told me that I had a unique skill: the complete inability to learn from my mistakes. I thought that was harsh, at the time. Too harsh. And yet, I was hesitating, heart pounding, thinking about the cash under the house. Enough for Afshan and Shahid to have a life. Enough for even bloody Kylie and Tyler to play farmers, and breed bloody Dexters.

The last time I had done something so foolish, it had cost me sleep, a paranoia-free existence, and my composure for the better part of a decade. Peace of mind was important, wasn't it? I'd put it all on my mortgage, giving me a semblance of security. Did that balance it out? The crazy with the sensible?

I ran to the bathroom and grabbed the plastic shopping bags from the cabinet. I couldn't hold my phone and grab the cash at the same time, so I propped it up on the crate, and worked in the semi-dark. By the time the toolbox was empty, I'd filled five bags and tied them off.

Sweat dripped and I buzzed with adrenalin. I snatched up the phone and it slipped from my hand. I felt around for it. My palm touched a corner. I picked it up and turned it round, hoping the crack in the screen wasn't worse. It had survived but was caked in mud, and something small was stuck to it, the size of a finger, soft and round. A cigarette butt with a gold band. Hero brand. Cuong's brand.

I put the butt in my pocket and threw the bags out onto the hallway floor.

I couldn't walk out of here with bags of noticeable cash. In one of the bedrooms, I grabbed an empty beer carton. I filled it with the plastic bags of money and folded the cardboard ends down. It was bulky and heavy, but I could manage it. I looked out the window to see if anyone was about. The street was deserted. The front and back door were deadlocked, so I threw the box, and my handbag, out the side window and climbed out. I dusted myself off and walked as casually as I could down the driveway, holding what looked to the world like a slab of VB, and my handbag slung over my shoulder. I closed the gate behind me.

In a neighbouring wheelie bin, I dropped the rubber gloves and the cigarette butt, then walked to Wright Street, heading east, towards home.

When a cab passed, I waved it down and offered the driver one hundred bucks to take me to Ascot Vale and forget I existed.

I stood across the road from Pine View, holding the beer carton, and watched my building for signs of intruders. I decided it was safe and climbed the stairs.

I opened a kitchen cupboard, plastic containers spilled onto the floor. Bags of cash would never fit in there. In my bedroom, strewn with clothes, I stuffed the carton under the bed. I thought for a moment, then I went back, took out half the cash, and stashed it in my freezer.

I poured myself a vodka and took out the manila envelope with the documents and passports. According to the details, Razz was nearly fifteen. And Cory's friend, the girl, her passport photo looked like a glamour shot, hair swept back off her face; she was even wearing a blazer. The other passport photos were of teenagers I didn't recognise. They all had studio hair and corporate attire, as though they were going to a costume party as a young liberal or a stockbroker. But no make-up in the world could disguise their terrible dull-eyed expressions, the kind I'd seen on junkies down on their luck.

I considered the best thing to do with it all. An anonymous tip off? But I couldn't be sure the information would be understood or acted upon. Some of those front-room cops were a bit thick. Anyone higher up was a possible Flower stooge. Clearly, going to the cops was off; we couldn't trust them. Also, it might incriminate Cuong. Also, as of this afternoon, me.

I did something out of character, I rang my mother.

'Sell the farm to Kylie and Tyler. They're good for the money.'

'Eh? What? You say they've got money?'

'They're good for it, yes.'

'All right. Good news. I'll tell that Farquhar to get on his bike.'

I smirked; it grew into laughter. The adrenalin of what I had just done hit. I jumped up and put Amy Whitehouse on my little-used CD player, cranked it way up, and danced around until Brown started bashing on the wall and yelling something about not acting like beasts, reminding me why I hardly ever listened to music at home.

The volume came down and so did I. All the files went back in the envelope, except for the passports of Razz and the others. Those I put in an old envelope. I would show them to Phuong tonight at dinner. I'd like to see her face when I told her what I did. Not everything, not the money part, just busting into their stupid lair and raiding their stash.

The rest of the documents I hid under a cushion on the sofa. After I had a chance to talk with Phuong, I'd give it to some media person who knew their outlaw motorcycle gangs from a hole in the road.

I was feeling pretty good, and went hunting for my DVD of *Blood Diamond* to finally see the ending. I ran an eye over the spines, stopping at *Crouching Tiger, Hidden Dragon*.

Li Mu-bai, warrior monk, a man full of quiet regret, who in the end wanted nothing more than to be a ghost, so he could be by the side of Yu Shu Lien. Was there a more melancholy figure than Li Mu-bai?

Brophy, maybe.

An uncomplicated, undemanding man. A man quietly struggling to live his dream. And what had he asked of me? Patience. Forbearance. A little faith.

Perhaps I'd been negligent in that.

Hell, no, a voice said. Nuh uh. Why help your nemesis? Your worst enemy? You should pour another vodka, go back to bed. I agreed.

But Brophy ...

I checked my phone. There was enough time to see Flicky and be back for dinner at Phuong's. Oh, alright. *Fine*. One last chore to do.

I changed out of the muddy jeans and into a dress — a pink shift — and slipped on a pair of black ballet flats. It was a wildly impractical outfit for my lifestyle, and some scars and plasters were exposed, but I didn't want to rock up to Flicky's looking like a tradie. I wanted to feel feminine this once. One thing ruined the effect: no pockets, there was nowhere to keep a weapon handy. I dropped the knife and the screwdriver in my handbag, with the passports, and ran out into the street to hail a passing cab. 'Williamstown,' I said, getting in the back. We flew to Flicky's, lickety-split.

The front door was chocked open and only a flimsy, tattered fly-screen protected the Sparks family from riffraff like me. Inside, a woman was on the phone, voice of an extrovert, shouty, raucous. It reminded me of my mother; she bellowed down the receiver like someone using a megaphone, like she didn't believe telephones actually worked.

'Of course, last year Cynth wore that chiffon *thing*, remember? And that hat, size of a beach umbrella, taking everyone's eye out. Plastered by two, Henry carried her to the car!'

I made a fist, and used a knuckle to tap the frame.

'Better go, hun. Someone's at the door. See you Tuesday, we'll swing by in the limo. No chicken, please, goes off in the sun. Bring flats — I am. Bye, sweetie. Bye!'

A thin silhouette in chunky heels clomped down the wooden hall. The screen door swung out at me and I took a step back, the better to take in this vision of well-preserved beauty queen. Mrs Sparks smiled. 'Goodness, you've been in the wars, haven't you?'

'I fell. It's nothing. Is Felicity home?'

'Come in, she's in the garden.'

'I'll wait here, if that's okay.'

She looked at me, the smooth face motionless, but the eyes darting. 'Alright then, I'll fetch Flick.'

I *knew* it. Flick. Tricky Flicky. She came bouncing down the hall and stopped dead in her tracks when she clocked me. 'Jesus, Stella. Are you okay?'

'Where's Brophy's money?'

'Excuse me?'

'The money you stole from him, where is it?'

'Is this one of your little jokes?'

'I don't have time for your denials. Just hand over the cash and the photos, too, and I'll be on my way.'

'I'm not falling for it. Peter told me all about your overactive imagination.'

'He ...' My face became warm. Overactive imagination, not a phrase he would use. Her interpretation perhaps. 'What did he say about me, *exactly*?'

'He said you possessed a highly imaginative aesthetic, something like that, I don't remember exactly. Basically, implying you're deluded.'

It sounded like Brophy had said something complimentary. I decided he had. It felt good. 'He told me you stole money from him.'

She looked stricken. 'I did no such thing.'

'Money went missing and you went into hiding. Coincidence?'

'Hiding? I'm right here.'

'Why were you unable to be contacted?'

She scoffed. 'I dropped my phone in the toilet at the Drunken Tweet. It's been sitting in a bucket of rice for two days. It only started working again this morning.'

'But you did steal the money.'

She folded her arms. 'No.'

This was a pointless exercise. 'Give me the money or I call the cops.'

She screwed up her face at me. 'I don't believe that Peter would even *think* I could do such a thing. I'm calling him.'

'Go ahead,' I said. 'I *dare* you.'

A second of indecision, then she pulled out her mobile and hit it once. Brophy was on speed dial. I gritted my teeth. She put the phone on speaker and held it out for me to hear. A child answered. 'Yo!'

'To whom am I speaking?' Felicity said.

'It's Marigold, Brophy's twelve-year-old daughter,' I said. She didn't know anything.

Felicity shrugged. I moved closer to her phone. 'Yo, Marigold, it's me, Stella.'

'S'up, shorty. I ain't seen you since we was gettin jam in the joint.'

The horror on Felicity's face was priceless. I felt I should explain. 'She means since we bought doughnuts from the Olympic Donut van. Which is about a month ago.'

'Is she American?'

'Pfft. *No.* She's young.'

'Hey, Marigold, is Brophy there?'

'Nah, he's taking care of his own, know what I'm sayin'? Hangin' his shit, yo, for Tuesday night.'

'Are you home by yourself?'

'Mos def.'

There were laws against leaving children unsupervised. 'When is Brophy coming back?'

'Didn't say. Been gone for hours. He's all, like, the exhibition, it's the only thing. That's how he be.'

'True that. Stay there, and don't start any fires. I'll come over as soon as I can.'

An unsupervised Marigold was a hazardous state of affairs. My suspicions about who had taken Brophy's money now took a new direction. That meant that, ugh, Felicity may have been innocent. She slid the phone in her back pocket and raised her eyebrows at me.

'That didn't help matters,' I conceded.

'If only Peter had a mobile.'

That thought had crossed my mind many times. 'Felicity, er. I may have ... that is, Peter might have made some assumptions about you.'

'Peter said that?' She looked heartbroken, I felt bad. I'd been pretty horrible to her.

'Don't get upset, here's a tissue.'

She took it from me with a sniff.

'Peter thinks you're a very good artist's model,' I said.

She gazed at me. 'Really?'

'Sure, yeah. I guess.'

'Come inside,' she said. 'I'll make some tea.'

'Thanks, Felicity, but I better go hail a cab and get Marigold.'

'A cab? Where's your car?'

'I had a bingle, it's in the shop until ... forever. That's not important. Thing is, I have to go.'

'Don't do that. I'll drive you.'

45

MRS SPARKS' ride was a white two-door Mercedes, six-speed manual with black interior. I estimated it cost more than I earned in a year. Felicity drove it like someone unused to the idea of forward motion. We jerked and kangaroo-hopped for five hundred metres before I said stop. 'What the hell, Felicity.'

'I can't drive a manual. Don't tell my mum. She thinks I've had lessons.'

'Are you kidding me?'

'Manuals are hard.'

'You wuss.'

She shrugged.

'This is hopeless,' I said. 'Take the car home. I'll get a taxi.'

'No, you drive it. It'll be quicker.'

I'd have to take Felicity home afterwards, which was a drag, but she had a point. We needed to hurry. I couldn't believe he'd leave Marigold alone in his studio. Brophy had been distracted lately, but that was negligent.

I drove the fancy ride like I drove my old Mazda, and like the Mazda, it went like the clappers. Unfortunately, the trip was spent in traffic and the whole sports-car experience was wasted. Maybe on the open road this thing would be fun.

'You took your time,' Marigold greeted me in the Narcissistic Slacker gallery with her hands on her hips. She stepped back. 'Oooh, look at you, all dressed up.'

'Is Brophy still not back?'

'Your face is a mess, girl.'

'I know. Is Brophy here?'

'See for yourself.'

'Answer the question.'

'Chill, yo. You seriously need to chill.'

I found some paper and scribbled a note to him saying I had his child and was taking her home. That, I figured, would get his attention.

'Okay, Marigold,' I said. 'Let's go. Downstairs. Now.'

'Um ...'

'What is it? I'm not in the mood.'

'Don't leave that note.'

'Why?'

'Dad doesn't know I'm here.' She sounded as close to contrite as I'd ever heard her.

Her clear blue eyes blinked at me. She was hiding something. 'Tell me.'

'I broke in. You can get in from the car park at the back, there's an old ladder that goes to the roof, then I climb down the hole and I'm in. It's easy.'

'Sounds like you've been breaking into your dad's studio a lot.'

'I get bored at home. Mum's boyfriend's a flog. She's all lovey-dovey, but I can't stand him. You should see the way he chews his food, the noises, ugh.'

'Where does your mother think you are?'

'At a friend's. When Dad comes back, I sneak out through the roof and go down the ladder. Don't tell. Please.'

'We'll talk about this later. For now, you better come with me.'

'Can't I just stay here?'

'No, now move.'

She didn't like this turn of events, and petulantly stomped her brand-new Doc Martens on each step. I knew nothing of parenting, but I imagined the way to deal with this child was to say no to everything, take away all electronic devices, and feed her on gruel for a week.

When she saw Felicity's mother's car, Marigold whistled. 'Sweet ride.'

Felicity pulled a lever, and the front seat shot forward.

'Nuh uh!' Marigold said and folded her arms. 'I call shotgun.'

'Get in the back or so help me I'll give you the first proper hiding you've ever had.'

'A proper what?'

'Get the fuck in!'

'Whoa, Stella, seriously. You need to chill.' She-who-must-have-the-last-word crawled into the backseat and put on her seatbelt, and, thankfully, shut up.

I checked the time. If I took Marigold to her mother's, there'd be enough time to drop Felicity home and take a taxi to Phuong's.

I headed for Marigold's mother's place, and on the way gave her a lecture about not talking things that didn't belong to her. Of course, I felt like an A-grade hypocrite for haranguing Marigold. I knew something about taking things that didn't belong to me. Thousands of gangster dollars to be precise. Not to mention that today was not the first time I'd done something like that. I was pleased to discover that it was considerably less harrowing the second time around.

46

I PULLED in at Marigold's mother's house. The Mercedes's tyres clipped the gutter, and we rolled up and off the nature strip.

'Way to park,' Marigold said.

'Quiet, you.'

'There is no cool way to mount the kerb, know what I'm sayin'?'

'We say "gutter" in this country.'

'I think kerb is also acceptable,' said Felicity.

'Oh, for the love of —'

'Off you go, Marigold,' Felicity was saying.

The child was stubborn. 'I hate it here.'

'If you need a break, you can come and visit me. We can make *kaddu bharta*.'

'What's that?'

'Mashed pumpkin.'

She groaned and slid out of the car like she was heading to the gallows.

And once more I was heading to Williamstown. The Mercedes purred into the Sparks's garage. 'Come in,' she said.

'Things to do.'

She seemed disappointed.

'But I'll see you around,' I mumbled.

'I knew we'd get along.' She beamed with affection that seemed almost childish. It made me uneasy, and I got out of there before the moment became even creepier.

I took a taxi to Phuong's place in Kensington. She let me into her apartment and offered me tea, telling me how she bought it specially for me, and about its health-giving properties.

'How kind,' I said. 'And I brought something for you.' I waved the envelope under her nose. 'But I reckon you need gloves.'

'What the —'

'Gloves, Phuong. You have to come out of this looking clean, like a surgical instrument. Like a comb in that purple liquid hairdressers use.'

'What liquid?'

'It doesn't matter, you just need to remain above reproach, okay?'

She took a packet of disposables from a drawer. 'What have you done?'

I tipped out the passports on her kitchen counter. She picked one up.

'Where'd you get these?'

'Ricky Peck's place, the one with the hydroponic set-up. There's a stash of documents and accounts. Crates of weapons.'

'You broke in.'

'I learned from the best.'

She went to the kitchen and heaped some dumplings on a plate. 'Someone saw you.'

'No.'

'No one watching the house?'

'Not while I was there.'

'I shouldn't have involved you. It was a mistake from the beginning. Someone will have seen you. You were probably followed back here.'

'No. No one followed me.'

'The Raw-Prawn people will find out. OTIOSE at Crown looking for Cuong. They'll put this together. I'll be sacked.'

She thrust the plate at me and a pair of chopsticks.

'Phuong, when you get stressed you turn into a drama queen. Have you noticed that? From Zen master to nuclear-powered pessimist in five seconds.'

'It's easy for you to make fun, you don't have a career.'

Ouch. That was uncalled for. I put it down to the pressure she was under. Besides, I was feeling tolerant and generous. The score at the house left me euphoric. I ate a few bites. 'I didn't get caught.'

She snorted, smothered a dumpling in Sriracha sauce.

After a moment I said, 'These are fraudulent passports, supplied by the woman we saw at Crown. Marcus Pugh said she was being blackmailed.'

'The Corpse Flowers blackmailed the woman, demanded she supply passports?'

'Yes, and like you told me yourself, they're all for teenagers. Those bikies do what they like. They sent the Guns and Gangs unit into disarray, then they pretended to disband. Then they quietly carry on trafficking unsuspecting kids to Burma.'

'Trafficking?' She chewed another dumpling, shook her head. 'This whole thing has been a travesty. Expecting Mortimer to clear Bruce's name is like asking Satan to babysit.'

'Not necessarily. I mean, I can't speak for Bruce. But it is possible Mortimer was working *against* the Flowers from the inside?'

She thought for a moment. 'Why would Mortimer do that?'

'He was the distributor for the youth demographic, remember?'

'That was just Peck trying to sound like a CEO.'

'Yes. But still. Mortimer *was* selling to teenagers. Maybe he formed a friendship with some of them. It could happen. What if he didn't like what Peck and Gorman were planning to do with them?'

Phuong held the bridge of her nose. She looked exhausted. 'What about Cuong?'

'I think Cuong was in on it. He and Mortimer couldn't go to the cops. So they undermined the Corpse Flowers's activities from the inside. We know it was a whistle-blower who blew up the passport scam. That might have been Cuong. Which would explain why the OTIOSE officers didn't detain him at Crown. She'd come to meet him, and brought evidence with her.'

'If that's true, Cuong should have come to me,' Phuong said.

'The Flowers have cops in their pockets. Even Blyton, who you vouched for. If Cuong came to you, word would've reached Blyton, then Gorman and you'd both be dead.'

Phuong was quiet. We ate in silence. Then she said, 'I'm going to the temple where Cuong is staying tomorrow. This time I'm going to get *everything* out of him.'

Later, she drove me home, and kept her own counsel. She was taking a huge risk protecting Cuong, and I guessed she was ruminating on the idea of unemployment — if she was ever found out.

Me, I was thinking about Brophy. And the cash getting cool in my flat.

47

I RACED up the stairs and put the TV on. The ABC announcer was telling viewers that Bunny Slipper's three-part series was coming up.

There was Bunny, speaking direct-to-camera: 'Before his death, enforcer Ricky Peck, and known thug, Luigi 'the Turk' Tacchini, had joined a criminal network stretching from Australia to Thailand and all the way around. South East Asia was their playground. Ice was in, and heroin was coming back with a vengeance. They dealt not only drugs but firearms and military-grade explosives.' Bunny walked towards the viewer, hands touching lightly in front of her. The background was the Australian Federal Police building in La Trobe Street, Melbourne.

'The Corpse Flowers are following those motorcycle gangs who have already expanded into Malaysia and have improved supply chains, after setting up in Cambodia and Laos.' Cut to vision of big tattooed Australian men being arrested by Thai police in neat, perfectly ironed uniforms. Ring-a-ding sixties druggy music played. Shot of a Thai girl dancing in a skimpy outfit.

'The obligatory bikini shot,' I said out loud and sighed. Bunny lost points there.

'Europol believes motorcycle gangs are expanding their empires, into other black-market enterprises, including the trafficking of human beings,' Bunny continued. 'In the meantime, the stage is set for Australia to be awash in drugs.'

When the credits rolled, I called the ABC newsroom. 'Bunny Slipper, please.'

'Putting you through to her voicemail.'

At the tone, I left my details and hinted I had valuable Corpse Flower information. I wasn't going to the police, and I would never endanger Cuong. But Slipper was an expert on the activities of

Australian bikie gangs in Asia. If I gave her a few juicy details, she might reciprocate with some background on Kengtung, maybe have a theory for the Flowers's scheme.

A moment later, an call came from an unknown number. I picked up. 'Hello?'

'This is Bunny Slipper. Am I speaking with Stella Hardy?'

Score! 'Yes. Thanks for calling back. I have some extremely sensitive information you will be interested in.'

'About?'

'About the Corpse Flowers, and Victoria Police. Can we meet?'

'I need to know the nature of the information before I set up a meeting.'

'I doubt this line is secure. You're going to have to trust me.'

Long pause, breathing at Slipper's end. I held my breath.

'Do you know the Drunken Tweet?'

I pumped my fist, and said I did.

'If you can meet me there in half an hour ...'

I replied, 'Oh, indeed.'

As I dropped my phone in my handbag, the Carpenters sang again. It was Raewyn Ross. 'Hi, Rae.'

'Senior Constable Ross, actually.'

'Right. Sorry.'

'Those two *suspects* you were enquiring about. I have a positive ID.'

'Excellent work.'

'All in the cause of love. Young one is Conti, Joe and the older bloke is Healey, Dan. Both stationed at St Albans.'

'Bless you, Rae.'

I splashed some water on my face, brushed my hair, and ran downstairs to hail a cab to Seddon.

'Two Mad Fucking Witches.'

The bearded youth who had drummed his fingers on our table

while we studied the cocktail menu, pronounced our order 'too easy' and whirled away to the bar.

'So, you're Stella Hardy.' Bunny studied me.

And I studied her. She was a confident woman, with a rare form of self-possession. Not to be confused with bravado, which was everywhere, but genuine uncommon self-assurance. She, I imagined, would never look down at her breasts laced with blue veins and sigh, or frown at rolls and spots and flab. She would never rue the ancestors who bequeathed her the wide face peppered with freckles, or praise the ones who gave her the penetrating grey eyes. She embraced it all and offered it freely to the world with — I now pictured her naked — hands on hips, saying to some adoring hopeful, 'You will never own me.' Every line on her face was a proud souvenir of a war zone, or a long journey to a secret location, or Persian Gulf uprising.

'Thanks for seeing me,' I said. 'I understand your time is valuable.'

'I'm flying to Laos next week for another series. But if your information is useful, then it's fine.' She tapped a spiral-bound notebook with a biro. 'Also, I'm kind of addicted to the witch juices here.' Dazzling smile.

I was about to play my useful-information card when Bunny pointed at my face.

'Colourful bruise.'

'Bikie punched me in the face.'

'I don't get it. You're not a cop, you said. How did a social worker get involved with the likes of Ox Gorman, number one Corpse Flower?'

I held her gaze. 'Long story.'

The waiter danced over with two tall glasses of blue magic and a bowl of caramelised popcorn, winked at Bunny, and scootered away. I removed the straw and drank most of it in one go.

Bunny frowned and leaned back in her chair. 'Come on. How are you involved?'

237

'Cops. I personally know two cops under investigation by the task force. One has ties to the Flowers. The other is mostly, probably, a bit innocent-ish.'

She sipped her witch juice. 'Who is the one with ties?'

I lowered my voice. 'Detective William Blyton. He and the late Jeff Vanderhoek, the junkie who died at the Turk's place on Saturday night, were lovers. Vanderhoek was sent by the top Corpse Flower, Ox Gorman, to act as an informant for the police, while in reality feeding information back to the Flowers. But Blyton got involved with Vanderhoek — they were both addicts, and Vanderhoek set up a dealer with a large stash to be arrested, so that Blyton could steal the drugs from the police evidence safe. They had plans to —'

'Slow down.'

I threw a couple of popcorn pieces in my mouth. Phuong refused to use this information, out of a desire to protect Copeland from implicit suspicion. I had no such desire.

Bunny continued scribbling, then looked up. 'I didn't say *stop*.'

'That will do for now.'

'You've got more?'

I nodded. I'd happily give her everything I had, starting from the night Bruce Copeland announced that Ricky Peck had drowned. Even the irrelevant bits, like Felicity. But not now. 'First, I need something from you.'

She smiled, like a viper. 'What do you want and what do you want it for?'

'I'll get to the point. A group of homeless kids in Footscray have been targeted by the Corpse Flowers. They've been offered rewards of money and some vague mention of a job to do in South East Asia. They name a town in Burma. What are these gangs up to in fucking Burma?'

'Burma, Laos, Cambodia,' she shrugged. 'The gangs are all over.'

'They were told specifically Kengtung.'

'That's wild Burma. Shan province. Lawless. Kengtung is a sleazy frontier town that is supported by China, but really, it's under complete

Chinese control because all the Burmese officials there are corrupt.'

'Drugs?'

A group of boisterous young women came in. In a sudden panic, I scanned them, fearing Felicity might be among them.

Bunny's eyes moved from me, to the group, to the door.

I took a deep breath, acted relaxed. 'I mean, drugs would be the obvious reason.'

'Yes. That part of the world is all about opium. But not just opium. More than half the young people use *yaba*, basically cheap ice with caffeine mixed in. I don't blame them. Their prospects are shit — either a form of slave labour on Thai prawn trawlers or prostitution. When I was doing research for the series, I hung out with some Australians working for an NGO over there, and even they were jacked. Pretty fucked up stuff is going on there.'

'Not just drugs then.'

She jabbed her witch juice with the straw. 'More than westerners hear about. There's huge resistance to western interference. The rebel groups despise the blue-eyed NGO-types. They just want to get on with business — drug trafficking, human trafficking, smuggling of animal products, tiger, monkey. Even illegal logging. The Chinese market is insatiable.'

I mused on that. Bunny was still, quiet, eyes down. At the next table, the women erupted into laughter. Meanwhile, the two of us were miserable. What horrors went on in the world while we sat here drinking in near absolute safety.

Bunny took a last sip of juice and wiped the blue from her lips. 'You're a fraud, Stella Hardy.'

I gasped.

'You got better intel out of me than I got with your corrupt-cop spiel.'

'The Corpse Flowers are also importing weapons. I personally saw a crate full of grenades. Think it's easy to get a crate of grenades into this country?'

She shrugged, unimpressed. 'I only have your word for it.'

'It's under a Corpse Flower house in Sunshine. There's enough storage room under the floor for crates, files. All the evidence the police need is under that house.'

She tilted her head to the side. 'The dope house where Ricky Peck died?'

'Not telling,' I said, mysteriously. 'But there's material on Kengtung there and about how Gorman and Peck were planning to send crews of homeless kids to South East Asia.'

I lifted my bag, pulled out the manila envelope, and slid it across the table. 'Fakes, procured by the woman recently arrested in Crown and under investigation by OTIOSE. Other documents here are in Chinese, some translated. I've only skimmed the things in English, which are mostly shipping statements, inventory. Some letters are addressed to *Mr Richard Peck*.'

She sat up, glanced around.

I went on. 'I have a contact inside the Corpse Flowers who is supposed to travel to Kengtung via Vietnam. He doesn't want to go through with it, but can't go to the police for fear of Gorman.'

She regarded me afresh, more attentive now. 'Gorman doesn't suspect him?'

'I don't know what they know.'

Bright-eyed Bunny, eyebrows raised. 'Is he your lover? Is that how you're involved? Did he give you that?'

I touched the bruise on my face. 'No.'

She shook her head. 'You seem like a rational, regular person. Yet you know all the Corpse Flower secrets. How did you get involved with this business?'

'I was helping a friend. But then something happened to a kid named Cory, and it keeps me awake at night.'

She lifted her pen. 'Cory who?'

'Fontaine. A teenager, sweet kid, charismatic, clever. The type likely to become school captain except he was one of those unlucky ones who spent his childhood in foster care, and his adolescence on the streets. Later, I saw his dead body sprawled on Ballarat Road. He'd been pushed into the path of a truck.'

She made a note in her book. She glanced up at me, pulled a bunch of tissues from her bag and shoved them in my hand.

'He was murdered because he didn't want to go to Kengtung,' I said, dabbing my eyes. 'Corpse Flowers are using homeless kids as drug mules.'

Bunny's nose flared; she'd picked a scent. Her eyes moved to the envelope.

I blew my nose. 'Cory told me, there was nothing I could do. I happen to think otherwise.'

'Me too.' She picked up the envelope. 'This contact of yours, the one about to leave for Burma, would he be willing to speak to me?'

'I'll ask.'

'My direct number is on the back.' She slid her business card across the table and left.

She was right, I thought, as I finished my drink, I should be dead. How the hell did things get so messed up?

Fuzzy-face the disco waiter picked up my empty glass, waved it at me. I nodded.

Phuong — no, Copeland — he wanted Mortimer found with no cops involved. I doubted it was for him to testify on Copeland's behalf. More likely, it was a stitch-up job. The Corpse Flowers wanted Mortimer dead for trying to sabotage the kids-to-Asia scheme. And the Flowers had certain cops in their pockets. Maybe they asked Copeland to find Mortimer so they could get rid of him.

If so, I almost helped Copeland do that. I shuddered and put my head in my hands, and remembered poor Jeff Vanderhoek. Tortured and murdered by the Turk for Josie, because she thought he had informed on her in Thailand. But who'd told Josie it was Jeff? Blyton thought it must have been Mortimer.

Cuong didn't believe it was Mortimer. And I believed Cuong.

I looked up and saw another Mad Fucking Witch juice waiting for me. If the government got wind of these drinks they'd be made illegal. I took a long drink and wondered if Jeff Vanderhoek really had ratted out Josie Enright. There must have been others who knew about the Thailand case, and that Jeff had been involved. Like maybe a cop, a cop who had informants. Blyton and Copeland worked together. Copeland knew Blyton was involved with Jeff. Could Copeland have told the Flowers that Jeff was the informant? From his relationship with Blyton, Jeff knew a lot about Copeland. It would be opportune for him to have Jeff out of the way.

Copeland, I was sure, was corrupt. But how to broach that with Phuong? I couldn't tell her anything. In the first place, she would accuse me of sour-graping her marriage, and hate me for it. And secondly, it would get back to Copeland.

In any case, she had her hands full keeping her cousin out of jail. Cuong was a tragic gambling addict, but an otherwise decent man, until the Corpse Flowers got their claws in him. Next thing, he was on his way to becoming an international drug trafficker, obliged to collect millions of dollars' worth of drugs from Burma.

And they did the same to the woman who counterfeited the passports. They were capable of bending all kinds of people to their will: junkies and vulnerable kids, sure, but also cops, a terrified mechanic, and a defenceless public servant.

I finished my second Mad Fucking Witch juice. They went down easily, and hit like a concrete truck. I was tempted to order another. If only I had taken tomorrow off like half the population of the city. I paid for the drinks and contributed to the taxi economy once more.

48

A FULL eight hours sleep and I was a new woman. In fact, I was early, so I dropped my phone off at a screen-repair shop in the plaza near work. Then I got straight down to WORMS business, firing off emails, making appointments, and reading *The Age* online. Boss snuck up behind me and stared at my computer screen. 'What are you doing?'

'Reading internet comments,' I answered, though it was unnecessary as he was reading them over my shoulder.

'What are you, some kind of masochist?'

I clicked the 'X' button and swivelled my chair around. 'What's up, Boss?'

'My God, Stella. What happened to your face?'

'Roughed up by a couple of bikies.'

'Everything's a joke to you, isn't it?' He pulled an empty chair over. This was a bad sign. I was hoping for a quick set of instructions for the day and to be left alone.

'I've resigned. Leaving at the end of the week.'

A part of me didn't believe he would really go. 'Does that make you feel better?'

'No.'

I was worried about him, hide-the-sharp-objects worried. 'I'm sorry.'

'I can't *give* you the job, Hardy. Procedures must be followed, hoops must be jumped through. But I can help you apply.' He hesitated. 'If you want it.'

I felt I *should* want it. I wanted to want it. It was complicated. If I was the boss, I'd have to work a lot harder. If I didn't go for it, maybe I'd regret it.

He touched my shoulder. 'I think you could do it.'

He was right, I could do it. That was not the issue.

The phone rang, and he rose wearily.

'Want me to take it?'

'Please. Whoever it is, I'm not here.'

Waving him off, I picked up the receiver, pressed a button, and said all the words.

'Stella Hardy? Jim from Talbot's Body Works. Your Mazda is ready.'

'What's the damage?'

'No damage now, love.'

'I mean —'

'Six hundred.'

'Sounds reasonable.'

'You gotta collect it now, we're closing up for the Cup.'

'Wednesday will be fine.' After this business has blown over.

'Um, I'll be ... on holidays. Closing the shop for a year.'

That sounded suss to me. Gorman probably put the mechanic up to it. He suspected I was still alive, and now he knew it for sure. If I went anywhere near Talbots, Buster would pounce. A car was no reason to risk death.

'It's not even my car. Belongs to my brother, and he's away for a while, so you can hang onto it for a whole year for all I care.' I hung up, thinking I'd rather lie back and feel the cold metal shock of a spring-loaded speculum than go anywhere near those thugs.

The phone on my desk rang again. This was getting ridiculous.

'Stella? Mum says I'm allowed to come over to your place. I asked because you said we can make that pumpkin mash one day. So she said I can come over and make it with you.'

'That's awesome, Marigold. Where are you?'

'Home. We got the day off.'

'How did you know where I work?'

'Googled you.'

A photo of me, with my name and occupation, was on the WORMS website. What an appalling lack of privacy.

'I'm a bit busy right now. I'll talk to you soon, okay?'

'Hey shorty, you don't sound fully rad.'

A responsible adult would remind her that how rad I was, was not her concern and to go and play with her friends. But when was I ever a responsible adult? She was a good listener, and there was no one around that I could discuss the situation with. 'Do you think art is futile?'

'No. It's a bludge from maths, and kids go crazy and we make a big mess.'

'Good answer. Do you think I should be the manager at my work?'

'Sure, you're bossy enough. But you'll need to be all serious and boring and probably get so busy that me and Dad wouldn't get to see you much. We'd miss you.'

'Another excellent answer. Okay, last one. There are some bad people in the world, people are dangerous. They even hurt people. And it is possible they will try to —'

'You got to muscle up, ya feel me?'

'You mean weapons?'

'Oh, indeed. And your posse.'

'Thanks. Um. Great advice.'

'So can we hang out? Do some cooking together?'

'Sure. When things settle down.'

'Thanks, shorty. Gotta bounce, yo.'

Muscle up. I wished. I finished updating a case file. The morning was quiet in the WORMS office, with not a single new client showing up. Or any existing ones, for that matter. I spent the morning putting together a work-skills training course; liaising with a local adult learning centre, covering CV writing, interview skills including role play, what to wear, what's expected; and highlighting job ads suitable for unskilled, recently-arrived residents.

And my skills? Bossy, erratic, moody, loyal. Did any of that add up to management material?

In need of fresh coffee, I plunged a French press in the staff room, sat alone, eschewed the crossword and the quiz, preferring to contemplate career suicide — staying put.

Senior Constable Raewyn Ross bounced in, aglow. Sexrisx or UzeHer must have come through.

'Coffee?'

'Not this time, I just came in to deliver some hot gossip. A bloke from the station here knows that cop from St Albans, Joe Conti. He reckons they're having a Cup Day barbeque at his place, all the local cops are going. I asked whereabouts that would be, in a super casual way. And he goes, Caroline Springs. Just like that, he blurted out the address.' She sang the word *address*, like Oprah.

'You sure this is ... appropriate?'

'Hell no! But the path of true love has to break a few rules,' she said, and started to write it down. 'You can totally just rock up.'

'Not me — my friend.'

'Sure, sure.' Rae winked. 'Your *friend*.'

'I have a boyfriend.'

She hadn't heard, or chose to ignore me. In any case, she placed an ingratiating hand on my arm. 'Get back in the saddle, Hardy.' And away she bounced.

I walked to Racecourse Road to pick up my phone, with its shiny new screen, and some lunch. On my way to my desk I was surprised to see a client in the waiting room. No, not a client. Flicky Sparks. 'What the?'

'I googled you.'

Boss had to take that webpage down. Immediately. 'To what do I owe the pleasure?'

'I'm going to drive you home.'

Felicity's timing was not fully rad. 'That's grand, except for two things. First, I'm not going home after work — I'm going to a temple in Braybrook.'

'No worries. I've been practising in the manual.' She steered an invisible wheel. 'Come on, you don't have a car, let me drive you around for practice.'

'And, two, I don't finish work for three hours.'

'Happy to hang around.'

It was a trap, no doubt. A voodoo thing. Next, she'd cut a piece of finger nail, take a stray hair from my shoulder, mix it with that cashmere-wood crap and *poof*! I'd be a slug.

'For three hours?'

'Yes.'

A definite trap.

Or was it? 'If you're going to stay, I have some work for you to do ...'

I set Felicity up at Shanninder's desk, and logged in on the computer. 'Since you're so good at Google, let's see you search for 'Kengtung' and 'methamphetamine' and maybe throw in 'trafficking' and, what the hell, 'outlaw motorcycle gangs', and report back to me.'

She acquiesced readily. Sat, adjusted the chair height, lightly placed her fingers on the keyboard. 'Is this a social-worker thing?'

'Yes.'

'For your work?'

'Not exactly.'

'A hobby?'

She was worse than Brown Cardigan's dog. If I didn't throw her a bone, she'd never shut up. I gave her a very truncated version of events. The story of Phuong needing to find a drug courier, and how I went to his house and didn't come home until next day, with burns, bruises, and a possible case of post-traumatic stress syndrome triggered by any Human League song. I left out names, but I gave her threads, leading up to passports for homeless children and an unofficial tour of Burma. This sent her walking around the room repeating 'Oh my God!' until I told her to stop.

She finally got to work, tapping and clicking and cutting and pasting. Meanwhile, I wrote a memo to Boss. I'd got to *unfortunately* ... when she stood at my side and coughed.

'How did you do?'

'The numbers were horrifying. Militias, gangs, and rebel groups, all involved. Millions of pills. Most of it goes to China.'

'China? Really?'

I followed her to the computer she was working on.

'This website has loads of data. It's by an organisation that monitors international drug trafficking. Drugs not sent to China go anywhere. Laos. Cambodia.'

Bunny was all over that. 'So much for the war on drugs,' I said.

'Plus, Kengtung has a roaring trade in local girls, mainly, sold into prostitution and sex slavery. They're snatched off the street or — get this — sometimes a man comes to their village with lies about good jobs in Thailand.'

I lowered my voice. 'Is there a demand for Australian teenagers, can you see?'

'I don't see that. But girls of any kind are targets for the sex trade, aren't they?'

'There's lots of poor, vulnerable humans in that part of the world,' I said.

'Wow, here's a story about destitute people selling their kids, or their organs.'

I read over her shoulder and there were story of bodies dumped, missing kidneys, heart, liver. A community serving as a human butcher shop.

'Is organ harvesting really a thing?'

I thought of Cory. He had hepatitis C — was that a deal breaker?

She sighed. 'It's business. If you have enough money, you can buy anything. Wealthy westerners on waiting lists get desperate and go to

China. They're notorious for using prisoners on death row. Outside of state-sanctioned arrangements, the black market for organs is huge it looks like.'

A rich person needs a kidney, do they want any old kidney, or a healthy one from a young body? Was that the Corpse Flowers's plan? The kids Raewyn Ross spoke to were worried that Ricky Peck was a paedophile. But why send kids from Australia for prostitution?

'What are you going to do now?' Felicity asked. 'Are you going to tell Brophy?'

I glanced up, distracted. 'Tell him what?'

'That I've helped you.'

'Yes. Sure. And you've been generous to me, too, under the circumstances.'

She did her cat blink. 'Have you seen him?' She asked in a way that made me uneasy.

'No, have you?'

'No.' She left the room, presumably to perform a nude Wicca ritual in the staff room or something.

I went back to my desk and saw an email from an agency alarmed by Marcus Pugh's HARM plan for homeless people. They'd gone over it, and it was nothing more than forced relocation. Hardly a solution. I couldn't concentrate on this policy stuff. I needed to talk to Cuong.

Boss had yet to emerge from the bunker in his office. To go now was, strictly speaking, earlier than the proper knock-off time. But Cuong knew more about what the Corpse Flowers had planned in Kengtung than he was letting on.

'Get your stuff,' I called out to Felicity. 'We're going to the temple.'

She jangled keys and said she'd meet me outside. I finished my letter for Boss and hummed a Kenny Rogers song about playing a game of cards while I printed it out. I signed it and left it in his pigeon hole. As I left WORMS, I felt a load lift from my shoulders.

'Stell-a!' Felicity yelled from the Mercedes. I made a sign of the cross and climbed in.

49

BEFORE LONG I was being kangaroo-hopped in the convertible Mercedes down Churchill Avenue, in central Braybrook. Wealthy middle-class Melbourne regarded this part of town as a socio-economic blemish on its otherwise flawless complexion, where manufacturing gasped its final breath, community workers outnumbered the residents, and hoons in muscle cars were followed by the police chopper. It was decided, by captains-of-finance types gathered in gentlemen's clubs, that it was better for the country (i.e. them) to lower the minimum wage, because people here in Braybrook weren't living close enough to the edge. Payday loans weren't offered in Toorak, nor were there pawnshops, with shop windows full of wedding rings.

I'd been here often over the years, and I liked its mess of contradictions: one part public-housing ghetto, one part aspirational immigrants, one part greenie first-home buyers. This was where Phuong's family had lived when they first arrived in Australia. It was her hood, her primary school was in the next block. Hard to find a more different childhood to mine. The security and predictability of my home life, with homogeneous white faces of the small Mallee town of Woolburn, against the hectic, vandalised volatility of Braybrook. Most public structures — phone boxes, bus shelters, kids' playground equipment — had at one time or other been set on fire.

Before they moved from the area, Phuong's family had frequented a local Buddhist temple. It was a converted house, formerly RAAF accommodation for the family of a worker at the nearby depot, later sold as a first-home-buyer opportunity, and finally bought by the local Vietnamese Buddhist congregation. It was a modest place compared to its famous rival, the Chua Quang Minh — a vast compound of temples, shrines, and housing for the monks, less than a kilometre away. The Dalai Lama had stayed there once.

'Turn here,' I said.

Felicity hit the indicator, lurched around the corner, and we had arrived.

The place looked much the same as I remembered it from visits with Phuong when we were students, back when we were both single and she still lived with her parents. It was a more fun, more simple time when all we had to worry about was having beer money. We could remain friends, despite any changes in marital status, if she didn't move too far away. Copeland would drag her away to the outer limits, some country residence in the hills that took two hours to get to. I shook off that line of thought and went to check out the temple. There'd been some improvements since I was here last. The community had installed a special roof with up-curved corners. And new decorative concrete lotus flowers adorned the brick fence. But the statue in the front yard, surrounded by pots of marigolds, was the same.

Phuong had been waiting in the temple doorway, and was waving us over.

'Inside and behave yourself,' I said.

'I just got here myself,' Phuong said, and directed Felicity to a rear garden.

Once Felicity had gone, she looked both ways down the street. Then she leaned in. 'Were you followed?'

'I don't think so, but Gorman knows I'm alive. One of his people rang me at work.'

'Shit. You can't go home.'

I'd worry about that later. 'Is Cuong here?'

'Yes,' she said. 'The monks said he could stay for a while.'

I nodded and we went inside.

Wooden shutters kept the interior cool and dark. Some walls had been knocked down, save load-bearing posts, opening the space up. Less was more — it was uncluttered and swept clean. The altar was elaborate, with many tiers and lights. At the other end of the temple, a large Buddha reclined, and all around him were offerings of flowers, groceries, and copious burning incense sticks.

'What about the Raw-Prawn investigators?' I said. 'They might be following you, too.'

'I often come here. It's not out of the ordinary.'

I could see why. Years of quiet contemplation seemed to have been absorbed into the structure. Calm came up from the floor boards, spread out from the walls.

Phuong linked an arm through mine and walked me out into the rear garden. Pathways meandered around shady trees and bonsai plants in earthenware pots. Felicity had wandered off to look at a life-sized Kwan Yin statue. A monk in blue robes and matching beanie gathered empty cups and ashtrays and stacked them on a tray.

'Hey,' I said to Cuong. He was reclining on a concrete bench under an old loquat. He was clean-shaven, wearing a fresh t-shirt.

I brushed back a stray hair.

'Stella found Ricky Peck's hiding spot,' Phuong said. 'We have the passports, the kids' files. Cards on the table, Cuong.'

He avoided my gaze. 'Peck asked me to look over his business plan. Hundreds of data sets, costs, travel, food, accommodation for the kids. I told him it couldn't be done. But they went on, obtained the passports. So I made a call to OTIOSE, named the woman. But I didn't mention the Corpse Flowers. And they agreed my identity had to be protected.'

Phuong was shaking her head in wonder. 'You couldn't tell OTIOSE everything the Corpse Flowers were planning? Right there and then?'

'Too risky. Mortimer, he hated their stupid scheme, too, and he told the kids to keep their distance. But Enright found out what he said …'

'So you hid him.'

A recording of chanted prayers started. Cuong took a drag on his cigarette. 'I let him use the empty flat next to mine.'

'And when Blyton went there?'

'Mortimer was hiding. I showed him the drug stash Mortimer had, for insurance, for income. I gave it all to Blyton and he left.'

We heard a crash and looked around. The monk had dropped the tray of cups. He was muttering to himself as he bent down to pick up the pieces.

'You gave heroin to Blyton?' Phuong said.

Cuong shrugged. 'Had to. To get him to leave me alone.'

'Is Mortimer still there, in the flat?' she demanded.

'No. He's gone. I don't know where?'

Phuong reached out and for a moment I thought she was going to do something drastic, like flip the table. Instead she took Cuong's cigarette and butted it out.

I looked from Cuong to Phuong. 'Who do we take this to? The federal police? Border force?'

'Yes,' Phuong said, then she frowned. 'No. It's too dangerous. Cuong's not safe until Gorman and the rest are in custody.'

'Bunny Slipper,' I said.

They exchanged glances.

'Don't tell me you've never heard of Bunny Slipper? The journalist? She's the one you want to speak to. In fact, I've already made contact with her. She can come here.'

Cuong hesitated.

Phuong looked dubious.

'Yes,' said Cuong. 'I'll talk to her.'

I rang Bunny's number and got her voicemail.

'When Bunny calls back I'll tell her you'll do the interview here.'

'Don't leave the temple,' Phuong said to Cuong. 'Don't ring anyone, don't go anywhere.'

I caught Felicity's eye, and waved her over.

Phuong walked us out, and leaned into the Mercedes. 'Sure you won't come and stay at my place?'

I gave her hand a squeeze. 'Don't worry.'

50

FELICITY REVERSED the Mercedes, skirted boot-first around a roundabout. And turned the wrong way into a side street. 'Where to now? Drop you at your place?'

'No,' I said. 'Hastings, Western Port Bay.'

Without a word of query or the slightest hesitation, she hit the accelerator, revved the German engineering. She put it into gear. 'So Monash Freeway?'

I entered what information I had into my phone. The name of Copeland senior came up as the owner of a boat-hire place in Somerville.

After an hour, as dusk turned to night and the street lights blinked on, we entered the marina. A faded sign told us we were in the home of 'gummy shark and whiting fishing'.

A few floodlights swamped the dark in places, and left it alone in others. A café and a restaurant were still serving customers. Copeland Boat Hire was in shadow, but a light within told me Copeland senior had not gone home for the night.

I told Felicity to wait for me at the café. 'Order me some chips. I won't be long.' Then I walked the length of the marina. 'Shack' was not an inaccurate descriptor, and the shabby, sun-bleached timber door hinted that the boat-hire business was not overly fruitful. I knocked.

Coughing. Then a whiskey-and-cigarettes voice growled. 'We're closed.'

'It's about Bruce.'

The lock turned, the door cracked on a chain, and the end of two barrels were shoved at my face. 'He's not here.'

'Phuong sends her regards.'

'Who?'

'Stand down, Dad,' Copeland junior said behind him. 'She has clearance.'

The shotgun withdrew. The door was closed, the chain removed, and I was admitted into the odour of blood and guts and bait. Senior was a slovenly mess, with white hair sprouting from his chin down his neck. His bald skull was laced with blue veins, and antagonism burned in his raw eyes.

'You're about to get married and you haven't told your father her name or anything about her. Where did Phuong stay exactly?'

'What is she talking about?' his father asked. 'What's a *foong*?'

'Let's have another drink,' Copeland said loudly. When his father went to retrieve the bottle, Copeland hissed at me, 'Phuong and I stayed in a motel. It's not what you think. He has dementia. Thinks everyone is a threat.'

'Then he is absolutely the right person to be holding a shotgun.'

'It's not loaded,' Copeland sighed.

'Drink?' More of a dare than an offer from the old fellow. He wore short shorts and a shirt with the sleeves ripped off. Faded soldier's tatts on his forearms.

'Thank you.'

He had the decency to tip out the dead fly from the jar before pouring four fingers of Corio Five Star.

'Dad, can you take a walk or something? Go see to the boats.'

Senior hawked and spat, muttered something about not fighting commies in the jungle so they could come over and sell drugs to kiddies. He went out with a slam that knocked the shotgun to the floor, without it discharging. Either Copeland was telling the truth or my luck was holding.

I waited for Copeland to inquire after Phuong. Instead he went with: 'What took you so long?'

'You spread the rumour that Vanderhoek informed on Josie in Thailand,' I said.

He lifted his head, as though trying to identify a far-off sound. 'No,' he said. 'The real informant did that to cover their tracks.'

I scoffed.

'There was a *real* informant, Hardy. When there's a bust like that there's *always* an informant.' He shook his head. 'None of it matters now.'

'It matters because Vanderhoek is dead. That rumour got him killed. So let's start from the beginning. Your cop buddy Blyton became an addict, and the Corpse Flowers supplied him.'

Copeland sat, looked blankly at me. Then he got up and poured another drink. 'Yes. He started on painkillers after an injury. He ends up using with Vanderhoek, and the two of them ... Anyway. Whatever, right? No one's business. They had a steady supply of heroin from the Turk. In exchange, Blyton looked the other way, did favours, gave information.'

'And you turned a blind eye to this.'

He grunted a cheerless laugh. 'The Corpse Flowers.'

'I take that as a yes. So how deep are you in with them?'

Copeland shook his head, the exaggerated movement of a drunk.

'Tell me about that night at the Spida Bar.'

'The Turk cuts off Blyton's supply. Out of the blue, there's no more. Poor bastard's hopeless.' Copeland blinked, almost teary. 'He sees the Turk at the bar, and he's furious.'

'Blyton approached the Turk?'

'He goes up. Makes demands. Turk says, *maybe, if you do a job. A paid job. Take care of Mortimer.*'

'You'd arrested Mortimer that afternoon. He was in remand.' I was on my feet.

Copeland watched me pace in silence.

'You and Blyton agreed to do it together. You let Blyton take the evidence, knowing Mortimer would get out. And what? You just go back to Norlane and make up some story about him resisting arrest?'

Copeland looked at me. 'The Turk gave us half the money that night in the underground car park. In a garbage bag. Fifties. Jesus.' He put his head in his hands. 'I've regretted it ever since. Jesus, Hardy, I'd never taken money from a crook before. Ever.'

I ignored his innocent act. 'Right, but when Mortimer gets out, he didn't go back to Norlane. He disappeared. You couldn't deliver on him. Couldn't you pay back the money? Instead of getting me to try and find him?'

'Money's gone. I owed thousands to my ex-wife. I just wanted to get the divorce finalised so I could marry Phuong.' He looked at me. 'It was for Phuong.'

'Phuong has no idea,' I said. 'But she's starting to suspect.'

'What does it matter?'

'Phuong loves you.'

'She's not loyal,' he slurred.

I went over and slapped him across the face, not hard, but sharp.

He stood up, tipped his chair over. 'Think very carefully before you do that again.'

'Stop whinging. Phuong's loyal. She actually thinks if I find Mortimer it will get you out of this mess. Why she should help you I have no idea. After you had threats painted on her car.'

He stepped back. 'Never. That was *not* me.'

'Some friend of yours then. The one who wrote her name on the bullets?'

He frowned. 'No. You don't understand, she's so fucking conscientious.'

'Not anymore. She gave me a transcript of the recording you asked her to delete.'

Copeland took that in with a bitter laugh. 'Told you, she's disloyal.'

'You overreached, getting her to delete it. There's nothing on the recording to convict you of anything, other than drinking. Your guilt got the better of you. That's why I don't believe your story about Blyton and the Turk and Mortimer. Like that was the first time you've ever done the Corpse Flowers's dirty work. You and Blyton were bent for a long time. But you treat Phuong's professional integrity as a small price to pay for your reputation.'

He flung his glass at my head. 'Get fucked.'

I ducked. 'Right back at you,' I said, and walked out.

Felicity was drinking tea in the café. When I walked in, she signalled the waiter for a second cup. She poured me a cup from the pot. 'How was your meeting?'

'Great.'

My phone sang 'Superstar'.

'It's Bunny. Do you have any idea what was in those documents you gave me?'

'Yeah, it's all weapons importation, about grenades, and setting up connections for drug trafficking.'

'There's letters here from the Xishuangbanna People's Hospital in China, that's near the Burmese border, right across from Kengtung, in fact.'

A hospital? That was troubling. 'I've got you an interview with the insider. There's a Buddhist temple —'

'Great. Sure. But you've got to get me into that house.'

'Peck's house, you mean? No. Forget that. You have to meet with the person I told you about. Tomorrow at two.' I gave her the address of the temple and I dropped my phone into my bag.

The teapot was empty, and Felicity scooped up the keys. 'Where to?'

'Home.'

She stopped opposite my building. I crossed the road, and spotted a blob of meat and fur in the gutter. Not Trotsky, please, not Trotsky. I went for a closer look. It was messed up. I bent down, peering in the shadows. A cat — fur was black rather than brown. Sorry, cat.

Felicity came over. 'You okay, Stella? You've gone white.'

To my horror, I'd started shaking. 'I can't ... go upstairs.'

'Of course not. Come on, you're staying at my place. Don't even think of going up there. We'll buy you a toothbrush. You can borrow some of my clothes.'

I was beginning to genuinely like Felicity.

51

I WOKE up, taking a few minutes to register that my phone was ringing, just as it rang out. There was a momentary fit of terror at finding myself in an unfamiliar room, until I noticed I was wearing Felicity's largest pair of pyjamas and remembered it was the Sparks's spare room. A missed call from an unknown number. It rang again.

'Stella Hardy?'

'Who is this? How did you get this number?'

'Shane Farquhar. Remember me? Your old school friend.'

'What do you want?'

'I've been talking to your mother.'

'That's nothing to do with me.'

'It has *everything* to do with you. I'm in the city. At Crown. Meet me in the food court on the ground floor in an hour.'

'I'm busy.'

'In an hour or there'll be hell to pay.'

'What time is it?'

'Ten. I've been up for four hours.'

The man kept seriously anti-social hours. A farmer's hours.

I had no desire to have it out with Shane Farquhar, and certainly not at Crown Casino. But the sooner this farm-sale fiasco was over the better. After that, I'd never have to deal with him again.

'Agreed,' I said, half-heartedly.

I went in search of breakfast. I expected the household to be asleep, taking advantage of the public holiday, but the Sparks were in a state of frantic activity, in preparation for the Cup Day festivities.

Felicity's mother stood at the kitchen bench making sandwiches. Dressed in a slip, she was deeply tanned and her white-blonde hair was done up, reeking of hairspray. She padded around to the pantry in bare feet. Felicity's father came out in his suit pants and a singlet. Shorter than I expected, but otherwise conforming to the image of a wealthy middle-aged man, greying hair, fit, muscular, good teeth. He asked for advice on cufflinks.

Mrs Sparks introduced me as a friend of Felicity's. Which I supposed I was now.

She came bustling past me. 'Breakfast?' She popped a pod in the coffee machine. 'Cups here, cereal there, help yourself.'

Good coffee and sourdough toast — I liked the way these people lived. Felicity came out in a white dressing gown. 'I put some toiletries and a change of clothes on your bed.'

I trotted off to see what she had in mind. A loose, cotton frock with an Italian label. I held it against my shoulders. It would fit. Just.

In the bathroom, I washed and slipped into Felicity's dress. Then I brushed my teeth with my new toothbrush and stepped on the pedal bin to dispose of the wrapping. As I did, something in the bin drew my attention. I reached in and pulled out a piece of a photograph, just a corner. It was only a headless shoulder, a hint of dark hair. The design of the shirt matched a shirt of mine.

I put the piece in my bag and went out into the kitchen.

'I'm meeting a friend in the city. Can you point me to the station?' I asked.

'I'll drop you in the city,' Felicity said. 'No trouble at all. I was going to do some shopping anyway.'

We were back in the Mercedes, me in Felicity's dress. With each favour, I was feeling more and more indebted to her.

'Forgot my phone,' she said and went inside.

I crossed my legs and kicked Felicity's handbag. I looked up to make sure she was not on her way back. Then I opened it. Wallet, lipstick, pen, nail scissors, and a spiral notebook. I flipped it open.

It was a list of dates and times.

10.50a.m. S > pumpkin
1p.m. P > S
11.30p.m. S > taxi

I looked up, saw Felicity coming out of the house, and threw the book in my bag.

'Crown it is.'

'Thanks, mate,' I said with a sidelong glance.

She let me out at the entrance to Crown. Impenetrable crowds, some already spectacularly drunk, milled around the entrance, in anticipation of Crown's 'alternative racing experience' — inside a tacky casino as opposed to mingling with a hundred thousand punters outside at Flemington racecourse.

'I'll be in the boutiques if you need me,' she said. I waved her goodbye, hiding my mounting feelings of mistrust. I would deal with her later. First, I had to get this Farquhar thing out of the way. I texted Shane to say I was waiting in one of the coffee shops.

'Hardy, you two-faced slag,' he said, sliding into the booth with a plate of chips. 'You've ruined my life.'

'That's a bit of an exaggeration.'

He seized a bottle of sauce and squeezed the contents all over his plate. 'How'd your fucking sister and her idiot husband get the money?'

'Through a family member. They got lucky. On the market. Apple.' Not strictly a lie. I'd been lucky *and* I'd been known to buy apples at the market.

He stabbed the chips with a fork and crammed them in his mouth. 'I had plans. Big plans and you fucked me over.'

'Hey, I resent that.'

'Yeah? Well, I resent you lying to my face.'

Jeez this bloke was hard work. 'I never promised you the farm.

All I said was that I would talk to Delia. And, frankly, this isn't my fault. Mum's been selling small parcels of the farm for years. You had plenty of chances. You blew it.'

'Waiting for the drought to end. Thought of selling up myself.' He ruminated on some dark notion, resentment all over the sunburnt face he was stuffing. 'I'll sue.'

'There was no contract. Nothing in writing.'

More stabbing and gnawing. 'I can make things very uncomfortable for your family.' He lifted his gaze from the chips to sneer at me, reminding me of Alma. 'The fuck happened to your face?'

'Nothing. Look, Shane. You have to take this like a grown up. Kylie is family. And you're ...'

'A long-standing member of the community.'

'Tyler doesn't have much experience. Maybe you could help him out. Mentor him.'

'Get fucked.'

'They want to breed Dexters, small Irish cows. They'll need advice.'

He sat upright. 'Dexters? Terrible decision.' A smirk crept across his face. And I didn't like the glint in his eye.

'What are you up to?'

'Nothing.' He pushed the plate away. 'Driving back. Never want to hit the city again.'

'Have a good trip.'

'You and your whole stupid family have made a big mistake.'

'Give my regards to your mum.'

'She always said your dad couldn't kick. Played for frees.'

I didn't bite. 'Off you go, Shane.'

I went to where the high-end boutiques were located, looking for Felicity. I looked in Ralph Lauren, Marc Jacobs, DKNY, expecting to find her checking out the handbags, or trying on sunnies. With no luck tracking down Felicity, I decided to see if I could crash Crown's Cup Day gig.

The event entrance was in the main foyer of Crown. It was sponsored by *Fregare*, the new fragrance by Caposala, a European cosmetics giant, rebranded when the old name scored negatively with consumers ever since a notorious incident when a bad batch of exfoliant removed numerous layers of skin, way too many layers. A class action lawsuit was pending.

A group of tall Barbie-esque women, in mauve — this year's Caposala colour — were checking tickets and handing out free samples. I pulled my work lanyard from my handbag and rolled back my shoulders, extended my neck and tipped my head up. Inhaling the clouds of scent, I made an arrogant mince towards the function entrance, swishing Felicity's floaty frock, and put out my hand for a sample.

'Ticket?' An improbably beautiful woman asked nervously.

'My dear, I'm Angora Rockford, I don't *need* a ticket. Here.' I flashed the WORMS lanyard.

'Oh, of course. Here, have two samples.'

And I was in.

Fregare was the feminine perfume. The male fragrance was *Fegato for Men*. The bottle was in the shape of Michelangelo's 'David', so not at all tacky. I pulled out the stopper. Notes of vetiver, musk, and cashmere wood. Interesting.

I dropped the bottle in my bag and went looking for food.

A big screen had been erected, and was showing horses and pretty people being interviewed. Food was laid on, and waiters in long, white aprons carried trays of champagne flutes. I mingled for a bit, and who should I spy but Pukus. He was in his natural habitat, hovering over the food, like a corpulent antelope grazing the vast tracts of canapes.

'What's good to eat around here?' I asked.

He welcomed me with a high-pitched snort. 'How did you get in?'

I smiled enigmatically.

He raised an eyebrow. 'How's Ogg-Simons?'

'He quit.'

'The twat.' He was already pink from champagne. 'He's a weak cunt.'

The language shocked me, and then it didn't. 'Boss is a good bloke.'

He finished a miniature gourmet sausage roll and dusted his fingers. 'He's weak. Leaving the agency. Why? Because of his *feelings*. I said to him, I said Brendan, get drunk and get laid like the rest of us, mate. Go to the footy and shout your cares to the wind. But no, he's sensitive. Prefers the company of his wife.'

'Yes. I see how that makes him unfit to be a man.' I selected a mini pastry with a cheese filling, and a piece of cucumber, a blade of grass balanced on top.

'You know the passport thing is about to go public,' I said.

'No, it isn't. It's all tight. They managed it very carefully. No media.'

'Okay, but the whistle-blower is about to give an interview to Bunny Slipper.'

Some of Pugh's face slipped down into his jowls.

'Yeah. Apparently, he's going to talk about how the passports were for homeless kids to go to Asia and have their organs sold to rich people with bad hearts, and dodgy kidneys.'

'What? Are you sure? Oh, no. PR's not ready for that kind of front-page disaster.'

'Oh, come on. You can spin it. You're very good on your feet.'

'Yes, er, thanks Hardy. But still ... this kiddie travel business. Looks bad.'

'So you'll honour your commitment to increase funding for homeless children?'

A young man behind a bar started pouring champagne.

'Oh, right, that scheme of yours. Makes sense, I suppose. I could make that announcement at the same time. Yes, yes. Very well,' Pukus said and pushed past me to join the other dignitaries gathered around that waterhole.

I ate my pastry; it was delicious. Tomorrow when Boss gave me a lecture for refusing to apply for his job, as per the letter I'd left in his pigeonhole, I'd be able to say that I can at least continue to hold Pugh to account for his promises.

So far, so good. On the giant screen, a race started. Several guests fell to raucous cheering. The security guards eyed each other warily. Judging when to chuck the buggers out was a delicate matter, especially if they were, say, the justice minister.

I looked up and saw Felicity coming towards me. How had she evaded the purple door sentries, I wondered? I flashed the David-shaped perfume bottle at her. 'This is the one you gave Brophy.'

She froze like a rabbit in a spotlight, light reflected in her large brown eyes. She tried to swallow. 'Is it?'

I considered the bottle, the brand. 'It must have cost a bomb.'

'Oh, no. I get them free.'

'What about cutting me out of the pictures you stole from Brophy's? And keeping a record of all my movements? That's why you've been so helpful to me — you're gathering intel.'

Guilt and tears welled in her eyes. 'Stella,' she sobbed.

'Admit it, you're *stalking* me, aren't you?'

Tears spilled as her face crumpled. 'God help me.'

'A-ha! I *knew* it!'

'I tried everything to get him to love me. I've cast hundreds of love spells. I brought wine to the modelling sessions, I flirted, I flaked out on his couch, but he never went near me. All he wanted was to paint.'

Brophy, you legend. I wanted to run around and high-five every fool in the place.

She blew her nose and went towards me. A hug was the idea. My arm went out and locked straight, fending her off.

Felicity Sparks. Well, well. To think I'd blamed Marigold for the photo thefts.

'So you admit you pinched that photo of Brophy and me?'

'Stella, I'm sorry.'

'And the spying?'

'So I could tell him you were seeing other men. Forgive me?' She raised her arms, moving towards me again. A mummy's girl, used to getting a kiss for every little booboo.

'Back off, Sparks, you treacherous, two-faced slag.' I was so angry, I found myself slipping back into the old Woolburn lingo, using a particular favourite of Farquhar's. 'Ring Brophy now. Make a full confession.'

Felicity pouted for a second and then, to my amazement, actually got out her phone. I waited while she tried his number. He wasn't home, of course. I checked my watch. 'I have to go. But you will tell him, *won't you* Felicity? Then you will leave us both alone.'

She sniffed, nodding, bottom lip turned out.

I was roaring inside with vindication. I'd turned the tables on that bully Shane Farquhar. Pressured that liar Pukus. And now Felicity. As if she stood a chance trying to deceive me and steal Brophy. It was possibly the best day of my life. The only way it could be improved would be if I managed to track down the Corpse Flowers, round them all up, and deliver them to Phuong.

I made my way to the exit. There was a hush in the foyer, and I checked the screen. Another race was getting set. The horses were at the barriers.

My phone rang. An unknown number.

'What?'

'It's Alma.'

'Alma! Finally. What's happening?'

'I'm going to go to the police, Stella. I realise I've been really stupid.'

'Great. Good for you.'

'But I thought it best to see you first. I was thinking, why don't I come over and you can help me talk things through? Where are you?'

It was a pretty clumsy effort, really. 'I'm busy right now.'

I thought I heard whispering.

'Really, doing what?'

An idea was forming, and I realised I was nodding and smiling. 'You won't believe it,' I said. 'But I was planning on going to Ricky Peck's house in Sunshine.'

There was a pause. 'Wait, what? When? How come?'

'Oh, in about an hour. I was just going to have a look around. His death was declared an accident, and now the evidence team have finished their search it's just sitting there empty. No cops around. It's in legal limbo.'

Another long pause. 'On your own?'

'Yep. All by myself. Sorry Alma, got to go. Don't tell Josie, okay?'

'As if. I don't even like her anymore.'

I ended the call and checked the time: almost one. I had an hour to get to Ricky Peck's house.

52

I RAN to the exit, tapping my phone and dodging punters. Finding a way out of Crown wasn't easy; their cheesy cardboard racehorses and Melbourne Cup replicas blocked my path. I kept trying numbers, but the networked seemed to be overloaded. I was staring at the screen and hoping for a connection when a text popped up from Bunny:

> Change of interview location. Ricky Peck's house. Film crew
> meeting us there if you want to watch.

No! *Bad Bunny!* Couldn't she just meet Cuong at the temple, like she said? Why did she have to complicate everything?

Now I had to get to the North Sunshine dope house before Gorman and the other Flowers, and help Phuong arrest them all, even though I hadn't told her any of this yet. And I needed to have the whole thing sorted before Bunny and Cuong showed up. If Gorman saw Cuong, he'd kill him on sight. When I hit the street, every taxi was full.

I stood on the corner, frantically tapping numbers.

Finally, Afshan answered, and he was in the city doing a delivery. He said he'd be happy to come and get me. I gave him directions and told him I owed him. Again. More than ever now. A few minutes later, he pulled up in a cloud of exhaust smoke.

I continued my futile attempts to contact Phuong as we fanged west, passing the docks and crossing the Maribyrnong at lightning speed. At a notorious bottleneck leading under a railway bridge and into Footscray, our pace slowed. Afshan kept his cool and manoeuvred the van to front spot at the lights. He assured me he

271

knew a faster shortcut. Soon we were in an industrial area, taking corners on two wheels and defying the laws of gravity.

On my last try, Phuong picked up.

I got straight to the point. 'The Flowers are heading to Ricky Peck's dope house.'

'What? How? Are you sure?'

'Yes, I think even the Turk will come out of hiding,' I said.

'He'd never do that.'

'He would to confront me.' I gave her a brief version of my conversation with Alma. 'Enright and Gorman won't be able to resist either. The fucking lot of them will be at Ricky Peck's house,' I said. 'This is the arrest of your career.' If all went well, I thought, an ABC film crew would be there to film the aftermath.

'I'm on my way. Stella, do *not* go to that house.'

I told her I wouldn't, then asked Afshan to hurry. The rat run took us directly to Sunshine North — and in no time, to the surprise of us both, the van pulled up outside the house in one piece. The street was quiet, no neighbours were about. There were no motorbikes or muscle cars parked near Peck's house. The sun was out and set to scorch mode, baking the road, killing vegetation, directing waves of shimmering heat onto my head.

Afshan wished me luck. 'If you need me I'll be at my office.'

'Right,' I said. 'Wait, what office?'

'Funky Town.' He swung the wheel.

I opened the gate, went up a couple of steps to the entrance, and peered in the front window. It was in much the same state as I had left it. The front door handle turned in my hand and the door swung in on its hinges. I hadn't left it like that.

My eyes took a moment to adjust to the gloom inside. The front room and the adjoining room were still strewn with the detritus of a hydroponic set-up: tubes and leads and ripped pieces of gaffer tape. The wardrobes in the bedrooms were open. I couldn't remember if I'd shut them. In the hall, I inspected the lino. This time, I easily spotted the loose square; it had been dropped askew, and the hole in the floor was visible underneath.

I crouched down, ready to climb into the subfloor cavity. I leaned over and a man's head popped up out of the hole.

We both uttered profanities of surprise.

'Who the fuck are you?' the man said.

I thought about going with the Marion Cunningham real-estate-agent ruse again, and trying to back away slowly like I didn't have a clue what was down there. But then I saw he had a face tattoo — the words *fuck yeah* scrawled across his forehead.

'Stella Hardy,' I said.

He seemed relieved. 'The social worker? Cuong's friend?'

I nodded. 'And you're Isaac Mortimer.'

He put out his hand. I hesitated, felt stupid, then I extended mine. He grabbed it in his meaty mitt and squeezed till my eyes watered. These blokes must work out their every muscle — arms, wrists, fingers.

'Everyone is looking for you,' I said.

'Yeah.' Mortimer gave an unconcerned shrug.

'You shouldn't be here,' I said. 'It's dangerous.'

'I'm looking for the fucking money. Thought I had it when I found the trapdoor in the floor. But I checked down there and if there was any money there it's gone now.'

'Money?'

'Peck's petty cash. Over five hundred grand.'

'Maybe Gorman found it.'

Then he scratched his head stubble. 'What brings you here?'

'Me? I'm trying to get the last Corpse Flowers out in the open. I didn't think *you* would be here, but you are, and now they're coming.'

'Good,' Mortimer said. He was still in the hole in the floor, and now he leaned back with his thick arms folded.

'They'll kill you.'

He pulled a large hand gun from his waistband and put it on the lino. 'We'll see.'

'Might not be enough,' I said, edging back slightly.

'Hold this.'

He handed me a heavy, olive-green, softball-sized orb with a pin. I was horrified. 'No,' I gave it back. 'You hold it.'

'Nah, you'll be right.' He winked. 'Let's wait for them out the back.'

He jumped out of the hole, replaced the cover, and shoved the gun in his waistband. I had planned to wait for them somewhere safe, like in the reserve next door, or across the road behind a wheelie bin. But Mortimer's confidence and serenity was contagious. I found myself sauntering behind him.

We went outside into the glare; the concreted yard radiated shimmering heat. The plants in the concrete planters were still dead, the green pond water was steamy. I scanned the shadows near the fence. Waste from the hydroponic operation, empty takeaway noodle boxes, scrunched up Madame Mao's Handmade Dumplings bags, a few pizza boxes. Piles of crushed beer and Jim Beam mixer cans.

We stood together in the shade of the fence.

I thought for a moment. 'Who killed Ricky Peck?'

My theory, it was the kids. Maybe a few of them together, say Brook and Ange and that boy. If they had all held him down …

'Cuong,' Mortimer said simply.

Damn.

'Had to,' Mortimer was saying. 'He and I agreed, Peck was psycho. He had to go.'

'Stella?'

I looked up and saw Phuong walking slowly down the back steps from the house in black leggings, a sports Adidas singlet, iPhone strapped to her upper arm, earbuds around her neck, and her gun in her hand. 'Easy now, Mortimer. Take it easy.'

'It's okay, Phuong,' I said. 'I've got a grenade.'

She paused, thinking, then she continued. 'Hands where I can see them.'

We both raised our arms.

'Not *you*, Stella.' She did her trademark half-smile. 'On the ground, Mortimer. Sit down. Hands on your head.'

'He's cool,' I said, but Phuong aimed the gun at Mortimer's head, and he lowered himself to the ground.

Her eyes moved to me. 'A grenade?'

'Yes. And Mortimer has a gun.'

Mortimer sniffed. 'Only fair, he wants me dead.'

A car engine revved in the street. A single car door slammed.

'I'm getting up,' Mortimer said.

Phuong frowned. 'Alright. I've put in a call to special ops. They're on their way.'

'You better hide,' I said to her. 'If they realise you're a cop, they'll kill you first.'

Phuong looked around at the ground. 'Get some of those Madame Mao bags.'

I picked out two dumpling bags still in reasonable nick from the rubbish pile. She put her Glock in one. I put the grenade in the other and gave it to her.

'What the fuck?' Buster came waltzing down the steps, orange fluff on his head wafting in the breeze, and holding a shotgun by the barrel.

Mortimer waved. 'Oh, hi,' he said, casually. 'How's things?'

Buster held back, confused. 'What are you doing here?'

'Mortimer's here to kill Cuong,' I said, the only thing I could think of. 'Gorman's orders.'

He pointed at me. 'You're dead.'

'Nah, I'm good. We just ordered dumplings. You want one?'

'Is someone going to pay me?' Phuong asked, acting annoyed. 'Twenty-five dollars!' She was playing the delivery girl. Fortunately, Buster didn't question it.

Unfortunately, her terrible overacting struck me as hilarious.

I couldn't look at her. I squinted at the sky and bit my lip, hard. If she said it again, I'd lose control, maybe wet myself.

Buster turned to Mortimer, confused. 'Ox said *I* could do it.'

'Change of plan,' Mortimer said.

He frowned. 'Jeez, I just spoke to Ox. He goes *we gonna pop a few cunts,* but he never mentioned *you.*'

'They never tell you anything,' I said, trying to sound sympathetic.

Buster hesitated, thinking that over.

Then Mortimer ran at him, shoulder down. Buster tried to raise the shotgun, moved too late, and Mortimer rammed into his side. Buster stumbled, bounced off a concrete planter, dropped the shotgun. He came up, fists swinging. But Mortimer blocked him, his fist up in front of his face, boxer-style. Buster swiped a right at Mortimer's ear. Mortimer absorbed the blow and countered with a left punch to the ribs. Buster staggered back, winded, then ran again at Mortimer, raining clumsy head punches, which Mortimer skilfully neutralised by moving in close. They wrestled, until both men fell on the ground.

While they struggled, I picked Buster's shotgun up by the barrel. I was better with those — in my teens, one summer in Woolburn, I'd killed a dog. It was a seminal moment. In that I now hated shotguns. I threw it in the murky pond.

Mortimer got to his haunches and bounced up on his toes. With his fists drawn martial-arts-style, he circled Buster, who was still on the ground.

Phuong retrieved her Glock from the bag, and showed it to him. 'Get up.'

'That's not a dumpling.' Buster got to his feet, scoffing. 'You don't know what to do.'

'Try me,' she said. 'Now, I want you to stand in front of me, and if you say one word when Gorman gets here, I'll shoot you in the head. Understand?'

'You don't owe these people anything,' I said to him. 'They're horrible to you.'

He pouted. 'Money's good, but.'

'Anyone home?' a voice called.

Senior Detective William Blyton stepped from the house into the backyard. He was as wired as I'd seen him at Afshan's place when he'd taken Cuong away. He paused and looked from Mortimer to Buster to Phuong, taking in the situation.

'On the ground, mate,' he said to Buster.

'Oh for fuck's sake.' Buster dropped obediently back onto the ground like he knew the drill. He lay on the hot concrete on his stomach, hands clasped at the back of his head.

To Phuong, Blyton said, 'Hello, Detective. You can put those on the ground now, please.'

Without a word, she set her gun on the ground and placed the dumpling bags on top of it.

'Let me guess,' he said to me. 'Stella Hardy, Client Liaison Officer, and colossal bloody idiot.'

I kind of deserved that.

He addressed Buster, still lying on the ground. 'She leaves her fucking calling card. Can you believe it? Normally, I'd give her straight to Gorman. Lucky for her, I intend to kill the bastard myself.'

Mortimer spat. 'Get in line.'

'Shut up, traitor,' Blyton walked around and put the gun to the back of Mortimer's head. 'Jeff would still be alive if it wasn't for you.'

'It wasn't him,' I said, carefully. 'It was Copeland.'

Blyton looked confused. 'Copeland?'

'Yes. He lied to Josie to take pressure off himself. He said that Jeff Vanderhoek had ratted her out in Thailand.'

'Bruce said that?' Phuong said.

'Sorry, Phuong, it's true,' I said.

A door slammed and voices shouted inside the house. Phuong bent down, reaching for the dumpling bags. Buster started to get up. Mortimer moved his hand slowly to his waistband.

'Nobody move,' Blyton growled under his breath.

Everyone stopped, and we all looked expectantly at the back door. Josie, AKA Philomena Josephine Enright, came trotting down the steps. She had a long-barrel weapon over her shoulder. As she approached us, she pulled out the clip, checked it, put it back in, pulled a lever down, pulled back and released a handle. Countless war movies, and documentaries about African rebellions, had taught me that Enright's weapon of choice was an AK-47. These bikies could get their hands on anything.

Blyton changed aim from Mortimer to Buster's head. 'Stop there, Enright. Or I make a mess of your goon.'

Buster whimpered.

Josie stopped two metres from where Blyton stood, gun vaguely pointed at the area of Blyton's chest. She clocked Mortimer, then her gaze moved to Phuong and then to me. 'What seems to be the trouble, William?' Her voice was calm.

'You ordered the hit on Jeff,' he said. 'You had him fucking tortured.'

She shrugged. 'Rats get what they deserve, William. You know that.'

Blyton let out a deranged laugh. 'Jeff had nothing to do with you getting busted in Thailand,' he said, arms locked straight, gun aimed at Buster.

She lowered the AK-47 a little. 'What?'

'Tell her, Hardy.'

Mortimer, I noticed, was moving slowly towards the dumpling bags Phuong had placed on the ground.

'It's true,' I said, struggling to keep the panic under control. 'The feds were all over the Thai operation from the start.'

She moved forward. 'The feds?'

I darted a sneaky glance at Mortimer. Crouching, moving slowly back.

'Of course,' Blyton was saying, defiant now, like something had broken free inside him. He, too, had known who ratted out Josie all along. 'And you went inside that fucked-up Asian slammer, and believe me, it hardly raised a sob,' he smirked. 'The syndicates running the distribution networks, that's who the feds were after.'

Josie muttered an obscenity.

Blyton turned, moving the gun from Buster to Josie. Buster scrambled to his feet and ran down the side of the house.

'You're lying.' Josie raised the butt of the AK to her shoulder, put her eye to the sight, and aimed at Blyton.

'No.' Blyton shook his head. 'You had Jeff killed on a rumour.' Tears streamed down his face as he raised the gun and fired two wild shots. The bullets struck the side of the house.

Josie ripped a hail of shots with the AK. Shells bounced at her feet.

Blyton fell back on the ground. His arms flung out at odd angles from his now motionless body. His bloody gut still pulsing rivers of red.

53

I REALISED I was screaming.

'Shut the fuck up,' Josie shouted at me, bringing around the business end of the AK to point at my face. 'What the hell is *your* story?'

I didn't understand the question. My mind was in pieces, part of me floating away. Phuong was acting like a shocked bystander, looking scared. But I knew she wasn't frozen in fear, she would be calculating her next move.

The wise thing would be to say nothing. But I found myself saying, 'My story? I don't have a story.'

'Then you're next.'

'But I know about the Thailand job, and the informant.'

'You're just making shit up,' she said, but she cocked her head, ready to listen.

'Sorry to tell you, Josie, but Jeff Vanderhoek never talked.'

'You're saying there was no informer. And the Thais just magically *discovered* all the details, the flights, our hotels — it all fell into their laps out of the clear blue sky.'

'No. There *was* an informer. And he told the feds, and they told the Thais.'

'Shut up, Hardy. That's bullshit.' The speaker had come into the yard from the driveway. He was a man I'd never actually met before, but I knew instantly who he was. I didn't need to check for the missing finger and the stab wound to know it was the number one Corpse Flower.

'Hello, *Gorman*,' I said.

'Ox?' Josie said, her eyes never leaving me. 'She's saying the feds knew about me before the job, that it wasn't Vanderhoek who told them.'

'Darling, we can talk about it later,' Gorman said. 'First, we have to get Mortimer to tell us where Peck's money is. Then we can *deal with him* and go.' He looked at me and then Phuong. 'Who's this?'

'Dumpling delivery,' Mortimer said.

'No shit? You cunts ordered dumplings? Excellent.'

Josie rolled her eyes. 'Ox, forget about the fucking dumplings.'

'Right,' he coughed. 'Come on, Morty. Where's the money?'

Mortimer sneered, but said nothing.

'Ox, ask her who the informer was,' Josie said.

'On second thoughts, forget the money. Spray the lot of them,' Ox Gorman said. 'I'll put the bodies in the house, and we'll light it up, what do you say, honey?'

Josie hesitated. 'Okay … but …'

'And then we get their fucking dumplings. What kind did youse order?'

'Let me check,' Phuong said, and bent down. I watched her scoop her hand under the bags. In one deft move, she lifted her gun as she picked up the dumpling bags.

Josie's face hardened to a grim stare. 'I want to hear what she has to say.'

I pointed at Gorman. '*He* let you languish in Thailand. He sent you there to set up a base. But the police were sniffing around, so he shut it down. And to shore up his position with the cops, he chucked you under a bus.' I was adding some colour, and a lot of shade.

'She's lying, honey,' he said, lightly. Gorman seemed desperate to avoid upsetting her. I could understand that.

'Pork and mushroom,' Phuong said, handing one bag to me. The grenade. 'And mackerel or —' she was holding the other bag in a way that concealed her Glock behind it, and took a big sniff inside, '— maybe squid?'

Way in the distance, a siren wailed.

'Hand 'em over, dumpling girl,' Gorman said.

'Ox, shut up,' she hissed at him, her face flushed. 'Let the fucking social worker speak.'

'Sweetheart, she's deluded.'

'How do you know this?' she asked me.

'From the cops. Blyton knew. All the cops know about Gorman.'

She looked down at Blyton's dead body. I kept my gaze pointed up at her face. If I looked at that horror, I'd freak out.

'Now let me ask *you* something, Philomena Josephine Enright. Are you happy with the trade in body parts?' I asked. 'Trafficking young kids. Are you happy about that?'

'Happy? I'm fucking rapt.' She was laughing. 'The money is *huge*. Per child, we're looking at over a million. Rich sick people, they fucking care *a lot* where their organs come from. No stunted political prisoners for those guys. We offer the whole package. Anyway, no one gives a shit about homeless kids. I mean, who is the real criminal?'

'It's you, Josie. You just blasted Blyton into pieces right in front of me. You sent Jeff Vanderhoek to the Turk to be tortured and murdered. You lure children to their death. You murdered Cory.'

She shook her head at me, like I was stupid. 'That's business. You assess the risks and you eliminate them.'

'Josie, we need to go. Shoot her, shoot them all, and let's go,' Gorman said.

She looked at him. 'Nine years. Nine fucking years, Ox. Did you do that to me?'

'Yes, he did. But he's too much of a coward to admit it,' I said.

Josie's eyes filled with tears.

Shouts inside the house, boots stomping. Gorman and Josie turned to look, Josie pointing the AK at the door.

Phuong raised her hand with the Glock now in it. I snatched the grenade from the bag.

Someone kicked the back door open. It swung hard, nearly came off its hinges, and the Turk stepped out.

'Is this where the party is? What's everyone doing out here?' he demanded.

Phuong swiftly reassessed the situation, and, changing her mind, hid her gun behind her back. I followed her example, concealing the grenade against my leg.

He clocked me and broke into a vile grin. 'Holy shit, the rumours are true, you made it out of there alive.' He turned to Gorman. 'Why are all these people not dead?'

Gorman looked exasperated. 'That's what I've been saying.'

'What about Ricky's money?' The Turk asked.

'Mortimer hasn't said,' Gorman said. 'Yet.'

Mortimer shrugged. 'It's not here.'

'You.' The Turk pointed at him. 'You fucking traitor. I've been waiting to catch up with you. Why'd you kill Ricky?' the Turk asked him.

'That was Cuong.'

'Yes, that was me.' Cuong emerged from the side of the house. Walking down the driveway with him was Bunny Slipper. Her eyes were wide, and behind her two women carrying camera equipment. They all looked terrified. Cuong moved in front of them.

'You killed Ricky? You bastard! Where's our money?!' Josie screamed.

'Honey, calm down,' Gorman said.

She rounded on him, the AK at her shoulder. 'Don't tell me to calm down.'

With her back turned, Cuong ran at Josie, shoving her from behind. She fumbled the AK and it fell to the ground.

That's when I held up the grenade. 'Everyone on the ground now,' I said. 'Or I pull the pin.'

Slow and reluctant, Josie, Gorman, and the Turk started to crouch down.

'Stella, I can take it from here,' Phuong said, aiming the Glock at Josie.

283

Mortimer was up and aiming his handgun at Gorman.

Sirens screamed in the street. Car tyres screeched to a halt.

I went to the Turk. 'Take off the watch.'

He glared at me and grudgingly unclipped his Cartier watch, and dropped it in my hand.

Car doors slammed, someone shouted orders through a bullhorn. The sounds of weapons locking and loading, people running through the house.

Without warning, Gorman scrambled up, and in a flash I realised he was charging at me.

I pulled the pin.

Gorman stopped dead, everyone did.

Then Gorman, Josie, and the Turk were running for the house. A logjam formed in the door, Gorman pulling bodies away to get in first. He held Josie back by the hair. She grabbed the Turk's belt. He had hold of Gorman's arm. Someone gave way, and they tumbled down the back steps. Mortimer, Phuong, Cuong, and Bunny all hit the ground. I tossed the thing into the pond and hit the deck, arms over my head. The grenade explosion sent shock waves out over my covered head; water, algae slime flew. Pond water rained down over everything.

Phuong was the first to recover. She flicked a piece of slime out of her hair and raised the gun at Gorman. 'I'm not your fucking dumpling girl.'

People in riot gear poured around and out of the house.

Cuong and I were ushered away to be checked over in an ambulance waiting in the street, as Special Operations officers secured the area. Bunny's camera crew were setting up, and Ms Slipper was excitedly running around asking random cops for an interview.

'Here,' I whispered to Cuong. 'If you have to go back to Vietnam, here's something to take with you.' I placed the watch in his hand. 'Keep it, sell it. Use it to hypnotise people. It's entirely up to you. You did a brave thing, ridding the world of Ricky Peck.'

'I didn't do that,' he said. 'I can't do that. He drowned. That's all.'

Well, *that* was a relief. I couldn't wait to tell Phuong.

'But what about the ghost? I thought perhaps that was your guilt over Peck?'

He shrugged. 'We all have things from our past we'd rather forget, don't we?'

54

LENNOX 'OX' GORMAN, Philomena Enright, Buster, and Luigi 'The Turk' Tacchini were in custody.

Mortimer was judged to be a credible source, and given protection. True to his word, he filled in the blank spaces. A pretty row of Flowers were named. That particular gang would stink no more.

Copeland was a slippery eel and immediately had his lawyer release a statement that claimed there was no evidence to convict him of any wrongdoing. In fact, it said, Detective Copeland was the one who had convinced Alma to do the right thing and testify against Philomena Enright. Mrs Dunmore had driven Alma to the police station. They, too, were offered protection and with a nod from her mother, the teenager's cynicism melted like a warm McFlurry. She told the police of Enright's reaction to the results of Cory Fontaine's blood test. That she had witnessed Enright confront him in the toilets at McDonald's about Cory's illness. Enright had then let the boy go, but had followed him outside and, when he was near the road, she'd shoved Cory into the path of the truck.

There were some chaotic scenes at the police station and the questioning seemed to go on forever. I gave the best account I could of everything that had happened, culminating in my presence at Ricky Peck's house that afternoon, but excluding any self-incriminating facts. At last, I signed my statement and they called me a taxi, on the proviso that I'd return if required. I rushed home, took a long shower, washing the pond slime and cordite from my hair.

An hour later, dressed in black pants, a black lace top, and black jacket, I entered the buzzing rooms of This Is Not A Drill. I lifted a glass of champagne from a waiter's tray, and took in the breathless crowd. I recognised a few faces from their publicity shots. The centre of this universe, Peter Brophy the commodity, was being interviewed by a journalist, and I took the opportunity to study his work in relative privacy. The paintings, about twenty portraits, were not the representations of erotic fantasy I had baselessly feared they would be. Painted in coloured translucent circular layers, the effect was of an x-ray, not of anatomy but of radiances within and around the body. Each figure was drawn upright, and dynamic, struck with volts of white, which lit up each composition. As if the figures were trying to dance off the canvas. This mix of abstraction and reality was a radically new concept for Brophy, with only small intimations from his earlier work. I hated to concede it, but having Felicity as a model had indeed altered his aesthetic eye.

He'd captured her recklessness, and her sensitivity. Nonetheless, he'd retained that Brophy straightforwardness. The figures appeared slightly at a distance, a little absurd, imbued with warmth and humour. A mad world made for twirling Felicities.

I looked among the patrons and spotted her, weaving through the crowd towards me, waving a champagne glass. A moment later, I picked up her scent, a mix of neroli, patchouli, and mendacity.

She touched her face with the cold glass. 'I told him,' she said. 'Everything.'

I sipped my champagne.

'No, really. I did. I admitted that all along I'd been lying to you about him, and that I had, er, I'd lied to him about you, too.'

I paused mid-sip. 'What? What lies?'

She looked stricken. 'That you told me you wanted him to focus exclusively on the exhibition ... and to leave you alone. Partly because you wanted to support him — I said that part to make it more believable — and partly because you needed space from him. I told him you thought he was smothering you ... and that ... you hated it.'

I looked across the room at Brophy, as that information sank in.

He was being posed by the journalist in front of one of his paintings, frowning uneasily for the camera. 'That is some cold-hearted shit.'

She blinked. 'My shrink said the same thing. It's related to a fear of abandonment, she reckons. And an unconscious rivalry with my mother, a life and death thing apparently, in which I desire her complete and total annihilation or something. But you and Peter should know that I'm aware of my destructive behaviour patterns now, and I'm going to transform my destructive tendencies into positive ones.'

'Great, Felicity.'

She stood there, clasped hands holding the flute at her chest, bouncing on her toes. I sensed some additional need in her, signs of an imminent request.

'What do you want?' I sighed. 'Forgiveness? Absolution?'

'Sure, *forgive, forget*, whatever.' She took her nail scissors from her handbag. 'And a hair, only one, for a ritual I'm performing. A small sample of your —'

I ducked and told her if she didn't stop I'd get a restraining order. Then I went around the space looking for friendly faces. Phuong was at home; she'd broken off the engagement and didn't feel like socialising. I hadn't told her the whole truth about my conversation with Copeland. But when she said they had *conflicting values*, I guessed she had some idea of what kind of man he really was.

Cuong was still at the police station. He was fully cooperating with the police and willing to testify against the Corpse Flowers. He'd been assigned a lawyer, and, well, he did have a lot of explaining to do. Whether the Immigration Department would take that into considerations on visa breaches, he would have to wait and see.

I was surprised to see Boss among the throng, inspecting a painting at close quarters. I half expected him to say it was worthless. But before I had a chance to ask him what he thought, he was patting me on the back. 'Hardy, how about these pictures? Don't get them, don't understand them, but I'm buying this one. This is the one.'

288

'They're not cheap. Are you sure? I mean, what's the point, right?'

He waved the question away. 'Point is I like it.' He straightened up to face me. 'You're going to stay put then?'

'You mean the WORMS promotion? I can't see myself sitting in the office all day, juggling budgets.'

He raised his glass to me. 'Good for you.' And then he was gone, off to see about purchasing some art.

Then someone was tapping on their glass and calling for a bit of shush. We all looked around to see what was about to ensue. I worked my way to the front. Brophy was standing in front of the largest portrait in the exhibit. He rocked and shifted, nervous arms folded.

He mumbled his thanks to the This Is Not A Drill gallery, and someone yelled for him to speak up. He raised his voice. 'I want to thank a lot of people, for their support and their belief in me, friends, my daughter, Marigold. Sorry if I've forgotten anyone, I hope those people know I appreciate their assistance. The process was somewhat fraught at times, but I'm proud of the results.'

A cheer went up. Someone shouted, 'On ya, mate!'

I cheered too, and then I made my way to the exit. This was his moment, to share with his admirers. And I'd made it here to see it. But as I told Brophy earlier, I had one last matter to take care of. Then he and I could, at long last, be together. I turned to give him a little wave and saw that he was pointing at me.

'But what I really want to say is my thanks to the woman who is my inspiration, not just in my art but in my life, a woman who is … the love of my life, and I wouldn't be here without her. Stella Hardy.'

We shared a lingering look across the room, which rapidly seemed to have become warmer — perhaps it was the champagne — and I blew him a kiss.

55

FUNKY TOWN was in party mode: Cup Day night was a good time for ten-pin bowling. The doors parted. I walked through into the foyer, and into the hubbub of the bowling alley. To the right was the cafe. Afshan and Shahid were waiting for me.

'Come on,' I said.

Afshan parked the van in the next street from the house. We approached on foot, and as we reached the corner, we could hear Conti's party was in full swing. Cars were parked all the way down the street. I took up position in the neighbour's front garden. Afshan and Shahid stood in the middle of the road, outside the house.

'Hey, Joe,' Afshan called. 'Come out, Joe!'

'Joe Conti! Come out and talk to us,' Shahid was yelling.

A few moments later, a heavy-set bloke came thundering out, wearing a *kiss the cook* apron, still holding a stubbie. Behind him, an older bloke, fit-looking and ready for a fight.

The men moved, somewhat sloppily, out onto the street.

I stayed in a crouch and moved closer.

One of them pointed at Shahid. 'Don't remember inviting any ragheads, do you, mate?'

His mate roared, laughing, then stepped to the side, bent forward and hurled up a cascade of undigested matter. He stood, unsteady but triumphant, wiped his mouth, and took a sip of beer.

The first one patted his pockets, pulled out a packet of cigarettes.

I moved silently out from the neighbour's garden and behind the parked cars.

'Excuse me, sir, we don't want to interrupt your party. But you have money that belongs to us,' Afshan said.

'Fuck off, why don't you?'

The other drew himself up, swayed slightly. 'We're the police, sonny. Run along.'

My phone was charged and ready.

'That money is ours,' Shahid said. 'We earned it, it belongs to us.'

The vomiter grabbed Shahid around the neck. 'You don't get it, do you, shithead. No one cares what happens to you. No one wants you here.' He released Shahid with a shove.

The other cop joined in. 'That's right. What's yours is ours. And there's not a damn thing you can do about it. If you don't like it, you can fuck off back to the Stone Age shithole you crawled out of.'

Afshan started undoing the button on his jacket. The two cops couldn't believe it. One went forward, swung a wild roundhouse. Afshan danced out of his way.

The older man rushed Shahid, who put two hands out and pushed back hard, knocking the cop sideways. The cop, angry now, turned around to run at Shahid again. Then he saw me crouched on the ground and stopped.

I stood up, and addressed the man I assumed was Joe Conti. 'You need to leave these men alone.'

'The fuck are you?'

'I'm the one with the incriminating video footage.' I showed him my phone. 'Stop bothering my friends, or we'll see you in court.'

The next day, I checked on the cash. There was four hundred and fifty thousand dollars under my bed and another ninety in the freezer. Sure, part of me was worried sick, and another part was exhausted from constructing elaborate rationalisations. But the largest part of me felt justified. This time, I deserved it ...

Kylie's phone went through to voicemail; I left a message offering to meet her and her husband and discuss a financial windfall in the family that had miraculously transpired. Then I took ten grand to work, wrapped up in a bag, and rang Afshan, telling him the good news: a small parcel with his name on it had been handed in anonymously at WORMS.

On the news a few nights later, Bunny Slipper delivered a long piece to camera, intercut with B-roll footage of Asian hospital exteriors, street scenes from the Burmese capital, the old Corpse Flowers clubhouse, the Australian embassy in China. It would take time, she said, for Interpol to fully piece together the extent of the organ harvesting racket across three, possibly more, countries. At the Australian end, the scam included the fake passport scandal, and the luring of displaced teenagers with promises of money and drugs. Those responsible were facing multiple charges, including for the murder of homeless teenager Cory Fontaine.

At a hastily convened evening press conference, the Honourable Mucous Pukus MP, in a rare display of actual honour, announced a funding increase of fifty thousand dollars for a program to secure accommodation for street kids.

I turned off the television and stuffed one of Madame Mao's mushroom and ginger tofu dumplings — I'd grown addicted to those lately — into my mouth, and started to pack: DVD boxsets, floaty frock, wicked platforms, a lacy number.

Brophy and I had a dirty weekend coming up.

Acknowledgements

I WISH to thank the following people for their help with this book: Lesley Halm and everyone at Scribe, Clare Forster, Stephanie McGlinchey, Imbi Neeme, Trish Bolton, Clare Strahan, Lucy Treloar, Kate Richards, Toni Jordan, Natalie Thomas, Ming Lu Chen, and Clinton Green.